IT'S MORE THAN HIS TASTE

IT'S MORE THAN HIS TASTE

Alan Jay Robinson

IT'S MORE THAN HIS TASTE

This is a work of fiction. Names, characters, organizations, places, events, and incidents are either the product of the author's imagination or are used fictitiously. Any resemblance to actual persons (living or dead) is purely coincidental.

Published by Alan Jay Robinson

ISBN: 979-8-9939237-1-0 (hardcover)

ISBN: 979-8-9939237-0-3 (paperback)

ISBN: 979-8-9939237-8-9 (digital)

Cover design by Diego Sanguino

Book design by Gecko Edit

CONTENT NOTE

This novel is intended for mature readers.

It contains aggressive language, graphic scenes regarding sex, and violence. Reader discretion is advised.

SUMMER
2012

1

WHAT I'M ABOUT to do will challenge every fiber of my being, of who I think I am.

Every. Last. One.

There's no going back after this. My phone back face down on the coffee table. My right leg bouncing up and down uncontrollably, elbows on my knees, hands over my face; eyes shut finally for a moment.

I'm out of control. This is out of control. I look up at the clock again on the wall across from me, above the TV. 9:46 a.m. My hand grabs, and I swig down that last bit of bourbon in a glass in front of me, left over from last night.

Jesus. Am I really about to do this?

I don't think I can—I shouldn't. I change my mind. I reach out, flip my phone over and tap the screen. The screen saver appears—no new messages. Just Lucy as my background. My arms cross, and my body leans back into the couch. Fuck. I don't want to change my mind. Not this time.

Music. That will calm my nerves. Take my mind off the reality of what I'm doing. I lean back up and click on the TV remote. A pop station appearing. Hell no, not this pussy shit. This will make me feel worse. I click through, finding the rock channel. Foo Fighters appears. I like this. This is man's music. This is good. I set the volume just to 10 so I can still hear the hallway outside the door to my apartment. It is silent in the building this morning. I haven't heard a peep from my neighbors on either side of me; above or below.

I light up a cig, lean back into the couch, and cross my feet up on the coffee table. I take a few puffs. Relax, Roy. You're good, it's gonna be good. I look to the left, outside my window at the buildings across my street—old, second-floor apartments just like mine, above bars and restaurants. How busy is St. Clair Street in downtown Frankfort, Kentucky, in the mornings? I don't know. I only moved here a few weeks ago. I should have thought about this before. Fuck. I don't see anyone home through their windows? I'm not getting up to check. In case anyone is on the street—what if they look up? Then they'll see me.

A feeling of shame comes over me.

It's quickly trumped by the adrenaline I awakened just moments ago. An adrenaline that I always thought would stay dormant, that I've known might secretly exist. Why am I awakening it now? What if somebody sees? What if somebody hears?

10 minutes out. My phone lights up with a new message.

My throat swallowing. I can't do it. The adrenaline spiking. I can't. I exhale, slowly counting to five. I repeat inhaling and exhaling slowly to try to bring the adrenaline down. I'm gonna have a heart attack, and I'm only thirty-four. Every cell in my body feels like the epicenter of an earthquake, all going off at the same time. This is insane.

Knock knock knock knock knock knock

My head whipping toward the front door, the sounds waves like a tsunami wiping my insides out.

What the fuck? It hasn't been ten minutes yet.

I stand up and walk quick to the door, passing by a mirror on the wall. I can't bring myself to look into it. I get to the door and stop for just a second.

Check the peephole. I look. Bobby? My neighbor's twelve-year-old son. What the fuck is he doing here now? I open the door just enough to show my face. "What is it, Bobby?"

"Sorry to disturb you, Mr. Stevens. By chance you got my mama's number? I forgot my key to get in my apartment, and I don't have a cell phone." His Catholic-school uniform makes him look nerdy. If I'd had to wear a tie every day at twelve and go to school looking like that, I'd have killed myself.

"No, kid. I don't. Now get on outta here—you're disturbin' me." I slam the door shut, lock it, and walk quickly back to grab my phone and check my messages.

Nothing.

I sit back down, reaching for my Marlboros in one motion. I quickly light up another. My ashtray on the coffee table in front of me with dozens of buds staring back at me. Two eagles propped up in the center, bodies intertwined like a braid, and their heads facing opposite of each other, with their beaks open at the top—like a couple having an argument: their heads and minds opposite each other, but tied down by their hearts. Black and green. The ashtray just two colors. Black as a pupil and green as a jade. It's quite beautiful, actually. The green and black colors spiral at the base of the ashtray, until they give way to individual features at the center, where one color follows each eagle head. Their beaks open just enough to perfectly fit my unfinished cigs above all the other dead buds. One of the few things I got to grab real quick from my Uncle David's place after his wife, Sheila, put him in that nursing home a few months back. I should go see him. I haven't been since I helped move him in. Poor bastard.

He did raise me, after all, at least for the part of my life that counts. Taking me in at age five, after my father, John, had died. Can't believe to this day I still don't know a goddamn thing about my mother, or my father, really.

I wonder how that fella that lived with my uncle and me is

doing? What was his name? He was my uncle's best friend, and roommate. Ah. Ramón.

I wonder what happened to him? Shit, it's been twenty years now since I've seen or heard of him. I'll never forget that evening after my Grandfather Walter's funeral, my whole life changing that day. Came home late after hanging with friends, and our whole house was packed into a moving truck with everything but Ramón's stuff; his room completely untouched. I still don't know what their fight was about? My stuff was already packed, and we took off the second I got home. And I never heard of or saw Ramón again, or that town again. What could have been so bad we had to race out like that at night? And why did my uncle choose to move us to Owenton, Kentucky? In the middle of nowhere? Uncle David hasn't said his name once since that day. I actually liked Ramón. He was cool.

This ashtray. Shoot, it's bringing up memories. Hm. I barely saw my uncle after entering high school after moving to Owenton. He was always working. I'd catch him for a few minutes sometimes on the porch, and he'd have a cig with me. We'd share this ashtray. Those moments being the very few moments we'd talk my whole high school life. It wasn't much. But still. In hindsight, his buddy Ramón spent more time with me as a kid than he did. I don't think my uncle ever really liked me.

Why am I saying that?

I should still go see him. Ugh. What if Sheila is there? Can't believe he's stayed with her all these years; married her that same year we moved—what was it? Hm. 1992. Some marriage of twenty fucking years…fucking bitch. She's already moved on from him. I always thought she kept secrets from him, from me too. It was no less than a week later that she moved out of their house after he got put in that nursing home; said she was "too depressed" to be all on her lonesome self, left in a big house, alone with nothing but silence now that he's out of it. Yeah, right. That dog won't hunt. Who are you really, Sheila? And what are you hiding?

I look back up at the clock. 10:02 a.m.

I'm really pushing it on time…My body exhales and my right leg begins to bounce again. Shit, I was finally relaxed somehow. Wonder if Bobby fucked off? I feel kind of bad. The kid seems nice. At least compared to how I was at twelve. I probably do have his mama's phone number written down somewhere here? But now ain't the time. I can't focus on anything else right now. I put my phone into my pocket and walk back to the door to check the peephole. Let's make sure he's gone.

All I can see is an empty hallway. Good.

Vibrate…vibrate

I pull my phone out real quick. A new message: **Just parked, walking up now.**

The adrenaline now back from my spine to my toes. I can't control it. I can't control myself. Should I run out of here? Hide in my bedroom? Really? *Hide in my bedroom?*

Hm. How about respond back and say, "nvm, fuck off"?

NO.

I can't ignore it or block now. It's too late for that. I can't. I also…don't want to…

My gut has taken the driver's seat that my brain always had. The discipline that has kept me at bay all these years, now out of sight and reach. Even if it were in sight, I think I'd look the other way. My longing and curiosity reaching a new peak, with no new height to climb, to hide behind, and now I'm forced to see and surrender to the alluring steep fall on the other side. What is at the bottom? I don't know. What will happen to me on my way down? I don't know. I can't see past the peak. But I have to go through with this. My body can't close again what's inside, not when I'm this close. There is still time to go back. But I don't want to. The journey up here was too vigorous. What's over this peak and on the other side, at the bottom, has to be worth it. Worth it for me? But what if it's not? What if I'm wrong?

Well, thinking about my uncle, Sheila, Ramón—all that was a nice little distraction, but now my heart is about to burst through my ribs like one of those fucked-up baby aliens from *Alien vs. Predator*.

I step to the right side of the door. Just look in the mirror, you stupid pussy.

My head and eyes follow up from my boots to my eyes. I check myself up and down more. I like these black cowboy boots—my favorite pair. Some light-blue baggy jeans and a white tight beater. I look good. I follow myself up back to my eyes. What are you doing, Roy? I don't recognize you.

Okay, that's enough of that!

I step back in front of the door quick, out of the mirror. My body swings, my back now landing up against the wall, perpendicular to the door. I put my hands into my pockets, head down, and I wait. My body now perfectly still, but my heart pounding at the speed and irregularity of horses' hooves hitting the track at Keeneland, fighting to win a high-stakes race.

Knock knock knock

Three quick, low knocks at my apartment door.

I quickly check the peephole and see a man outside in the hallway. I open the door quick halfway, look at him, and nod. "Come in."

2

———————

HE STEPS INSIDE to his left, barely making it in as I shut the door and lock it fast. I step back from the door and look at him more. What do I say? The mix of adrenaline and the beats of my heart numbing my ability to think or talk. "Uh, I only got 'bout thirty minutes…so we gotta make it quick." What did I just say? My eyes bouncing from his eyes back to anywhere else. He nods at me? Or is he just checking me out too?

Eye contact is made, but then he looks down at the floor. "Yeah…yeah, me too."

I like his voice. Not too gay. Sounds like a regular fella. Chill. How is he so chill?

He's much more chill than I. He must have done this before. Of course he's done this before. I guess I didn't ask him. Jesus. I feel like a stupid, silly virgin that doesn't know what they want.

I guess I am that.

I turn and walk toward the living room, my head down, and stand between the couch and the coffee table. He follows behind. I turn around and face him. He's standing close. Just three feet away.

"What do you wanna do?" Words coming out of his man

lips, they excite and scare me at the same time. I don't know? What do you wanna do?

I glance at him, then at the inside of my apartment door I just shut behind him—where I just let him in and locked us in here. Ask you to leave I think? No.

"Um…uhh…umm." My brain not firing anything. My hands sliding into my back pockets.

He nods and smiles. "Maybe we should take our shirts off?" Okay…yeah, that's a start. I can do that. His smile actually calming me a bit. Can I really trust him?

I nod back, begin to take my white beater off. He takes off his black Nike ball cap first—revealing his bald, shiny head underneath. Huh. I guess I never got a face pic. I'm not bothered by it. I think I like it actually. He takes off his gray T-shirt, "MC" on it in small letters on his chest. His initials? Max Canterbury. Sure, that can be his name. Is it weird I don't know his name? Should I ask him? No. We just met off Grindr, both saying we're horny and discreet. We don't need to know each other's names. I don't think? Is that rude?

His head turns toward the direction of my TV. "Is this Foo Fighters?"

"Yeah." I look and see the TV screen is black. Hm. He knows their music. That's cool. I guess some fags do listen to alternative rock too? Could've fooled me.

"Cool, they're my favorite too." He smiles at me. They're not my favorite…feller. Whatever.

Just take your pants off.

I want to see everything.

I remain standing still with a black expression, my eyes lost on him. He's like, movie-star chiseled. My chest moving erratically. His eyes flicker from my pecs back to my eyes. He steps one foot closer and extends his hand toward my chest; my arm swiping it away from me in a quick jerk. Shit!

"Woah!" He steps back and puts his hands up. "What are…"

"Shit. I'm sorry, I'm just really nervous." Both my hands up now in the air in front of him, along with his; mirroring each other—calling a truce. God, this is not how I imagined this going. "Here, uh, I'm putting my hands down. That won't happen again, I promise." I set my hands down against my thighs and hold them still. I nod at him. I'm ready. Imagine my wrists are tied with rope to an anchor screwed into each of my thighs. I'll do that. Cement them in. Keep them there. I take a big breath, and I close my eyes. "Go ahead, try that again."

My other senses so much stronger now with my eyes closed. My bare skin on my torso can feel the brisk air still left from having the A/C on all night. I can hear his breathing; it's much softer than mine. I like his cologne, or is that how he naturally smells? Did he just move closer to me? Just then I feel his cold palm touch my chest. Colder than the air around us. My torso jumps slightly in reaction to it, and then continues to tremble as he places his hand just over my heart. Keep your eyes shut, Roy. Focus on the idea of your hands tied to anchors at your thighs. I'm afraid of how I will react if I open my eyes. The trembling now seemingly uncontrollable, like a drummer in my diaphragm with no end to his song. My arms start to shake naturally, following the movements of my torso, but I continue to imagine the rope getting tighter on my wrists. His hand feels good there.

"It's okay, you can trust me." His voice soft, but also so loud, echoing in my head.

Can I? I just met you. I just met you, and I already like the way your cold hand feels on my bare skin.

He begins to move his hand slowly across my chest, making it to the other side. I can feel his rough, calloused hand travel through my chest hair. Are all guys' hands this rough? Are mine this rough? His hand now feeling warmer all of a sudden. How much time has gone by? Are we heating up together? Just from this contact only? My dick starting to grow beneath my belt buckle…*Woah.* Holy shit. I'm getting hard. I'm getting hard quick. I'm slightly surprised. Drummer boy now calming his tune within. The man moves his hand back from left to right across my chest, and then continues back and forth in a soft, oval-like track formation across my chest. Hm. Keep doing that.

"Does that feel good?" he says.

"Yeah, it's good." My body visibly calming down.

His hand then coming to a stop at the center of my chest, then starting to travel down slowly.

This is it.

He reaches the top of my stomach. I feel the sides of his fingers as he maintains contact while he flips his hand over. I feel the hairs on the tops of his knuckles on the surface of my stomach. I love it. Who would have known something as simple as the back of his knuckles on my stomach would get me going. He continues to travel down. Fuck, I'm not ready. Am I? My dick erecting further, he's seconds away from reaching my belly button. He's almost there. I CAN'T.

My eyes open, my right hand shoots up from my leg, anchor and rope released by a grenade that had a hidden timer; grabbing his wrist to freeze his travel. Now eye to eye and holding his wrist with my hand in an iron grip. "Turn around."

"Yeah, sure," he murmurs.

My left hand relaxes off my thigh, and now with both hands free, I grab his shoulders and spin him around in front of me.

Now pressed behind him, I slide my thumbs between his body and the inside of the top of his jeans. I push so they fall down to his ankles. His shoes still on, he's locked into place. His toned, smooth legs—so fuckable. Do fags grow leg hair? Or they shave it? Either way, I could just get off squeezing his thighs together and sliding my dick through those. I undo my belt buckle and unzip my jeans. I pull out my hard dick and place it right in the groove of his smooth, bubble ass, which sits beautifully perched up on these gorgeous legs. Woah. The head of my dick is inches from his hole. I've never fucked an asshole before. This is it. I put my hands on his hips and pull his ass closer into my cock. This is finally it. Fuck, I think I could cum right now just from the heat of his ass on my head. I continue to pull and push his ass in front of me, watching my head kiss the surface of his crack. Holy shit. I didn't know my dick could even get this hard. Look at it! I continue to watch the tip of my dick as I push through, in and out of his cheeks. My mouth drooling in awe. I spit down on his ass cheeks. I spit and rub more through my shaft, sliding my dick across the spit splattered on his cheeks. I start to push through further to press my tip onto the tight lips of his hole. Finally they meet. His breathing now a little louder, and his back arched, positioning his ass high. The arch tells me everything. The body doesn't lie. I mean, look at my own.

"Do you have any lub—ahh!" he blurts out as I push through his tight blockade.

"What?" My head now in him. Pushed through, I can feel his hole stretching, yet clenching? This IS tighter than a pussy. Woah. That's fucking hot.

"Nothing, just spit more, can ya?"

Oh. I can do that for sure. I look at my hard shaft I can still see: veins about to pop, the rest of me now succumbing to the warm sensation of the inside of his hot, tight ass. I drop more spit, keeping both hands on his hips. Looks like I found some new imaginary anchors to tie onto that I like a lot more. I thrust forward, and slowly watch my dick disappear further into him. He takes me inch by inch.

"Oh fuck." He exhales. I assume he likes it?

My dick now fully in, with my balls pressed up against the back of his ass. I keep in him for a second or two, then start to pull out. He shoots an arm back to grab my ass with his hand, pulling me back forward, into him, forcing me to stay deeper…I guess he doesn't want me out.

I agree with him and keep my dick all the way in. I slither my hands up his stomach from his hips, cross them as I get to his smooth, hairless chest, and pull his body back further into mine, pushing my dick even further up his hole. "Fuck me, that feels good." My eyes closed, and I can feel a smile spread on my face.

My head is to the left of his ear. He starts to shimmy his ass left and right. You must be happy, ain't you? Should I say something? Ask? His ear is right there. My arms still on his chest, embracing him into me, I begin to whisper, "You like that?"

Without hesitation: "Oh, fuck yeah." His body relaxing further into mine.

"Is this what you want?" I start to pull out a bit to then thrust forward. "Tell me what you want."

"Oh fuck, yes, it is." "Yes, sir." Sir? He pulls his pelvis forward, keeping my tip in—my shaft feels air—and slams his pelvis back to take me whole again. "Fuck, that feels good." I love how much he loves it.

He continues his motion back and forth. "Fuck, daddy, your cock is big. Fuck my tight little hole."

Daddy? And sir? He looks my age? Uh. What do I say? "You like that, *boy*?" I begin jackhammering his hole. Full on fuck mode, like an addict, hands on hips, dick in and out of ass, just plowing. I can't take it anymore. I'm gonna cum.

"I'm gonna cum," I blurt, and I keep my rhythm. "I'm gonna cum." I continue to jackhammer him.

"Okay."

I'm right there. The adrenaline, nerves, now transferred down to pressure building in my scrotum, about to burst in a release of pleasure. I can't wait. He starts to fuck me with his ass the same rhythm I'm jackhammering him.

Clap clap clap clap clap clap

"Fuck, baby, fuck, fuck, fuuuuuuuuuuuck, fuck!" My dick bursts with cum deep in his ass. "Fuckk!" "Fuck!" I can't stop shouting *fuck*. My hands still on his hips, forcing his ass to be at the mercy of my load, my dick still draining inside him. "Fuh-hhk!" A final last *fuck* and exhale. Shit, that felt amazing. Wow.

My dick still inside him, I look to my left up at the wall clock. 10:25 a.m.

A glare on the clock

That must be coming from outside!

Holy hell. I never closed the blinds to my apartment window behind me. My hands still on his hips, I jump back and push him forward. He falls forward to the ground, landing on his knees and hands, not able to stop himself because his ankles are locked by his jeans. Whoops.

"What the hell, man!?"

My back now on the wall, hiding next to the window. I flip my dick up, button and zip myself up. I grab the cords and aggressively close the vertical window blinds. I get the blinds to position in four motions, then spin the tilt wand so the blinds turn and shut. He's there on the floor looking up at me, his red bare ass too. The blinds rattling back and forth, fighting each other to get to their resting positions. I step out from the corner behind the window, just as the blinds make it still. I take my finger and slide a blind just a sliver to peep through and check the apartments across the street.

Janice is standing at her window, talking on a cell phone. Fuck.

Did she see anything? She lives directly across St. Clair Street from me, on the same floor. Eye level. *Son of a bitch.* Panic coming over me. A panic I've never felt. I snap back around and look at the man still on the floor, now trying to put his pants on. "You gotta get outta here. You gotta get outta here right now." I point at the door.

He starts to get up and grabs his T-shirt to put it on. "All right, calm down."

You're not moving fast enough. "Hurry up!" I shout, my left arm still in the air, pointing at the front door of my apartment.

"All right!" he shouts back, getting both hands through his T-shirt, pulling it down now across those rock-hard abs that I just came inside under. "All right," he says again, softer, fully clothed now and looking at me. Why is he still so chill? When you tell someone to leave your home, get the fuck out. I just pushed him to the ground seconds ago—is this a game to him?

His eyes travel from mine to my left hand in the air. His eyes light up. What?

Shit. My wedding band.

Another tsunami comes unexpectedly, though my insides were already taken out earlier—so, what next?

He looks back at me, an energy shifting in his eyes. "Are you married?"

Without hesitation, I grab the first thing in front of me on the coffee table and chuck it across the room. Being the hardest baseball pitcher back in high school comes handy right about now. I still got it. The object milliseconds away from him. "Get the fuck out!" It strikes him on the right side of his forehead. "Go!" The object shattering all over him—an explosion off his face, dust all over him, and debris shot all different directions.

He turns around and walks toward the door. He's unbalanced. As he stumbles by the mirror, he pauses by it and looks at me through it. His hand over the right side of his face; blood visible between his fingers. He grabs the top of the mirror frame and rips it down from the wall. The mirror crashes to the floor, the frame disassembling and pieces of mirror glass shooting across the hardwood floor.

He turns to face me—"Fuck you!"—revealing a thick gash of blood next to his right eyebrow, at his temple.

"Get out." I jolt across the room toward him.

He exits through the door just as I'm hopping over the coffee table. I lock it and look through the peephole. I don't see him. My sweaty dick shriveling uncomfortably. I adjust it. Hm? I'm curious. I take a whiff. *Not bad.*

I look down at the mess in here. My eyes scattering over the floor. What did I just chuck at him that exploded on his face? Broken glass everywhere. Hm. The coffee table is always a mess of used mugs, mail, remotes, etc. Was it my uncle's ashtray? I scan to find—

Knock knock knock knock knock

You gotta be kidding. The sound of his knocks again, right

behind my head, flooding anger through my veins. Does this guy have a death wish?

I turn around and open the door quickly, my hand closed as hard as a rock, ready to throw a punch through his right temple. "Bobby?" I poke my head through the doorframe and look down the hallway left and right. "Get in here."

Looking at me puzzled. He hesitates, and then steps into my apartment.

I step to the left, and as he passes through, I shove him forward by the back of his shoulder, forcing him quicker into the apartment. Hurry up, kid. I close the door, shut and lock it. Now one hand holding the door handle, the other hand on the dead-bolt in the locked position, my head facing the door. "What are you doin' here, Bobby?" Did he see something?

"What happened in here, Mr. Stevens?" Fuck. My apartment.

"What are ya still doin' here? Don'tcha have school today?" I turn around and put my back against the door.

Do I ask Bobby if he saw him? No.

He begins to scan my apartment. "Why is it so dark in here?" His voice is light and kinda screechy, like how most boys sound not having been through puberty yet. He hops across the living room, landing in open spots to not step on any glass. He stops next to the window and reaches for the cord to open the blinds.

"Bobby, no!" I shout. "Don't open those." I hop over, following his same path. I arrive at the closed blinds and peep through the same sliver. *Janice is still standing in her window.* I look back at Bobby. "What are you doin' here, Bobby?" "I already told you that I don't have your mama's phone number."

He continues to scan my apartment, now from this side. "That's okay, Mr. Stevens. Hey, ya mind if I hang out here for a while?" Are all kids this fucking spacey and weird? No, you cannot. "Bobby, I gotta get to work; you can't stay here."

He puts his head down, discouraged?

Is he going to move?

I look back at the front door, and just before I can speak my next thought, I hear sirens in the distance behind me, coming through the window, from the street. Oh…shit. That fucking pussy called the cops on me.

Think…think…I look back at Bobby. Hm. "Okay, kid, I got a deal for you. Listen quick." I lean in and face him. "You can stay on three conditions."

He lifts his head up with a smile at me. "Yes." "Sir, what are they?"

My conditions spit out quick off my tongue. "Do not answer the door for anyone, and I mean anyone. I don't care if it's Santa Claus, or your best friend from school. This is my apartment; no one is allowed in but you."

The sirens now louder behind me

"You understand?" I face him and walk backward toward the door. The glass on the floor splintering more under my boots. "Second. Make sure you are out of here by four p.m. Four p.m. sharp. If you are not out of here by four p.m., I'm gonna personally tell your mother you skipped school. Bet you don't want that, now do ya?" Across the room now from him, I see his eyes widen, and his hands clench the straps of his backpack he's holding onto.

The sirens behind him on St. Clair Street loud as day

Thank god my car is parked in the back. I gotta get the fuck out now. I open the door and peep my head out to look quickly again, left and right. Nobody. I turn back around to look at Bobby. Now the strange kid I'm all of a sudden trusting with my life. "Last condition, clean up this shit, and don't open those blinds."

3

Just outside my car, the fuel pump trigger pops.

The inside of my car so silent, my shoulders hiccup in reaction to it.

How have I made it this far today? Every time a new fella walked into my bar, I was on pins and needles. Hiding behind the storage room door, peeping through a hairline crack to assess each one before calling it safe and walking out. No cop did come for me. So why did I hear those sirens from the street outside my window? Maybe I'm being too paranoid. The fella didn't even know my name. How would he know where I work? But he now knows where I live.

That's probably worse.

I should just take off from here. Tell no one and just drive until I land where the tank runs out. I got plenty of cash to last a while. I don't deserve anyone, or anything for that matter. I'm disgusting. Vile.

What about my uncle?

Would I regret taking off now, just before he dies? I can't leave him in his final days. What's the difference? I haven't been there anyways. What about Lucy? My wife.

She is better off without me too.

Lucy can find someone new. Someone her daddy finally approves of. Since the moment I met him, he's always kept me at arm's length. I never gave him a reason not to like me.

Is this selfish of me? To just…leave? Leave them in the dark, not knowing whatever happened to me? Lucy and my uncle are the only two people that truly love me. But they wouldn't love me if they knew what I just did—the sinner I am. The disgusting animal that lives inside of me, no longer tamed. Don't go there, Roy.

You. Are. Not. That.

You're not.

I'm not that! Today was just a…fluke.

I'm just confused, somehow. I've confused myself today about who I really am. This guilt though—can I live with it? This…secret. What are my options? Hurting them by disappearing all of a sudden, or hurting them from the police or that asshole exposing me. Exposing us for what we did. What I did.

That. Cannot. Happen.

The police didn't come to my bar today. That has to be a good sign? Maybe he called the police, but the police didn't believe him? I got connections at the station. Sergeant Keaton knows me well there. And I know things about her—things that she'd probably prefer I didn't.

Fuck. Janice too! Son of a bitch.

JANICE

Incoming call from Lucy Stevens

My car speakers ringing, Lucy's name popping up on the dashboard next to the clock. 5:02 p.m. Fuck. I have to pick it up. What if she made it home before Bobby left? I haven't heard from her all day. I guess normally I don't. I'm overthinking it. Take the call from your wife, you idiot.

My thumb puts pressure slowly on the answer button on my steering wheel. *Click.* "Hey dear, what's goin' on?"

"Hey darlin', how was your day?" Her voice cheerier than it

usually is. "Just callin' to see if you could pick up a few things from the market on your way home. I'm goin' to make your favorite dish tonight, steak and potatoes." *Steak and potatoes.* Hm. Her mother's favorite dish too. She hasn't made that dish since her mother died last year. Why tonight?

I feel so turned inside. So sick. I don't know what to do with it.

It's nice to hear her voice, though. "Of course." A soft smile across my face. But why my favorite dish? Her dead mother's favorite dish? Maybe she's missing her mother today? Or, oh my god, did I miss a special occasion AND cheat on my wife on the same day? "My day was good. Same ol', same ol'. I just finished pumping gas 'n' can stop by the market now. Can you text me your list?"

"Okay, great, I will text you. What time do ya think you'll get here?" Still cheery and a little pep in her voice too. Why is she so…excited? "The place looks amazin' by the way. What got into ya? I've never seen you clean this nice."

"Ah." I stutter and stare at the clock in my car. "It's a little after five now; I should be back no later than six…Yeah, you like how the place looks?" Good thing to hear she didn't come home to find Bobby, at least, or with glass all over the floor. Bad thing to hear Bobby maybe took my cleaning condition a bit too seriously. But, hey, if that's the least of my problems, I'll take it.

"Oh my goodness. Yes. It's one of the reasons I want to make you a special dinner."

One of the reasons?

"Okay, great, well, I love ya, and I'll see ya in a few."

"Love you too."

Click

One of the reasons? It's definitely not our anniversary. Hm? My insides in a full twist. Made it through my first conversation with her, the guilt a thick knot around my heart. How will I undo it? How will I make it go away? Will it ever go away?

4

JUST A FEW BLOCKS away from our apartment. My eyes scour each intersection I pass. Coast must really be clear. Right? Wife sounded great. I blocked that guy's profile on Grindr earlier. Nothing from the police. Everything looks…good, like my life can just return back to normal. Just like that. Can it? Yes, yes it can.

Maybe…

Just one problem, though.

I can't stop thinking about *him*. How hard my dick got with him.

My dick now slowly getting hard again from just thinking about him. Fuck.

Yeah, there was the whole scene with the gash of blood on his temple, broken shit everywhere in my apartment, and Bobby interrupting…but I can't stop thinking about…being inside of him. Everything about him, really. How his body looked and felt—while I was inside him. My first time ever with a guy. After all this time, all these years. My eyes rolling in the back of my head from the image of his pants falling to his ankles, his ass floating above, hungry for me. The combination of thrill and guilt swims through my veins in synchrony, with thrill just slightly leading the race. The knot around my heart less tight.

I want it again already. So badly. Is this how addicts feel? When they first get hooked? An addiction they didn't even know was possible.

A new, sick curse I can't shake.

One that you've maybe heard of but never thought you'd experience. One that you see and hear of those around falling ill to but never think it could happen to you.

But what if it is happening to me?

Fuck me.

Why now? I didn't ask for this. What about Lucy? She didn't ask for this. I love her so much. She is my wife—my everything. How can this be? How can I feel these two things at the same time? Can she help me break this curse? Is it part of her responsibility to bear, because we are married, to help me break it? I don't think God intended this. Maybe if I just focus on her, like I always have, this other…beast inside of me will go to sleep forever. How do I knock it out forever? This has to be a mistake, a disease, unnatural, *curable*. Something wrong in my brain or something that can be cured through prayer or maybe meds. Or maybe prayer AND meds. But I can't tell anyone. So how am I gonna get meds?

I should visit my uncle.

I won't tell him what happened. But visiting him might make me feel…better? Maybe less confused and lost than I do now. My apartment door now in front of me. I open up and walk in. One hand on the door handle, and the groceries my beautiful and doting wife asked me to pick up in the other—my wife that wants to make me my favorite dinner. She is my home, my peace, my everything—has always been. And I don't deserve her.

She greets me from the kitchen as I enter our apartment. "Hey, dear, how was your day?"

"Hey, hun, it was good." I make my way to her, walking

from the living room into the kitchen. The apartment is…spotless. Goddamn. Bobby really wanted to skip school today and not fuck up. I scan the living room area from the kitchen entryway. I've never seen our hardwood look this clean. The coffee table is cleared, with nothing but a candle and TV remotes. It smells fresh in here too. A freshness never scented before. Where did he find or get that? Makes me feel like this can be a new, clean slate. Thank you, God. This is exactly what I need.

I step further toward Lucy as she's mashing potatoes on the counter next to the stove. I set the groceries down on our kitchen dining table behind her. I lean in to give her a kiss on the cheek, now standing pressed right behind her. "How was your day?" I lean back, and our eyes meet, but quickly I turn back and step to unload the groceries. "Smells good. What are ya cookin'?"

She looks back at me while continuing to mash. She looks cute in her favorite red-and-white-checkered cooking apron. A white T-shirt underneath. A classic country look that always looks hot on her. She'd look hotter naked underneath. "A little kiss on the cheek?" She smirks. "You deep clean the apartment today and greet me only like that?" She turns back to her potatoes.

I quickly hop back over and squeeze her tighter from behind. I hold on for a few seconds and kiss her on the side of her face repeatedly, up on her cheek and down her neck.

"Roy, stop. Why are you being so affectionate today and nice?"

"Today? Am I not always affectionate with my beautiful wife?" I cock my head out from kissing her, look her in the eye, and give her a grin while still holding her.

"I mean, you are." She returns her attention coyly back down to her potatoes. "My day was good. You know the post office is boring, nothing ever new. The apartment looks great… what got into ya?" She looks back up at me. You mean who did

I get into? Jesus, I'm a monster. Don't laugh. This is so awkward.

"Nothing." I smile and let go of her. Did I say that too quick? "I just felt like a good ol' summer cleanin' was needed." I turn from her again, and step to the dining table and start to unload more groceries. I set a bag of onions down; one rolls out over a piece of paper. My hand pops out to stop it from rolling off the table. What is that? The onion just stopping over:

FRANKFORT POLICE DEPARTMENT
WITNESS INFORMATION REQUEST

My hand hovers over the onion, grabs it, and lifts it up at the same time that my other hand grabs the piece of paper to bring up to my face.

Date: June 10th, 2012
Location of Incident: St. Clair Street, Downtown Frankfort
Time of Incident: Approximately 10:30 AM

Dear Resident,

An incident occurred near your residence on the morning of June 10th, and the Frankfort Police Department is currently investigating. We believe someone in the building may have seen or heard something that could help us better understand what happened.

If you were home during this time or witnessed anything unusual (such as suspicious activity, arguments, loud noises, vehicles, or individuals in the area), we are asking you to contact us as soon as possible.

Even if you're unsure whether the information you have is relevant, we encourage you to reach out—what may seem small could be important.

Please contact:
Sergeant Keaton
Frankfort Police Department
Phone: (502) 555-2813
Email: OfficerKeaton@frankfortpd.gov
Case Reference Number: FRPD-12-2433

All information will be kept confidential. We appreciate your cooperation and assistance in helping us keep our community safe.

Sincerely,
Frankfort Police Department

Son of a bitch.

I thought this was over? I thought I could just move on. Come on! Act confused. She might be looking at you. "What's this?" I turn her direction.

She glances back, then back forward to her potatoes. "Yeah, did you see or hear anythin' this mornin'?" "I found that on our door when I got home." "You were home at the time, weren't ya?"

"Uh." I turn back to the table and set the onion and paper down. "I was not—looks like the incident happened at around ten thirty. I was already at the bar by then." "Had inventory work this mornin'." I shuffle sideways toward the living room and exit the kitchen. "So this was put on everyone's doors on St. Clair Street?" I holler back as I make my way toward our bedroom across the apartment. Did Janice get it, too, across the street?

"I guess?" "Hey." "I'm makin' steak tonight; how would you like it?" "Medium rare as you usually like?"

"Yeah, please. You know how I like it. I haven't changed on ya."

Well...shit. A blank space in my head. Should I ask? I have to. "What's the special occasion?" I holler from our bedroom, looking for clothes to change into. "And what time will dinner be ready?" Found out your husband cheated, and you're gonna ask for a divorce after making his favorite meal? That's ridiculous, Roy. Okay, back to logic—

So the police are looking for witnesses. So the sirens were here for something, and the police did not come to my work today, and not just my apartment alone, only looking for me. They have nothing.

I hear Lucy say something. So they don't have a direct connection to me about what happened earlier. What witnesses could maybe speak? *Bobby.*

I holler back, "What did you say? I can't hear you." Did Bobby see him when he ran out?

Her faint speech coming again. I cock my ear up and move toward the bedroom door, continuing to undress.

"Well, I wanna talk to ya about somethin'."

I finally hear what she's hollering back from the kitchen. Somethin'? Hm. Somethin'…

My shirt midway off from removing it and my head cocked out from my torso. My body freezing. Fuck. She knows. Wait, no she doesn't. How would she know? What does she need to talk about, then?

Now in some fresh clothes, I make my way back to the kitchen. "What is it, hun?"

"You cleaned up the house today, huh? What, are ya tryin' to get lucky tonight or somethin'?" She smiles at me as she mixes beans on the stovetop, the other hand gently placed, flat over her stomach. Get lucky? Yeah, that would be nice. But, I shouldn't have to deep clean the apartment just to get laid from you. But…now that you mention it—maybe get a blow job out of it? I grin at her.

"Is that what you wanna talk to me about?" I smile and chuckle back, looking at her. I glance back at the letter that I left face up on the table.

"No…actually." She sets down the spoon that she's mixing

the beans with and looks up at me. "I wanted to…well, I have something to tell—"

Knock Knock Knock

Three loud, powerful knocks come from the apartment door, interrupting her mid-sentence.

My body jolts too.

"Jeez, Roy." "It's just someone at the door. Are you okay?" Yeah, just a cop to arrest me, and tell you that your husband's a fag.

No, I'm not.

"Yeah." "Nothing. Nothing at all." "I'll get it." I smile, and turn around and walk toward the door. Who could it be? "You relax and continue cooking." I get to the door, and lean in to look through the peephole.

Knock! Knock! Knock!

I bounce back, jolted again from the noise. Fuck! This *is* police knocking. Strong. Aren't they supposed to announce themselves? Is it too late to jump out the window? Grab one of my loaded pistols inside the apartment and shoot myself where I know I won't wake up from it—opening this door to face what's on the other side will be the death of me anyways. With a bullet I at least can control my own fate.

From the kitchen: "Roy, you answerin' that or what?"

"Yeah." "Yeah, I'm right here." I have no choice. Open the door and face it like a man.

I quickly open the door. Bobby to the right and his mother to the left. Bobby makes eye contact with me for a second, and then his head shoots down. His dehydrated, prune-looking mother. Her cracked, brittle lips under her fluorescent-pink lipstick. Her face pinched at me.

"Uh." "Hello…" I gesture with my hand open toward them and smile.

"It's Lynette, Roy…We've been neighbors for two years now." Her raspy smoker's voice like a rattled out-of-tune guitar from a year in the 1600s. Maybe that's generous. "I live here to your left." She nods her head down the hall in the direction of their apartment. "This is my son, Bobby." She nods down at him. "He lives with me too. Ring any bells?"

Why the attitude? I look at Bobby. Give me some kind of clue, kid. Nothing.

"Yeah, Lynette, of course I know who you and your son are."

He remains with his head down, she hyperfocused on me. Not a blink or flinch.

From the kitchen: "Roy, who is it?" Lucy inquiring with her innocent curiosity.

"Oh, it's just the neighbors, Lynette and Bobby," I say clearly while looking at Lynette. Her face gleams a smile against her will.

"I got a call today from the Catholic private school that I pay a lot of money to send Bobby to." "They say he didn't attend school today. I just came home now to find him in his room, wearing this." Her arm rises up from her side, a black Nike ball cap in her hand, now in the air in front of me, between us. My eyes drop to the cap.

Okay? A second more looking at it.

FUCK.

Blink. Look natural and not surprised. "He says it's yours. Did you give my son this hat?"

In my periphery, I see Lucy exiting the kitchen and coming toward the door. I quickly close the door just enough, allowing only my face through—that bald fag's hat inches from my eyes. "Lynette, I don't know why your son missed school today, 'n' that is not my hat." I avoid looking at Bobby. That little fuck. "You're disturbin' our dinner now; y'all have a good night." I shut the door, Lynette continuing to speak more as it closes. I lock it and turn to face Lucy, just as she arrives.

"What did they want? No one ever knocks on our door." "Was it about this note from the Frankfort Police Department?" She's holding it in her hands.

No! "Uh." Think, Roy. "Lynette wanted to know if I saw Bobby today. I guess that little punk skipped school." I look down at the note in her hand. My hand flies up to scratch the back of my head.

"Oh? Well, that's weird; Bobby seems like a good kid. Never thought of him as a punk. Always dressed nice, clean." Her posture relaxes. "Why would she ask us? Both of us were at work today?"

"Yeah, I don't know." I glance up at her, shrug my shoulders, and make my way to the bathroom. "When is dinner gonna be ready, hun?" I holler back as I enter it and close the door behind me.

I stand at the sink, leaning forward, with my hands pressed down on the hard, cold top; my head down. Fuck. How did I miss that stupid asshole leaving his *fucking hat behind*?

My whole life destroyed because of one Nike ball cap. One little mistake. One little oversight.

If Lynette knocks on that door with that hat in front of me and Lucy one more time, what do I say? Lucy knows every piece of clothing I own. Our apartment isn't big. And what did Bobby tell his mother? Why did they come here? Is she knocking on every apartment door on this floor? How relentless is Lynette?

I'm such an idiot. I'm such a fucking idiot.

Why would Bobby take it? That little shit!

All that money toward Catholic school and his mom can't buy him a twenty-dollar fucking hat, so he has to steal one? Wonder what else that little fucker stole from here. This is why I never want kids: can't trust them with anything. Thank god we don't have any, and thank god Lucy has never gotten pregnant. I offer him a deal because he wanted to skip school, then he goes and fucks me like this. I slam my fist on the sink countertop, causing a loud thud.

"Roy? Everything okay in there?"

"…Yeah, I'll be out in just a second." I'm collapsing inside, a swirling tornado of chaos. How do I calm down? I don't know what more can swirl before it ejects out of me. Keep it in, Roy; learn to calm it down. Channel it somewhere far below. Bury it again.

I open the bathroom door to find Lucy standing just right of our apartment door, observing the empty wall space where our mirror once was. "Roy, where is our mirror?"

It's a hurricane now. A category five. I clench my teeth. Contain it. Think of something to say. Hold. Your. Ground.

5

———

"Yeah, uh…it broke."

"It broke?" She steps directly in front of the wall, slides her hand up where the center of the mirror used to be, and then looks back at me. "How did it break?"

"…Well." How did it break? "When I shut the door leaving today to go to work, I heard a crash behind me. I opened the door to see the mirror on the floor, all broken 'n' shattered 'n' shit."

"That's weird." "I hung it up myself and don't remember a loose screw?" She looks back at the wall, sliding her hand over the hole where the screw was ripped out and circling it with her finger. "Weird." "Okay, if you say so." She turns and walks back toward the kitchen.

I can't do this.

She passes under the kitchen doorframe before disappearing. I look back at the empty wall and imagine the fella with the bloody gash in his temple fleeing. Lynette and Bobby on the other side of our apartment door still standing in the hallway; standing there holding his hat to give me.

Did Bobby see him run out of my apartment this morning? And would he tell his mama? What would I do at twelve?

"Is that what got you goin' to cleanin' the apartment then? 'Cause the mirror broke?" I hear from the kitchen.

I really can't do this.

I don't know how many more lies I can tell or hoops I can jump through right now. I gotta get out of here. I just need a second to think. Get my story straight. "Listen, I'm gonna go visit my uncle for a bit, and then I'll come back for dinner. That okay with you? I feel guilty I haven't seen him 'n' it's gettin' to me today."

"Now?" She sounds annoyed from the kitchen. I stay silent. "Uh yeah, is that why you asked me what time dinner will be ready?"

"Yeah." That's exactly why…I make my way to exit.

She emerges under the kitchen doorway and walks toward me. She grabs my face with both hands. "Of course, I'm happy you want to visit your uncle. Go." She lets go of my face. "Text me later when you'll be home, and I'll start dinner back up so it's ready before you get here, fresh 'n' hot off the grill." Why does she have to be so perfect?

I smile down at her. "Thank you, hun. You are the best wife a guy could ask for." "After all these years together, I wouldn't change a thing." I kiss her on the cheek and exit our apartment.

6

———————

WHAT AM I going to do? I can't escape this feeling of disgust with myself. A disgrace so dark—

Adultery.

And with another *ma*—I don't even want to bring myself to say or think it again. To finish that line. I park my car, exit, and start walking through my uncle's nursing home. My soul feels torn out of me, and shattered like that mirror across my apartment floor. Can I repair myself back to normal? Or will the cracks where it broke always show?

Among the people I see is Sheila, walking the opposite direction, toward where I just parked. Great. I nod a "don't talk to me" hello as I walk past, hoping she doesn't stop me to chat. She almost pretends not to notice me. An awkward smile and her head down as she passes me. They get in a fight or something? Or what other secrets are you hiding now? I turn to look as she continues walking. She doesn't look back.

My uncle was a hard worker, and the free time that he did have, he spent with her. The only memorable interactions I had with him were partially those moments of silence enjoying a smoke together, but mostly all the times he would tear into me, beat down my ideas on things. Things I wanted to do or have. I remember a burgundy pair of cowboy boots that I wanted for my sixteenth birthday—told me no nephew of his would dress like sissy show cattle. Who would've cared? All the other kids in school wore cowboy boots. Why couldn't I? I wanted a white pickup truck—shot that down, told me I should only buy cars in black; said only chicks and fags drive white trucks. I'd cross my legs the wrong way he didn't like—he'd make me stand for the rest of the time where we were at, didn't matter where; happened once at a restaurant. He made me leave the table and told me to stand outside and wait until he finished dinner with his date. That's how I got into smoking cigs. It was winter, and I was cold. I didn't eat dinner that night. I was ten. I kind of understand that one now, because when I see fellas cross their legs like that, they always are a little faggy.

I never understood our relationship. Sheila did tell me once that my uncle had never wanted kids. Whether that is true or she was just trying to be a bitch and get in my head…It's not his fault my dad died and my mother wasn't around. There was Grandpa Walter, but he was too old at the time. Either way…I still love my uncle. He's the closest thing I've had to a father; made sure I had food, clothes, and a roof over my head. He never came to my baseball games, or graduation, but made sure I had the essentials to make me a man. What more does a man need in a father, anyways?

Knock knock

A heads-up I'm entering his room.

His body lying in the bed in the dark, with just the light from the TV above cast over—I'm assuming left on after he's fallen asleep? "Uncle David? Hello…" I walk further in, making it to his bedside. That show *Friends* is playing in the background. *Asshole never let me watch that growing up.*

"Uncle David?" I lean, whispering near his face. "Uncle David, are ya asleep?"

I lean back from over him and take a moment. One minute he's walking and talking, the next he is paralyzed in this bed after a stroke AND finds out he has stage-four lung cancer. How fucking crazy. I still can't believe it.

He actually looks pretty peaceful. His eyelids closed and relaxed over his big, round eyeballs. His breathing a steady, calm pace. He's definitely asleep. Maybe I don't need to feel that bad I haven't been here. He looks fine. "Okay…I'll let ya rest a little, then, but I'm gonna be right here when ya wake."

I turn my attention to the chair just right of his bedside and take a seat in it. How long should I wait? Lucy's waiting on me. Maybe he will wake up soon? I haven't been to visit him. I can make the effort now. I'm in no rush to return home.

Knock knock knock

Three quick little knocks echo to my right at the entry of my uncle's room.

Guess I nodded off. My body wakening abruptly, excited, fully reclined, with my legs out and torso leaned back. Andrew, one of my uncle's nighttime nurses, is now standing in front of me. I've only met him once. But I vividly remember him.

I was just dreaming of that man. I can't believe it. This time we were fucking in my car, and he was riding my dick in the back seat. Oh my god, it was hot. So hot that the dream made me hard, a chubby now clearly visible through my pants. Did Andrew see it? He's standing right there.

"Hey, Andrew, how is it goin'?" I lean up fast, the reclining chair follows, and my body goes back into a sitting position.

"It's good, you know. Same old, same old. It's nice to see you. I feel like I haven't seen you in a while, and your uncle always talks about you."

"He does?" I look at my uncle, resting.

"Yeah, well, I mean he mostly asks about you, and I tell him you're doing all right." Andrew looks at me and smiles. I guess that's nice of him. A little weird to speak for me, though.

His big brown eyes seeming even bigger and browner tonight. How can brown eyes be that captivating in light this dark? Maybe it's his darker features too. His super-dark-brown hair, like a dark chocolate. It's always cut sharp. His eyebrows are thick and dark too. Not too thick that he has a caterpillar on his face dancing when he talks, but…just thick enough. He has long eyelashes for a guy too.

My boner going down now, slowly, from the conversation. "Well, thank ya for doin' that; that's very kind, and not required of ya."

"Of course, Roy, anything for you, and your uncle."

I look at him and give him a hesitating, small nod.

He walks to the other side of my uncle's bed and begins to wake him. I remain in the chair and watch quietly. He grabs my uncle's hand with his and shakes my uncle's hand softly. "David," he says, and repeats it while leaning over him, closer to his face. "David. Wake up, David. It's time to take your evening meds." My uncle's eyes start to slowly open; his head is positioned forward. "Hi, David." Andrew smiles down at him, hand still holding onto his. "I have a surprise for you." Andrew's smile, so big after making eye contact with him, now engaging with him closely. "You have a visitor. Look who came to see you." My uncle's eyelids now cracking open further and recognizing him. He smiles back at him.

Andrew seems to be…very comfortable with my uncle?

"Huh?" my uncle murmurs. Clears his throat and shuts his eyes back. "Who?"

"Your nephew is here. Remember your nephew? Your nephew, Roy, is here to see you." It's only been a few weeks since I've come to see him. *Remember me?* This is exactly the reason why I don't come. Is he going to even know who I am? His head still positioned forward, and his eyes now opening back up further and looking at Andrew. I stand up slowly from the chair and take two steps to stand next to the bed across from Andrew.

Andrew turns his attention from my uncle and looks at me across the bed and nods. "Here he is, right here, your handsome nephew." And he looks back down at my uncle.

Did he just call me handsome? I dart Andrew an intense

look. He notices, retracts off my uncle's hand, and stands back up to a straight position, his smile gone. He looks back at my uncle.

My uncle then turns his head right and sees me. I try to put my hand on his shoulder calmly. But I'm now pissed and confused. I'm happy to see the old man awake, though. Does he recognize me? "Hey, Uncle David. Nice to see ya." I smile down at him and nod. How far sick is he now?

"Ah, there is my boy. It's about time you come see me." I can't hide a wide smile spreading across my face. Thank god he still remembers me.

"All right, David, I'm just going to give you your evening meds, and I'll get out of your way so you can visit with Roy." Andrew makes eye contact with me again as he marks on his clipboard. If I hear his voice and/or if his faggot ass looks at me one more time, I'm going to pop his head off.

I watch as my uncle opens his mouth for Andrew to place his evening meds on his tongue.

Disgusting.

Why doesn't my uncle have a nice lady nighttime nurse? Andrew has a cup of water ready in the other hand. He then brings it to his mouth for him to wash the meds down. My uncle drinks the full cup of water, Andrew angling the cup more as he drinks. "Thank you, Andrew." My uncle finishing and taking a breath. "You take good care of me, and I appreciate you." He what?

I can feel myself wanting to throw up.

Andrew leans the empty cup back away from his mouth slowly. "You're welcome, David. Enjoy your visit." Andrew exits the room. He doesn't look my direction. My eyes follow him out.

I turn back to my uncle. "Did ya hear that? Did you hear that faggot call me—"

"'—handsome'?" He interrupts me abruptly.

"Yeah…What the fuck is that about? I should have knocked

him off his ass right then, teach him a lesson on talkin' to me like that."

"Roy." "Now why would you do that?" His voice soft, looking at me like I'm crazy. Is he for real?

My mind starts to race. This is coming from the guy raising me since I was five to always hate faggots. Every time there would be anyone that came across with a little sugar in their tank, he would murmur under his breath, *Fuckin' faggot* or *Fuckin' fairies*. I remember every time. I don't know why, but I do.

Telling me if I ever behaved in any way like them, that he'd reconstruct my face to the point people would no longer recognize me as Roy.

When I was in third grade, I remember an awkward teenager at Sunday service sitting in the pews across from us with his mother. They were new that day to our church. He had a light-purple collared shirt on; a clean head of hair, super blond—maybe unnatural, come to think of it; shiny lips; and his legs crossed the way all fags cross them. I don't know why I remember all these details about him. But I do.

And my uncle made sure to point him out to me, told me boys that dress and look like that are faggots and shouldn't be let out of the house—that's the first time I understood what the word meant—and that God did not create boys to behave and look like that, and that they are living a sinning life; a real-life, living example of the devil's work.

I took note. I didn't want to be like that, to have the devil corrupt my soul.

After the service, my uncle went up to the mother in the parking lot, with me by his side, and her boy was next to her. He told the mother God did not welcome them in our church and that they needed to find a new one, and threatened that if they didn't, he would take matters into his own hands. I never saw those two again.

Silence still between us. I look back at him, realizing my eyes have been on the floor, lost in memory. I can feel the grooves in my forehead tightening.

I'm gonna say this loud and clear: "Why wouldn't I? I'm surprised this whole time you've had a faggot takin' care of you, touchin' you, seeing you naked. It's disgusting, it's wrong, and it's vile. Are you sick in the head too?" "Have you lost your goddamn mind?"

He maintains eye contact with me. "No…Roy, I'm not sick in the head too. If anything, I'm seeing things more clearly now than I have ever." His reply calm and stern.

He must be tired, or is this how his body has gotten now? He needs to rest between sentences as he speaks. "Lying here in this bed…alone, reflecting on my life, spending my final hours every day watching *Friends*, eatin' shit food, and just maybe wonderin' a little"—he takes a big breath—"wonderin' what if I made…ahem." He clears his throat. Jesus, get on with it. His eyes begin to water, and he looks away from me.

Huh.

I have never seen my uncle's eyes water. Not ever.

I look down at the bed. "I'm sorry for raisin' my voice." Clearly he is not himself. This must happen to people that are getting closer to death. Who knows what these meds are doing to his brain too. I have an idea.

I look back up at him. "I'll get you a new nurse, one that is respectable and not a fag, a proper woman, one that will not confuse you of who you are."

"Damn it, Roy!" His mouth opening in a snap of anger. "I don't need a new nurse!" he yells, then starts to uncontrollably cough. Shit, did I break him? Please don't die in front of me.

I extend my hand to set on his, and he turns his head opposite me and continues coughing. I look at the cup of water left on a tray next to him, where Andrew was, on the opposite side. It's empty. I turn around to exit the room. I'll go find him some water. *Andrew* is already entering the room with a fresh cup.

"What did you do?" Is he accusing me of something?

I step in front of his path to block him. "What did you say to me?" He stops. My uncle continuing to cough behind me. "I didn't do anything." "What did *you* do? How about you do your job right, and my uncle wouldn't be coughing like this."

His bottom jaw falls a little, and he puts the back of his hand against my arm and shoves me—"Can you step aside, please?"—and takes a step to walk through.

"Don't ever touch me, you faggot." My reaction loud, my body squirming from his shove and touch. I turn and look back down at my uncle. "And don't touch him anymore, too—you've done enough."

He passes, ignoring me. He gets to my uncle's bedside and feeds him water just as gently and delicately as before, *like a woman*. My uncle's coughs coming to an end. He starts to walk back my direction to pass me and exit the room. He makes eye contact with me. "You're not my patient; I don't take orders from yo—"

My foot sticks out, and I push and trip him over it. He lands on the floor in the direction of the door. I take a step toward him and get to knee level. "I know that you are a faggot, and I know that tomorrow I'm reporting you for…violating my uncle." I then spit on him. "Now, get."

"Roy!" I hear behind me. My head and Andrew's head turning at the same time, responding to his voice. Andrew and I both stand up, facing him. "Roy, I was wrong."

What did he just say? "Uncle, what are ya sayin'?" I step toward the foot of the bed. "What are ya talkin' about?" I turn my head back to look at Andrew. "What are ya still doin' here?" "Get the fuck out!"

I see my uncle make eye contact with Andrew. He nods at him. I notice Andrew nod back. What in the Kentucky-fried fuck is going on here? Andrew turns around and walks out of the room. I look at my uncle. I say again to him, "What are you talkin' about, Uncle?" "What is goin' on?"

His attention now on me. "Take a seat, Roy." He nods at the

chair to his right, where I originally was. I step over to the chair, double-check the entrance to the room to make sure Andrew ain't still standing there. I sit down at the edge of the chair, next to my uncle's bedside, and lean in. "What is it?" I try a softer voice with him. "Tell me what's goin' on here. Tell me the truth." "Are you okay in here?" "I'll find you a new place if not."

He looks at me. "You know I don't have much time left… I've spent enough time runnin' and lyin' all of these years." You have?

"Runnin' and lyin' from who?" my body barks back quick. Why am I so angry? His breathing becoming more timid. His eyes look…lost, like he doesn't know who he is or what he's going to say.

"Uncle, whatever you have to say, I'm here; I'm here for you right now. Do you need somethin'? I'll do whatever ya need. You're the only family I have, 'n' I love ya." His eyebrows rise. Is that a thought he'll finally share? "What is it, Uncle?"

"Do you remember Ramón, Roy?"

Ramón. That's weird. I was just thinking about the fella earlier today.

"Yeah, I do." "He was your best friend and a cool fella to have around. I was actually pretty upset when you moved us when I was fourteen in 1992, and I never saw him again, or got an explanation about it." Silence between us again. I stay still. Is he gonna say more? I watch him search for words. "Did you owe him money? Did you fuck one of his broads? Did he fuck one of yours? Did he have a sister you fucked that you weren't s'pose to? Why are you bringin' him up? I haven't heard ya say his name in…well, twenty years, actually. Since the day we moved quick that day—leaving him and everything in his room behind." "Like ya wanted to disappear on him or somethin'?" "Why?"

He continues to lie there in front of me, silent. What could be so difficult to say? He looks up at me, then at the entrance to the room behind me, then back at me. "Ramón was not just my roommate. He was…more." "I loved him."

Did he just say *loved*? "What?" I reply. "I've seen you with broads since the day I was born. You've been with Sheila since the year we moved to Owenton. I just saw her here a few moments ago as I walked in."

"Sheila was here? I didn't see her today." His reply confused.

"Yeah, Uncle. Sheila, *your wife of twenty years*, who you love, that is a *woman*, was here just earlier today by your bedside. Are ya thinkin' okay? I don't think you know what you are sayin'?"

He now looking weaker and paler than when I first walked in. The lines in the skin of his face so tense, versus when they were relaxed while he was asleep, looking so peaceful. "Maybe you are right, Roy." They begin to relax. "Maybe I am losin' my mind after all. Just ignore everythin' I just said." Awkward silence now between us. I don't know what else to say? He shuts his eyes and rests his head further back into his pillow. "You go on home now, back to your wife. I'll get some rest, get my brain workin' right."

"All right, have a good night." I get up and walk to exit his room. I turn around as I get to the door. "I love ya; sleep well." He's right. Lucy is expecting me for dinner. I need to go home and be with my wife.

But I kind of like a different idea more.

7

———

I DON'T WANT to go home. I'm not ready. My head shaking, I pull out my phone as I leave my uncle's room, my thumb swiping through different messages on Grindr.

> Sup

> Looking bro?

> I'm at the motel 6 off interstate 64, looking to suck.

> Yo

> Hey

> Be my bitch?

> Heyy, what's up

> hi

> btm?

Too many messages to go through now in a public hallway —what am I thinking? But I'm horny again. Is it because of the dream? I start walking and messaging, bouncing attention from my phone to my surroundings every few steps to make sure no one can see my phone and that no one is approaching or coming up behind me. I click on the Motel 6 guy and reply with a pic of my dick and ask him if he can meet now. I put my phone back in my pocket, look up and realize I'm lost in the nursing home. Must have been too distracted. I stand in confusion, turning around and looking all over.

What the fuck *is* going on here?

That faggot Andrew probably inspired these crazy and delusional ideas in my uncle's head. Maybe because a fag is taking care of him in his final days, it's rubbing off somehow on him— his mind now confusing Andrew's twisted kindness with the good memories of his past with his best friend, Ramón. I don't know how else to make sense of it? How could my uncle say that he *loved a man*? I should figure out the mix of drugs that he is on. I want what he's having!

I need a fucking drink, and now a hole to fuck.

Or I guess a mouth to use will do.

I continue walking. I look right as I pass by the cafeteria. No fucking shit, as I live and breathe, right in front of my eyes: Sheila sitting down, laughing with a fella, and two full plates of food in front of them. I stop in my tracks, surprised yet not surprised, and stare at that evil, conniving bitch. The guy she is eating with looks like my uncle's doctor. I've met him a few times. Wow. I mean, fuck, my uncle doesn't really have that much time left; she couldn't have waited a few more weeks? Shacking up with a man under the same roof he's dying under? Jesus Christ. At least I'm not the only one committing adultery.

I charge through the cafeteria doors. A loud *click* sounds. Only a few other folks are inside, so our audience is small. Sheila and Dr. Pingree both turn their heads toward me and keep focus as I walk toward them. Sheila mouths *Oh fuck* as I make my way to their table. Dr. Pingree's chin is down, but his eyes are up at me. Hey, you little bitch.

I get to them, set my hands on the table between them, and lean my head down to their level, Sheila to my right, Dr. Fuckaroo to my left. "Good evening, you two. How's your dinner?" Smirking, I turn left and right to make eye contact with both.

"We were just having a bite and talkin' about your uncle's health," Sheila says most confidently and casually, adjusting her legs, crossed under the table.

I then see Dr. Pingree's body shift after hers. They playing footsies or some shit here too? "Do I make you nervous, Dr. Pingree?"

"No, sir…I mean Roy, not at all," he replies, maintaining eye contact with me and taking a sip of his water. "Why, uh, why would you make me nervous?"

"Hm." "Just a thought. Good. I don't know why you would need to feel nervous 'round me, especially if there is nothin' goin' on here." I remove my hands from the table, lean back up to a straight position to stand tall above them, and cross my arms—shaking my head in a way to mock them. "So, my uncle's health, then, is it that you are discussing? What is the latest update? How is his mind?"

"His mind?" Dr. Pingree looks up at me. "His mind is fine. The stroke, as you know, has taken most of his mobility away, and the cancer continues to…spread from the inside, but his brain is perfectly healthy for now."

Hm. "Is that so?" I look at Sheila.

She puts her hand on her chest. "Why are you lookin' at me?"

I can feel my eyes sharpen at her. "I don't know; you are his wife." My shoulders shrug.

I turn to Dr. Pingree. "Thank you for the information, Doc. How much time do you think he has?"

"Um, well, I can't really predict too accurately." He takes a bite off his plate. What type of bitch doctor is this? Nervous. Can't give me details. Hiding behind chomps of food in his mouth. Shagging my dying uncle's wife, probably because he can't get his own because he's a dweeb.

"Dr. Pingree, I just need a ballpark." I open my hand and toss my arm in the air in front of me and him, then drop it back to my side. I tilt my head his direction. "Please." I give him a fake polite smile, removing my smirk.

"Well, he's been doing very good, so it's very hard to accurately—"

"Dr. Pingree!" I shout. He just about makes me as mad as Andrew does.

"Yes, um, I would say your uncle has several weeks to maybe a few months left." He clears his throat and looks down at the table.

"Several weeks to a few months?" Sheila gasps out loud. What are you so surprised about?

My head cocks her direction. "You just can't wait to get rid of him, can ya?" She pushes her lips closed and tries to remain still. "That's what I thought." "You know, one day, my lady, you are gonna rot in hell." "You're nothin' but a gold-diggin' bitch." Before she can speak, I turn around from the table and walk back through the doors I came through.

I. Need. A. Drink.

I always need a drink.

I check my phone, 8:12 p.m. All right, I should text Lucy now that I'm on my way back. I finally recognize the halls I'm walking out through. I swipe back on Grindr to see if I have any new messages:

Lookin

Sissy boy needs hole filled

Hey :)

Yes, I can meet now, park on the dark road
behind the motel 6, message me when you
get here

I tap on the Motel 6 fella again. This is a bad idea, but I
can't shake it:

okay coming now.

8

I EXIT the nursing home and make my way to my car. Am I really doing this? Yes. I am. My nerves and excitement all over again controlling me, directing me.

I can't stop it. I don't want to stop it.

But I need to stop it.

Right as I grab the door handle to the driver's seat of my car, my eyes look up and I see catty-corner to me—is that a person sobbing? Their truck turned off and parked. Sitting in the passenger seat. That guy looks familiar. I stand for a second next to my car and continue to look. I can't tell who it is. I open the door, get in, and start my ignition. My automatic lights come on, lighting up the dark parking lot. It's a guy. He looks my direction, and then I recognize who it is.

Andrew

I put my head down to avoid him. Did he see me? Does he know it's me?

I find and take a swig of whiskey from one of the flasks I have on the floor in my car and start scanning through more messages on Grindr. There are a whole new bunch of profiles here. I guess I haven't had this app for long, so I'm still learning about it all. I just downloaded it only a few weeks ago. Kind of shocked how you go from one town to the next and it's a whole new batch of horny, sick fags; all hiding. Lurking around underneath everyone's noses. My profile is blank; I just have my height and my weight—just like a lot of them.

I look back up in Andrew's direction; he's still in the passenger seat of his truck. Why is he in the passenger seat? Sobbing? But the sobbing now seems to have stopped.

What's his fucking deal?

I turn off my car, step outside, and walk toward him. Fuck. What am I doing? He notices me when I am a few yards away. He watches me, still, like an owl in headlights, as I walk in front of his truck, making it to the driver's side door. I open it.

"What do you want? I'll call the cops, Roy. I swear," he screeches, but I'm not threatened at all by him. His voice just a sad whimper to me, really. And cops don't give a fuck about people like you in this town, anyways.

My hand still on the door handle, I open my other hand in the air in front of him, over the driver's side seat, and lean my head into the truck. "I'm not…" "I'm not gonna fuck with ya. Can I sit?"

"No." He turns his head away to look out the passenger-side window.

I look through the window he is looking through. What is he looking at? Nothing. It's dark out, and no one is around. I then slowly sit in the truck next to him, watching him carefully as I get fully in and close the door. "What are you lookin' at?"

"Nothing. Why are you in my car?" He turns to look at me, his eyes and face red.

"Well, I was mindin' my own business, about ready to leave this shithole you call your work, 'n' saw ya a mess in here."

His brown eyes sending a warm vibration into me; a new gloss over them I haven't seen before. "You just called me a faggot and tripped me to the ground, Roy. Why are you now in my car, trying to act nice to me?"

My lungs expand quick for a breath, and my hand jumps in

the air, then falls back down and slaps my lap. "I don't know. I hate people like you. You're right, I don't know why I'm in here." I grab the car door handle with my other hand to open and exit. My leg swings out. I turn my head back. "Is that really why you're crying?" "I've done way worse to people." I turn my head back to exit. "Bye—"

He grabs my right hand, on my lap, with his left hand. "Stop."

My body stops just as I am about to transfer my weight onto my leg already outside the truck. I feel his cold hand on top of mine. My eyes dart down to see if it is actually true. His hand is on top of mine, and he has a small squeeze over it. I don't mind his touch. I actually might like it.

A picture shoots across my mind of his hand on my uncle's, just like it's set on top of mine now. A fast blink, and my eyes make contact with his. "Let go of my hand…right now." He lets go and puts both of his hands open in the air as if I have him at gunpoint. My right hand swings across my torso, away from him; with it now free in front of my face, I look through it, through the windshield, and see my car. I look back at him. "I gotta go. Good night."

I exit his truck, and as I shut the door, I hear, "Roy." No screech or whimper, but loud and demanding. I keep walking and hear again louder from behind me, "Roy!"

I turn around now at the front of my car. "You stop shoutin' my name out loud." "Faggot!" I yell back at him across the parking lot. I scan to see if anyone is around. Still no one. He's still in the passenger seat of his truck, with his window rolled down, staring at me. Just as my head follows my body, swinging into my car, I hear from his direction, "Good night."

His resilient voice. *Good night.*

There's a softness about it I like—*and* hate.

I immediately start my car and gas it out of the parking lot. Where is that flask? My hand finds it, digging in the back seat as

I drive quickly, controlling the steering wheel with my knee. I take several swigs and open up Grindr on my phone.

A couple photos have been sent, and a new message:

Where are you?

I type a reply fast:

I'm on my way

9

JUST PARKED, I type out…This new adrenaline back. This time a little bit tamer. Why? Maybe because this is the second time? Maybe because it's dark and I'm not meeting at my apartment? My insides feel like bubbles multiplying, about to pop. I'm not sure what they'll release. My thumb now hovering over the send button. I followed his directions where to go. My car sitting with its lights off on the side of an abandoned, narrow road behind the Motel 6. This guy has a beard in his pic. I don't know if I'm into it. He just wants to suck me off.

I need it.

A quick release down his throat, and then I'll get home quick. Lucy won't know a thing. My right leg bouncing. Is the car shaking? I can't believe I'm doing this again.

This spot does seem pretty hidden, with no traffic. Unkempt branches from trees and bushes run overgrown on the sides of the narrow road, perpendicular to the back of the motel. It feels almost too hidden. Is this safe? If he is a serial killer, this would be the spot to send me to meet him. If I were a serial killer, I'd target the fags too.

Worst case scenario, I'm sure I can take him. Ugh. Shit. What if he really is a serial killer? My foot back on the brake and hand on the ignition key to start the car. Maybe I should get the fuck out of here. I can't. The sexual urge inside me is far too overcoming. Wow, not even the idea of possible murder or a mugging can get me to turn this car on and go.

Or does this actually make it more exciting and arousing? Hooking up with a stranger in a world hidden and forbidden from others. Taking a quick chance to release a nut, with a possible exposure that would ruin me. Ruin us. The tip of my dick now controlling my thumb.

Tap

An impulse. Do or die. I say do. Message sent.

I set my phone face up on my lap. A few minutes go by, and my phone vibrates, illuminating with a new message: **walking now.**

My lungs exhaling slowly. How long was I holding that breath? My body adjusts itself in my seat. I should leave. Two times in one day? What am I doing? I can take off. I can drive away. Drive, Roy. Turn the car on and run. Go!

I don't want to. I grab my flask and take a swig, and a few more.

Vibrate…vibrate…

A text message.

Lucy

> Hi dear, hope your visit with your uncle is going well. Checking in on a time you might be back? Asking because I want to make sure dinner is ready and hot for you!

Damn.

I look at the time on my phone. 8:47 p.m.

WHAT AM I DOING? Lucy just texted me, and it's near nine o'clock. DRIVE HOME, Roy. Just do it…I can't. I'm far too excited, nervous again. It feels like a new side of me that I can't ignore has just been awakened today. My body tensing up at the thought.

Up ahead of me, about half a football field's length down this narrow road behind the back of the motel, a few lights expose beat-up dumpsters. This guy must have met other guys here before. Who would come back here? His directions were so specific, and I can't imagine anyone uses or knows about this road.

A figure appears from the side of one of the dumpsters. Jesus.

Okay, that's actually kind of creepy. Maybe this isn't that arousing. Is that him? I slump down into my seat, hiding behind the steering wheel, like a kid hiding behind a pillow they're holding upward in front of a scary movie they shouldn't be watching.

But this is real life, and I'm not a kid. And I also shouldn't be here.

My eyes peeking through, just over top of the wheel. The dark figure is walking in my direction; he's walking to me. I keep my position. That has to be him. He just messaged, walking now. I watch as he continues down the road toward me. His shadow then disappears into the darkness of the road. Shit. The light cast off from the back of the motel no longer exposes the road between my car and him. My right leg unable to sit still. What the fuck did I just agree to? This is insane! I should turn on my lights. No. I can't; that would expose the dark path and draw attention. But who's around? *Only me.* Should I turn on my interior lights? No, he will just be able to see me, and then I really won't see him approaching. My body adjusts itself up higher in my seat, now nose level with the top of the steering wheel, to get a better view in front of me.

What is hiding behind my steering wheel like a little bitch gonna do? I need to face him head on, or at least be able to quickly turn the car on and floor this son of a bitch and get the fuck out of here. I keep my foot over the brake pedal and my hand over the key in the ignition.

There he is! About twenty yards ahead.

I clear my throat and crack my window to breathe in some fresh air. My eyes watching his every move as he inches closer. He's wearing all black, a hoodie, with both hands tucked in front and the hood over his head. Fuck me. What weapons do I got in here? A few empty flasks behind me, one half-full flask to the left of me in my door—that one at least has some weight in it if I need to strike him. I take a swig of it. Okay, now a little less weight. I chuckle to myself. He's now seconds away from arriving at my passenger-side door. I can hear his footsteps approach as the stones and sticks on the road roll and scratch beneath his feet. Everything is so dark—outside, his clothing. It looks as if a dementor is arriving to suck my soul out—well, actually just my semen.

What could possibly go wrong?

I like Harry Potter; this is a good sign. The dementor-fuckery figure lifts the car handle to open the door, and he struggles. Whoops. I left the door locked. Smart man. I quickly unlock it, and he lifts the car door handle again, opens the door, and sits right next to me.

"Hey." He takes off his hood and looks at me. "How's it going?" His beard really hairy on his face.

"Good…" I look at him and nod. I look back forward at the motel up in the distance, and at my side mirror. No one. Am I into it? I don't know what the fuck I'm feeling anymore. How do I get out of this?

"Cool, cool." He then leans over and extends his arm across and grabs my crotch with his hand. His manly hand.

My body freezing except for my head. My chin dropping down to look at his heavy hand over my crotch. My head turns slowly right to look at him, his eyes focused on his hand on me. He doesn't even look up at me. He starts pushing his fingers around and through, massaging my dick and balls just underneath my zipper. The strength of each finger pressing and pulling in all directions. It feels good. My right leg finally losing its Adderall, relaxing. My eyes still on him, watching his eyes enjoy what he's seeing and doing.

Ugh. Unzip me.

"That feel good?" He puts more pressure from his hand, now using the width of his palm and extending his fingers to grab and work deeper.

"Yeah…" I realize I'm holding my breath again, and I exhale. "It's good." I bring my head up to a forward position and set my eyes on the far-off dumpster he appeared from behind. My dick now starting to get hard from his touch.

Damn. Who would have thought a dumpster dementor could be so erotic? So far…

"You can relax, man." Shit, is it that obvious? My leg isn't bouncing anymore, and I thought my breathing was back to normal?

I look back at him, and he finally looks at me. A desire and excitement in his eyes. He glues them back to his hand on my crotch, like a sexual fiend addicted to this adrenaline, too, like me. I get it. My nerves—of him making a move to kill me—now a thought out of mind. "Yeah, okay."

He leans over my center console, with his lips forward. I stay still. He continues toward my neck. "Woah." I raise my arm up to block him; my head cocks left, away.

He doesn't bounce back or react physically at all to my block; he just pauses in place. "Hey, you don't like kissing, no problem. Sorry." He smiles and looks back down to focus his eyes on my crotch again. I like seeing his eyes just focused there. His hunger and curiosity extending down, expressed through his hand touching me. It makes my dick harder.

"Yeah…no, I'm uh, not into that." My head still cocked left, away from him, I bring my right arm back down from blocking him. I know he can feel my hard dick.

He looks back up at me. "Why don't you put your seat down a bit." "Relax."

"You want me to relax? How do I know you don't have a

knife on ya or somethin'?" My body shifts to the left side of my seat. His hand slingshots back to his side. My left hand on the handle of my door.

He chuckles. "A knife?" I remain silent and in my position. His voice light. He then settles down. "Dude, I don't have a knife. I'm not here to stab you; I'm just here to suck your dick real quick." "That's it."

Wow. His forwardness and words are…Just wow. "Okay, yeah." "Yeah, I know." "Uh, sorry." I shake my head. "Uh… what I do…do I—"

He interrupts me. "Put your seat back. I'll do the rest, sexy."

Sexy? I look at him and somehow feel…trust? How the fuck did I go from fear of a possible shank seconds ago to, now, trust? Or am I just really needing to get off, and my dick is deceiving me, from the spell of this dark, phantom, hairy creature massaging my balls again? It is the first time I've heard a man call me sexy. Must be his eyes…"Yeah…okay." I let go of the car door handle and pull the lever on the side of my seat base. I lean my seat back a bit. Maybe forty-five degrees. This way I can still be upright in case I need to react to something. Fuck it, I'm putting the seat back all the way. Let the dumpster dementor take the wheel!

My eyes now looking up at the beige cloth ceiling of my car. The touch from his hand to my dick and balls now feels warmer somehow.

"How does that feel?"

"It's good." I push my chin down to my chest to look at him. He's now positioned his head over my cock and is massaging heavier. His hands are strong, and his face just above my crotch is…so fucking hot, patiently waiting to suck the cum inside out of me. I let out a soft *ahh*. "It feels very good." I put my head back on the seat and set my eyes back on the ceiling of my car, my dick now getting harder from the sight and touch of him. My hesitations and thoughts of danger now completely gone. Nothing else matters. I have no concerns.

I shut my eyes. He's now rubbing my shaft through my pants, grabbing it with his warm palm and still giving my balls attention with the thick tips of his fingers. My jeans begin to unzip. Finally.

Shit. I didn't shower today after first fucking that guy earlier and then working all day. I just remembered.

My head lifts up to look over at him; he's already pulling my dick through my boxers, and then he engulfs it whole in one swing. I'm inside his wet, hungry mouth. He lets out a grunting moan as he takes all my dick, over his tongue and down his throat. His manly beard I was afraid of is slightly tickling my balls, and I like it. I think it makes me even harder. My dick now down his throat, he inhales through his nose as he pushes his face through my balls and nuzzles in my inner thighs.

I exhale a long *fuck* as my head falls back on the seat.

I hear him moan again as he then begins to take my dick in and out of his throat, but keeping my head always in his mouth. I guess he doesn't care; maybe he likes the dried-up cum and ass sweat from hours ago.

My skin-stained sex scent from earlier.

A hand of his cupping my wet balls. The saliva he's leaving behind drizzling down my shaft. He's working my shaft with his tongue, circling around my sensitive tip. He then pushes his head down and opens up for the tip of my dick to push down his throat again. His Adam's apple wanting to fight my tip for space. But I'm winning.

My eyes keep rolling from the back of my head to forward, back up at the ceiling of my car. The glass in the car has already fogged. Jesus, this is so hot. This is so fucking hot. Literally I'm hot too. My head springs back up to watch.

I grab his forehead with one hand, the other grabbing the back of his head. I hold his head in the position I want, hovering just above the length of my dick, keep my tip kissing his wet lips. I force my heels down into the floor of my car and thrust my hips up. My dick follows the wet track of his tongue and back down his throat. But this time, at my control.

I keep his head in position with my hands and begin to face fuck him. He begins to grunt more, struggling to breathe through his nose, as my dick chokes him. I think he likes his throat being forced open. Little slut. My hands then force his head all the way down, my hips still thrusted up. I keep pressure down, my dick forcing his throat to expand. His lips now at my balls and his wet beard sending sensations through my thighs. He chokes, and saliva spits out from the sides of his mouth. I release him from my grip. He can have a breath.

"Holy shit, dude." His eyes on my cock and his hand jerking me off. He lets out a loud moan, opens his mouth to take my dick again. He's now using the strength of his grip on my wet shaft to get me going. His warm mouth; tongue still swimming in and around my tip; jerking me off and blowing me at the same time. Holy fuck, I'm gonna cum so hard.

"Fuck, man, you're gonna make me cum."

He looks up at me. We make eye contact. His devious desire. I love seeing his face as my dick travels through the inside of his mouth, swishing over his tongue and pushing through his cheeks. He closes his eyes, grabs the base of my dick further, and I watch as he opens his throat so he can slam his head back down on my dick and hold it there. My head falls back down onto the seat. I feel him start to jerk me off with that perfect rhythm again, and he puts his mouth in that perfect position just hovered above. Waiting. When I cum, I want to watch him swallow everything. I want to see my dick pulse, and his face while I pulse in it.

"You want my cum, huh?" I lean my head up.

"Mm-hmm," he grunts.

"Fuck, that feels so good…Shit." I close my eyes, keeping my head up. I can feel myself getting close. "Fuck, just like that, keep doing exactly that." His pace has increased, his rhythm so good, just faster. My car windows a steam room. I grab his head again the same way I grabbed it before, dig my heels back in the floor of the car, and rapidly face fuck him more. My wet balls now slapping the side of his face as I jackhammer my dick down his throat. My eyes closed, I hear him choke and spit more, but I keep going; he doesn't tap out. His grunts just get louder—turning me on even more. "Shit, I'm gonna cum, fuuck. I'm gonna cu—" I force his head down to feed him as deep as I can down his throat. My eyes popping open from the release—flashes of red and blue are illuminating the inside of the car. My insides vacuumed out, like the devil himself has just plucked out my soul.

My hands rip and push his head off my dick, his head banging into my steering wheel; my cum spewing up onto his face like water exploding out a loose nut on top of a fire hydrant. He looks at me in confusion and disappointment; murmuring? My cum still pumping out of me, now landing on my shirt. He falls back to the passenger side. I continue to watch his reaction in silence. He then notices the colors flash in the fog on the windows. I put my seat up slowly. We're both silent now, stuck in the smell of my sweaty cum. Caught. Committing faggot acts. We're fucked. *I'm* so fucked. I've never been this terrified in my life. What do I do?

10

——————

"You said this road was abandoned," I whisper as I look at my window, still cracked open.

He whispers "fuck" repeatedly at the red-and-blue fog while slamming his foot up and down, then puts his head down into his hand, the other hand clawing like a cat on his thigh.

"Sh. They can't see us. So maybe they will drive away?" I turn around to check that all the windows are fully fogged. There is no visibility—except through the crack in my driver's side window. The red-and-blue flashing is the strongest to my left. I'm guessing there is just one cop car, to my left and in front of me.

"Roy Stevens, step outside of the vehicle."

The bearded man and I both look at each other as we hear a cop speak through her mic. Did I just hear my name? The devil returning my soul, the beat of my heart back, pounding under my ribs.

Oh my god. *This morning* They finally caught me. Found me.

Have I been followed?

"Are you Roy Stevens?" he asks me.

I remain silent. Thinking. The disturbed fella then raising his voice. "Who are you?"

I whisper back quick, "Sh." "Calm down." I raise my hand flat in the air in front of him. "They probably just ran my license plate and got my name that way." For fuck's sake I hope that's what it is. That's got to be it.

"I can't stay calm. My wife and kids are in that motel. I can't stay fucking calm." Is he about to have a panic attack or something? "Maybe I can run into the woods and they won't find me."

Did I just hear "wife and kids"?

"Roy Stevens, I'm only gonna ask ya one more time." We lock eyes, still, listening. "Step outside of the vehicle or we will be forced to enter." We? There is more than one cop? Fuck. Why do they need to enter? WHY?

"I can't get caught." He puts his hand on the passenger door handle. He starts to open the car door. In a flash I ignite the engine; put the car into drive, and gas it.

The car catches him back into his seat; he was almost halfway out. I keep the steering wheel a little to the right. I'm driving blind; hopefully I won't hit a cop. The shrubs smack his door back shut and the car shakes. We can hear branches breaking and scratching along the right side of my car as we speed blindly forward. Fuck it. How far have we gone? I glance at the speedometer.

37 mph

I think we made it past. I open my window and put my head out to see in front of me. No cop cars, and the dumpsters behind the back of the motel still up ahead. We made it! I turn my head back and actually see two cop cars. Holy shit. Whew. I throw my hand up and shout into the air, "Hoo-wee!"

"Whoa! Stop! Stop the car! What are you doing?" My scaredy-cat, dick-sucking dementor screeching.

I turn to look at him, keeping my head outside the window so I can still see the road. "No. We are not getting caught out here." I turn the heat on full blast to get the fog off the glass windows inside the car. "Running into the forest? That was your best idea? Shit. There were two cop cars back there. If you were gonna flee the scene, anyways, what's the difference?"

"The difference is I don't know who you are." His hands flying up in the air, his eyes bulging out of his skull.

"Well." "I'm Roy Stevens! Weren't ya listenin'?" I yell and give him a grin. Is that my cum on his beard? That's hilarious.

Where's my flask? I reach down into the car door to find it and take more swigs. I turn to him. "You want some?" The windshield now just barely giving us clearance to see through near the vent. I tuck my head down close to the top of the dashboard to see through the little pocket of windshield finally clear. We are seconds away from crashing into a dumpster. I whip my head back out the window to see the road more clearly. We arrive at the back of the hotel from the road. I turn the steering wheel right, hard. The car swerves, my back bumper nearly clipping the dumpster.

"No. I don't want any. Stop and let me out." He opens the door—to jump? But he doesn't. I think the car is going too fast for him. Pussy.

"Go ahead, jump. I ain't stoppin'. I'm gonna lose them cops. I know this town like the back of my hand. You wanna jump 'n' meet your wife 'n' kids with a few cops and my cum on your face, you go on ahead." I let out a laugh as I zip around the side of the hotel and gun it after turning right onto a country road.

He closes the door and puts his seat belt on. "Where are you taking us?" He turns back to see if the cops are following behind. My eyes in the rearview mirror, waiting to see the flashes of red and blue appear. My windshield fully clear now. Where should we go? I glance at my speedometer.

92 mph

Speed limit is fifty-five miles per hour on these roads. We are about half a mile east of the motel now. How did they find me? Can the cops really be after me for making some fag bleed a little this morning? Come on.

"Where are we going?" he shouts at me.

"I don't know. Shut the fuck up. Give me a fuckin' second." And then I see it, those terrifying flashes of red and blue in my rearview mirror. Fuck.

The cops are definitely following us. A road appears up just in front, almost as soon as I see the red and blue lights. I veer right, hard.

"What did you do?" "Who are you?" My cum still on his beard, winking at me from the flashes that bounce off it from the streetlights we pass. I crack a smile and begin to laugh again. I step further on the gas…

"This is funny to you?" Freaking out and flustered. "This is funny to you!?" he shouts, then lunges at the steering wheel with both hands. "Stop. Stop the car!"

He's trying to get an actual grip and will crash us. I grab him by the neck with my right hand, press my fingers down hard, and flex my arm out to keep him away. "Stop. I have an idea," I say. He starts hitting my right arm with both of his hands to make me break loose. "Stop. Would you calm down?" I press further, bend my arm and then thrust it forward, releasing my grip and throwing him into the door. He puts both hands on his neck, breathing heavily.

Maybe that was a little aggressive.

"I'm sorry, okay. I'm freakin' out, too, but you don't see me bitchin' like a woman, do you?"

He's frozen against the door, as far away from me as possible. "I'm not gonna hurt ya. I was laughin' because my cum is still on your beard, okay?" "Dumbass." "No, this is not funny to me." I glance in my rearview mirror. Nothing. I recognize the intersection coming up just ahead and now know where I am. "Listen, I have an idea." "Trust me."

He takes the inside of his shirt below his neck and wipes his beard aggressively, then looks at me. "Dude, I don't care who the fuck, or what the fuck, you are. Can you just stop the fucking car, please, and let me out? Please. I have two kids."

An intersection quickly approaching. I turn left at it. As I make the turn, I look out my window and still see no flashes of red or blue coming from behind. "Look. I lost them." I gun it again, bringing the car from a skidded left turn to seventy-plus miles per hour up and down the hills.

"Listen, I know a place two more turns. I'll get us there. I'll turn off the car lights, and we can hide for a few. I'll take you back to your kids 'n' wife. I promise."

"Fuck that. I'm not going anywhere with you."

"Seriously? You have a wife 'n' kids! I'm trying to help you. You want them to find out about whatever the fuck you were just doin'? Would that make them happy?"

"I don't need your help. What makes you think I need your help?"

The next intersection approaches and has a stop sign. I slam on the brakes, causing the car to skid again, this time to a full stop.

Well, fuck you, then. I extend my right hand over him. He jolts back in his seat. I reach past and grab the passenger door handle, pull it, and push his door open. "Get the fuck out, then." I throw my right hand up in the air in front of him. He swings his legs out, looks right to see the dust off the road in the air behind us, looks forward and then left and right to see darkness and woods in all directions. "Go! You said you wanted out; get out." He turns to look at me, his eyes widened. What is he doing? He's wasting my fucking time. The cops could still be trailing behind us.

"Where are we?" He looks at me, almost half his body yet again outside the car.

"Get the fuck out. Or I'm gassing it again and that door is going to break your legs." I hold my foot on the brake and hit the gas. The back wheels start spinning, and the car begins to shake. "What are you gonna do, cowboy?" "Now or never. Decide."

He swings his legs back into the car and shuts the door.

"Okay, go." He puts his seat belt on. "You better get me back."
"Please."

"Jesus Christ." I let go of the brake and turn the steering wheel right. The car whips off, now southbound, and we continue. Silence now between us. Finally. My speed a little down now.

Both of our eyes scouring all mirrors at every second, searching for any sight of red or blue flashes. Nothing. An incoming call from Lucy comes through the Bluetooth. Her name appearing on the center dashboard. Fuck. I never texted her back.

I notice him see her name on the screen and look at me. "Who is Lucy?"

"She's nobody. Mind your own business." I keep my face tight and stern.

I let her call continue to ring and go to voicemail. Not a peep more from the fella. I'm gonna have to come up with something clever to explain to her why I'm so late for dinner… and why I didn't get back to her either…"We are approaching the house now." No streetlights around, because on this road there are just a few houses for every mile you go. Did we actually make it? An old black aluminum mailbox appears on the left, with a dirt driveway just before it. This is it. I turn into the driveway. Double checking again that no cops are coming from behind or ahead. Nothing.

"Where are we? Why did you take us here?" He puts his right hand back on the door handle.

"I used to live here, moved here to this house when I was fourteen." I look at him and take a swig of my flask. I swing the car around the back of the house, passing a narrow, shadowed path to my right. Lying on the forest floor, it's a path that only someone that has lived here would know about. Ain't that something? Another narrow path for him and me to hide in. I should write a love story. Hopefully this one gives us more luck. I set the gear in reverse and turn my head back. I drive the car backward, following the narrow path between the tight trees and shrubs, coming just inches from hitting both mirrors off as I reverse us back deeper into the woods. My rear lights bounce a soft red light off the large tree trunk just a few more feet backward. The trunk now at my back window, I turn the car off and keep our windows open.

"You wanna smoke?" I reach over and grab a pack of Marlboros from my glove box. I open the pack, put a cig in my mouth, light it up, and pass the pack to him.

"I don't smoke."

"Okay, well, shoot yourself, then." I go to set the pack in the cup holder between us.

"All right, fine, fuck it." He grabs the pack from my hand and grabs a cigarette. He takes it out and sets the pack down in the cup holder. He looks at both ends, and then looks at me.

"Haven't you smoked a cigarette before?"

"Yeah. I have. It's just been a while." He inspects it and then puts the right end in his mouth. "You got a light?"

"Of course I do." I extend my arm across the car and light the lighter in my hand in front of his face. I can't help but watch his lips as they pucker and suck near my flame, my hand. The cigarette finally catches. He leans back into the seat and blows the smoke outside his window.

I take another swig from my flask. "What's your name?"

"You don't need to know my name. I never share my name." "You actually share yours?"

"Well, shit, I was just makin' conversation. Sorry I fuckin' asked." I turn my head to the left to look out my window. I look up through the trees at the night sky and see a bright full moon. "Not a cloud in sight tonight." I turn back to him. "Well, this turned out to be some shit experience, but at least we got ourselves a full moon." I give him a cheesy smile.

He leans forward to look up through the windshield, and then his attention shifts forward. "Can you see the road from here?"

"Can you see the road from here?" I look forward, mimicking him. I can barely see the back of my uncle's house in front of us from the narrow path I drove us back on.

"No, I'm not blind; I'm just asking, Can we see if a car is coming or not, from, like, their headlights?"

I shake my head. "I don't think so." I look at my car clock. 9:43 p.m.

Lucy Stevens then appears on the center dashboard again. The stereo in my car: *"Incoming call from Lucy Stevens."* Shit. I sit and stare at her name on the screen in the dashboard and take another swig of my flask. I turn the volume to zero and turn my head back left to look out the driver's side window at the sky. I stare at the full moon. Lord, get me out of this.

"Who is Lucy? Why has she called you twice?" His words finally calm. "You have a wife and kids, too, don't you?"

My head snaps quick. "No, I don't have a wife. I'm not a fuckin' piece of shit like you. Again, it's none of your fuckin' business." "Be quiet." *Lucy Stevens*, still on the screen illuminating the car.

"All right...Well, I guess she's your sister or something. Whatever." "Must be lucky to know a guy like you." "A badass that thinks he can outrun the cops."

"Lucky?" "You think your wife is lucky to have you?"

He pauses and looks down. "Why would you ask me that? Of course she is. I take care of her; I'm good to our kids. Yeah, we fight here and there, but I do my best to make her happy." "All couples have their things."

Things? "Does she know you like to suck fellas off behind motels?"

He lets out a laugh. "You're joking, right?" He looks at me, his smile then fading off his face after realizing, I guess, my question is serious.

I take a puff of my cig and exhale. "No, I wasn't, actually. I was just curious." A few moments of silence go by. Doesn't he feel any guilt like I do? Will this knot around my heart be attached to an anchor I have to drag my whole life? And what if the anchor eventually gets stuck. How will I move then? "You don't feel any guilt? Runnin' around…hookin' up with fellas… betrayin' her?"

"Dude, I'm confused? How do you go from choking me to now this weird pillow talk?" We make eye contact and hold it for a moment. No more fear or panic in his eyes. God knows how I fucking look. His face lights up a bit. "Lucy *is* your wife."

I shake my head. "No. She is not." I pause, and he sits in silence looking at me, with my head now down. Should I just fucking tell him? Tell *someone*? It might make me feel better? "Okay…she is. We were high school sweethearts. Everyone expected us to get married." "We're actually trying now to have kids…and I've never done this before." A new vibration rattles inside me. My head turns left to look back up at the moon. A tear I can't hold falls from my left eye down my cheek. I quickly wipe it with my hand and take a swig of the last of my whiskey. I don't really feel any better. I think I feel worse.

11

———————

1:02 A.M.

I look above the car dashboard—

A car's headlights flash across the side of my uncle's house. Shit.

The car now coming up from the left side of the house, following the same pathway that I took to circle the house before I reversed us back into this spot. Did I leave any tracks? Fuck, I didn't think about that.

We're both huddling now in the center of the car, next to each other, with our eyes just peeping over the dashboard. The car stops right where I stopped to reverse us back in here. Directly behind the house. The red taillights so bright. The only light, illuminating the thick woods and grassy ground with a red hue. This is it. The death of us.

Just go, keep moving. Come on.

The taillights going out

I'm trying to make out what type of car it is. I can't. "Can you tell what type of car it is?" "Is it a cop car?" What other type of car would be here? Is it Sheila's?

He shakes his head as he squints. "No, I can't tell."

"Neither can I."

Our breaths hold as we wait for our eyes to adjust back to the dark after staring at the electric red.

The car door opens. A figure steps out.

"Is that a cop?" he asks me.

"I don't know."

I see the figure disappear forward, past their car, and then it's gone. Son of a bitch.

"Where did they go?"

"I don't know." We remain in silence, and then I see it again. The figure appears, walking around the house, following the path they drove in on. I point slowly so the guy can follow my index finger to see him too. The figure gets back in his car —we hear the door open and shut. And we see the red lights back on. Whew. The red lights now giving me relief. We made it. I think we made it? The car starts to move slowly forward, and we watch it disappear around the house, and then it's gone.

We both let out sighs of relief. Feels like both our hearts stopped beating there for a second as we saw our lives flash before our eyes. I wonder why the cop circled the house on foot? Maybe they wanted a closer look.

"All right, let's go," he says, trying to command me. "I gotta get back to my wife. She's probably wondering where I'm at. I told her I was just going out for a walk to get some air; now I reek of cigarettes and have been gone for hours. Shit, those cops are probably out now looking for me and not you—knowing her, she probably called them herself."

"No. Not yet. That was probably a cop; we need to stay here for a few until they find something else to distract them with." I take a moment to think more. "There is a pool hall near your motel. Let's go there. That'll explain the cigarette smoke. You can tell her ya went there."

"My wife is not going to think I've spent the last several hours at a pool hall and did not let her know. I don't even play pool."

Okay, what else, then? "Hm." "I have an idea…You might think it's crazy." I bite my lip. This is kind of exciting.

"I don't know what crazy else thing you could do that would surprise me at this point, *Roy Stevens*." A cute smirk on his face.

Hm. A fella saying my name like that. Is he flirting with me now?

"I'll drive us to the pool hall. I'll park my car there. I'll walk back with ya to the motel; meet your wife—you can call her when we start walkin' after we park, tell her you made a friend 'n' got distracted, and that's why ya been silent."

His eyes flash like gas on a flame. "You're fucking crazy." "You're not meeting my fucking wife."

"Look. I'm offerin' ya a great scapegoat. You've been silent on her now for at least four hours." "Who knows what story both our wives are tellin' themselves right now. If your wife at least meets me, I can be your excuse—your scapegoat, your best new pool-hall friend that you got too fucked up with from all the shots I made you do with me." I nudge his arm. "Showed you some true Southern hospitality." "What would you rather have her think?" "Hm?"

He sits there thinking. Shaking his head, and then he nods it softly. "Your idea…could work. It's fucking crazy, but it might be my best option." "How can I trust you?"

"Well, you've trusted me so far, and look where we are at. I outran the cops, and I haven't killed ya." A quick laugh erupts out of me.

"You're right, what's not to trust? I'm in the middle of nowhere with a bipolar, drunk, gay country hick. And you're right, I'm still breathing, and you haven't killed me…yet." His head points up to the ceiling of the car, he closes his eyes, and he draws an imaginary cross using his hand over his face and torso.

"Ha ha, very funny. And I'm not gay." "This is just a one-time thing." God, that word immediately made my blood boil. *Gay.* "And I have just as much as you do to lose if caught."

"Probably more: This is my town, not yours." I set my hand on the inside of his lap. "After I walk over 'n' meet your wife for a second to say hello 'n' show her what distracted ya, I will walk back to my car 'n' be out of your life forever." "Promise." I nod at him.

He nods back. "Okay, let's do it. But if this is going to convince my wife, we have to be drunk out of our minds."

My other hand now over my face, biting my middle fingernail. "That car had to be a cop car." Who else would be circling my uncle's house at the wee hours of the morning? "Let's stay here a little while longer, and then we will go."

"I agree." "And I mean it—drunk out of our fucking minds."

"I'm out of whiskey, but I can act like a drunk fool for ya." I look over and wink at him. "No problem, baby."

I quickly turn my head away from him. Did I just call him baby? I don't even call my wife that.

Don't overthink it, Roy.

12

———————

Two strangers now walking down a road only lit by moonlight, the motel just up ahead a football-field length. That drive back here was nerve racking. I went just below the speed limit, both he and I looking left to right, back to front, in silence. On edge waiting to be caught. Not one word was said.

Had we gotten pulled over, what would I have done? Two men with wives, caught in a scandal together, having been hiding in the woods—like lost, rabid wolves that should be shot. Hm. Maybe they would have taken us out of our misery, shot us then. Kept us from coming clean to our wives, the world. Maybe we should have gotten pulled over. That would have been easier.

It's a little bit after 2 a.m. Who knows where the cops are at now? They ought to be staked out to prey on the bar crowd coming out soon? Hopefully they are busy with that.

What are the odds I'd run from the cops twice today? And actually get away with it? The guy is to my right as we are walking. I like walking on the left, feels…lighter, closer to the open road rather than the dark and dead woods to his right. Actually, we should be walking along through the dark and dead woods—not on the open road like lost tweakers.

Why isn't he talking to me? Seems timid: his head down and

face so serious. Ah, there is that beautiful moon again up above us. How could you feel a problem in the world when you look up and see such a gorgeous night sky? Up ahead I see lights from a car getting to the intersection at the hotel. Should its headlights turn this way, I will drop to the ground faster than a hot shit out of my ass, crawl into the woods, and make a run for it like he wanted to earlier. Wouldn't that just be a full-circle moment. Maybe I should have let him run out of my car before? Nah. This is way more fun.

Okay. How is this going to go? What are we going to say? I don't know a thing about him, other than that he loves to suck dick. And that he's great at it. Can't bring that up to his wife. A chuckle blurts out of me. Or maybe he learned it from her? And she'll like the compliment?

Several yards up ahead to our right, bushes swish and tree twigs crack, startling both of us. We both stop in our tracks. We look where the noise came from, hunching our backs lower, as if that does anything, fucking morons. I don't see anything. We look at each other. Fear back in his eyes from the noise, or is it because I'm about to meet his wife?

I step forward to start walking again, and he follows. "That was probably just a deer." "Come on, let's go." I turn back and look at him. "Uh…ya should probably tell me your name now that I'm gonna meet your wife." I push him on his shoulder to get him to relax a little bit. "Maybe some other details about ya, somethin' that we might have in common?"

He ignores me, keeping his attention forward, scratches the back of his head with his hand. "Um, yeah, I guess you're right." "Um, fuck." "…My name is Dorian."

"Dorian?"

"Yeah, it's Greek."

"Oh, okay. Well…*Dorian*, I've never met a…Dorian, and I've never met a Greek person either. All I know are Johns, Davids, Bills…Randys. Why don't you have an accent if you're Greek?"

"I was born in the US." "Both my parents are from Greece."

"Oh, okay." More silence follows. What else can I ask him? "What else should I know about Greeks, then?" The motel appearing larger as we continue getting closer to it.

His silence persisting. He's staring at the motel approaching, not looking at me at all. Then he quickly glances my way. "I don't know, man…Family." He shrugs his shoulders. "The Greeks always put family first. Haven't you seen *My Big Fat Greek Wedding*? We're exactly like that. Except for the Windex thing. Everyone knows everyone's business, and you don't have one second to breathe alone." "Ever."

"Nope, I've never seen or heard of it."

We go back to our silent walking. I think he's nervous. I feel pretty good at the moment. I guess, How would I feel if he were about to meet Lucy? Yeah, that's a thought. Like that would ever fucking happen. I don't know if it's just the whiskey or if I'm excited about the challenge? This little skit is keeping me away from dealing with my own blown-up shit too. But hey, I'm also doing this guy a solid by helping him out, so there's one good deed for the day.

"You know what? I just remembered a fact about ancient Greeks." A jump in my step from excitement…"Some regulars at my bar rambled the other day about how in ancient Greece, warriors would bond from blowing each other. Based on your performance tonight, you're definitely Greek!" A grin splats across my face, followed by a laugh, and I push his shoulder again.

"What the fuck is wrong with you. Is this all a fucking joke to you?" He stops us on the road and turns to me. "This is my life." A beat of silence as we stare at each other. Fear back in his eyes, a glaze of goofiness probably over mine. Get it together. "You know what, this idea is fucking stupid. Turn around and go back." He puts his hand over his face, eyes shut underneath. Is he about to cry? Goddamn it, please don't cry.

"Dorian," I say calmly. I grab his wrist to pull it away softly from his face, forcing him to look at me.

He shoots his arm up after my hand touches his wrist, pushing my arm away. "Don't touch me." "You're twisted." "I can't believe I'm in this situation because of you."

"Because of me?" Not missing a second: "The ancient Greek in you wanted to swallow my load tonight—that's on you."

He then pushes me with both hands into the street, away from him. He signals with his left hand the direction where the pool hall is. "Go back." "Leave me alone."

I put my hands up with open palms. "Dorian. I am going to help you." I put my hands down to rest at my sides. "You just told me family is important to you." "I'm sorry for being a jackass." "I'm gonna make sure your family doesn't know anythin' happened tonight. We are doin' this for your family." "For that wife of yours 'n' kids."

His breathing all over the place. He looks at me, looks back down the road toward the pool hall that we came from, looks back to the motel up ahead, and then looks back at me. We are here doing this again? More seconds of silence as he thinks and breathes. He nods. "Okay, yeah." His reply not sounding all that confident to me.

He turns toward the motel and continues walking, and I follow. I hear him speak from a few steps ahead. "My wife's name is Iris." I speed up next to him to follow his new pace. "I have a son—his name is Damian—and a baby girl; her name is Penelope." I start to rehearse the names in my head so I can remember.

Iris, Damian, Penelope.

"Okay, got it." The lights of the motel now on us, we are no longer lost shadows on the road. We walk across the parking lot toward the first-floor rooms. The motel has the rooms lined up in front of the parking lot, with bright-yellow doors. We step in front of room eleven from the parking lot.

He turns right and starts walking alongside the rooms. I follow behind.

Here. We. Go.

"Hey. Remember we're drunk, okay," I shout out from behind him, then kick him in the butt.

He turns his head back, unenthused. "Yeah, yeah." Nods and looks back forward.

Which lucky yellow door will we be arriving at? Ah. His pace slows as we pass *thirty-one*, and he stops in front of thirty-two. No turning back now. Room thirty-two must be it. I turn around and look to scan the motel and parking lot one more time. Silence. Not a person or thing in sight.

He goes to slide his hotel card in the door to open it. He pauses. He stands there for more seconds, frozen in thought? What is he doing? We are deer in headlights out here. I look beyond and turn to scan our surroundings again.

I look back at him as he puts the hotel card back in his pocket and takes out his phone. Two feet next to him, now in front of the door, I lean in, whispering anxiously, "What're ya doin'?"

He takes his phone and chucks it onto the cement ground. A loud *smack*.

I see his screen shatter…He looks at me. "Get out of here. I don't need you anymore." He bends down, picks up his phone, and stays down inspecting it. The screen still turns on. What is he doing? We had a great plan? I stay standing, watching and confused. He then again forcefully smashes his phone into the cement. This time the phone ricochets into the motel door. His face now nearer to the door as he tries to catch it, his phone landing to his left, just before my feet. "Shit!" he hollers, then covers his mouth with his hands. A blink, and the door is open. A woman rocking a baby, asleep in her arm.

Iris

The woman looks down on him. "Where the hell have you been?" Sheer anger in her voice. He stands back up, and she looks at me. "Who the hell is this?" A little boy then appears at her side in his matching white-and-light-blue-striped pajamas. He stays hugging her side, his head just tall enough to reach her waist.

Damian

"Daddy!" the little boy shouts in excitement to see his father. The woman grabs Dorian by his shirt. She steps, angling herself to allow space to then pull him into the motel room. He falls to the ground behind her, and she steps back forward—now facing me. "Who the hell are you?" Her Greek accent is strong, her voice…powerful.

Shit. Who am I, again? Ah. "Good evenin', ma'am." I nod my head and smile. "Looks like your husband got himself into some trouble here at our town bar." "I was just trying to bring him back home safe to ya." The baby still sound asleep, rocking in her fuming mother's arm.

Penelope

Be careful with that rock…you'll wake the damn thing. The curious boy at her side. She looks me up and down like I'm a talking scarecrow. "Well…thank you. I've been trying to contact him for hours." She looks back at Dorian, still on the floor behind her. I look at Dorian and try to signal for him to say something. Anything? Jesus.

He gets up from the ground, swaying his body a bit, and gets next to her. "Um, yeah…I'm sorry, my love…I got carried away…and I lost my phone." He's trying to sound fucked up, slurring his words. Hm. Lost his phone? Her attention on him now, I quickly shoot down to grab his phone at my feet. I put it in my back pocket.

She puts her free hand on his cheek and leans her head into his. "I'm glad you're okay," she says endearingly. She then extends her arm out and whips it back quick to slap the shit out of him.

SMACK

Woah. Jerry Springer, where you at with the cameras? Get a shot of this!

The loud smack causing even me to bounce back a little, and I'm not the one hit. Dorian falls into the door behind her but remains standing. "You're a fucking drunk, always leaving me alone with these fucking kids. If it weren't for our parents setting us up, I would have never married you." Oh my god. A real arranged marriage in front of me. I don't think I've met anyone like this.

She looks back at me. "I'm sorry you had to see that." She smiles and throws her hand in the air, the baby still asleep somehow in her rocking arm. Is that thing even breathing?

"He leaves me with these kids all the time and gets drunk with his buddies. I thought the few times we take a family road trip to visit his parents in NYC, he could behave without his buddies around." She taps her forehead with her fingers and throws that hand higher into the air, "But noo, of course he finds more buddies to go get shit-face drunk with." She gets louder: "AND conveniently loses his phone."

I look at Dorian, standing behind her, his face red like the hue on the woods we just escaped from. He remains silent. Does this guy have any backbone? I look back at her. I have an idea. "It's Iris, right?"

She shakes her head and closes her eyes. "I'm sorry." Her voice now shaken. "I just completely word vomited to you, and you did a nice thing tonight. Thank you, and I'm sorry again, and…" She pauses with her mouth slightly open. "Wait, what did you just call me?"

"Iris. Am I sayin' it correctly? Ee-rees?" I reply calmly, smiling at her.

She nods and cocks her head. "Yes, that is my name. Why?" She darts a quick look behind her at Dorian, checking him out. She looks back at me.

"Dorian told me all about you…uh." I look down at the baby and the little boy. "In fact, all he could talk about tonight was how much he loves his family. I'm assumin' this little fella is…Damian? 'N' in your arms is your beautiful baby girl, Penelope?" I look at Dorian behind her. "But hey! He forgot to mention y'all are headed to NYC. That should be a lot of fun; I've never been." "Thanks for leavin' that one out, buddy."

Dorian's voice cracks. "Yeah." He coughs and clears his throat. He steps closer to his wife from behind. His hands sliding and appearing over her stomach, he pulls her into him. "We are going to celebrate my parents' fortieth anniversary in NYC this weekend."

"Well, you know what, bud, perhaps you did 'n' I'm just more drunk than I thought 'n' forgot." "Silly me." I chuckle and smile at both of them. "Y'all have a good night, now, 'n' enjoy your trip." I look at Dorian and signal a wave with my hand in the air. "Nice to meet ya, bud." I look at the woman and nod. "Ma'am, have a nice night."

I smile, turn around, and walk back the way we came, alongside the rest of the motel doors. I hear their door shut behind me. Door eleven arrives on my right, I turn left and walk a few steps between two cars parked. Just before I step past them, I stop, lean my head out, and scan the parking lot again, looking for anything. Not a human or thing in sight. I guess a perk of fucking around this late at night—or early morning, I should say. I hustle quickly across the exposed, lit parking lot and dart back into the dark road Dorian and I just walked up from. Next stop, pool hall, get my car, and get the fuck home to face my wife.

The light of the motel complex now behind me and darkness in front. I turn to look behind and still see no activity, then look back again forward. My pace increasing, I check my phone. 2:37 a.m.

6 missed calls
2 voicemails
Several texts
All from Lucy

Shit. At least a little bit of a relief to see her last attempt to reach me was a few hours ago, though. Hopefully that means when I get home, she's asleep. I'll have to come up with some story to tell her in the morning. I've never gone silent on her like this…She's probably called everyone looking for me. How am I going to get out of this mess? The guy kept bitching for us to get back sooner. His wife was blowing up his phone as I drove us back to the pool hall too. Shit! My right hand shoots back to grab my ass. His phone still in my back right pocket. I stop on the road and turn back toward the motel. Should I put it somewhere for him? Wait…He just tried destroying it. I think he's fine without it. A small casualty worth maintaining a big lie?

I'm nearly halfway to the pool hall. Wow. I can't believe I just saw his wife slap the shit out of him. Damn. I swear I'd never hit a woman, but if Lucy ever hit me like that—not that I EVER could see that happening—I'm not sure how I would react. How could he just stand there and take the hit with no reaction? Interesting. No effort or reflex to defend himself, verbally or physically? To just take a blow to the face from your wife like that? Maybe it wasn't the first time? I mean…I get dealing with an angry wife. Lucy and I have been together for what seems like forever. She and I have had our fights, but nothing like that. Nothing physical. And to strike him in front of the kids…

My eyes bounce up from the gravel, a darker mass tucked off the road just before the pool hall.

I stop in my tracks and get down low slowly.

Is that what I think it is?

I crawl in the grass off the road and into the edge of the woods, maintaining a visual on the mass. I find a large tree and step up behind it. I think I'm hidden good. I lean my head out and take a deeper look. *That's a cop car posted outside the pool hall.* Fuck. How am I going to get past it? AND drive my busted-ass car home?

I guess I can make my way through the woods? But if their

windows are down, they might hear me. The woods ain't that deep here before you hit the river. I bring my head back in from leaning it past the tree trunk. I turn around, putting my back against the trunk, and my knees give. Who knows what other cop cars are posted on the other side of the pool hall too? Can I catch a break? I slide down, and my ass hits the forest floor.

Ouch

I forgot about Dorian's phone in my back right pocket. I take it out and stare at it.

Through the spiderwebbed screen, his phone still works and lights up. His background photo a picture of what looks to be his newborn, Penelope. *Son of a bitch.* An idea comes to mind. Will it work? It has to work. I need it to work.

I can't do it. What other options do I have? Yes, I can. I have to do it.

I tap *emergency call.*

I tap *9*

1

1

And the *green button.*

The operator answers—

"This is 911; what is your emergency?"

"Help me! My wife is beating me and going crazy! I don't know what I'm going to do. She has the kids, and I'm locked in the bathroom," I plead, trying to remove my Southern accent as best I can.

"Sir, okay, calm down. What is your location?"

"I'm in room thirty-two, at the Motel 6 off 64. Please! … Hurry!" "My kids!"

Tap

My thumb hits the red button.

13

———

I can't believe that worked. Thank god it worked. My pores now sweating out the alcohol from the steam in my hot shower like I'm a whore sitting in church. I was able to slip into my apartment as quiet as a ghost. Lucy has to be in our bedroom, asleep; she wasn't up waiting for me in the living room—thank god again. My body swaying left and right under the water. Careful. My drunk ass is about to sway into the shower curtain and trip over this tub and break my face. Whatever. I fucking deserve it.

Hm. How long have I actually gone silent on her before? Maybe this isn't that bad. I peep out of the shower curtain to check the bathroom clock. 3:02 a.m.

My dirty clothes from the day on the bathroom floor; hanging just above on the wall, a fresh towel on the rack. Yeah…shit. She hasn't heard from me in like nine hours now. I've never been gone that long. I turn the faucet handle more to the left, increasing the heat of the water, almost to the point that it feels like I'm burning myself, but not yet. The burning sensation feels good.

Well, hell. Maybe this can be like a mini baptism. Lord, rinse away all my sins from this past day. A quick chuckle pops out. The hotter, the cleaner! I'll delete Grindr off my phone, go to bed, and start tomorrow—new.

I did it, I tried it, nothing good came out of it, and nothing good would come out of it again. The cops are now out to get me. I'm surprised they weren't waiting for me here when I got home. The right side of my car is fucked, and god forbid Lucy finds out—my whole life will be FUCKED. If I lose her, I have nothing to live for.

I grab the soap bar, swish it around in my hands, making a wet, lathery paste. I scrub my balls and dick aggressively. Ouch. Maybe that's too aggressive. I should wash my hair too; get everything clean and new, a fresh scent. A new, clean me. I grab the shampoo, rub some in my hands, shut my eyes, and start spreading it into my hair.

Creak

Did I just hear something? I rinse the suds out of my ears.

Is that the bathroom door opening?

"Roy?"

Lucy's voice

Shit. "Yeah." "Honey."

"Where have you been? I tried callin' ya and textin' ya hours ago." "Several times."

I put my head under the shower water to rinse and scrub away at my head, buying me some time. "Yeah, I'm sorry about that. Uncle David isn't doin' too well." I raise my voice a bit to fight through the water running down in front of my mouth. "And then I got distracted because you'll never guess who was there: Sheila, actually, 'n' she was flirting with my uncle's doctor. Can you believe that?"

Zing! The sound of the shower curtain flying open. My head pops back from under the water.

I clear the water off my face with my hands. Lucy is standing on the other side of the tub, with her face leaned in to me.

"Whoa." I cover my dick with both hands. "Hun…what're ya doin'?"

"You were at the nursing home until just now?" "Till three in the mornin'?"

"Ahem, yeah." My eyes avoid contact, checking my legs to see if they are clear from soap.

"Why were you there so long? Why are you now showerin'?"

I turn the water off, reach past her shoulder to grab the towel hung up behind her. Droplets of water from my arms fall on her; she doesn't flinch or move.

"Well, you know, I haven't seen him in a while, and I guess felt guilty." "I told ya that before I left." I remain standing wet in the shower and start to dry my head and face first, talking now through the towel flapping in front of—and hiding—my face. "I'm showerin' because…When is the last time you've been in a nursing home? Hm? They're nasty, hun." I bring the towel down from my head to dry my chest, and she steps into the shower with one foot, then puts her nose right on top of my mouth.

"You were drinkin' with your uncle at the nursing home too?" "Huh?"

"Uh, no, I mean, yeah…I had a flask in my car that I had a couple sips out of…Why?"

She leans back away from me. "Why are you lyin' to me, Roy?"

"What are you talkin' about, Lucy? I ain't lyin'." I step outside the tub, onto the floor mat. She steps out and back, and I continue to dry myself. "Why do ya think I'm lyin' to ya?"

"I've known you since you were a boy, Roy. I know when you're lyin'. I just don't understand why?" She turns around and walks out of the bathroom. I finish drying myself off and step to follow her, my towel wrapped around my waist. She appears back at the bathroom doorframe in front of me, just before I get out, holding fragments of something in front of her at her waist.

The fragments are large enough that they cover her hands, and look like a brown color? What is that?

"What happened to my mother's urn?" She stands still, bringing her hands a few inches higher. Eyes locked on me.

Holy. Shit.

I look down at the fragments, realizing she must be holding the broken remnants of the object I threw that exploded on that guy's face. I forgot about that little urn. She'd refused to put her mother's urn anywhere else but on the coffee table, to be with us all the time. How could I have forgotten about it? That has to be it. I stare at her hands in disbelief. Get it together; say something.

"Uh? Where did you find that…like that?" "Wasn't that on our coffee table?"

"IN THE GARBAGE!" she shouts at me. "I was makin' dinner for us earlier and noticed it when I went to throw away the onion skins in the kitchen garbage bin." A scary moment of silence. I don't know what to say. What the fuck do I say? How the FUCK did this happen? My mind racing for answers, but nothing is landing or making sense.

"Roy, are you serious? You broke my mother's urn today and just tossed it, along with her ashes, in the trash? Are you going crazy?" "Why would you do that?"

My bare skin now cold from the air and caught in a lie, this damp towel around my waist not helping. "Lucy, I am so sorry." I step to her side to get past, then walk across the hallway into our bedroom to put on some clothes and warm up. She follows me and then stands at the doorframe at our bedroom.

"You're sorry? That's it?" Her wrists now bent down, dangling the weight of the broken urn fragments in her hands. Her *mother's urn fragments*. Jesus Christ. "What happened? How could you try to hide this?"

I manage to get a hoodie pulled over my head. "Well, like I said, I was doing some deep cleanin' today, and I just bumped into it, 'n' I guess it fell and broke. I didn't have the heart to tell ya, and I freaked out…I'm sorry." "It shouldn't have been left on the coffee table in the middle of the living room, anyways."

Her attention lost in her hands, her cheeks reddening. "Why didn't you just pick up the broken urn fragments, and then her ashes after? I could have maybe fixed this urn, or put her ashes in a new one." She begins to softly weep.

I walk over to her and embrace her. "I'm so, so sorry, Lucy. I'm so, so, so sorry." I embrace her tighter. "I don't know what I was thinkin'. I wasn't thinkin' at all today."

She pushes me off from her using her arms folded under my embrace. "You threw away her ashes, Roy." She lets out a loud weeping sound. "Her ashes! Just thrown away into the trash, like nothing, like fucking onion skins and old boxes of cereal."

Wow. My wife never swears. A good church girl brought up here never swears like that. Especially in front of her husband. I sit down at the corner of our bed, closer to her, as she remains standing in the bedroom doorway. She begins to weep louder. "How could you do that? How could you think that makes any sense at all? What is going on with you?" She throws the fragments down to the floor and turns around and goes into the bathroom, slamming the door behind her. The fragments rattle on the hardwood at my feet, and she weeps louder from the bathroom.

I can't believe it. I can't believe the object I chucked this morning—well, technically yesterday morning—was MY WIFE'S DEAD MOTHER'S URN. I slap myself in the forehead. Fuck that Bobby kid. Well, maybe he didn't know what it was. Fuck, I didn't even know what it was until now. Everything happened so fast. Why did she have to leave her urn on the coffee table? It's been so long since her mother's funeral, I just forgot about it.

Where is my phone? Let me make sure I delete Grindr before we get any other surprises. Ugh! It's in my pants pocket on the floor in the bathroom. I jump up from sitting on the bed and walk to lean up against the bathroom door.

"Lucy?"

Knock knock knock knock knock

I give soft, rapid knocks.

"Go away," she wails.

"Hun, can I come in? I just need to grab my phone." She then opens the door as quickly as a lightning strike.

"I know you weren't at the nursing home all night." Her eyes and face in different shades of red and black.

"What?" Her changing from sad to stern so fast catches me off guard.

"I CALLED THE NURSING HOME, ROY," she shouts. "I asked around for you, and no one had seen you." Her tears now gone, her voice confident. "I got a hold of Andrew after transferring to your uncle's room, and he told me you left a bit after eight p.m." Fuck. Fucking Andrew. Another reason to kill that fucking faggot.

"Okay. I went to the bar after I left the nursing home. There it is. There is the lie!" I raise my voice back. "You happy now? You caught me. I didn't say anythin' because ya told me you had a special dinner planned, so I felt bad makin' ya think I was ditching ya to drink with the fellas. I'm sorry." "I'm an alcoholic —what d'you expect?"

She adjusts her posture taller. "I called the bar, Roy, and texted some of your friends. No one has seen you. So you're lying to me now." "Again." A beat of silence. "WHY ARE YOU LYING TO ME?" Her shout louder than before.

I enter the bathroom and lunge to grab my dirty clothes on the floor. Jesus. I really can't catch a fucking break. "I don't know what friends you texted, but the fellas I was with tonight, none of them were on their phones." I turn around and walk back to the bedroom, retrieve my phone, and put it in my pocket.

She follows behind me. "So what are these *friends'* names? It's a small town; I'm sure I know them?" I turn to face her, her arms now crossed.

"They're new."

"They're…*new*…What? New to town? How convenient." She steps closer. "Tell me about these new friends, Roy. Can I meet them? I would love to meet your new friends that are more important to hang out with than your wife. Come on, what are their names? Tell me!"

"Ah, okay. Ron, Danny, and I can't think of the other guys' names. They were here travelin' for work. Only in town for one night."

She steps now just feet in front of me. "I don't believe you." I remain silent. She hollers again, "You're lyin' to me again." Now at the top of her lungs: "You are a liar, and I don't beli-"

SLAP

The back of my right hand swipes Lucy across the right side of her face.

"I'm tellin' ya the GODDAMN truth, woman!" My hand falls back to my side. Both of hers now covering the right side of her face as she stumbles back away from me. "What more do ya want me to say?" "What more do ya want from me?" My swing and words all bursting out of me like water over-flowing from the top of a glass under a faucet that can't turn off.

A still silence persists, with timid breathing and eyes locked from the both of us. "The truth." Her body now trembling irregularly.

I extend both arms her direction. *"Lucy."*

She puts out her hand in the air, flexed. "Don't. Touch. Me." "Don't come near me. I don't know who you are." Her other hand still covering her face. "What is wrong with you?" She weeps. "What is wrong with you, Roy? You just hit me." "You just hit your wife."

I sit at the center of the foot of the bed and put my head into my hands, giving my breathing a second to calm down. What did I just do? I can't believe I just struck her. She is right. What *is* wrong with me? My phone vibrates in my pocket. Who would be messaging me this early? Grindr is still on my phone. Fuck.

"I'm gonna go." I get up from the bed and race out of the bedroom.

"What? Roy, no. Don't go." Her voice following behind.

I pass the coffee table, grab the cigarettes, lighter, ashtray— anything there—real quick and throw it in a grocery-store plastic bag I grab from the kitchen. What else do I need?

"Roy!" Lucy exclaims. "Where are you goin'?" I don't look at her. "Roy. You can't just leave me. You can't just leave when…" She covers her face with both hands.

Leave when…*what?*

I'm not gonna look at her. I can't look at her. I look past her feet into the bedroom floor at the fragments of her mother's broken urn. "I just have to go. I'll be back," I say to the floor.

I exit our apartment. Before the door shuts behind me, I glance up at her. "I'm sorry." The door shuts, and I lock the door from outside. My forehead lands on the door softly, and I begin to weep; my jaw drops for a breath through it. "I'm so sorry." I weep more and cup my mouth to control the sounds from waking up the silent hallway. I push myself off the door and force myself to walk. You're an animal, Roy. A fucked-up, out-of-control wild animal with rabies.

14

THAT ANDREW HAS no fucking business talking to my wife about my whereabouts. That motherfucker. He better not still be at the nursing home. Fucking with my uncle and now fucking with my wife. I'm gonna fucking kill him if I see him. My hands reaching all over the car from the driver's seat. One by one I grab and shake violently each flask, checking for any swigs left. I'm pretty sure my uncle's nursing home has limited visiting hours, but that's where I'm going, so they are about to deal with at least one visitor. I glance at the clock in my car. 3:40 a.m.

Any cops still out? By this hour they got to be processing everyone they've caught over the past few hours? Why am I thinking about this again? If they were after me, they would have just come to my work, been waiting for me at my home. Whatever. I don't get it. Not one car light beam on the road at this hour. Every intersection, flashing red only for stop-and-go traffic.

I look at the knuckles on my right hand on my steering wheel. A loud wail breaks out, my body sobbing uncontrollably. Get it together, Roy. Sometimes men hit their wives. It happens. It's not like you actually *hurt* her. You're never gonna do it again. NEVER. Okay? You're gonna apologize again tomorrow, and she'll forgive you. Wives forgive their husbands for stupid shit they do. Tomorrow you can go to the store and buy ingredients to make her a homemade shepherd's pie. That is her favorite, and she'll love that. She is going to forgive you, and you guys will get through this. You're going to remind her of the doting and faithful husband that you are. Remind her how much you love her and how much she means to you. More tears break out and stream down my face.

You're gonna fix this. My eyes glance at myself in the rearview mirror. Coward. I pull into a dark spot, away from the lit entrance of the nursing home. The entry lights are on. So I must be able to walk in? My cig about halfway done. I dig in the plastic bag to take out that ashtray, extinguish the cig in it, and roll down my window and blow the ashes off the tray, outside my car. The green and black eagle heads have a little glow from the light cast behind and between them, coming from the nursing home entrance. I wonder?

I enter the nursing home with my hood on. Both hands in my hoodie pocket, right wrist bearing the weight of the plastic bag as it flaps, hitting front to back on my right leg as I walk. I keep my head down. I can get to his room from here without looking up, maybe just a few quick glances when I need. The front desk to my left. No one. I continue my way. The cafeteria now to my left, someone there in my peripheral vision through the windows? Don't look. I probably look like a thug right now. Black hoodie on just like that guy, only I also have a white plastic bag with god knows what anyone will think. Meth. Meth is what they'll think for sure. A tweaker right off the street, finding a room to shoot up and squat for the night, maybe shoot my shot with a sexy nighttime nurse trying to get her fix too. Jesus, I need help. I turn right to enter B hallway, which my uncle's room is on.

Shit.

A nurse now a few yards from me, standing up ahead to my

left in the hallway. Keep walking. Head down. I'm just about to pass her.

"Excuse me."

My head stays down, and I keep walking. I think she's talking on the phone?

"Sir, visiting hours are not until seven a.m.," I hear behind me. I keep walking.

"Sir." She now must be several rooms behind me. "Sir. If you don't answer me…" "Sir!"

I feel close to my uncle's room. My head still down, I look up to check the room numbers on my right. B11. Got him. His door is slightly ajar. I squeeze through the opening to get in, and face it to shut it fully, a soft *click*.

I turn around and walk slowly to my uncle, freeing my hands from the hoodie pocket and removing my hood.

"Uncle David," I whisper as I approach his bedside. "Uncle," I announce a little louder. He's sound asleep. His mouth wide open, taking in-and-out, soft but rugged nighttime breaths. The TV now off, but a little light fills the room still, shining through the cracked-open blinds from the parking lot lights outside his window. Jesus. How hard would it be for Andrew to shut the window blinds completely? It's not rocket science; didn't this fella go to school? I remain standing in silence over my uncle and drop the plastic bag next to the reclining chair on the floor. The noise startling me and him a little in his sleep. He takes a gulp; his breathing adjusts, along with the position of his head, now facing the light from the window. Whoops. I walk over slowly to the window, making sure I don't bump into anything and create any more noise. Damn, I hope he doesn't wake up, actually. I'd probably scare the shit out of him, scare him right into a heart attack, and then he'll actually die.

I get to the window, remarkably without stumbling into anything, and peep through the cracked blinds. *Son of a bitch.* My breath taken out from me. I can't believe it. A black SUV squad car rolls just outside, from my left to my right in the parking lot. He's going the direction of the entrance. Seriously? Fuck me. I quickly close the blinds, and my chin drops to my chest. Where can I hide in this place?

Click!

A loud noise from behind me. I drop to the floor, diving next to my uncle's bedside to hide. A figure enters the room.

Click

The noise softer.

The figure coming my way.

"Roy." A loud whisper comes from…? "Roy." "Are you in here?"

Is that Andrew? That fucker.

I stay lying on my side, huddled just under the window-side edge of my uncle's bed. Maybe he will go away. I can't kill him now if I see him—the fucking cops are here. He appears at the foot, leans his head out to find me on the floor. "Roy? What are you doing?" His words fast.

I quickly bounce up, one index finger springing in the air at him, the other in front of my mouth. "Sh. He's sleeping." "Can't ya see that, or are ya retarded too?"

Andrew smacks my hand out of his face and points back at me. "You got bigger problems, Roy. What are you doing here?" His hand now points to the door. "Our head nurse called the cops, saying a stranger in a hoodie is roaming the halls." "I only knew to check here first because I heard a nurse say she saw the guy enter this room. Are *you* retarded?"

"Fuck." I turn away from him. Think. Where can I hide? Should I jump out this window?

"Roy, is there something going on?" "By the way, *retarded* is not socially correct anymore."

Is he for real? "Nothin', Andrew. Stay out of my fuckin' business. You got a crush on me or somethin'?" "Why would ya follow me in here at this hour?"

"What are you talking about?" "That's the problem with

you straight, egotistical, closed-minded men, thinking when another guy calls you handsome that he's, like, gay and obsessed with you." "What makes you think I'm gay, anyways?"

A laugh bursts out through my teeth, and I cup my mouth and look at my uncle. I turn back to Andrew. "Sh, lower your voice, you idiot." "I know you're a fag—look at you. You are as scrawny 'n' feminine as the silly broads I meet 'n' fuck at the bar."

"Oh? So you want to fuck me?" "Also, you're married, you asshole."

Click!

The door hatch sounds an alarm to both of us. I dive down back to my pathetic position, hiding on the floor behind my uncle's bed. Andrew remains standing. I can see through, under the bed, to the floor in front of the door. Light shines through from the hallway, and shadows appear, walking in. Fuck me. Fuck me. Fuck me.

This is it. This is *really* it.

"Andrew, what are you doing in here?" *A person's voice I don't recognize.* "Did that guy come in here?" I keep my position, still, listening to them, now staring at the two new pairs of feet just arriving next to my uncle's bed on the other side of me. "David Stevens is your patient. Who would have come into his room at this hour?"

"I'm not sure, Tracy," Andrew says. "No one else has been in here but me."

The stranger speaking again. "Why are you in here, Andrew?"

"I, um, well…David's family hasn't been showing up a lot lately, and I guess I've grown to care for this patient a bit more than others." "You know how that can happen." "So, I was just checking in on him. Sometimes his pain meds wear out and he'll wake up a bit earlier from the pain." This son of a bitch disrespecting me in front of my uncle while he is asleep and while I'm stuck down here.

A response—from Tracy, I guess? "I see. Well, quick; I need you now. A different nurse said they saw that guy enter this room. If he's not here, we need to check the other rooms quietly, and fast. This is Sergeant Keaton. She's already identified the car outside, and they are actually already looking for the guy from an earlier incident."

The guy? Sergeant Keaton *knows* me; we have each other's cell phone numbers. If she identified that the car outside is mine, why isn't she sharing my name? She has to have put two and two together that this David Stevens is related to me. It isn't hard math?

"No shit." Andrew says. Disbelief in his voice.

Abrupt coughs interrupting them just above my head; the bed slightly shaking

"Hi, David," Andrew responds, back to his brighter, faggoty ring.

I hear my uncle clearing his throat just above me. "What's going on?" "Who are these people?"

"We are so sorry to disturb you. Our apologies, David. There was an incident, and we thought your room was affected, and now just realized it is not."

"What incident?"

"…Carbon monoxide," Andrew blurts out. "We thought there might be a leak, and we are checking all of the rooms." Damn, he is actually pretty good on his toes.

"Yes, Mr. Stevens." Tracy speaking. "You are all safe, and we are all set here. As Andrew said, we are so sorry to disturb your sleep. We are on our way out now. Good night." The feet lift and escape my sight, their shadows decreasing in size until there's just light on the floor. The room returned back to darkness as the door shuts behind them.

I get up from the floor and get next to Andrew. "Why did you do that?"

"Roy?" My uncle surprised to see me pop up like a goblin

hiding under him. "Why were you on the floor?" "What are you doin' here?"

"Hey, Uncle, sorry; didn't mean to scare ya or cause a ruckus. I just needed to come here." I double tap the top of his hand in the bed and lift off.

"Listen, I have to go; that nurse is my manager. You stay here, and I will be sure no one else enters this room the rest of the night." "Okay?"

A few seconds of silence between Andrew and me. Can I trust him? I give him a nod. He starts to walk away. "Why are ya doin' this, Andrew?" "I've asked you now twice."

Andrew stops, his body remaining forward toward the door. Is he going to speak? Turn around and cry? My uncle interrupts: "Thank you, Andrew." And Andrew continues forward and exits the room.

I watch until the door closes, and then look down at my uncle. "What is goin' on between you two?" "Why does he care about ya so much?"

"Is it that bad that someone cares about me here?" "Does it make you feel guilty or something?"

Fuck. Maybe? A new weight in my stomach. "No. I mean, I just don't understand, that's all."

"It's okay, Roy. It's my fault you don't understand. It's not yours." He breaks eye contact and drifts into silence, staring at nothing but darkness in front of him.

"…That I don't understand…*what?*" I walk around the foot of his bed to his right to sit in the reclining chair next to him.

"Why was there a cop here?" He returns back from outer space and looks at me.

"Uh, I don't know." I break eye contact and look down at the plastic bag I brought. I grab it off the floor and set it in my lap. "You know, I had the stupidest idea. Well, I've had stupider, but look what I brought." I pull out the ashtray that he and I used to use when we'd have cigs together, and a pack of opened cigarettes, and I toss them on the bed next to him. "I thought, fuck it, that ol' man would probably like a smoke just 'bout now." He looks at the ashtray and cigarette box and releases a chuckle, followed by a couple of coughs. That's a win. I haven't seen him chuckle in a while. I crack a smile back at him.

"Thank you." "A smoke sounds great right now, but let's not draw any more attention this way, yeah?" "You also do realize we can't smoke in here." "Right?" "I didn't raise you to be so reckless."

"Yeah…yeah." "I'm sorry, it was a dumb idea." My mouth remains closed with a smile. I shake and scratch my head. Silence proceeds, and I focus my attention on the door to listen for anything. Nothing. "Uh, I'm also sorry…" "Ahem…ah."

"Sorry for what?"

"Well, I guess, I could have been better, you know. Shown up for you here more. Been a better…*son* to ya. You did so much for me growin' up." "These past few months, I really haven't been here for ya like I should have been." "Like I should be."

"Yeah…that's true." "It's okay, Roy." "I know life can sometimes get…complicated, and people get confused on who or what they should be."

"…Are you sayin' that I'm confused?"

"No…I'm saying that people get in their own way, and yeah, I guess lose sight of what's truly important. Most people let fear determine the outcome of their lives, rather than say…love." My uncle deep in thought, staring at the ashtray. His eyes changing depth in the haze. "Do you know who gave me this tray?"

"No. I thought Sheila picked it up at one of 'em flea markets?"

"No, she did not." He pauses. "Pick it up and read what you see underneath."

I grab the ashtray I threw on his bedside. His eyes are fixed on it. I turn it upside down over my lap, but the room is too dark to see anything. I pull out my phone and use the light from the screen to scan the black bottom. "I don't see anythin'?"

"Trust me, it's there, written in a different shade of black. You just have to find the correct angle to see."

"The whole bottom of this tray is black."

"I know. Continue looking."

I adjust the angle of the tray to the light off my phone, now going slower. I make my way to the center and think I see something. "Is it cursive?"

"Yes."

I stretch my neck further, leaning closer into the scribble, adjusting each hand by a fraction of a millimeter to get this legible. I think I see it. I read out loud without reading in my head first. "Love, R."

Who is R?

My phone and ashtray collapsing in my lap immediately after I say and think it. "What is this?"

"What do you think it is?"

"I don't know, Uncle; you tell me. I don't know up from down, left, or right, anymore."

"Ramón gave me that ashtray before you were born."

"What?" "Why?" "*Before* I was born?" I didn't know they'd known each other that long. Come to think of it, I really don't know anything about your life before you took me in.

"Because." "Well, because he was the love of my life."

"This?" "Again!" "Why are you sayin' this crazy shit."

"Sh." He coughs more. "You heard Andrew to be quiet."

"Fuck Andrew," I say louder.

"That anger inside you, resentment you hold against others like Andrew. It's my fault. And I was wrong with so many things."

I'm not listening to this bullshit again. "You know what? It's late. I should go, and you need rest." I toss the ashtray back at him on his bedside and get up.

"Roy." "Don't go." "There is a cop out there, and god knows what trouble you got yourself into now." I look at the window across the room. I can fit through there; might have to break the screen, though.

"I'm not in any trouble, Uncle."

"Okay, say I believe you. Why don't you just rest here until the sun comes up, then. Sleep in the recliner. Andrew promised no one would enter. I'll go back to sleep too."

I stare more at the closed blinds. Just a very dim blue hue from the parking lot lights still remains. "Yeah, I guess you are now one to trust a fag, ain'tcha?" I look down on him. "Your life ends now at the mercy of a fag wiping and touchin' your ass, 'n' turns out, you probably fuckin' love it, you sick, twisted bastard."

"Fuck you. You ungrateful little shit." He raises his voice, spits at me, and coughs louder. "Get caught then. Run. Go," he shouts. "I'm done protecting you." "All my life I have protected you, 'n' for what?" "For nothin'." "I've done it for nothing."

The lightning change in his voice pushes my body back two steps; I hop forward in one. "Shh, shh, sh, sh, sh." Both hands in the air in front of him. "I'm sorry." "I'm sorry." "I'm sorry. I'm a fuckin' mess." "I know." "Just, please, lower your voice." My head tilts left to listen for any movement outside in the hallway. If they are still anywhere nearby, I'm fucked.

"Sit the fuck down, then, and rest here a bit. I don't wanna hear another fuckin' word." His voice at the depth it would be right before he would kick my ass as a kid for fucking up on something. *Still sends chills down my spine.* I grab a cup of water that's been left near his bedside. I put the straw between his lips for him to sip.

"Yes, sir." I sit back down.

I remain silent, thoughts racing. How long did you know Ramón if this ashtray was given to you before I was born? I thought you ran from Ramón? Why after all of these years, all of a sudden now this is coming up? Is it even true? How CAN this be true? You were fucking a *man* that shared a bedroom wall with *me?* There is no way. Is it hot in here? I feel hot. My right fist clenching. Okay. Calm down, Roy. Take a breath.

What is it with Sheila, then? You immediately married her within months of moving us to Owenton. I have to ask. I don't want ya yelling again, though…

His eyes are shut, and his chest is moving up and down slower. I clear my throat, breaking the silence in the room. "Ahem." "Can I…just ask you one more question?" "Then I promise I'll go to sleep."

"Sure." A curt reply, but that's a go.

"Say I were to *believe* this…this…

"I don't know what the fuck this is…

"…But say I were to believe you actually, uh…lov—uh." I can't say it. "Liked to fuck Ramón when you couldn't get laid elsewhere." His eyes open, and he darts a look. Old man can't whip my ass anymore when his limbs are out. But I know what fury comes next after that look, so let's not press him further.

"Get with your question, or I'm going to make sure that cop comes back here, and I personally will find a way to get you arrested if they don't have good enough reason already." *Yeah, well, they don't.*

"I'm not hiding from that cop." "Whatever." "Yes, okay." "Why leave him?

"Why did we leave town that night so abruptly in 1992? After Grandfather Walter's funeral? And leave your so-called lover behind? You made me leave all of my friends, my baseball team—I was the number one pitcher in the area for my age, if you remember; my fastball touched eighty-two miles per hour that year. I was expected to do big things at that high school I was going into. You didn't give me time to say goodbye to anyone; blindsided me at night that we were takin' off. Do you know how much that sucked for a fourteen-year-old kid about to enter high school with everyone he grew up with?"

He's silent, refusing eye contact with me. "Ramón's room was untouched? Why wasn't he home with you when I got home that night? And when I asked you about him then, you shunned me away from askin' again. Forbid it." "Love of your life? What happened then?" "Whatever he did to you changed my whole life; obviously it changed you too." "I deserve to know."

Silence proceeds. A few blinks and a small head shake. "I can't tell you." He turns his head the opposite direction of me.

"What?" Are you serious? "You're here now pretty much lyin' on your deathbed, 'n' you can't tell me the truth?" "No offense." My fist clenching again, harder. "Isn't now the time you're unveiling all of the secrets, hm?"

Will sarcasm work? "You can tell me you like dick but can't tell me why the fuck we ran? Hm? Tell me that the love of your life all of a sudden was a man years ago that lived with us? Actually, kind of helped raise me, if you think 'bout it, 'n' your sickness was under my nose the whole time?" He remains turned away from my direction. "That's why you like it here: That Andrew is probably suckin' you off here every night, 'n' you fuckin' love it." "You're finally gettin' your fix in after faking it all of these years with Sheila." "You're disgustin'." "You're a sad 'n' lonely faggot."

His head snaps my direction. "No, I can't tell you." "That's exactly right, and the head Andrew gives is the best goddamn head you'd only get in your fucking dreams." I shake my head. Fast little movements left to right, back and forth. Just when I thought maybe I'd understand. Coward. Coward! My uncle is a fucking coward. I'm in disbelief. Is this what shock feels like?

"You got to ask your little question. Now shut the fuck up and go to sleep." He shuts his eyes and leans his head back into his pillow, tilted opposite from me, again.

"Yeah, well, I'm reminded why I don't come here." "That was a shit answer, and you're a coward"—a final comment I can't keep from slipping out under my breath. If it weren't for Sergeant Keaton in these halls, I wouldn't be caught dead in a room next to you. Next to a fag.

15

CLICK? *People chatting far away?*

No, go back to sleep. You don't hear anything. It might be something, though? Sh, you're tired. This position is too good. Just sink back into the impression you snuggled into. All is okay. That was exciting! What was I dreaming about again? Oh yeah, evading the cops. Where was I? Yes, driving down the road, speedometer reading ninety-two miles per hour, this time my passenger being…really? Andrew? Fuck that. Ugh, whatever. He looks kind of cute in my passenger seat. One cop gaining on us in my rearview mirror, their black front metal bumper right on my ass. The glare of the sun on their windshield. I can't see who the officer is? What is Andrew doing with a map pulled out in his lap? Stop looking at me like that. *"Roy."* He points up ahead through the windshield. All I see is road and an underpass coming up. What is he pointing at?

Click

Okay, I think that was the door.

"Roy."

I gasp for air and open my eyes. My body jumping from the loud whisper shot in my ear. Andrew leaning just above me.

Andrew? Oh shit. It is him. "Get up." He grabs my hands and pulls me up. "Get up. Get up. Get up."

He gets me standing up in front of him, his hands now cupping my shoulders, and his face in mine. I'm so tired, he can do whatever he wants. What does he want? "You need to follow me right now. The day nurse came in here just a few moments ago and saw you. She reported, and the cops are going to be back here any second."

"Okay, okay, um, where we goin'? What's your big plan?" My brain a fog from just waking up.

"Just follow me, and I'll get you out of here." He nods. "Trust me, okay?"

"Trust you? You were supposed to make sure no one entered this room, bucko."

"Stop being a stubborn ass. I can't control the day shift nurse starting her routine. It's seven fifteen a.m. now." He grabs my hand and lunges for the door.

I jerk it back and turn toward my uncle. "Uncle David." He awakens from his sleep in a quick jerk and looks toward me a little frightened. "Good morning, sir. Looks like I have to go."

"Why?" He clears his throat and shuts his eyes back.

"Roy. We have to go now." Andrew from behind me in a frantic whisper.

"Andrew?" "Where are you?" My uncle's eyes pry back open.

"Yeah." Andrew raises his voice just a bit. "I'm here behind Roy. I got to get him out of here."

"Okay." Soothed and unbothered, my uncle looks at me. Nothing else to say? I'm not sure when I'll be able to sneak back in here again.

Andrew behind me—"Roy!"

"I'll be back, Uncle. I promise."

I turn to face Andrew and follow him out.

"Bless your heart, boy." I hear him say. I exit and glance back at him as my last step takes my body into the hallway. At the same time he turns his head forward. Yeah, well, bless your heart too.

I look forward to Andrew's head. "Andrew, where are we goin'?"

"Stay right behind me and move quick, don't make eye contact with anyone, and keep your head down."

"Where are we goin'?" I say louder.

"Sh." He whips his head back to me, then looks back forward. I haven't been on this side of the nursing home. I have no idea where I'm at or where he's taking me. He turns left down a hall; I stay right on his ass.

"Good night, Cheryl," he says to a woman as we pass by.

"Good night, Andrew. See you tomorrow, babe." I take a quick glance. I can't help it. Babe? What female nurse here is calling this scrawny fella babe?

"Is that your work crush, *babe*?" "She's pretty. Tell me, how do you like her?"

He whips back again. "I told you to shut up. What is seriously wrong with you? You have Energizer Bunny batteries as brain cells or something?"

"I don't know what that means."

"Of course you don't." He stops abruptly, just as we get to the end of the hallway. He pokes his head out to check down right.

"Whatcha lookin' for, *babe*?" I lean into his ear.

He turns quick, sets his hand on my chest, grabs my face with the other, and pinches into my face with his thumb and fingers on my cheeks. "Shut up." His mouth on top of mine, making me inhale the intense whispers of his frustration. God, I haven't seen his eyes this close. He's kinda hot when he's upset. I'm not even mad about this feminine manhandling. Hm. "I'm trying to help you, again." He turns quick back to his spot for a peep; his hands drop off me. That was kinda fun. Do it again.

"Wow." "Pretty boy has some moves and some strength in

those little bones." "I'm impressed." He turns his head back at me. A hollow stare, then…Is that a smirk?

He puts his attention back on the hallway. "Yeah, well, only in your dreams, cowboy. Come on, let's go." Ha. That's funny, only in my dreams…very funny. He grabs my hand, hops out from hiding behind the edge of the hallway, and rushes down a new hallway.

I yank my hand from his grip. "Stop doin' that." I follow quickly again behind. Are all fags this clingy?

"Hurry up." "The exit is just up here." I cock my head out to the left and look up to see an exit sign past his dark-brown curly hair. God, I'd like to run my fingers through, lock those curls into a spiral mercy grip, and yank his head back. Anytime, and all the time. He'd probably like it. I can tell.

We arrive at the exit, and he turns to face me. "Here, take my keys." He opens his hand with car keys in his palm.

"What?" "Why?"

"Take my keys, go to my car, and hide out there for a second. I'll be there soon and explain. Trust me, there's no time."

I shake my head. "Andrew, I don't—"

"Roy. This is the employee parking lot." He pushes the exit door open. "Go." He shoves me from behind my shoulder to get me out the door. "Go!" "I'm right behind you." My body now outside. He shuts the door and darts off.

Fuck. Which one is his car? I start walking. The cars are parked just up ahead. I hit the lock button several times and listen for a beep. A little silver two-door Sebring flashes and beeps down yonder. Hm. I don't remember this being his car? Whatever. I get to the driver's side door, unlock it, and let myself in. *Andrew's got some style.*

Vibrate…vibrate…vibrate…

My phone against my leg in my pocket. I take it out.

Incoming call from Lucy

Shit. I can't talk to her right now. I hope she's okay. My battery at *2%*.

What other notifications do I have? Texts from Sergeant Keaton: **Roy** and **Give me a call.** Both from several hours ago. A text from Lucy several hours ago: **Where are you?** Some of my buddies from the bar letting me know that Sergeant Keaton stopped by the bar last night, asking about me. And, of course, Grindr notifications, still.

Two missed calls from Sergeant Keaton as well, no missed calls from Lucy…well, not at least until now.

Vibrate

Lucy left a voicemail

Screen turning black

I toss my phone into the cup holder and look up. Andrew is now coming from the sidewalk off the back entrance I walked out through. He makes his way to the driver's seat, notices me already sitting here, and shakes his head. Is that another smirk on his face? He changes his direction in a quick step, arrives to the passenger-side door, and lets himself in. "You gonna start the car or what?"

"Yeah, you got a phone charger in here?"

"I think so." He stops in thought. Checks the pockets behind my seat and his, then goes to open the center console. "Yes." A white cord spiraled up inside. He grabs it out and looks where to plug it into the console; leans further to see which hole is the right match. Does he never charge his phone in here? He finds it. "Ah, there it is." Plugs it in and then strings the cord through the fingers of his hand until the metal connector reaches his clean fingertips, then extends it my direction. "Here." He smiles. "Now start the car; I'm freezing my ass off."

"What ass?" I blurt out. I can't help myself. "Sorry, ahem." I grab the cord and plug my phone in. It ain't no colder than sixty degrees out. He must run cold. I press the brake and turn the key in the ignition. The car fires up, and he adjusts the blasters and temperature to high, all pointing his direction. Now that he's good, I turn my attention to the back entrance he just came from. "Are we okay here, or do I need to drive us somewhere?"

"No, we're okay here. No one recognized or said anything while I walked you out. Just Cheryl, and she's not a gossip." He puts his hands in front of the vents.

My left leg shaking. The idea of seeing another squad car pull up this direction has my nerves bubbling up again…I can't control them. "Yeah, we gotta go." I press the brake, grab the gear stick, put it into drive, and take off.

"Whoa. Okay, calm down, Roy. Didn't you think about the cops possibly being right in front? We have to drive past the front to exit to the street. I just said we were good back here." He thinks I don't trust him. Which is true, or I think he's naive. Either-or, I'd rather take my chances to keep moving than be a sitting duck back there. I'm not risking getting caught from Cheryl Ain't a Gossip.

"I trusted you; now you can trust me. We need to move." We pull past the nursing home on our right from the employee parking lot. Two squad cars parked out at the front entrance with their lights off. They must be inside the building. I don't see any bodies in the cars. I look to where I parked. I don't see it. Where's my car?

"Looks like we just missed them," he says as we ride through toward the street. Where am I going? I get to the street and make a right.

"Why did you force me in your car?"

"What trouble did you get into after you left here last night?"

"Uh." Ha. "I can't believe it."

"What?"

"You are smart, you know that? I witnessed all of your little lies earlier to your boss 'n' Sergeant Keaton." "Now here you are: have me trapped in your little two-door car right where you want me." "Try to have your way with me like you have your way with my uncle. You got a park somewhere around here you want me to drive to and fuck you in?" "What's it called?"

"Is that really what you think?" "God, you are so clueless and relentless." "Roy, I'm just trying to help you." "Also, I don't meet in parks." "But I guess now I know that's your thing."

"Why?" I adjust myself in my seat with a shout, head facing him, eyes bouncing back at the road ahead to make sure we don't crash. "Why are you trying to help *me*?" "You don't know me; you don't know my uncle; you don't know my family." "You're a paid nurse—to do a job to take care of sick people— that has crossed the fuckin' line." "That's what you are."

He pulls his hands away from the vents, crosses his arms, and looks out the passenger-side window. My head turns back forward.

"Has your uncle told you anything?" he says to the window. "Also, where are you taking us?"

"What do you mean? What has he told you?" Hm, what does this little shit know that I don't? Did my uncle confide something to you? I am his nephew. I am family. Not you.

He looks down at his feet. "Has he told you anything about…Ramón?" Andrew then looks back up at me.

I can feel my eyes screw tighter like drills in my pupils. A heat wave back in my chest. Hands squeezing the wheel. "How do you know that name?"

"Where are we going?"

"I don't know!" I shout. A new intersection approaches; I accelerate and turn left, hard, through the yellow light. Silence between us. I can feel him staring at me. Don't look at him. I see the speed limit signs at thirty-five miles per hour. I take my foot off the gas to slow down.

"I've been taking care of your uncle for a while." "And he's mostly been alone, besides you visiting once and Sheila every now and then." "Sometimes us nurses are all patients have to talk to…rely on, socially."

"Oh, is that so?" "What are ya tryin' to say?" I shoot him a quick glance.

"Roy, I'm not here to fight with you. Don't make it that. Turn right up here. I'm just trying to help you, because I care about your uncle and I know your uncle really, really cares about you."

"How are ya helpin' me?" "Sounds like both you 'n' him are keepin' secrets from me of god knows what." "A right up where?"

"Yes, here." I turn the car right onto a street he points at. I haven't been in this neighborhood before. "Where are we goin'?"

"First off, I was able to keep that cop from finding you earlier. Second, I'm here now getting you out of the nursing home before the cops were coming to arrest you." "Third, I smuggled you in my car now, because they towed your car earlier. Figure I could give you a ride to where you needed to go next." "Which, by the way, looks like you don't know where to go next, so now, four, I'm taking you to my place." "Anything else the fugitive needs today?"

"Your place?" I slam on the brakes, bringing the car to a screeching halt. "I'm not going to your faggot home."

"Jesus, Roy." His chest jumping forward, his seat belt locking and catching him. "You are in the middle of the street in morning traffic, trying to escape the cops, and you pull this? You're fucking crazy. Do you think?"

Shit. He's right.

"And enough with the *faggot* word. What are you? A closeted man stuck in the 1950s?" "Read a book or something."

"I don't know what that means, and I read plenty of books." But shit. He's right. My foot pops off the brake and slams it forward back on the gas.

"Okay. Again. Not causing attention is the goal. Take a chill pill; slow down." "Turn right up here." "And it doesn't seem like it." He points with his index finger at the entrance of an apartment complex.

"Fine. But I'm not going inside."

"That's fine; I didn't invite you inside, and I don't care. We are at least off the street." "You know, you're not the only one taking on risk here. I could lose my job for helping you out today." "Did you think about that? Probably not."

Could he? He just helped a fella see his dying uncle in the middle of the night? What's so wrong with that? At least, that's what he thinks he helped me out with. I turn right into the apartment complex. "My place is just up there on the left." "Riiight here."

I slow the car down and pull into a spot in front of the apartments. Let me see if my phone will turn on. I hold the power button down, and the white Apple logo appears on the screen. Lucy's voicemail still there waiting for me, and another text from Sergeant Keaton: **Roy, you need to call me now.** Fuck. My right hand holding my iPhone still, turning the screen down over my lap. What am I going to do? Think. *What the fuck am I going to do?*

"What did Sergeant Keaton say to the nursing staff about me earlier?"

"You remember her name? She didn't say much, just directed us to check the rooms with her. She seemed calm, wasn't frightened about the call. If anything, she was maybe a little confused because a call like this hasn't happened there." Hm.

"Confused? I see. Okay, good."

"Why? Is there something she should have said, warned us of?"

"No."

"Mhmm."

"You know, your attitude makes me want to sock you in the face. But I'm not gonna do that because I guess you are takin' good care of my uncle, 'n' that's the least I can do—not get in the way of that." "You're probably the one good thing in his life at the moment." "And that's." "Sad." "Really fuckin' sad."

"I also just saved your ass, but sure, go ahead, forget that already." His hand springing in the air in front of me. "Why are you such a dick to me?" "What have I ever done to deserve you acting like such a. Fucking. Dick?"

What has he done? Well, (a) being a faggot, and (b) taking care of my uncle with his faggot hands, and (c) being alive. Okay, maybe (c), I guess, is too far. You're right, you did just save my ass. I guess. Could have just jumped out the fucking window had my uncle not manipulated me. Ah, fuck it, maybe I can be a little bit nicer. "Nothin', you haven't done a thing...I don't think." Silence proceeds, the inside of the car finally feeling warm. I'm not going inside his apartment. Fucking weirdo, getting me here. I should just go to work. How am I going to get my car back?

I adjust the blowers down from their high speed. "Tell me, what do you know about Ramón?"

He murmurs quick, weird little noises under his breath. Huh? "I-I actually don't know."

"What do you mean you don't know? What do you know of that is something that you don't know?" "You're the one that brought his name up. Not me." "You know something."

"Well, I know your uncle's time is..." He pauses. "Is, ah..." Please, don't be a pussy like Dr. Pingree. Please, for the love of god. "Nearer," he proceeds. Okay, that's definitely better and more direct. Points for you, Andrew.

"How much more time?"

"I'm not a doctor, Roy."

"Yeah, but you see patients like this all the time. You can make a decent prediction. Can't ya? Or can ya not?" "Are you incapable?" "Not as smart as you lead people to think?" "Hm?"

"Roy, I'm capable." "Fine. I would say maybe three months. Soon his needs will transition and he will be transferred to hospice."

"Does he know this?"

"Yes."

"How?"

"Because he asked me the same question as you, and I respect him enough to give him my truthful answer."

"Are you in love with him or somethin'?"

"Jesus Christ, Roy, you are so delusional." "Really?" He shakes his head and looks out his passenger-side window, away from me again. "A lost cause, for sure."

Huh? "I know." My voice lowering. "I mean, I don't know much about that *delusional* part, but I'm, ah, well, I feel like shit, actually. I've done nothin' for him 'n' have treated him…well, like shit." "My whole life, he never asked a thing from me— raised me pretty rough, though, to be honest, BUT never asked a thing. I wish I'd been better to him, especially now."

"Really?" "Why now?"

"Because he's dying, you fuck." "Why else?" "What type of question is that?" "You think I would just say somethin' like that for the hell of it? Especially out loud in front of you?" "He's the only blood family I have left."

He sighs. "Well, if that's really true, there might be something still left that you can do for him." He turns his head back my direction.

I look at him. I feel my eyes flicker from the opportunity, my insides reset like an interior panel board switching back on after being off for a hot second. "Really?" "What?" "Tell me." I can't wait. I'll do anything.

"…Several days ago your uncle asked me to write a letter."

"A letter? Who writes letters anymore?"

"Yes, well, as you know, your uncle can't move his hands, and the person he wanted to write to, he doesn't have their number but recalled where they live—or I should say, *might* have lived."

"Okay." "Go on, who was the letter written to?" "What did it say?"

He looks down at the gear shift, still in drive. "Can you put the car in park, please? No one is coming here, and we don't have to flee." My foot still on the brake from pulling into the parking spot. Whoops. I swing the gear shift up into park, phone still in hand on top, and look back at him. "Go on."

"It was addressed to Ramón."

"Really?" "…He had you handwrite a letter to Ramón." "What did it say?" "And why you?"

"I can't tell you that."

My phone drops into my lap. What the fuck is up with everyone telling me they can't tell me things today? I grab his hand and squeeze. "Andrew, what did it say?" "You're gonna tell me right now." "Or else I'm going to brea—"

"Let go of me, Roy." He keeps his eyes on my hand grasped over his. "Or else…What?" He turns to me and his eyebrow pop up. Is he mocking me?

Louder I respond, "What. Did. It. Say."

"You can't bully me into telling you. I won't. The contents of that letter are private, between your uncle and Ramón, and I respect them. Would you want someone reading your letters between you and…whoever?" "That's actually a silly question; do you even know how to write?"

Who does he think he is? Talking to me like I'm some dumb country hick? "This is different, and you know that." "And you already know what it says because you wrote it."

"No. It's not. And I had to. It's an honor that your uncle trusted me with this request." "Information I will take to my grave out of loyalty and respect for the trust he gave me."

"Yeah, I bet it fuckin' was." I let go of my grip on his hand. Motherfucker. "You are in love with him." "Aren't you."

"Sure, whatever you need to tell yourself. I am most definitely head over heels in love with a man like five times my age." "Can you handle me as your stepdaddy?" I'm gonna punch his teeth out. I'm gonna punch his whole bottom jaw out. Right fist clenching. Fingers flexing. Clenching. Flexing.

No! I can't do that. Won't do that. HE DESERVES IT. Calm the fuck down.

I pick my phone back up from my lap, check the time. 7:57 a.m.

Lucy's out of the house by 8 a.m.; Andrew can drop me off after. I'll change and holler at a buddy for a ride to work after. I'll have plenty of time. What about the cops? Will they be there this time looking for me? "Can you take me to my apartment?"

"Is that really the best idea?" If this fella questions me one. More. Time.

I click on Lucy's voicemail and bring the phone up to my ear:

"Roy." Her voice in a shallow shudder. *"I'm still in shock from last night. After you left, our neighbor Lynette came to our door. She knocked, and I answered quick, thinkin' it was you. I guess she heard us yellin'."* She begins to weep. *"She saw the mark on my face, Roy."* Her weeping louder, with more distance between each cry, as she tries to catch breaths between. *"She called the cops, Roy. They came, and she forced me to tell them what happened. I'm so sorry. I'm so sorry."* It's okay, hun, it's okay. I'm sorry too. My eyes on the verge of tears themselves, listening to her hurt. Hurt that I did. *"Where are you, Roy?"* Her voice less shaken. *"The cops told me they found your car behind the Motel 6, and that you fled from them earlier?"* The hairs on my spine flex to the sky. The cops told her that? *"They are looking for you, Roy. Just, please, please, come home to me, and I will take back what I said to them. Please. We will figure this out together. I love you."* I set my phone back down on my lap. I can't go back. I can't go home. I can't go…anywhere here.

"You don't think the cops are there waiting for you? I think they are looking for you, Roy."

"Shut up, Andrew!" Could he hear Lucy's voicemail in my ear? Or is it that obvious already? "You said there was a way I could help my uncle." "You never said what it was. What is it?"

"Oh." "Well, the letter he wrote. The letter your uncle wrote to Ramón." "It didn't make it."

"What do you mean, 'It didn't make it'?"

"The letter came back with a stamp, 'Return to sender.'" "I guess where your uncle thought Ramón still lives is not the case. He must have moved. So I still have the letter."

"What?" "Why?"

"Well, as I said, your uncle's time is nearing." " I thought it would be better for him to think that his letter made it. For him to die with a little more peace thinking his final last words got to Ramón."

Silence between us. I guess that makes sense. But also not. "So you still have this letter…unopened?" "You think it's better for my uncle to die thinking Ramón didn't want to respond back?"

"Yes, it's right here." "And, yes. There is no guarantee Ramón would have written back, anyways." He opens the passenger-side glove box; a letter falls out to his feet, and a gun that lands on the backside of the glove box door. *He owns a gun?* He quickly shuts the glove box; I hear the gun bounce back into it. He grabs the letter at his feet and sets it on my lap. "I've kept it with me in case I changed my mind, but it's only been a few days that I've had it."

"You own a gun?" My hands not moving off my lap. "Why do you own a gun?"

"It's Kentucky, Roy." "Like you said, I'm a faggot." "All faggots own guns in case we need to shut an asshole up." Is he fucking with me?

A "ha" pops out, and my head shakes. I guess they'll let anyone own a gun in this country.

My eyes travel down to the letter in my lap. Well, I'll be damned. He's telling the truth. Lo and behold, my uncle's address on the top left, addressed to Ramón Ramirez in the center, a New York City address under his name, and stamped on the side, *Return to sender*. Guess it wasn't meant to be, then.

"…Okay, so what am I supposed to do with this? Show up in

New York City to this address and ask around for a Ramón Ramirez?" I shake my head, shrugging my shoulders at him.

"Yeah." He nods, still. Oh my god. He's serious. "I mean, you said you wanted answers. Here is your ticket for that too."

"You're right." "I do want answers." And they are in this envelope, set right and perfect in my lap. "I should just open this letter now 'n' get the answers directly 'n' avoid this whole bullshit."

"You said you wished you'd been better to your uncle; now is your opportunity." "If you leave now, you'll get to New York City by nightfall. It's just a day's drive. I've looked it up before."

"I don't even have a car, Andrew." "This is crazy talk." "Even for me."

"No, it's not, Roy; it's selfless, and…romantic." My stomach churning. *Romantic?* Between my uncle and Ramón? Disgusting.

"Something important to your uncle, important in his life, that you can help him now with." "Even if you think you don't agree with it."

Silence between us. Don't look at him. You don't wanna get sucked into whatever crazy bullshit this is, Roy.

"You can borrow this car." "My car." What did he just say?

"You're just gonna give me your car?" "You know the cops are lookin' for me; I called you a faggot 'n' pushed you to the ground earlier, made you cry, 'n' you just…now want to give me your car…to flee across the country in?" "To fulfill some sick, nasty last deed of my uncle's?" "Now look who is the insane one."

"…I have another one."

"You own two cars?" "What other car do you own?" *A truck.* A scattered memory filtering through from finding him last night in it. Damn, I need to lay off the booze if I can't even clearly remember a detail from twelve hours ago like that.

"Does it matter, Roy? I'm offering you a car." "Just take it."

He turns his head to look out the passenger-side window,

away from me. His right elbow into the door's armrest, and his right hand closed, just hovering over his mouth. His chest moving up and down differently. Is he about to cry again? Why do I always make this fella cry? I roll my eyes.

"Your boyfriend break up with you or somethin'? You steal his car, and now you're giving it to me to get back at him?" "Sending me off to NYC to clean up your shit with my uncle so your conscience is clear?"

He turns to me, hand removed from his face. "No!" he shouts. "It's my fucking car, and I don't need it right now." He turns back to his window and begins to sob. What the hell?

"Okay…" "What nerve am I hittin' here?" "I'm confused? Why are you cryin'?" My hands flail in front of me, halfway up. Why am I asking? I want this conversation over.

"It doesn't matter."

"Okay." "Well, don't bitch that I didn't ask—"

"My cousin was in an accident earlier today—well, technically yesterday morning," he says to the floor. "He was sick anyways, but now I'm not even sure I'll get to speak with him again." His sobbing continuing.

"Okay…" Do I need to ask? Huh. "What happened?" I rub my hands up and down my thighs. I really don't have time for this. He notices.

"Nothing, Roy." "You know what? Now it's your turn to stay out of my business." He gets in my face. "How do you like it?" His voice loud; strong. "Don't ask me again." He controls himself from sobbing more.

"Great!" "I don't need to know the details of your sad life." "Thanks for the car." "Get out."

"Get out?" His face pink and nostrils expanded. "You are so infuriating." "If I lend you this car, promise me you are going to New York and coming right back."

"I'm not promis—"

"Promise me!" he barks like a chihuahua you wanna punt

into the river. "I'm not letting you have it unless you're going." "You can do this." "Do this one last thing for your uncle."

Am I about to accept orders from a fag-barking chihuahua? Or should I grab that gun and just drown the both of us now?

16

———

I just *HAD* to complain that I hadn't *done anything* and that I *felt* bad for not being a better nephew to my uncle. Now look where I am, flying east on I-64 toward West Virginia to god knows where.

I've never traveled east past Lexington, Kentucky. I glance at the letter staring back at me, face up on the passenger seat.

I can't believe it. All this time. All this time that has gone by, and he thinks now is the time to write a letter and bring up all this shit from his past? Does he think Ramón will actually write back?

I bet I could just read it, and then write him something back like I'm Ramón responding.

How hard could it be to write an end-of-life love letter to someone you knew so long ago? I hate to admit it, but Andrew has a point about respecting privacy. A man should respect another man's privacy, even if he is a closeted fag living in sin.

Is that what I really think?

That fags have rights too?

I guess? Sure.

Maybe it just brings peace to his conscience thinking that Ramón will receive it, like Andrew thinks. I can just call and ask him. Andrew isn't there to get in my way. I don't know who the day nurse is? But I'm sure if I call and introduce myself as a relative or something, she would put him on the phone. Andrew doesn't own him or control who talks to him. Regardless of how close they've gotten.

I pick up my phone and start to type in his nursing home in Google so I can tap and make the call. Shit. I can't do this. The nurse would know I called. Find out that he wrote a love letter to a *man*. Fuck. I can't believe Andrew helped him with this shit. I hate him so much.

To somehow convince my uncle to say out loud all these things about Ramón, to then write it down…on paper. Seriously, what meds are they pumping in him?

This is fucking crazy. I grab the letter and bring it in front of my steering wheel. *626 Waverly Place, New York, NY.* They really haven't spoken in twenty years? *Return to sender.* What are the chances he's there? Probably none. Hence the return to sender.

My uncle's home address in the top left corner. Wonder why Andrew didn't put the nursing home as the return address? I guess receiving a letter from a past lover with a return address of a nursing home might not excite someone to open it. Wait. This was returned back to my uncle's house. How did Andrew get it? I push my left knee into the bottom of the steering wheel and hold. I grab the top of the envelope with both hands; pushing one hand and pulling the other slightly.

Rip it and turn around, Roy.

What good can come from this? Nothing.

This is sick. This is…ugh…Fuck! I can't. I chuck the letter across the car toward the passenger-side window. It hits. The letter falls to the floor, landing face down. Thank god the window is closed. I guess thank God? What does God actually think about all of this? I already know. A sin. And now, what of me? Helping carry out this sin? Turn the car around, Roy.

I can't. Turn around the car and go back to what?

I glance at the clock at the center dashboard to check the

time. 10:01 a.m. My speed a bit past the limit at eighty-six miles per hour. Okay, slow it down. I got all day, and this ain't my car.

I should call Sergeant Keaton back. It's getting a bit too suspicious now that I haven't returned her messages. All right, let's brainstorm this real quick. I still don't know for sure what happened about twenty-four hours ago, when that fella stumbled out of my apartment after I put a crater in his temple from chucking my dead mother-in-law's urn at his face—and left Bobby alone to clean it up and told him not to answer the door to anyone. Did that fucker answer someone?

Lucy found a note left on our door when she got home from work; the cops asking if there were any witnesses that saw something outside the apartment building on St. Clair Street. Witnesses for what? Everything happened inside my apartment only. They have to be separate things.

Onto the next then—

The cops I fled from in the night…I can tell Sergeant Keaton that my car was stolen…They already have a concrete record for where my car was. *I was there.* Hm. So I'm calling now to report that my car is missing this morning? Okay, that works…What about Lucy? Fucking Lynette. That's the second time that bitch meddled in my business in one night. Lucy said that she would take back her statement. Is it just that easy? I guess she and I need to come up with something…a reason for the ruckus. Get our story straight—why I was gone when the cops showed up after Lynette called them, and why she had a mark on her face near four in the morning…

I'll text my boss that I'm sick; that will at least buy me a couple days off from work. One thing easy at least. Okay, Lucy first.

I don't want to call her. Fuck. I need to.

I grab my phone. Scroll to her name.

Tap

Ring…ring…ring…ring…

Don't pick up. I can just lea—

"Roy?"

"Hey, hun."

"Ah, hi." "Where are you?" "Are you okay?"

"Yeah, why wouldn't I be okay?" "Are you okay?"

"Yeah, no, I'm good, um." A breath and beginning to weep. "I'm just happy to hear your voice."

"I'm happy to hear yours too." "Ahem." "But, ah, listen." "I gotta do a thing for my uncle, so I'm goin' to be out of town for a day or two."

"What?" "What are you doin' for him? Where are you goin'?"

"It's, ah." "Well, it's a private thing." "A loose end that needs tying up." "But don't ya worry." "I'm gonna handle it 'n' come right back." "Turns out a demon from his past has come back, and I need to help him out with it." Why did I just say that?

"A demon from his past?"

"Yeah." "It's a long story. I'll tell ya when I get back."

"Okay…" "Roy, where were you last night before you came home?" Shit. This again?

"The cops told me your car was found parked behind a Motel 6?" "And that you fled from them in a high-speed chase?" I mean, they barely kept up; I wouldn't call that a chase. Her weeping increasing. "Are you cheating on me?" A big breath and louder wail. "Is that why you hit me?" Fuck.

"Lucy." "I'm not cheatin' on you." "You are my wife." "I love you. I would never think to ever cheat on you." "I respect you, god knows. You are my world; you are my everything." "I can't begin to explain to you the guilt I feel…" Silence continues; I listen as her cries lighten.

"Roy, there's something you're not tellin' me."

"Lucy…" "Uh."

"Roy! I can't take the lies; I just can't!" "You've never lied to me before. What is goin' on with you?"

"Lucy." "My car got stolen last night." "Okay?" "That's why

I was on edge." "I didn't tell ya because it was late 'n' I didn't want to upset you."

"Your car got stolen?"

"Yeah."

"Where were you when it got stolen?"

Where was I? "I was hangin' at the bar with those new friends I told ya about, 'n' when I went to leave, my car was gone. I then got a ride home, 'n' I'm now handling it this morning. After this call with you, I'm gonna call Sergeant Keaton 'n' let her know, okay?"

"Okay…"

"Okay, well, good. I'm gonna hang up now. I'll call ya later tonight. I love you."

"Love you too."

Tap

I don't need to help my uncle to make my own place in hell; I'm doing it just fine all by myself.

I toss my phone into the cup holder. How many hours until NYC? I grab it back real quick. GPS says nine hours and forty-seven minutes. I throw it back. It's gonna be a long drive.

Last time I was on a road trip, Lucy and I went to Florida, two summers ago for our anniversary. That was a nice trip. Besides the fact that we really didn't fuck. But that's also how it is between us at home anyways. I can't remember the last time we did fuck? What should I have expected? Her pressure on me of wanting kids now; me always putting it off. This car is lonely without her. She's been my gal forever now. I'm thirty-four, and I've been with the same person for twenty years. God, her father was such an ass to me. Wouldn't let us get married. Until somehow it finally happened. Poor Lucy had to grow up with a strict father, the town's favorite pastor. But at least it did finally happen. Men around me would kill to have a wife like mine. She's gorgeous and sweet as a rich apple pie. A true man's dream come true.

High school sweethearts and inseparable. Both our families attending the same church her father preached at. I guess, what difference does it make? Married or not, she and I were still together: fucking like rabbits at the time, always; happy. If she were here right now, she'd be singing along to some tunes and pushing me around, giving me a hard time to get me to loosen up and sing with her. To not be so serious all the time. She'd want to stop every hour to pee and god knows sightsee things that no one else gives a shit about. But I love that about her. That she has curiosity and gets joy out of even the simplest things. While I'd just be a grump and want us to get to our destination as soon as possible.

I guess I'll get to NYC sooner without her, but having her here would be nice and maybe even worth all the small, little setbacks. How do these truckers do it? All day, every day, on the highway, alone. Bunch of lone wolves. Am I gonna be one of them?

Wait a minute. Truckers have to fuck too. At some point they have to get off on the road. But where, when? I guess at a stop in West Virginia I could take a long…lunch? Can't get caught out here, now can I? No one knows who I am or where I am from. I can be *invisible* out here. Huh. I guess I understand you a little bit more now, Dorian.

Okay, Sergeant Keaton. You're next. I grab my phone and swipe to her text thread.

Tap

Ring…rin—

"Roy." "It's about time. Where are you?"

Okay, Roy. Keep your story clean, tight, and simple like this two-lane highway. "Hey, Sergeant Keaton…uh, sorry for the delay. My car was stolen last night, and this morning has been a zoo figuring all that out."

"It was?"

"Yes."

"I'm sorry to hear that. Sounds like you're in a car now? Whose car are you in, then?"

"Uh, yeah, just a friend of mine has an extra car and dropped it off for me just shortly ago."

"Nice friend you have. I'm sorry to hear your car was stolen…Did you report it?"

"Thank you." "Actually, not yet. That's why I'm callin' ya back now, as well as saw your texts."

…Silence on the line. She gonna say anything?

"So, uh, why the text last night from you?" "And, can you start a report, please, for my stolen car, please?"

"Sure thing, Roy, I can help you with that." "Where were you last night, by the way?"

"I was at the bar, left 'round one-ish; noticed my car wasn't there, 'n' then I had a friend take me home."

"So you were at the bar for the night, left around one a.m., and found your car missing in the parking lot, and then had a friend take you directly home. Is that correct?" Shit, am I missing something? Why is she asking me these questions?

"Yes, ma'am."

"And what happened with you and your wife at around four a.m.?"

"What do you mean?"

"Roy, you know it's a small town and I'm a sergeant here at the station. A 911 call came in, and I know two of my officers went to your apartment in the early morning." "Now, you and I have history…I can maybe help you if you tell me the truth. If you don't, there's not much I can do for you." Fuck. What do I do? I can't tell Sergeant Keaton the truth. Over my dead fucking body. The truth will never come out. I'll die before that truth comes out.

"I'm not sure what you're gettin' at, Sergeant Keaton."

"Did you hit your wife, Roy?" "Did you hit Lucy?"

"No." My throat clears. "I did not hit her." "Why would you think that?" Stern and confident.

"Okay." "Well, what happened then?" Fuck. What do I say? …Shit. Shit. Shit. Shit! I'm taking too long to answer. Uh…

It's bubbling. It's bubbling. Words have to come out. I have to say something! "It was self-defense," I blurt. "I, uh." Throat clears again. "She, well, she's been on some meds for quite some time because…because we've been having some fertility issues." "And her mood changes a lot 'n' swings different directions, 'n' she had an episode last night because I came home so late from the bar, 'n' was angry at me." "She got really loud and in my face, and…'n' she hit me first."

"She hit you first?"

"That's correct, ma'am." "Sergeant Keaton, I swear, you know me." "I would never, ever hit a woman. Intentionally. I hit her out of an instinct, an uncontrolled reflex. I was drunk, and it was an accident." "I swear it." "She slapped me first, and my right hand just popped up from my side." Technically half true.

"So you did hit your wife?"

"Yes, it was out of self-defense, a reaction." "Weren't you listenin'? She hit me first."

"I heard you. A second ago you said no, that you did not hit her. So I'm just making sure I'm getting the truth now." "What did you do after?"

"What did I do after?" I? I? "I sobbed like a baby." "What man hits their wife? The shock took over me. It doesn't matter that she hit me first. She is my wife, and I instigated the situation 'n' should have been home earlier, or let her know when I was gonna be comin' home. The whole thing was my fault."

"What did you two do after you sobbed, having realized you hit her?"

"We, uh…Well, Lynette, our neighbor, came knockin' at our door. I guess she heard us fightin'. Lucy answered. Lynette said she was going to call the cops. I was still drunk and not thinkin' clearly, so I got scared 'n' took off."

"You *took off?*" "Where did you go?" Where did I go? Um…

"…I went to see my uncle." "At his nursing home." "I…uh."

"I know visitin' hours are not allowed at four in the mornin', but I just thought it wouldn't be a problem if it was just me, sittin' in a chair next to his bedside quietly while he slept." "You see, I haven't been there much for him."

"Whose car did you take?"

"Mine."

"You took your car? The one that was stolen and missing hours before at one a.m.?" "And you drove drunk?"

SHIT

Fuck.Fuck.Fuck.Fuck.Fuck.

"I mean, Lucy's! I say *mine* because—it is technically *her* car —but I am using it today." "And I was pretty much sober by then."

"Okay, Roy, I see how this is going to go." "I'm sure you know, your car was found at the nursing home and towed away a few hours ago. Do you take me for a fool? We have it. Now I don't know whose car you are in now, and I don't know why you are lying to me, but I bet if I call Lucy right now, I'd be able to find out real quick."

"Go ahead, call her!" "I'm tellin' you the truth."

"Roy." "I don't think you understand. There is now a warrant out for your arrest for domestic violence. Okay? You hear me? You need to come in to the station. If you are telling me the truth, then I can help you clean this up."

My uncle's frail body hijacking the sight in my mind, now in front of me with his soft, jagged breaths. The open, tight, two-lane highway gone, and I realize I'm in a bumper-to-bumper backup.

"I can't do that." "I can't do that, Sergeant Keaton." "You see, I'm actually on a very…important mission right now."

"Roy." "Let me speak more clearly." "My officers will find you and bring you in if you don't voluntarily come in. Do you know what a *warrant for your arrest* means? Every officer here at the station is aware and has eyes out for you. Don't make this harder than it needs to be."

"I'm sorry, Officer." "'N' good luck findin' me."
Tap
New York City, here I come.

17

WHAT IS it about men that is so…alluring to me now?

Why now? WHY? I've gone this far without. Is it because I'm traveling? No. You just cheated on Lucy back home, you idiot. Am I having a midlife crisis? Do people fuck the same sex when they have midlife crises? Maybe the fucked-up ones do.

Okay, be honest with yourself.

Haven't you always had a thing for guys?

No. The fuck not.

Yes, you have.

Remember that new kid in school in fourth grade? You had never seen a boy with such pretty eyes. Pretty eyes? Who cares about pretty eyes? Just because I think someone has pretty eyes doesn't mean I wanted to fuck him. I just liked his eyes.

Hm.

BUT maybe there was something *more* I liked about that boy. Maybe I did like him…more? But in fourth grade? My stomach churning again. This time it's worse thinking about myself versus my uncle. It's so disgusting. So fucking vile to think. To be a fucking pervert in fourth grade. Is there a difference now at thirty-four if I like men? As an adult? Is it still perverted even though I'm a grown-ass man? Yes. It's worse. You're a fucking pervert.

"Another, sir?" The bartender pointing at the empty whiskey glass I'm holding in my hands, finding me lost in thought. I bring it up to my face and watch as the last bit of joy slides down the side of the glass, not enough left to find a channel to ride to my lips. I set the glass back down. A noise as the heavy bottom clunks with the granite bar top. A few patrons turn their heads at me across the bar, perpendicular to where I am sitting. Like the view? The men dressed up in long-sleeve button-ups, the women in dresses made of thick, colorful material that covers their tits fully. Me in my raggedy clothes that I ran out on my wife in…

"Yeah." He starts to pour me another neat.

This one looking heavier than the last. Or is he just pouring out faster from the bottle? Maybe the lighting changed. How long I been here? "Rough day?" He looks at me through the pour.

"Ha." "I guess you could call it a rough day." "Happy to be here, though." A quick, cheesy grin shines from me as he pulls the bottle up to top me off. I grab the glass and signal a cheers with it, then take another gulp. I set it back down. Slower this time. A softer tap. A third of it gone. I pull out my phone. Hey, you other perverts—What you got going on tonight?

Pic for pic? Sure, send me one first, moron.

Looking? *Face pic in a T-shirt.* Not really my type.

Hey man. Sure, I'll respond to him: Hi.

Hey. *Pic with his head cropped off, fully dressed.* He might be hot. I type: **Hi.**

Bottom slut looking for tonight, interested? *Hairy ass-and-hole pics.* Maybe? No. What am I? Fucking wookiees now too?

Block

Looking to suck. Damn, how many fags like to suck dick? Seems like a lot. Good thing for me, I guess. A quick chuckle pops out. I glance up to see if anyone's watching me.

Yoo. Sure. I type: Hii.

Top here. Not a fat chance in hell.

Couple looking for a third, hosting in our hotel room. *Pics of them shirtless flexing together in different bathrooms.* How many bathrooms do these guys have? These guys are really, really gay. Too gay.

Block

> Hey dude, horny as fuck. Where are you?

No pics, but his profile only has his age and weight listed, just like mine. Hm. Another incognito man like myself. Let's try him:

> I'm at the Courtyard by Marriott Basking Ridgge
>
> Traveling
>
> Where aree you

Immediate response

> Nice, I know exactly where that is.

Does he, now?

Ding, ding, ding. We got a winner.

Are you really gonna do this again, Roy? Yeah. What the fuck else am I gonna do at this random hotel in New Jersey? Was stuck in Andrew's tiny-ass car all day, horny as shit again. This whiskey now touching my soul just right. God, I love it.

Can't run into any more trouble with the law or Lucy here. Shit. *Lucy.*

I told her I was gonna call her later. Can I push it until morning? I'm exhausted. And now drunk, and also about to commit more sin…Now isn't really a good time.

What if she calls me? I can call her in the morning after I

get some rest. Tell her I crashed as soon as I got to the hotel. You know what? I'll just text her.

I swipe over to her text thread:

> Hey, hope your dsy was nice. I'm jusrt getting into my hotel and amm gonna crashj. I'm exhausted.

> Ill call ya tomoroww

What time is it? 8:36 p.m. I put my phone face down on the bar top. It's a little early to be crashing for me, but hopefully she buys it. I have been on the road all day, and she knows I didn't get much sleep from last night. *She was there.* I chuckle to myself. God, there is a special place in hell for men like me.

The patrons down the way from me laughing, with drinks in their hands, now excited from their food arriving. Looks like a group of three couples. I wonder why they're at this hotel tonight too? I grab my phone back up and swipe to Grindr. I scan real quick to my left, right, and behind. No one near. Should I put a picture up? Maybe just a pic of my arm or pic of my crotch through my jeans? There's a bit of everything these fellas put on here. Maybe I can put something a little more than just my height and weight?

No, nothing at all, not even in my clothes. People know what clothes I wear.

Okay, I'm in the middle of nowhere, miles and miles away from home.

No. It's not worth the risk. A shirtless pic? I mean, I'm hotter than 90 percent of the dudes on here. I don't know—maybe if I get just a little more drunk, I can have me a little photo shoot in my room. Get a good shot to put on my profile before I enter the big city tomorrow! Fuck, I'm a fucking mess.

I'm not going.

Yes, I am.

I AM going to New York City tomorrow.

Eh. But hey—my shoulders shrugging up to my ears—I will be a drunk HOT mess. A LAID hot mess. Yeah, baby!

A blank profile with just my height and weight is still fine… It's not like I'm having any problems with fellas hitting me up to meet. Fucking feral animals.

I guess it's no different from my fellas picking up broads at the bar. I swig another gulp. But those women at least play—a coy game; well, most of them. These fellas are just relentless. Do any gays ever play coy like how women do? Tease the men, pretending to act as naive prey like women do? I like that game. I like the hunt.

Those smart women know what they're doing; prey that knows they're being hunted, and they like it too. They control the hunt more than the hunter ever realizes. Those women are the true masters of the game, if you think about it.

Are the gays all hunters? Hunters fucking and chasing hunters? Is that possible? The two I've hooked up with weren't hard to get at all. Wait, am I the prey? Nah, no way. I am the hunter, and they were easily hunted down by me. Roy is nobody's prey.

Wait—would it be that bad if I was someone's prey? I just made an argument that prey can be in more control than the hunter himself. Whatever.

I might be prey to this whiskey, though. Hahhahaha, yeah, sir, Johnnie Walker Black, fuck me up, baby. I'll be your boy, you can be my daddy. I'll swallow every last bit of your dark, silky, smoky cum. A laugh blurts out of me; the bartender gives me a look like I don't belong here. Yeah, yeah, go back to whatever the fuck you're doing. Johnnie and I are having a moment.

A new Grindr notification. I tap through the app:

> Nice, I live nearby and prefer travelers. Pic?

> Sure

I send him the two pics I have. Me in a white T-shirt and

light jeans, face cropped out, but you can see the bottom of my neck. The photo cropped tight.

You

Face?

No, I don't send those

Discrete?

Yeah

Can you not tell by now? Jesus.

Oh, okay. Me too. Perfect Do you want to get fucked?

No

Not ever.

Do you want to fuck me?

Yeah

When are you free?

My screen changes—
Incoming call from Andrew Boyd
Finally that fucker calls me back.
Tap
"Hey, what took you so long?"
"Roy, I'm at work." "You okay?"
"Yeah, but I called you more than two hours ago." My words drawing out—hadn't noticed until now because I haven't been talking to anyone.
"Roy, the beginning of my shift is always the busiest. I greet all my patients, get updates from the day nurse, aid with dinners,

administer evening medications. I'm sorry I missed your call; I'm calling you back now. What's up?"

"Put my uncle on the line—I need to talk to him."

"Are you drunk?" Is it that obvious?

"No." "Why would you say that?"

"You sound…agitated, and a little slow." "Your speech is slurring."

"*DoOoo IIIIIiiiIII?*" "I've had a few whiskeys…Nothin' out of the norm, baby." "Johnnie and I just hangin' out like good ol' pals; maybe we'll jerk each other off later, who knows." "Not like it's any of your business." "Actually, wait, you'd probably like to see that."

"*Baby*, eh?" "Okay, well, baby, what happened?" "Did you find Ramón?" "Who is Johnnie, and why are you about to jerk him off?"

"Not yet." "I'm resumin' the mission, back to…tomorrow mornin'." "Johnnie is also none of your business. Why you askin'? You wanna join, cowboy? Sure, you could drive up here tonight and meet me in this fancy-schmancy town." "The room has a king bed."

"Mm, are you okay?"

"Yes, Andrew, I. Am. Fine." "Peachy as a fat girl's ass that's had too many Twinkies in her life." "And Johnnie." "Johnnie is my daddy." Another laugh blurts out. This time the bar-goers, along with the bartender, darting looks at me. Yeah, well, fuck you guys too.

"Okay, well, drink some water." "I'm sure you don't want to meet Ramón smelling like a drunk mess." "What do you think of New York City?" "I bet it's amazing, isn't it? I bet it's so different from here." "I dream one day to move to a big city."

"Sure." "Will you put my uncle on the phone? Pretty please."

"He's asleep now. Want me to call you back if I find him up? Where are you now? Are you sure you're okay?" "Who is Johnnie?"

"Yeah, I'm fine." My voice erupts loud. "Stop askin' me if I'm okay." I turn my body alongside the bar, putting my back to everyone. The bottom of my phone closer to my mouth. "I just need to talk to him."

"What's going on, Roy?"

"Andrew." "I just want to talk to my uncle. Not you." "Okay?" "Fuck off and stop askin' your little questions."

"Okay, well, you can talk to me too. I don't bite. Unlike you. Fucking pitbull over there on the other side of the line." "Getting blitzed god knows where and with who."

"I'm a lion." "Honey." "I ain't no little pitbull shit that stays controlled, locked in a house, waitin' all day for some owner to come coddle me." "…Like you."

"Oh yeah?" "I know that's not the case. Trust me." "And, lion…really? Could you be any more of a cliché when identifying with an animal you'd be if you had to be one?"

"A cliché? What would you be, then?" I turn my body back forward, putting my elbows on the bar top. The couples all still there down the bar, away from me, eating their dinner, now chatting with the bartender, taking quick looks my direction and then back to their food—exchanging more laughs and smiles. What's so fucking awesome, huh? You guys enjoying Johnnie too? He's the best. I grab my glass and signal a cheers their direction.

"Me? Oh, I'd be a dolphin, for sure."

"A dolphin?" "A giant, ugly, bald-looking fish in the ocean that comes up and does cartwheels to please everyone?"

"Cartwheels? What type of dolphins have you seen—can you take me? Yeah, those exactly, I would be those kinds."

"Nothing, I just saw a show with Lucy a few years ago in Florida on a trip. The dolphins were trained and did tricks with their trainers." "Like a dog, ha, like a pitbull." "Of course you'd choose to be a sea dog." I let out a laugh. "Get it?"

"Yeah, yeah." "So funny." "So my animal pick is fun, loyal, and brings joy to people." "Yours is…?"

"Mine is at the top of the food chain, baby. Scary. Idealist to all, whether they know it—strong, the alpha." "A representation of how all men should be." "Lions."

"All men should be?" "I wouldn't say all…Are you drinking water yet?" "You're slurring your words even more." "Do all mighty lion-men, such as yourself, can't speak clearly too?"

I clear my throat. Grab another swig of whiskey. Clear my throat again. "Of course you wouldn't." "Why?"

"Lions are just a bunch of big, insecure pussycats with bigger claws and teeth. Mindless, only hunting for food and water to survive out of instinct. Versus: Dolphins have social skills, rely on family and connection. As well as hunting, instinctual skills to survive." Is Andrew telling me he's a hunter?

"Instinctual skills to survive? What crack are ya smokin'?" I take my last gulp of whiskey. "Dolphins can't survive for shit. They are hunted by sharks and orcas. Where did you go to school?" "No one fucks with a lion. Dolphins get hunted." "Your animal is prey." "You are prey." "And haven't you ever heard of lion packs before?" "You don't know what you're talkin' about."

"Yeah, well at least compared to a lion, dolphins' life experience on earth is far more reaching than a lion could ever dream about. I bet a lion couldn't even dream of it at all." "What's better? To live long and not know what you don't know? To be stuck in a mind and environment that limits you from more? Or to live shorter and know and experience everything imaginable that you want?"

"Okay, I don't know what fag shit you now led this conversation down to." "Just call me back when my uncle is up. 'Kay?" "Ya hear me?"

"Yeah, sure."

"Bye."

Tap

I swipe back to Grindr.

Hello? You there man?

8 minutes ago

Yeah, sorry, I'm here. Want to come now?

An empty glass in front of me again. I look up. "Bartender, another." *Drink water.* Andrew's stupid voice left in my head. "Can I have some water too?"

I can come at midnight, that work?

Yeah, I'm in room 432

Don't stop at the front desjk or anything, just come to my doorr.

I know the drill.

Okay

The drill? Well, that's good. At least one of us does.

Gives me a few to drink a bit more. I should probably eat something too. What if he's ugly? Shit…Well, I brought Andrew's gun into the room with me. Not that I'm going to actually use it…

I'll check the peephole first. If I'm not into him, I guess…I'll call the front desk, tell them there is a hobo outside my door in the hallway, banging on doors. They'll have him on camera at least banging my door? Wait. *He's gonna be on camera coming to my room.* You're out of town, Roy. It's fine.

Hm. I'm excited. The bartender comes back my way, finally. "Same thing, sir?" I nod. He tops me off again. "Thank you." He's kinda cute. Maybe I should invite him up, too, yeah? My first three-way? Why the fuck not.

I'm on vacation.

18

———————

Knock knock knock

Did I just hear…? Eh. My body turns the other direction—away from the noise.

Knock knock knock

Again? My eyes trying to peer open. Where am I? I turn to look at the back of my hotel-room door. Fuck, my head hurts. Oh shit. Someone is here. Who the fuck is here? The cops follow and find me here?

I lean up from my hotel bed and glance at the alarm clock on the nightstand—

It's blinking 9:19 p.m.

That can't be the time? I grab my phone and see Grindr messages and the real time. 11:57 p.m. I then fix the time on the alarm clock. Oh, that guy! No way, he actually came? Ha. Fucker is early to be knocking so loud like that. I look back at the nightstand. *Ramón Ramirez.* My uncle's letter to Ramón that I brought in and set next to my bed. Why did I bring that thing in with me?

The top of my forehead resting in my palm for a second, as if the pounding pain in my head will transfer to my palm and then out of my body through my fingertips. I still got three minutes. Leave me alone. You can wait. I rub both hands over my face and eye sockets. The room slightly spinning. Feels good. I spring up from the bed, trying to swing into balance on my two feet. No. He can't wait, you idiot. The cameras! A rush of panic—go get him. "Comin'," I holler.

I make my way to the door and trip on my shoes, nearly face planting into the wall next to the door but catching myself with a loud slap on the wall. I open the door without even checking the peephole. "Hey, come on in." My left hand swinging across the shoes I just tripped over, gesturing for him to enter. "Welcome to my abode." Abode? Really? Who am I?

"Hi." His voice extremely deep. Wasn't expecting that. I guess, what was I expecting? He walks past me with his hands in his pockets. A red ball cap on. My height. Light features. Face clean shaven. He passes me, and I check him out more from the back. His ass thicker than the last. Juicier. Yum. I want to bite into that right now. I close the door, keeping my eyes on him.

He stops at the foot of the bed, his head continuing to move around, scanning? What is he looking for? Maybe he's just as paranoid as me.

His legs and ass planted still, just for my view. Hm. Is *he* prey that knows his power? Or is he a hunter that knows how to watch his back? Either way, I don't care. Take all the time you need, babe. We already agreed who's fucking who. Regardless whether you're a hunter or prey. I like what I see. He then turns around. "Traveling alone, I take it?"

"Yeah."

"Cool. I'm discrete, too, so I prefer to meet guys that are traveling." Yeah…I'm noticing that theme. I walk over his direction, trying to not come across as drunk as I am. As I get nearer to him, Lucy pops into my mind—how she smelled alcohol off me in the shower. Do I reek of it now?

"You, uh, need a glass of water or somethin'?" I walk back a few steps and dart into the bathroom. "Hey, I'm gonna brush my teeth real quick; been a long day. You chill for a sec," I holler out.

"No. I'm good, thanks," I hear outside as I run the faucet cold and gulp down two glasses. Fuck, I don't have a toothbrush or anything here. What else I got? I scan the counter and look at the mini shits the hotel provides. No. I'm not putting miniature shampoo or a soap bar in my mouth. Maybe hot water will work? Kill all the germs? I turn the faucet until the water comes out steaming hot. I fill the glass and slowly add the water to my mouth, swish and spit, and repeat. My sensations a bit numb from the alcohol, I can't tell if I'm just burning all the good shit that needs to go or I'm actually burning myself. Better than nothing.

This hotel room got any mini bottles? I step outside the bathroom after wiping the water off my face with a towel.

A quick jolt from his body, now leaned, relaxed, against the desk across from the foot of the bed. Behind him his jacket set on the desk next to the coffee maker. Did I just see that or am I imagining things? Maybe he's nervous too? Wait. Am I nervous? I step toward him. "One second." I step past him and lean down into the minifridge. Nothing. I turn my attention back to him and lean up. "You got any liquor on you?" His appearance casual, ass half sitting on the desk.

"Why would I have liquor on me?"

"Uh, I figured I'd ask 'cause I'm out."

"No, I don't drink, actually."

"You don't drink?" "Ever?" Who doesn't drink?

"I mean, I used to, but nowadays I rarely do."

"Okay." "Ah." "Why don't ya?"

"Come closer to me." Stepping off from the desk, he's now planted back to standing by the middle of the foot of the bed. "Where are you from?" His deep voice drawing me in, turning me on.

I step closer to him, now just maybe two feet in front. "Kentucky."

His face lights up, and he nods. "Ah, Kentucky." Smaller nods continuing. "I think guys from Kentucky are hot."

I nod, staying quiet.

"Why are you discreet?" He steps closer to me, leaving now only a small distance between our noses. His lips slim and angular like a Disney character's.

"Um…I…have a wife." My head drops, eyes landing on his feet. I wonder how big they are?

My head pops back up. "Why?" "How about you?"

"Hey, no need to feel bad at all, man. Me too—I get it." His eyes, and the tone of his voice, creating a sincere spell. Does he actually *get it?* Maybe he's done this more than I have. He's gotten used to masking the guilt better than me? He wraps his hands around my arms. Thumbs pressing up and down on my biceps.

I nod slightly and look away. I look back. "I mean, you're hot, so…" My shoulders shrug.

He then slowly drops—eyes locked onto mine, opening his mouth at the pace of his obedient descent—lands on his knees, and pushes his fat tongue fully out over his bottom lip and chin. The spell continuing. His tongue now a meaty platter for the tip of my dick to dangle over and tease. My body positions my crotch just above. My hand extends from my side, sliding fingers under his chin, making it down past his Adam's apple. I then shift my fingers softly in different directions, feeling the hollow channel of his throat. Warming it up. Cupping the bottom of his jaw with my palm. Pulling my whole hand so his tongue now makes impact on top of my jeans. My dick starting to get hard underneath. His eyes still locked to mine. His seduction. His submission. His mouth. This is exactly what I need. It's all that I want.

My head rises up, eyes released from his spell. That newfound adrenaline my body now craves returning with lightning strikes a dozen. My focus jumping to the peephole of my hotel-room door, in front of me across the room. I'm still trying to maintain my balance. I closed it. Right? Yeah, I did. My eyes shut. My focus on the grip my hand has under his jaw. My knees bend slightly. My dick getting harder. The pressure building up. I need to free it. I grab his face with both hands and smash it into my crotch. His head swishing in different directions against my force. Down, boy. I am in control. Not you. He's pushing his lips and breathing heavily into and through my jeans. My dick and balls feeling the heat of his lust. I'm exhaling quiet moans. I can let him know I'm enjoying this.

With his nose pressed under my balls, he takes both hands to my belt and unbuckles. Swishing his face left to right, and again. He pulls my belt off, snapping it across his left to land on the bed. He unbuttons and unzips my pants and pulls them down with my underwear all in one motion. His head kept still. My dick pops out, landing on his forehead. He smiles and lets out a groan. Now taking the left side of his face up, down, and through my sack. Petting my balls with his left cheek.

My head hovered over him, enjoying what I see. "You like my balls?"

"Oh yeah." A grunt from below. He looks to his right and runs his fingers through his hair. He puts his face back in that position and begins to add his tongue. My dick now fully hard and knees giving further. I can't take it like this much longer. The sensation of his hot, fat tongue just makes me think of how the inside of his tight, hot ass is gonna feel. Fuck face-fucking him; I want to feel his hole now. "Get up." I step back, grab his head with both hands to pull him up. His face now next to mine. He lunges in with eyes closed, mouth open and tongue flickering out. My hands set strong on his face, blocking him from reaching my lips. I spit in his mouth. "No, I don't do that."

He opens his eyes. "Oh, fuck." He smiles, with grunts coming from behind his teeth. "No problem." "Can I eat your ass?"

Can he eat my what? "Like how I eat pussy?" His eyes draw

a blank, and my grip lets go of his face. "Nah, you ain't touchin' my ass."

"Yeah, yeah, no problem." "Sorry I asked."

He turns left and steps toward the foot of the bed, his head forward. He takes off his T-shirt by grabbing it from the top of his back and pulling it over in front of him. His back muscles angular, too, just like his lips. Tight and just large enough to grab. The two lamps turned on in the room, giving just enough light for us. He's taking his time—control now, it would appear. It's good though; I like the show. I'll watch.

The tops of his shoulders are perfect handles for my hands to grip, soon, to send force that will travel down his back as I push my dick in from behind him. I stay standing in my position, trying to keep my balance still. Fuck, I should have drunk more water like Andrew said.

He takes both his hands and slides them down the sides of his legs, taking down his sweatpants and revealing a red jock-strap. He's so confident. Like a woman seducing a man in her lingerie, knowing that he's hooked for her slow tease and unraveling dance. He turns his head right and looks down at my dick, still erect, not too far behind his now-exposed, lifted, candy apple ass. I wanna bite that jock, pull it with my teeth, and snap it back on him. His sweatpants now down at his ankles, he steps out of them, swings his right hand back to grab my dick. His right profile sharp, a confident smirk sending a dimple to his right cheek. He pulls me from my dick closer to him, forcing me to step up behind him. His body shifting forward, putting both knees on the bed and cocking his ass up.

His right hand still on my dick, he leads the head of my cock right to his hole. My hands at my side now lift and grab his hips. The pressure of his now-opening ass as my tip pushes through. His head stays turned right my direction. Eyes closed; his confi-dent smirk shifting to a softer expression of delight; his lips pushed out; an exhaling moan. His jock strap is so hot. My first time seeing it on a fella—fucking a fella in it. I don't know what it is. Like a piece of lustful, shiny jewelry he's wearing just for me. And only for me. It's not meant for anyone else. Worn underneath his clothing all day around everyone, and I am the only one that knows—that underneath he's my little whore. Always dressed for my eyes and pleasure only. A slutty strip to show off his assets, just for me. I chuckle. The last piece of clothing, resembling his last wit of dignity, that he's ready to strip off, just for me, before I defile him. To salivate over and worship how it looks. To then use it how I choose. Grab and snap. Cup his balls and squeeze, so he knows I own everything on top and underneath. Yeah, it's his last piece of clothing left, the last mask covering his vulnerability, and it's all designed and intended for me. And he fucking loves it.

My head getting sucked in by his eager, warm rim, the top of my shaft following through slowly. He exhales and moans as he takes me in inch by inch. His ass feeling like a tight, wet pussy. Wow. This is the tightest fucking wet pussy I've ever had. Do gay fellers' asses always feel like this?

Did that *MC* guy feel this way? I don't know; it happened so quick, and I was so nervous. But I'm not nervous now. I'm hungry. Eager.

He's so…wet and ready. His ass crying for the dick it craves, like how my dick cries with precum, craving it back. My shaft now fully submerged inside him, his ass cheeks pressed into my lower stomach. I fucking love this feeling. I love the way it looks too.

He lets out another moan. "Fuck, you feel so good inside me." He then opens his eyes, turns his head further back to send me a smile and share quick eye contact. He extends his right hand back, places it on my ass, pushes me so my feet step a little left. He snaps his torso down to the bed and tilts his ass further up.

Are you comfy now, cowboy? Stay just like that for me.

19

———

CLAP CLAP CLAP CLAP
   Moans from him
   Clap clap
   Grunts from me

"Ugh." This is the greatest sex I've had in my life! How is that possible? Don't overthink it, Roy. He feels fucking amazing.

The whole hotel floor has got to hear us. My inhibitions are too gone to care, though, but not too numb that my dick won't work. His hole the last well left on earth, satisfying my thirst. He's taking it like none ever before. I've never fucked anyone this hard. My hands on his hips, looping each side of his jockstrap through for a tighter grip. He shifts his body to the right, and I continue fucking with not a beat missed. We are in sync. *Fuck, I'm gonna cum.* "I'm gonna cum."

"Yeah?" From face down on the bed, he lifts his head up right. His right profile back to seducing me, with his smirking, angular lips pursed and sharp jawline flexed from his bite. His toned back muscles shining from the sweat we've worked up. My face drops down; my tongue out, licking the grooves of his back, going in a zig-zag motion, traveling up, crossing back and forth over his spine. Kissing, licking, biting my way up. He flexes and stretches so the top of his spine gets close to my face as I inch my way to the top, his hands now fisted into the bed, knuckles down, pressed into the sheets, propping him up. "Cum in my filthy hole," he grunts. "Yeah?" "You like my filthy, tight cunt?"

"Fuck, yeah, fuck, I'm gonna—I'm fucking cumming in your dirty cunt right now." My fucking now at rapid fire like a relentless AK-47; my dick pulsing and flexing, squirting last drops of cum out of my balls and into his ass. He holds still, right profile still turned at me, eyes down at his own ass still perked up. He winks. "Fuck, yeah"—loud and proud.

I step back; my dick slides out of his ass. He springs up; turning a 180 in one motion. His face now feeling the heat from my dick. He cups my balls with one hand gently, grabs my dick with the other, and squeezes to work more cum out. He looks up and shows me his fat tongue again. He gently places my dick in the middle of it, keeps it there, and circles in slow motions. Like a twister sucking everything up. Now squeezing at the base of my dick and pulling. His mouth closes to suck my head back in. "Ah, okay there, buddy." Shit now hurts. I step back more, removing my dick from his grasp. "Uh, it's a bit sensitive now." I need water, and he needs to leave. I exit to the bathroom to get some more water. My balance better now. The fucking and sweating must have helped sober me up a bit. "You want some water now?" I holler out.

"Sure. Yeah, I'll take some." I come out of the bathroom. He's standing between the foot of the bed and the desk again.

Did I just see a flinch again or something? Same feeling as last time, like déjà vu. Is he a bit jumpy, or is my vision dizzy still?

I hand him a cup of water. "Thanks." He nods. He takes a few sips and sets the cup in the coffee maker tray. I step past him and put my jeans back on. I sit at the foot of the bed. Silence between us. I watch as he puts his clothes back on, giving me small glances and smirking still as he picks up and works each piece on. I'm gonna miss that red jock.

"What brings you to town?" He adjusts his T-shirt down over his stomach, which has a little happy trail. Hm. Didn't notice that before. He takes his phone out of his pocket and scrolls with his thumb.

"I'm, uh, passin' through."

He glances up at me, not impressed with my vague reply.

"It's a long story."

He puts his phone back in his pocket, sits down next to me, sitting on one leg crossed under his body. The other dangling over the end of the bed and swinging slightly in my direction. "I got some time. Tell me." "Wouldn't be going to New York City, are you?" My ear perking his direction. How the hell does he know that? "I just saw a letter over there, an address to New York City." He signals toward the nightstand behind me. *That's right.* I forgot I put my uncle's letter there next to the alarm clock when I checked in.

"Yeah." I nod. "I'm goin' there tomorrow to meet a…friend I haven't seen in, well, twenty years." My shoulders shrug, and I give a cheesy grin. "Gonna be a big day." "Can't wait."

"Twenty years? That is a long time." He pops up off the bed and walks across and behind me. My head follows his path. He reaches, grabs the letter, and turns toward me.

I pop up from the bed. "What are you doing?"

He looks at me. "Nothing." The letter in his hands, between us. "I just have some friends in NYC, so I was curious about the address."

I pluck it out of his hands. "I don't need your help."

His peppy energy fleeing his body. "Oh." "Okay." He walks past and behind me; my eyes and body follow, shifting back to us both standing at the foot of the bed, toward each other.

"It's time for you to go."

He looks down at my hand holding the letter. "What does it say?" "Who is it to?" His question intrusive, just how Andrew is. Did he not hear me tell him to leave? What is with these fags and their questions? They're relentless.

Do I shout at him to get out? Tear up the letter in front of him to end the conversation? End this delusional saga here and now? Tell Andrew that I was robbed and the thieves stole the letter, my dignity, and my cum? Thing is, fella—I'm just as curious as you are to know what the fuck I'm holding in my hand.

"Did you not hear me?" "I just told you to leave." My right hand rises, using the letter to point at the hotel-room door behind him. An expression on his face as if I'm speaking math to him in Chinese. Blank. But attentive.

He slowly raises his left hand, mirroring mine. Reaches to the bottom corner of the letter with his thumb and two fingers. He clenches softly once making contact. My hand steady, the letter levitated between us. "Can I read it?" His peppy energy a tiny bit back. We both now holding the weight of this letter together in the air between us. *Can he read it?*

"Now tell me why that would make sense?" "No." I retract my hand, the letter following, pulling it out of his soft clench and tossing it onto the bed. "I asked you to leave." "Now get."

"Why wouldn't it make sense?" He shrugs and smiles. "We just had hot sex." "I like you; you like me." "I'm a writer by trade is all." He puts his hands up. "I don't mean to pry; I just saw it earlier when I stepped in and have been curious since." Yeah, well, get in line, buddy. My whole life has been turned upside down from this little piece of writing sealed inside that envelope.

"Yeah, I'm fuckin' curious too." Murmured under my breath. I can't help it.

"What?"

Hm. I'm never gonna see this guy again. In less than twelve hours I'll know what it says, so what's the difference? If I know now, or within twelve hours? Actually, what if Ramón doesn't want to share what it says? Then I'll never know and be even more confused AND pissed that I've come all this way for fucking nothing. My head turns back to the letter. It's upside down on the bed. Now seeming just like only blank, empty white paper. A white packaged piece of innocent paper.

Irregular shakes erupt inside me. What *if* Ramón doesn't share with me what it says; what *if* I cannot even find the fucker. What if he's dead. I glance at the alarm clock. 12:26 a.m. It is already the next day. The day the letter is meant to be opened. The day the truths and contents within are revealed. What about Andrew's point? *Fuck Andrew.* This is his fucking fault. AND he still hasn't called me back. Fuck him and his manipulation. And fuck my uncle too.

My hand reaches to pick up the letter. I turn it over. *Ramón Ramirez*. Eyes dash left. *David Stevens*. Two men's names written so close for the world to see, contents within exposing a forbidden lover's lifetime secret that proves my life was a lie around me. I extend my hand out toward the fella. Go ahead, grab and open it before I change my mind.

If he reads it, technically I didn't read it. *I* didn't open it. *I* followed the rules. He reaches out to grab the letter. I let go, and he holds it still, with both hands in front of him. Should I sit? No. I can't sit. "Okay, you can read it." "But a couple conditions—"

"Sure." "What?" He turns the letter over, positioning his hands to open it.

My hands spring up. "Open it as carefully as you can." "It needs to be resealed, as if no one has opened it."

"Of course." "I see now 'Return to sender.'" "Okay, yeah, I can do that." "Is your name David?" He turns to the desk, places the letter down next to the coffee maker, and grabs a pen. I watch as he slowly takes it to open the envelope. Millimeter by millimeter.

"Uh, yeah, my name's David."

Hm. Maybe he's done this before. He's doing a good job, now shifting his body to cover his process so I can't see any more. That's fine. I'll sit down. I should relax. Where's my water? I look for it, find it, grab the glass and gulp down the rest that's in it, and wait patiently, sitting behind him on the bed.

There's still time; I can tell him to stop. I can hear Andrew in my head yelling at me. The man's probably already halfway through opening it? Fuck. "Hey, actually, maybe—"

He turns quick, holding the folded letter pridefully in the air. "Got it out." Against my full will, a smile—agreeing with his excitement—pries through under the tight skin of my scared face.

There it is. Folded. Still all contents hidden within. I can stop it now. I can tell him to put it down. His face so lit up. Why is he so excited? Maybe it's a writer's thing?

"You ready?" He nods, looking at me. This is weird.

I return a small nod. "Yeah."

He steps a little to his left and opens the letter slowly. The page unwrinkling, becoming flat before his eyes. A blank white paper still to me, but a story and the hidden truths about my uncle's life in front of him.

His last breath in before he can read out loud—my final millisecond to stop him, and I can't:

My dearest Ramón,

I know you haven't heard from me in years, and God willing this letter gets to you.

You won't recognize the handwriting. But it is me, these are my words. I just have help with the writing. I would have handwritten myself, you know I love to write, but that's just not a possibility for me right now. Truth is, I don't have too many more days left, and it's taken me getting to my final hours, to finally realize how wrong I've been my entire life.

To realize how some of my biggest choices were my biggest mistakes. Mistakes that took away the one real thing in my life that was good, and true—you.

You need to know. That day I left with Roy in 1992, after my dad's funeral. Frank found us. He was there. He saw you, and he saw Roy.

I picked a fight with you that day, and left with Roy to protect all three of us. It was the only thing that made sense in my mind at the time. To run, and hide. I was scared. I'm sorry.

I've spent my whole life running and hiding, thinking I was protecting everyone I loved. But now at my end, looking back, I think—this was the wrong choice.

I was a coward. You were never a coward. You were fearless, one of the many things I loved about you. I hope you can forgive me—If I'm even a thought still left in your memory to forgive.

And, you were right by the way—I should have listened to you on how to raise Roy. You were stronger than I, wiser than I, you would have been a better father figure to him than me. I'm sorry I didn't see it—believe in us. Believe that we were worth fighting for, living for.

As I lay here paralyzed from the neck down, waiting; thinking. I know it would have been. I hope you're healthy and found happiness in New York City.

Love, D.D.

"You go by D.D.?" He looks up from the letter. "And you don't look paralyzed to me?" "Why are you lying about that?"

"What?" I look up at him, my eyes lost in the carpet on the hotel-room floor. *Raise me how?* AND who *the fuck is Frank*? I don't remember ever hearing that name. Not ever. Lightheaded, I think I'm gonna pass out.

"The letter is signed D.D." "I was asking if that's how you go by?"

D.D. My god. *D.D.*

All of a sudden I remember that name being said. Why?

D.D.

It's now repeating over and over in my head. It's what Ramón sometimes called my uncle. D.D. My uncle's middle name is Dixon. And D.D. was Ramón's nickname for him. The memories now flooding back into me. Ramón cleaning dishes— "Thanks for dinner D.D.; it was great"; "Hey D.D., you got some mail today from your father, Walter." It was always said soft, never in a fight, or a holler—not ever in public either. Behind closed doors in our home, Ramón called my uncle *D.D.*

"Um…" My head shakes.

He sets the letter down on the bed next to me. I look down at it and see the handwriting. It's true. The words he just spoke are written right there. *Love, D.D.* at the bottom. "Uh." "Yeah, I go by D.D." I look up at him.

"Okay, but why are you lying about being paralyzed? And who is Roy, and why did you have to run from Frank?" "I'm so confused."

Me too.

Who's Roy, and why did I run from Frank? My mind is gone; I can't even think of lies to answer those questions. I'm numb. Confused, and my head is starting to hurt again. I thought the letter would help answer questions. It's just left me more anxious and confused.

Vibrate…vibrate…

A sound comes from his direction, standing up in front of me. He doesn't move.

Vibrate…vibrate…

I look behind me at my phone face up on the nightstand next to the alarm clock. Is it me? My screen is black. I turn back to him. He's standing there, having grabbed the letter back up from the bed while I looked away.

Vibrate…vibrate…"Are you gonna answer that?" *Vibrate… vibrate…*"It's not my phone; has to be yours."

He reaches into his front pocket, slowly. The vibrating noise now stopping. He puts his phone to his ear. "Hello."

He continues holding the letter with one hand in front. What more is there to read? "Yeah, I'm hanging with a friend. What's up?"

*Vibrate…vibrate…*The noise continues more.

His head cocks slightly back and right. Where is that coming from? I know he hears it too. "No, I'll be done soon and can head out your way."

Vibrate…vibrate…

He shuffles in his stance and glances at the coffee maker across from me. I look across at the glass of water I gave him that he set in the tray, and at the jacket he brought in bundled up and set on the desk next to the coffee maker. Is the vibrating coming from there? I pop up from the bed and step forward. He puts his phone in his pocket and steps between me and the desk. The vibrating still continuing behind him. Something is off.

"I have to get going. Thanks for having me over." He sets a hand on my chest, turns, extends his other hand to grab his jacket. My hand stretches over from behind his shoulder and cups the front of his neck. I step left, pulling my hand back parallel with the floor, throwing him back into the bed from his neck. His jacket in his hand that he was able to grab going with him.

I take a closer look at the coffee maker. Where is the vibrating coming from?

I look at the sides of it and *see…*Is that…a phone camera sticking out? The edge of the back of an iPhone? The camera visible, propped up, facing the direction of the foot of the bed we were just fucking on. My hand reaches behind the coffee maker and grabs it out.

It's *another* iPhone.

Incoming call from Dennis Fitzgerald

My body flushes with all fight. A fast instinct taking over, my other hand pulls open the top drawer of the desk, grabs Andrew's gun I brought inside my room. My body then swings around toward the bed; I lock eyes and point the gun at him.

"Don't ya fuckin' move." He's frozen, on his side; his hands open over his face, shaking. His second phone still vibrating in my hand. I tap the green button, bring the phone to my ear. "Hey." In a deep voice, mimicking his.

"Holy shit, babe, that guy was so fucking hot. Where are you now? Hurry home. I'm horny and wanna fuck a load in you next."

20

---

626 Waverly Place

THE ADDRESS IN BLACK CURSIVE, stamped into a cement plaque just above the front door, grand and tall with white thick and historic-looking woodwork around. His building an orange-like brown brick; tall—six stories high. I look left and right as I stand in the middle of the sidewalk in front. People of all different kinds swerving around me fast.

Their subtle shoves and unimpressed glances as they pass me. My feet shift me back out of the center of the sidewalk, landing near the edge of the street, out of their busy paths. The street filled with cars parked behind me, alongside the sidewalk; mine parked several cars down. Good thing I didn't kill that fella; hiding a body here would have been a challenge.

I've never seen so many different people like this before in my life, and the way the buildings look too. I guess I've seen all of this in movies, but it feels different in person.

It's exciting!

Or am I just nervous to meet Ramón? I don't know why I would be nervous? That's stupid. It's not like he means anything to me. He just meant something to my uncle, and I'm just doing a good deed here. One good deed I can do that's in my control. I'm not gonna get caught up and twisted today in more bullshit like I did last night...My task is very simple—find Ramón, deliver this letter, maybe get a response from him? And then go home and put this all behind me; help my uncle die with peace.

Gay Street

Of course his building is right at the intersection with Gay Street. I hate that I'm even standing near it.

Okay...should I go up and knock? What do I say if he is home? I pull out my phone to check the time: 11:11 a.m. Ha! Make a wish.

I wish...I wish this fucker is home so I can deliver this letter and leave this place forever.

Several Grindr message notifications listed, too, under the time

I did open the app once I parked here a few moments ago; why not?

Who knows when or if I'll ever meet anyone that lives in New York City again. Not that I'm planning on meeting anyone...The thought already pissing me off. Freaking me out, really. I can't believe that fucker last night recorded me and sent it to someone. At least I got him back a little bit—scaring the shit out of him, having him think I'd blow his brains out, and taking his phone. Maybe I can sell it here in the city and make a buck while I'm here. I do need more cash. I can't use my credit card; how far does that warrant go, allowing Sergeant Keaton to work to find me? I can't leave a paper trail.

I knew I'd get Grindr messages, even without my face. Ha!

Nothing from Lucy...No missed calls or texts. I wonder what she's thinking? I should have called her on my morning drive here into the city. I guess I just didn't want to overload myself with too many things. Pussy. I could have at least thought of something and texted her.

I slide my phone back into my pocket. Okay...let's go.

I check left, then right and step forward. I cast myself into the currents of people. I make it to the first step in front of his building and set my foot up on it. Shit, what do I say?

Jesus, you think I would have thought about this more in my lonesome drive getting here. The letter folded in half in my pocket. I take it out and read the top of the envelope.

Ramón Ramirez, 626 Waverly Place, Apt C, New York, NY 10014

I look up again at the address plaque on the building, the front door still several steps up from me.

626 Waverly Place

This is it. Just fucking go. Go!

I fold the letter back into my pocket and leap up the steps in three hops. The front door now in front of me, I look through the glass pane and see a foyer, along with another door. I look left and see a board with labels that have names and numbers, alongside call buttons to buzz up. Ramirez. I scan for Ramirez. Anything? The board having maybe a few dozen apartment labels…I don't see his name. What about apartment C? Look for that. I scan fast, but the labels are not in any logical order. What the fuck is wrong with this place? No wonder the mail didn't get delivered. How do you find anyone here? I glance back at the street, with the zoo of people on the sidewalk; the cars zipping by, honking at each other. New York City is fucking chaos. My eyes back to the board.

C. There it is. Near the bottom. *Scott.* Hm?

The last name on the label tied to apartment C is Scott. That's pretty different from Ramirez. Check again. I scan the board again, looking for Ramirez, now taking my time, line by line, pointing with my finger, hovering over the labels traveling down. Well…I'll be damned. Scott in apartment C is all I got. I don't know what I was expecting? Fuck it—I press the button and the buzz goes off.

Click

Is that the front door unlocking? I turn right to look at the handle. Did I just hear that?

I turn back to the board, looking for any cameras. None. No

one's voice coming through the intercom? Someone just unlocked the door for me to enter? Whatever. Here I go. I grab the handle, swing the door open, step inside the foyer, and grab the next door.

It's unlocked too. Hm.

I step through the second door and find myself at a landing. Stairs in front of me to my right to walk up, a hallway in front of me to my left to walk forward. An apartment door in front of the stairs, to my right. *D.* I look left and read the apartment letter on that door. *A.* I look forward, down the hallway to my left and see another apartment door, in the back-left corner. Well, C is between A and D…Must be down there. I step left and walk down the hallway. I arrive at the door in the back-left corner. *B.* Fuck. I'm close? I think? My head whips right to find the last apartment door on this floor in the back-right corner. *C.* There it is!

I step forward to it quick. My hand pops up next to the *C* to knock—

The door is already cracked open?

My hand stops just before my knuckles bang into the hardwood. Should I just enter?

Fuck it.

I knock five quick times, push the door open, and step through. "Hello?" I step right into a living room? The kitchen behind across the way, a window over the sink, on the other side of the window another brick wall. I step more into the room, leaving the apartment door open behind me. "Helllllooo-OOOOoo?" I say louder. "Anyone home?"

"In here."

A voice to my left coming from another door, cracked open off the living room. I turn back to the open apartment door behind me and look at the hallway I just came from. I look back at the cracked door off the living room inside the apartment. What?

Did the voice come from that door for sure? Maybe I should turn back? No.

I walk through the living room, passing in front of a couch. "I'm looking for a"—I land at the door along the wall of the living room and push it open—"Ramón Ramir—HOLY SHIT!" A naked man with his bare ass set high at the edge of his bed, with nothing on but shin-high socks and a tight, black mask over his head. I grab the door handle and slam it shut. "Sorry!" I shout and step back. I trip backward into the couch, and my back lands on its seat.

His door pops open. "What the fuck is wrong with you?" "We agreed, no talking, just come and go." A short, hairless, bothered fag, standing full-frontal naked in front of me, with the mask removed. I feel my mouth drop open. "Uh." I leap up off the couch to the front door. "Sorry, fella, I don't know what's happenin' here? I was just lookin' for a Ramón Ramirez, and someone buzzed me in."

"So you tricked me on Grindr to fuck me anonymously because you're looking for my friend?" "That's fucking psychotic." He runs back into his room and appears back in his doorway in a flash, now with something in his hand. "I got pepper spray, you fucking creep. Get out!"

"Wait!" "You do know him? I swear I don't know what you're talking about." "I'm not a creep, I promise." "I just need to find him."

"You look like a creep." "Your body doesn't look like the photos you sent me; you fucking catfished me." "Only fucking creeps catfish people." "Get out or I'm calling the cops."

The cops here care about fags?

"No, you don't understand." "I just need to deliver something to Ramón. Can I leave it with you?"

"No. Get the fuck out!" He holds the pepper spray in front of him at arm's length and sprays it into the middle of the living room, toward me.

In a flash I leap out of the room, closing the apartment door behind me. I keep my hand pulled hard on the handle, pulling the door my direction to blockade myself from him. "Listen, I'll be outside on the front steps," I holler. Can he hear me through the door? "Please don't call the cops. I really need to find Ramón. I'm sorry about walkin' in on ya." I listen for a response—nothing. I knock hard three times. "Did ya hear me?" No response. I press my ear to the door...

"All I wanted was an anon fuck. Fuck!"

I push away from the door and stare at it. What the fuck just happened? I should go. Is he really gonna call the cops? I did leave. I move quickly down the hallway, back to the front entrance of the building. I open the first door into the foyer, step in, and open the main door to step outside. As I pass under the main door, I see a guy standing and scanning the board just as I was. My height, in a tight tank with popping muscles underneath; his nipples hard. Wait a minute...

"Apartment C, right?"

He looks at me while I hold the door open for him. His head tilts as he checks me out. He smirks. "You joining too?" Uh.

"Nah...uh...not this time, but thanks. He's...my roommate." "Have fun." I continue to hold the door open and nod for him to pass through, and I smirk back.

As he passes me, he puts his face close to mine. "Too bad, we could have tag-teamed him."

"Ha-um, thanks." I awkwardly smile with my face down, and I step forward as he steps in. I scan the New York City street and trot down the steps fast.

"Have a good day," I hear behind me. I don't look back.

I dive back again into the currents of people swirling around and choose a direction of a few to follow with their pace and path. WHAT THE FUCK. What are the fucking odds arriving at the exact same time?

He said Ramón is his friend, though.

This is the only trail I got. I have to go back; I have to talk to him again. How long does it take for a fag to get his hole wrecked anonymously in New York around lunch? A minute? An hour?

His ass and legs were…hot, positioned like that. Shit. Had I known what I was walkin' into, I would have already had a hard dick to fill him as he wanted. Lucky bastard, that muscle guy. Maybe I should go back to the steps and wait for him—maybe he'll be nice because the guy that was supposed to fuck him actually did fuck him? Because of me. Well, shit. I can check being a pimp off my NYC tour list! I chuckle and shake my head to myself. Some people on the sidewalk notice and send me looks. Yeah, I guess I do look crazy.

Where am I going? I look across the street and see a US Postal Service up ahead. Hm. Lucy works at one back home. They have to deal with address changes all the time, I bet, and have to know where people have moved? Let's try it.

***

"Next in line."

"Good mornin', ma'am, or maybe afternoon, I should say." I glance at the wall clock behind her: 11:52 a.m.

"Sir, how can I help you?" Her response dry and direct. I like it. Let's get to the point.

"Listen, I know it's probably a long shot, but I'm lookin' for a Ramón Ramirez. Ya see"—I pull out the letter and give it to her; she grabs it and scans it with her eyes—"I drove all the way here from Kentucky yesterday, 'n' as ya can see, this letter was undeliverable, and I'm tryin' to do right by findin' this Ramón guy 'n' deliverin' this letter to him. Can you help me find him? Please?"

She looks up at me. "Sir, this address is just around the corner. You can try knocking on the door. That's the best I can help you."

"Funny you should say that…" I chuckle. "I tried that 'n' it didn't go too well." "Trust me, I'll spare ya the details." "Don't ya have a system that ya can tell me where this guy lives?"

"Sir, people can forward their mail with the USPS, but that forwarding address is private information protected under federal law. Even if I were to look it up, I couldn't share that information with you."

"So you're telling me there is a way you can find where this Ramón fella lives?"

"Yes, if he did change his address with us within the last year and requested for his mail to be forwarded, but, like I said, I cannot legally tell you that new address if he did." She looks past me. "Next in line?"

I step into her sight. "Ma'am, ya don't understand. This letter *really* needs to get to this fella." I smile at her as kindly as I possibly can. She pauses in a stare at me, and then looks down to her computer and starts typing, glancing back at the letter. Is my Southern charm working or what? Come on. Tell me something good.

"Sir, I typed in this address to view the activity in name changes. There is none on record. Even if I was able to help you, I couldn't—there is no record." "Again, I am sorry, and best of luck to you." She looks past my shoulder again to the people behind me. "Next in line." Jesus! Fucking New York. Fucking bitch. Okay, back to plan A. I grab the letter and put it back in my pocket. I'll go back to the outside steps and sit...like a *creep*.

626 Waverly Place. Back here again with my foot on the first step. I take my phone out of my pocket.

12:02 p.m.

More Grindr messages popping up

Cops around? Did he call? I scan the zoo around me, from the people on the sidewalk to the cars in the street, but I don't see any. Must have been a bluff. Okay, I'll just wait for him to come out, or maybe buzz in again? I'm afraid to buzz in. I'm afraid to walk in. Just sit for a few and think, Roy.

I walk up a few steps and sit in the middle.

Let's view some of these messages—see who's around. What can that hurt? I won't meet anyone this time. I just wanna see.

21

———————

Whats upp?

Hey.

Good Morning

Top here, interested in a morning fuck? Maybe, not with you.

Hi

Taking loads ass up in my apartment, send pics and I'll send address. What a little slut. That's kinda hot, actually.

Hey sexy

Pnp? What does that mean?

Looking? DDF here DDF? What's that?

Want a bj? Always.

Jesus. So many more messages to go through. Do these fellas here work? I guess it is lunchtime…

I scan more through the messages and profiles. Men from what seems like all over the world here. So many flavors. So many opportunities. This app like an order-in Wonka candy store. I love it; I could sit here all day and hunt, and wait for this fella to come out of his place behind me. I reply to several, and say hi to several more.

Wait a minute…let's go back—

Where is the taking-loads fella?

I swipe back up through the messages. There he is.

Taking loads ass up in my apartment, send pics and I'll send address. I tap on his profile. A couple pics of his legs and ass. I think that's him!

67 feet away

Okay, it has to be him.

I tap back to send him a message:

> Hey!

I send him the two photos I have.

> It's me, sorry I don't have any face pics, but I'm messaging you now so you can see I didn't catfish you.

> This is my profile.

It says he's online…I'll wait. Hm. One more thing I should send him:

> Oh and don't call the cops. That was an honest mistake.

My phone in my hand and Grindr open. My messages sent to him seven minutes ago and no reply. Come on. Hm.

Let's try this:

> Did that muscle fella fuck you good? I let him through as I walked out, figured that's what you wanted, sorry about the mix up again.

My phone vibrates, a reply from him:

> You wanna fuck me next? You on the steps?

Are you kidding me? Is he for real? Uh. If fucking you gets me to Ramón the fastest, whatever. Can I get hard with this guy? With all that just happened?

I click to view his pics on his profile. Fuck. He is hot. I think so.

Okay, fuck his brains out real quick, then give him the letter to give to Ramón. Win for win, double whammy! Nice to meet you, New York City! See you later!

I reply:

> You gonna be ass up on the bed with that mask on again for me?

Let's see what he says…A response appears quick:

> Yess.

Ah, two *s*'s—he must be excited and have liked what he saw then. Though he acted pissed and scared at me. The building door a few steps up from me opens, and I look back.

That muscle guy in a tank coming out. He trots down the steps; winks at me as he passes. "Your roommate is hot." He lands on the street, looks back up at me. "Next time you better join, and we can spit roast him." He then takes off, walking away.

Well, there's a thought…

I don't hate it…Oh my god, my nerves trickle with excitement.

Jesus. I look back to my phone with the chat still on my screen. **Yess.** His two *s*'s sending enthusiasm to my dick.

My fingers reply back quick:

> I'm coming, I'll buzz up now.

I walk up the steps again, find the label with *Scott* and *C*, and press the button.

Click

I'm all of a sudden more nervous than excited. What the fuck? I was so confident typing, and now that I'm walking past the door, I'm also ready to run out. Should I run out? No. I pass through the second door of the building and make my way down the hallway again.

C. I find the apartment door cracked again, I hesitate just before I push it open, but my body moves forward through. I'm back in his apartment. I close the door behind me and look right to the cracked-open bedroom door off the living room. Didn't he yell at me for talking before? He did. That's fine. We don't need to talk; well, not until after. Let's see if he followed my directions. I pass by the couch, arrive at his door, and push it open.

There he is. A smooth, peachy ass propped up at the edge of his bed, my view the side of his arched, beautiful body as I walk toward him. His black mask on, completely covering his whole head, his face down into the bed. How does he breathe in that thing? His black-striped white socks almost to his knees; his toes pointed toward the floor, dangled off the edge of his bed. My body stops in the doorframe as I make my move to enter.

Go! What are you doing? You want to be inside his ass so bad, and it's so hot seeing how much he wants it—just look at him.

He speaks. "You gonna fuck me or what?"

Shit. He must feel I hesitated. Heard me open his door, but hasn't heard or felt me walk up behind him.

"Yeah, baby. You're lookin' good." Get over your nerves, Roy.

I force myself to step further into his room and stand right up behind him. I take both my hands and slide them under his ass cheeks, touching first with my fingertips, and then my palms cupping each cheek and feeling the back of his thick thighs. I play a little with his ass, and then spread his ass cheeks, showing his pink, tight hole. I just stare at it.

Lost in it.

Damn. I want my dick in that. I want to watch it go in. See him stretch for me; watch his body quiver with pleasure as I press into him. My dick now getting hard, and him relaxing further back into my touch, leaning his ass and body more my direction. You want me to stretch you out too? Don't you?

I keep my hands pressed away from each other. I start to salivate, releasing spit to drip down and splash onto his hole. Bull's-eye, baby! I continue salivating and dripping more down —bull's-eye after bull's-eye. His hole responding to each hit, pulsing at me after each splash. My right thumb sliding across his ass and circling my spit over the top of his hole. Preparing it. He starts to moan from the touch of my thumb on him. I swirl my thumb around until it lands in the center, and I push. My spit the perfect lube. My dick aching hard under my jeans. I slap his ass hard with my left hand, so hard his body jolts forward. His moaning louder. "That's right." "Good boy."

"Ahh, I want your load," I hear from the cloth black mask attached to this hot, naked body. My eyes glued to my hand with my thumb inside him. Huh. I wonder how many loads he has in him already. Fucking slut. My dick grows harder.

"Yeah, you like being a little slut?" I slap his ass more, jolting his body forward again. He leans his ass right back.

His head turns right from being face down in the bed. "Yeah, daddy, fuck me, please. Fill me up with your cum." His voice hungry for me.

Wait a minute…My dick all of a sudden losing its thrill.

I don't like this. This is feeling too familiar. I start scanning his room. My horniness turning into paranoia.

I step back, pushing his ass forward away from me. "Hey, you're not filming us, are you?"

He turns his body around, lands in a sitting position on the bed, takes his mask off, and looks at me. "Are you okay?" His eyes an ice blue that pierces right through you; an intensity so alluring, yet terrifying.

"Yeah? Why wouldn't I be?"

"Why would you ask me if I'm filming you?" "That's a pretty fucked-up thing to assume I would do."

"Do what?"

"Film someone fucking without consent." His voice catty and annoying to me. Great, I think I pissed him off again.

"Yeah…I agree."

"If you agree, why would you ask me that?" "You think I'm some trashy bottom that films guys filling me up all day with loads or something?" *Are you?*

Is this a trick question? "Uh…no?"

He stands up out of his bed and slides on a pair of dark-green booty shorts from off the floor. "You can go now. Thanks for nothing…again." His faggoty attitude I've only seen in a few movies before. Wow, these people are really real. They're kinda scary, actually. Especially when I'm sexually confused about them.

Yeah, I should go. I'm a fish out of water here, but Ramón? Fuck Ramón. I gotta go…I exit his bedroom into the living room, pass the couch, and make it to the apartment door. I hear some movement behind me coming from his room.

A thought comes to mind before I exit. "Was that real pepper spray earlier? I don't smell anything." I turn to look for him.

He's standing in his bedroom doorframe. "No, it wasn't real pepper spray."

"Nice, well, you fooled me."

"And you fooled me, twice."

"Because I didn't fuck you?" "Twice?"

"Yep."

"Okay." "Sorry about that. I got a lot goin' on."

"I don't care." "You don't unload your shit to an anonymous Grindr hookup."

"Okay." I look down at the floor. Uh? So guys just don't ever talk when they meet, or?

He starts speaking again. "Where are you from?" His arms and legs crossed, shoulder leaned into his doorframe, chin up, looking at me with curiosity all of a sudden.

"It doesn't matter." "And you're right, my bad." I grab the door handle and open the door.

"Ramón will be at Eighth Street tonight," he says to my back.

I stop and look back at him. "Why are you tellin' me this?" "Thought you were pissed at me?"

"I don't know, you seem lost and…skittish." "Perhaps today is your lucky day and I feel like being nice to a stray."

"A stray?"

"It's an expression, to my point exactly." "Again, if you're looking for Ramón, that's where he'll be." "Goodbye."

"Okay." "Well…thank you, I guess." I nod at him and exit his apartment. Lost and skittish? A stray? Like a stray animal? What does a hungry, horny NYC fag taking loads on lunch think he knows about anything? Well, he at least knows one thing, the one thing I came here for. Eighth Street, that's easy to remember, and that's where I'll go.

See you tonight, Ramón.

22

———

RING…RING…RING…

Come on, hun, pick up…

Ring…rin—

"Hello."

"Hey, hun." "How are you?"

"Roy, you were supposed to call me back later yesterday… What time is it?"

My phone drops from my ear so I can look at the time. "It's eleven thirty-seven; did I wake you up?"

"Eleven thirty-seven?! It's almost midnight the next day. Where are you? Why haven't you called me back?"

"I know…I'm sorry. Things haven't gone as planned 'n' I got delayed."

"Delayed?" "Delayed with what?" "Roy, you're makin' me lose faith." "Where are you? And what is goin' on?" "You tell me the truth now." I want to, but I can't.

"I'm…" In New York City, could you believe it? Neither can I. "I'm just out of town for a few days, and coming right back."

I hear her shifting around quick and the click of the bedside lamp turning on. "What business do you have with your uncle that you need to be 'out of town' for a few days?" "And who are you with?" "You tell me right now."

"Here with?" "Hun, I'm with no one."

"Stop callin' me that." "Stop callin' me that right now." "Right now, I am not your hun."

"Okay…I know, you're right; I fucked up, 'n' I'm sorry." "But you're still my hun, 'n' I mean it when I say it."

"Roy!" "I mean it—"

"I feel like life is pullin' and tearing me into all different directions 'n' I can't make no one happy." "Not you, my uncle." "Myself."

"Roy, what are you talkin' about?" "Is this about us not gettin' pregnant?" "Huh?"

"What? No." "I mean, maybe? I know you want a baby real bad."

"I want a baby real bad? You told me you wanted them too —with me." "Remember?"

"Yeah, I mean, I do." "That's been the plan, right?" "Ever since we met back in high school." "A plan set in front of us, to marry, have babies…grow old together…"

"Yes, that has always been the plan, and I've been happy with that plan."

"Mhm."

"Do you not want that anymore?" I'm not so sure if I always did, now.

"Of course I do." "Why would you say that?" "I love you."

"You do?" "Are you sure you do?" "Most husbands I know that love their wives don't keep secrets from them, run out of town on them without calling…hit them…"

"For god's sake, Lucy, goddamn it!" "That was one time in twenty fuckin' years that I snapped and my arm just flew up. One time! Can't I have some fuckin' grace for royally fuckin' up just once?" "Hm?" "Is that so much to fuckin' ask for?" "It's not like you didn't do anything at all to provoke me."

"You're sayin' it's my fault that my husband hit me?" "Is that what you're sayin', Roy?"

"I mean…you were yellin' right in my face 'n' you knew I was drunk."

"Wo0w." "Okay, Roy." "You're not actin' like the man I married." "The man I've known." "Maybe we got hitched too young."

"What are you sayin'?" "Hm." "Who have you been talkin' to?" "This doesn't sound like my Lucy?" "My wife."

"Your Lucy?" "The Lucy that waits on you, hand and foot? The one that cooks and cleans for you?" "The one that loves you so unconditionally that she would even be so stupid to turn a blind eye to all your flaws, at the cost of her own black eye?" "I know what Lucy you are talkin' about." "I know her very well." "Well, I knew her very well."

Wait. What?

"Lucy…" "I gave you a black eye?" "It was just a reflex, I swear it." "That silly slap from the back of my hand?" "There's no way *I* gave you a black eye."

"Roy, just…stop. Stop!" "Roy, you listen to me right now." "I have so many unanswered questions." "From finding my dead mother's urn in the trash, to not knowing why you were found behind a Motel 6 past three a.m. or whatever time it was, to fleein' from the cops; to hittin' me while you were drunk, to now hear you are 'out of town' to god only knows where and with who? Yeah right. You're a liar." "I don't know you." "I don't trust you." "You are not the man I married." "I'm done."

Click

"Lucy!" My home screen of apps in my hand in front of my eyes versus her name on a call. She hung up on me. She fucking hung up on me. I tap on the phone icon, tap her name to call—my phone back on my ear…*Ring…ring…ring…ring…*Pick up! *Ring…ring…ring…Her voicemail…*Fuck!

I bring my phone down to both hands in front of me. I swipe and tap to text her:

Call me back, please.

My phone vibrates in my hand and the screen changes from Lucy's text thread to an incoming call, an unknown number, *314-555-1516.* Who the fuck is this? Where is 314 from? I'm not answering. I press the power button once, silencing the vibrating, and slide the phone into my pocket.

It starts to vibrate again—is it her? I pull my phone back out—

Incoming call from 314-555-1516. Who is this? I slide the answer button.

"Hello?" "Why are you callin' this number?" "Who is this?"

No answer on the other end…

"Hello?"

"Roy?" On the other end, an old feller's voice I don't recognize. I stay silent for a second. "Is this Roy Stevens?"

Shit, this is one of Sergeant Keaton's people trying to get a hold of me? Can they track this call to find me where I'm at?

"You got the wrong number."

"Hold on there, son. Don't hang up. I'm looking for Ro—"

Tap

My phone back in front of me in my hand, call ended by the red button. Son of a bitch. How many others did Sergeant Keaton give my number to, to harass me?

I swipe to Lucy's text thread. Nothing back from her. Let me try again:

Lucy, come on baby, it's me, it's your Roy, the one you know, you do know me, you do love me, and I love you, please. Call me back.

I slide my phone back into my pocket and stand up, my ass sore from sitting on a hard stone ledge in the middle of nowhere for too long. Well, not absolutely nowhere. I look across the street: **EIGHTH STREET**. It looks like a dive bar.

I do know where I am, but also feel like I'm nowhere at the same time.

Ramón should be inside there. I need a drink. Surprised I made it this far in the day without one.

Hm. Getting drunk at a gay bar in New York City...Is that a good idea? Yes.

Probably not.

This should be a quick thing. In and out. I feel a vibration in my pocket and grab my phone back out. A message from Lucy coming through on the lock screen. I click fast to our text thread:

Just leave me alone.

My thumbs positioned to type, my brain sending no words to them. Fuck! Okay, I got it. My thumbs tapping quick all across the screen keyboard: **Listen, I'll be home tomorrow. We can talk then. I love you.**

Send

Incoming call from 314-555-1516

My phone vibrating back in my hand and the stranger's number on my screen. Fuck this guy! I hold down the power button at the top right corner, then slide on the screen to power off my phone. Good night, you bastard. To all you bastards. Go call and harass someone else worth actually fucking catching.

A New York City couple walking past me on the sidewalk. All dressed up for the night. High fashion, I guess, the lady in rhinestone heels and a silky, skintight black dress. Her arm dangled through the gap of her fella's arm, him with his hand in his pocket. He's dressed in fitted black clothes and a cool-looking hat. A style of hat I've never seen. I guess a simple ball cap won't cut it out here. His shoes with no laces and an off-white color. They look happy. He looks good...I miss my wife. I had all day to call her back, and I didn't. Why?

Maybe if I did earlier, she would have been in a better mood? She also didn't call me back either, though?

So…what does that mean? I can't believe what she just said. Maybe once I get through this night, I'll be able to think straight again, and then I'll see her tomorrow and have the right things to say and a plan to fix all this. Yeah, that makes more sense: Come up with a plan then. I don't know. I'm so lost.

I did have a thought already about escaping and never coming back. Would that be better for her? For me? For the both of us?

Is this my chance? To escape?

…That's an interesting word to think. Is my life one I think I need to escape from? Or is it just guilt that I'm running from? If it is guilt I'm running from, how long can I bear it? What am I doing? Here I go again, diving into my emotions, and look where it gets me. A confused fucking idiot. I am not a confused fucking idiot. I know who I am. This is stupid.

I slide my phone back into my pocket as I walk across the street. I wonder what bourbon they got in here? I arrive at the door, **EIGHTH STREET** now above my head, and I enter. Let's be done with this.

23

———

THIS IS IT? This bar the size of a McDonald's is the finale of my short time here in NYC?

Decent crowd…I think? All fellas my age or older throughout: from sitting at the barstools to standing at the bar, to sitting at high tops around the walls of the joint. A mix of colorful couches and funky-looking chairs in between it all. Are all these men…gay? I've seen so many different ones today.

Why would Ramón hang here on a Tuesday night anyways? How am I gonna find him?

I think I have a vague memory of what he looks like, but that was so long ago. Now he could look like any other old geezer in this…fruity place. There's a seat up at the bar in front of me. Good. I'll get a drink and just plant there in the front, scan like a falcon from the top of the bar, and not have to dive further in. Maybe I'll see that masked fella again and he can help me…hopefully. Would he wear that thing out here?

Maybe I should have gotten here earlier, but I got distracted walking, just walking around everywhere. How could I not. This city is amazing. Unlike anything else, I think, in this world.

"Hey, handsome, what can I get ya." The bartender smiling at me, and not my type at all. I don't smile back.

"Bourbon." "Neat, whatever your house is." I nod, maintaining a straight face.

"Sure thing." He mimics my nod and pours it quick, not having to travel too far away behind the bar. He places the drink in front of me. "Our house is Jim Beam; have you had it?"

I pick it up and take a gulp and set it down. This is made in Kentucky, my friend; of course I've had it. "I have. It's good." "Thank you."

"You're welcome." "Where are you from?"

Uh. "I'm from…" My eyes shifting from his to a guy across the bar…*Who is that?* "Hey, who is that guy over there?" I nod past him in the direction of the fella sitting at the opposite end of the bar from me. He's got to know who I'm talking about. This fella's face is…Wow. I can't stop. I'm like a baby falcon diving from the sky for its first-ever-seen prey. The prey being the only thing it sees, the only thing that makes it move—a nose-dive, straight down.

Get it together, Roy.

The bartender turns to look. "Of course, yeah, that hottie over there is Eugene."

Eugene. My brain excited to learn what my new favorite prey is called.

The bartender pointing real quick with his thumb. The guy noticing us talk about him. Shit, I think he saw me. Was I just… gawking? I look down and stare at my drink. Don't look back up. I want to, though.

I focus back on the bartender, still standing, staring at me. "What's your name? You work here a lot?"

"I'm Steve, and yeah, I'm here most nights a week." "How about you?"

"Nice. I work…in the industry too. I know the workload is a lot." "By chance you know a fella named Ramón Ramirez?"

"Of course." His face lights up. "Everyone knows Ramón." "He's a legend around here, and we are all excited about his new place that he's opening up." "Are you meeting him here for business?"

Do I look like a businessman? "Uh, yeah."

"Yeah? That's awesome." "I bet you're one of his investors, aren't you?"

I stay silent, with a blank expression. Investor for what? Who is this guy?

He speaks again at me. "No worries, you don't have to tell me. I'm just excited, heard it's nothing like this hole-in-the-wall here—which, don't get me wrong, I love, and many locals love; but we are looking forward to the new spot that you guys are opening up in Hell's Kitchen." "So thank you for being part of it." He tops off my Jim Beam without me asking.

"Ah, Hell's Kitchen, right." I nod and take another gulp. Just go with it, Roy. Free booze.

"Hey, don't knock Hell's Kitchen; it's the new hot spot in the city. But I'm sure you already know that." "Otherwise, you wouldn't be investing in it."

"Nah, I haven't made it out there yet." Shut up, Roy.

His face tilts. "You haven't made it out to the space?" "Well, you should." "Sorry, I'll stop pestering you; you're here to see Ramón, not me." "You want another?"

My drink is full.

"Nah, I'm good, but thanks—"

"What if I buy it?"

A fella appears and sits next to me on the barstool that was open to my left. "Would you do another if I buy it and join you?" I look and…

It's him. It's *Eugene.*

What do I do? What do I say? I grab my bourbon and take a gulp.

Two feet away from me now instead of twenty. I can see all of him more clearly. Well, his face. Come on, Roy. Say something, you idiot.

"Hi." My glass traveling back down in front of me, off my mouth.

"Hello." He smiles and nods back.

What next? …My words all a fog in my brain…again…He nods at Steve. "Two more." He leans over to look at my glass. "Crown Royal?"

I chuckle and look at Steve; I don't drink that fake bullshit. "No, please don't." My hand swipes flat across the top of my drink in front of them. "I won't drink that shit, ever." I look left at the guy.

"Well, what do you want, then?" What do I want? My thoughts unable to land an answer to his intrusive question—I hesitate, fogged again and now confused. *What do I want?* Now I'm in my head about hesitating. What do these fellas think of me? Well, actually, Steve thinks I'm some secret investor, and this guy…*Am I his prey and he's the baby falcon?* Is this what this feels like?

His attention so direct, so narrowed on me…I look at Steve, hand still over my glass. "Huh."

More words from the guy to my left. "You look confused; here, I got you." He pops his right hand up, flat in front over me, and his knuckles tap my chest. He looks back at Steve— "Two vodka sodas, please"—nods, and smiles. "Tito's is good." Winks at Steve and looks back at me.

Two vodka sodas? Are we twelve-year-old chicks?

I wouldn't be caught dead drinking those back home. His attention glued back on me. "Is that better? Can you live with that?" He smiles. Is he gawking at me in the same way I feel like I gawked at him earlier? Or is it in my head? I can't be that delusional. I've only had a few sips so far tonight. Unless sober me is delusional, and then we really got a problem. I chuckle to myself and grab my glass to take the last gulp of my Jim Beam.

"What's so funny?" "Didn't think you would meet anyone tonight, and here we are?"

I'm speechless again. His directness. What the fuck is his

deal? His teeth, his lips, the shape of his ears, his eyebrows—everything cohesively moves so mystically together when he speaks to me. Tie that together simultaneously with when he looks in my eyes—I am a drunk twelve-year-old chick on her twelfth vodka soda, and terrified there is something in my teeth or that my hair is messed up. Is it messed up? Am I high? Did someone drug me? Did Steve the ugly bartender put something in my drink because he wants to fuck me?

I swivel on my barstool to look at the front door that I came through, behind me, then look back at Steve and then the man. The two vodkas sodas now set down in front of us from Steve. Icey, bubbly, and thick lime cuts floating on top. They do look… refreshing. Simple. Very faggish.

The man grabs both, sets one closer in front of me, and keeps the other in his hand. "I'm Eugene." He cheers his drink with mine. I swivel back.

I look at him and pick it up. I look at Steve again, who's glancing at the both of us, back and forth. The clear fizzing drink in my hand, a sight I've never seen. This whole place is a sight I've never seen. Actually, the majority of these fellas are drinking clear, fizzy drinks. I see a few martini glasses across the bar, a couple beer bottles too. But mostly all fizzy, clear drinks.

"Take a sip; try it. It's good, I promise you." He smiles and nods, pushing his agenda to get me drunk. I know what you're doing. I'm literally the same as you. And you ain't fucking me tonight.

"What makes you think I've never had a vodka soda?"

"I mean, you are hesitating like I'm drugging you or something."

"Are you?"

"What?" "No, unless—do you want me to?" His eyebrows bounce.

"Excuse me?" My body shifts his direction in my swivel barstool, and my hands set on the bar top slightly with clenched fists. He notices, glancing down at them.

"I'm joking!" "I just think you're hot and came to say hi and buy you a drink like a normal person does."

His expression seeming sincere? He's probably just curious about me. Like the rest of these fellas I catch looking at me. Makes sense. I definitely stand out here in this joint. Everyone in here with fitted clothes, clean, or tanks with their muscles out. I'm still in a frumpy hood, light jeans, and cowboy boots, which I have not seen one New Yorker wear in all of today—and I saw a lot of New Yorkers today. Wait, how the hell does Steve think I'm an investor in what I'm wearing? He must be an idiot.

"Sorry, I, uh, I recently had a fag"—I stop myself before my voice releases the *guh* sound too hard—"guy"—I nod and he squints—"record us having sex behind my back, and that kinda fucked me up."

"Oh shit, man." "That is fucked up." "I'm sorry to hear." "Did you at least get a copy of the video? I'd pay to see it." He bumps his shoulder into mine, grinning and maintaining his stare.

I smile a little back. "No, I deleted it, and I stole the bastard's phone from him." "He's lucky I didn't kill him." "Hey, you know a place I can sell it and make some cash?"

"Um…damn, man, you're pretty hardcore, aren't you? I like it. I like a bad boy." His grinning and eye contact now immersing me further into a mystic, unknown attraction. And did he just call me "bad boy"? I don't think I've ever experienced this before. *Is this attraction?* What is this? I know what attraction feels like with Lucy. But this is new; this pull to be by him; this desire for him to continue his stare at me—say "bad boy" again to me, I'm watching your lips. It's all wildly polarizing. I'm caught like a fish with a hook in its mouth, now down its throat. If you rip it out, you rip my insides out, too, and I think I might die. So keep the hook there. I don't want to be released. Not yet. I like that I took your bait and you're reeling me in. Do it slow. Tell me more, and don't look anywhere else but at me.

24

LET's try this stupid sissy drink.

"Well, be careful what you wish for…Eugene…" I grab the glass, clink it with his—"I'm probably too hot for ya to handle" —and take several gulps of the vodka soda, the carbonated aftertaste sending a burning sensation up my throat. I'm not used to it.

…It's not…bad…

He leans back, staring me up and down. "I can handle a lot." "More than you would ever know."

I see. So this supernatural experience is a spell from some unknown creature that is full of secrets, confidence, and an ego. What could go wrong—or right? I think the sex would be hot. Did I just meet my twin?

I lower my head in a nod, and I smile. "Well, my time here is short. I'm out of cash, and I can't stay in the city too much longer."

"Out of cash?" "I might be able to connect you with a job here, if you're looking for one?"

Here? Looking for a job? To stay and work here in New York City? …An opportunity here? My eyes lost again in his, he can tell I'm considering his proposal—or at least tell I'm lost in deep thought or confusion. Who knows what my eyes are telling him?

"A job…a job doin' what?"

"Hey, Eugene. You said you'd be on by midnight. Come on! Leave that poor guy alone." A bar-goer shouting from somewhere in the crowd behind Eugene. Eugene turns his direction, looking for the fella. He just called me a "poor guy." Hm. Guess I am the prey.

He looks back at me. "Listen, I'm up…but will you stay? I'll be here." "Have any drinks you want; it's on me tonight."

He gets up from the barstool, starts to walk away, and then turns back to look at me. He smiles and disappears into the crowd. Up? What is he *up* for? I look at the drinks in front of us: he left his drink here too. Where did he go? Come back. Come back and talk to me. Come back and let me get lost in your electric, hazel eyes again. Don't release me. I wasn't ready. Shoot.

"Good evening, ladies and gentlemen. We're gonna start off with one of my favorites, Norah Jones, 'Come Away with Me.'"

What?

A smooth voice coming through the speakers, replacing the music that was coming through them before. I didn't really notice what was playing; didn't pay attention. That's unlike me. I love music.

Is that…him? Did I lose his sight but gain his voice? I scan the bar, standing up a little on the barstool footrest to see across the heads of everyone. I don't see him anywhere. A soft guitar melody now coming through the speakers above my head.

I look up at the speaker, and then I look at Steve standing behind the bar. Steve's looking at me and points with his finger at the back corner of the bar. My head shifting in various directions, trying to see through everyone else…I found him.

There he is.

There standing is Eugene with a guitar and a mic that blocks me from seeing his lips. I can see every other bit of his face, though. Lock eyes with me again. Look over here.

What is he singing? His voice a soothing wind against my heart the second his first word comes out. His mouth right on the mic, his eyes forward. The lyrics I can't 100 percent make out?

A woman sings this?

His beautiful voice continuing—sending chills across my forearms. Oh my god. Wow. He is a singer. And he plays guitar.

Norah Jones sings this!

I sit back down on my barstool. I'm gawking again, I know it. I don't care this time, though. We met, and he gawked at me *too*. None of these men know who I am, and I don't know them.

But what's this song called? He finally looks my direction and smiles.

His arm bent in front of his guitar and his fingers dancing over the chords.

Ahh. There it is: "Come Away with Me." Yes, yes I will. Oh fuck.

He's so good. His voice…smooth, sexy, light but also edgy. I down my vodka soda he insisted on, and then take a gulp of the one he left behind. The burn from the carbonation now feeling kind of good. Exciting.

Steve notices the empty drink in front of me, nods to ask if I want another. I nod back. Yes, yes I do. Keep them coming.

I should turn my phone back on. What if Lucy changed her mind? What if she texted me back?

25

INCOMING CALL from Andrew Boyd

My phone vibrating in my hand, another vodka soda in the other. Which number drink is this?

1:47 a.m. at the top of my screen. Shit. I should answer. It's been more than twenty-four hours since Andrew and I last spoke, when I was at the hotel bar, wasted in New Jersey. I look up, scanning for Steve.

"Steve." A bit far from me, he looks my direction while he's shaking a mixer in the air. "I'll be right back," I holler. I point at the incoming call on my phone and exit the bar.

"Hey, how's it goin' over there?"

"Hey." "It's good, I'm just on my lunch break now and am checking in on you." "Haven't heard from you all day." "Did you find Ramón?"

"How's my uncle?" "You never called me back last night." Not that I would have answered…

"Yeah, I'm sorry, my night got crazy busy. Another night nurse called in sick, so I was on double duty; I barely had time to even eat or take a crap last night." "Do you want to talk to him now?" "I can wake him up for you."

"Uh…yeah, go wake him up."

"Okay."

"Actually, no." "Don't wake him up. I'm coming back tomorrow and will see him in person then."

"You are? So you found Ramón and gave him the letter? How did he react? Is he going to send you with a message back to your uncle?" "That would be so romantic."

"Jesus, Andrew, is that what this whole fucking thing is to you?" "Some romantic story?" "It's bullshit. This is all bullshit."

"Sorry, you're right." "That was a silly comment." "I know you're going through it."

"You know I'm goin' through what?" "Hm?" "What am I goin' through?" "Because if you have any knowledge or thoughts, please feel free to share them with me now."

"Um, I don't know what you mean. I barely know you, Roy."

"Yeah, you do barely know me, but you act as if you do know me."

"Well, I might know you more than you think, I guess."

"And what does that mean?"

"It means that I know you and your uncle are more alike than you'd probably like to admit."

"Hm?" "And what makes you think that?"

"I don't know, just a hunch."

"I don't believe you." "What did my uncle say to you about me?" I read the letter. I'm sure my uncle said more to you about me. "And don't fuckin' lie. I always know a liar."

"Don't threaten me, Roy, okay?" "Can't you tell by now that I'm on your side?" "I literally gave you my car, am calling to check in on you—give me a fucking break."

"Yeah, you're right, you've done some nice things for me in recent hours." "That doesn't mean your intentions are good."

"My intentions?" "Why are you such a cynic?"

"Yes, your intentions."

"Roy, my intentions are to help your uncle as much as humanly possible." "This may sound weird to you, and you may hate it, but he's important to me." "Your uncle's important to me."

"Why is he important to you? More important than other patients?" "I heard you say it before to your boss." "Just tell me that you're in love with him, and maybe I'll get it."

"What?" "Jesus, Roy." "This? Again?" "No, I'm not in love with your uncle."

"Why is he so special to you, then?"

"…Well, it's as simple as he has listened to my stories and I have listened to his." "We are friends." "He has a lot of regret, and I know in the end, here, I can play a part to help him fix that bit of regret."

"Play a part?" "See, this is a fuckin' game to you." "Your intentions aren't good." "You're just sittin' there on the sidelines, watchin' mine and his life explode, eatin' popcorn."

"You have no idea what is going on in my life." "Just like you say I don't know you, well, you don't know me." "So just stop talking about things you know nothing of."

"Stop talking?"

"Yeah, Roy, for once shut the fuck up." "You're pissing me off tonight."

"You're a little bitch, Andrew." "A sissy-fag cock-suckin', uncle-fuckin' bitch."

"Good one, Roy." "As if you calling me a fag and tripping me to the floor wasn't clear how you felt about me before— thanks for the subtle reminder. Jackass."

The line disconnecting

Did he just hang up on me? My phone's home screen is back. He *did* just hang up on me. A faggot thinks he can hang up on me. Fuck!

Shit.

Maybe I am the problem? That's two now hanging up on me tonight. I swipe to my calls and click his name to call back.

Ring…ring…

My phone back pressed against my ear. Pick up, you bastard, I'm fucking sorry, okay? Just pick up…

Rin—

"What?"

"I'm sorry." "I'm sorry for being a dick." "I'm sorry for callin' ya a faggot—many times." "It ain't nice." "I won't do it anymore. In fact, I'll stop saying the word altogether, okay?"

"Did you find Ramón or not, Roy? What time are you coming back tomorrow?"

"Did you just hear me? I just apologized to you. Don't ignore that; don't ignore me." "I never apologize to anyone."

"Yeah, I heard, I got it."

"So we're good?"

"Yeah, we're fine."

"Okay, good."

"When are you coming back tomorrow? If it's before my shift, you can drive to my house and then I'll give you a ride back to yours to drop you off, or you can have Lucy pick you up at my place or something."

"Uh, I'll give ya an update in the mornin'." "I'm about to meet Ramón in a few, 'n' then I'll leave tonight, or in the mornin' to come back home."

"Okay, well, I have to get back to work." "You sure don't need me to wake up your uncle real quick for a chat—you seemed pretty agitated last night."

"Yeah, I'm sure." "Let him be." "This is all almost over." "Perhaps by this time tomorrow, I'll be in front of both of you in his room with a letter back from Ramón, or at least a message to give, and we can all move the fuck on from this."

"Okay, well, good luck meeting him, and talk to you tomorrow morning."

"Yeah, thank you. Talk to ya tomorrow mornin'. By—"

"Wait!"

"What?"

"Someone…strange came to visit with your uncle tonight. I've never seen him before." "I almost forgot."

"Someone *strange*?"

"Yeah, an older man with a black cane." "Maybe in his late fifties." "Have any idea who it could have been?"

"No." *Probably another closeted geezer.*

"You sure?" "After he left, I checked in on your uncle." "He seemed…disturbed."

"Andrew, I don't have time to think any more about my uncle's messes." "It was probably another faggot lover—I don't know, giving him one last blow job." "I gotta go."

"You just said you wouldn't use the f-word anymore."

"Good night, Andrew."

Tap

Who else knows my uncle is in that nursing home? Who else would visit him?

"Well, well, well, my creepy stalker that can't keep it up actually showed…"

I look to my left on the street, and walking my way is that catty boy. No mask tonight? He came. Thank god. All right, let's get this over with.

"Hey."

"Hiya, fucking weirdo. Did you say hi to Ramón yet?"

"Uh, no, can you take me to him?" "Is he here?"

"Sure…yeah, I'll take you to him." The boy texting on his phone. Is he messaging him right now? He glances up at me quick, then back to his phone. "Hey, you're not a hit man or something—are you?"

"Uh, no." "What gives you that impression?" That's a first.

"Well, you're not from around here—you don't look or sound like you're from around here." "You're kinda rough looking—which is hot, by the way; you can get it. I'm still pissed about earlier, by the way."

"Pissed? Pissed because I didn't fuck you…right?"

"Yeah, what else would I be pissed about—you do something else I don't know about? Steal something from my apartment too?" His right hand on his hip, eyes on me.

"No, no." "I haven't done anything, I swear." "Uh, you called me skittish and a stray earlier, and it is my first time in New York City, so I guess I feel like a fish out of water."

"So you're a hit man that has never been in New York City?" He smiles. "Whoever hired you is either super smart or a dumbass, because you're not very discrete for a hit man."

"Princess, I'm not a hit man."

He pinches his lips up at me. "Yeah, I guess we'll see about that." He passes me to pull open the front door of the bar, bumping his shoulder into mine on his way. "Let's go, princess. I'll take you to your prince now so you get paid." I follow behind him back into the bar. He turns his head back as he continues forward. "And if you are a hit man, I want a piece now for delivering you to him, 'kay?" He smiles at me again. Jesus, is this guy for real? He's a fucking nutjob.

"Sure." "You can have a piece—a piece of nothing because I'm not a hit man." I holler so he can hear me above the noise of the bar: "I'm not a hit man." His head staying forward—did he hear me?

We continue walking. I pass my spot, my vodka soda still at the bar, Steve zigzagging behind as he works the crowd lined up. It's a packed house, and he has only one barback. I look to make eye contact with him as I pass; nothing, though. Maybe he isn't attracted to me?

Up ahead on the left, Eugene is still serenading the bar. Where is this fella taking me? I scan the little groups of old geezers around. They all look the same in this dark lighting. I don't know if I would have been able to find Ramón without this crazy chariot. Even if he's a psycho, I'm glad he's here.

I see him. There is Eugene!

Will he see me in the crowd? I don't want him to think I left. My chariot still navigating us through, now putting our track to pass Eugene, right in front of him. Yay. We pass him swift and smooth, walking through the crowd. Eugene first locking eyes with the fella leading me, then me, and then back at the fella. Hm. Did Eugene put a load in this guy on lunch today too? We pass Eugene, and I turn my head to lock eyes with him again. He keeps his head forward, singing into the mic. Son of a bitch. Did I ruin it? Does he think I'm chasing this fella now? Fuck.

"Hey." "Do you know that guy we just passed?" I grab the fella's arm, putting my lips closer to his ear. "The singer tonight, you know him? Eugene?"

"Yeah, I do. Why?"

"Nothin'. We chatted earlier, and I was just askin'."

"Chatted earlier about what?"

"Ahem—it was quick. He sat next to me. I thought he wanted to drug me, but I think he was just flirting." I shrug my shoulders. "Maybe?" Was he flirting?

He squints and cocks his head. "Where did you say you are from again?"

"Do you want a drink?" "I'll buy. What do you want? Vodka soda?"

He hesitates for a moment. "Yeah, fuck it. Make it a double, daddy." A grin in his eyes. I order us two drinks with Steve once he makes his way down to us. I receive both, pay with the last bit of cash I got, and turn to hand one to the fella. Maybe I should get his name?

I look up from his drink in my hand to his face.

"Hey, this is Ramón." His hand flat, tapping the chest of a man—a *gentleman*…well, a geezer gentleman with a thick salt-and-pepper goatee—standing right next to him. My body freezing; both drinks in my hands. Unfreeze! Unfreeze!

"Ra-Ramón?"

He nods.

"Would you like a drink, sir?" I extend both drinks out, one in front of the fella and one in front of Ramón.

"Thank you, but I don't drink that."

The fella grabbing his out of my hand and downing half of it.

"Hey, well, what do you drink?" "It's on me." I have at least one more twenty in my pocket.

"Ramón, be careful with this one—I think he's a hit man. He showed up at your old place looking for you today." My head turns to face this catty motherfucker.

"I already told you I'm not a fuckin' hit man." My index finger extended, digging into his chest. He smiles and takes another gulp of his drink, finishing it, swinging his head back to down that last gulp. So dramatic. He comes back up, grabs the other drink out of my other hand and takes a sip, eyes grinning at me again; his chest a firm blockade—if anything, his pec muscles pushing back toward my finger.

"Oh, Mr. Tough Guy with cowboy boots and an accent." "I'm so scared." "What else can you do to me with that finger?"

I draw my hand back off his chest.

The old geezer shaking his head next to us. "Richard, leave him alone." I lock eyes with Ramón. Does he recognize me? I don't think so? His eyes also don't feel too familiar to me either. I look back at the fella: *Richard*.

That's your punk-ass name. Got it.

"So Richard is your name, huh? Now I at least know your name so I can stop callin' ya a catty bitch in my head."

"Oh, honey, *catty bitch* is a compliment to me. Tell me another—what else you got pent up in there that needs releasing?" "What else do you wanna call me?"

"Richard," the geezer cracks. Is this really Ramón?

"Sir, are you Ramón Ramirez?"

"Who's asking?"

"What do you mean? I'm askin'?" "I'm standin' right in front of ya, askin'."

He and Richard glance at each other.

"Is there somewhere we can chat private? Less noise?"

"See! Hit man!" Richard blurts out, then covers his mouth with his hand, trying to catch a piece of ice slipping out of his mouth.

My right hand pops up and grabs Richard's chin. "I'm not a fuckin' hit man, you fuckin' idiot." I pull and push, jerking my arm like a slingshot, pushing his head back on his neck.

He steps back one pace, my grip on his chin released, and he simulates cracking his neck, then licks his bottom lip. "I like it rough." Smirks and sips through his straw. "What else you got?" This fella is playing me like a fiddle.

Wow.

I mean, am I impressed by this? Kind of, actually.

I would never expect a catty bitch boy like him to have hunting skills, and here he is teasing me like I'm his little snack. Luring me in with his jabs. I can't believe it. This is his seducing dance. This is what other men go for.

"Boys, that's enough." Ramón interrupting us. "Yeah, we can chat in the office. Follow me." Ramón walking between Richard and I, headed toward the back of the bar.

He's several steps ahead. My legs haven't moved yet.

"What are you doing? Go." Richard pushing me Ramón's direction. I start walking.

Ramón stops at the very end of the hallway, in front of a beat-up black door. **OFFICE** written with stickers in the top center. He turns to check for me—now a few feet from him— sees me, and opens up the door, and I follow behind him.

26

"What is your name?" He walks alongside the desk.

"My name?" "Why do people keep asking me that, and other questions?" The door shuts behind me, and I walk a few steps in. "Is it that obvious I'm not from here?"

He lands behind the desk, grabs a glass bottle of dark liquor off it. "Well, I think asking for someone's name is typically the first thing two people do when they engage in conversation, and is quite normal." "Don't you?"

"Uh, eh." "Yeah, I see your point."

"So, you know my name is Ramón, and for some reason you need to speak to me in private." "I've now made time for you out of my night—to a stranger, I may add. Go on with it." "What is your name, and what do you want?"

Huh. He's a straight shooter. I see why my uncle liked him. No bullshit. No games. Just like how my uncle is. Well, used to be, before I realized everything was all bullshit.

"My name is John."

"John what?" Quick, without a beat, his nose up at me.

"John Pingree."

"Your name is John Pingree?"

"Yes, sir." I nod as confidently as I can. Make him believe it.

Why the fuck did I just give Ramón the name of my uncle's doctor?

"Okay, and what does John Pingree, who looks and sounds like he's from the South, have business with me about, up here in New York City?"

The letter in my jacket pocket.

That's the business I have with you.

A single piece of paper that has flipped my entire life into a twist. A letter with absurd accusations. Making what I thought was originally true just a cover-up, an act. A letter that reveals great regret, sorrow; pain. A letter that gives access to my knowledge on something you don't know or have knowledge of?

Do you deserve it? I just met you. I don't know.

But these are my uncle's last words and wishes on this earth. For you to know, and read. That is the business I came here for.

Why am I hesitating?

My right hand pops up, sets on top of my jacket, placed over the letter underneath.

"What are you doing?" He grabs a glass on the desk, places it in front of him.

"What?" "What do you mean?"

"Why'd you place your hand over your heart?" "You're not about to tell me some bad news, are you?" He opens up the bottle of liquor and starts to pour himself a glass.

Fling

The door abruptly opening behind us.

My body hops one step forward, my hand off my chest and into my jeans pocket.

"You murder him yet?" Richard stumbling through, passing me on my right and collapsing on a red beat-up love seat. The amount of gay sex that love seat has probably seen. I hope the dried-up cum somehow poisons you and you don't wake up.

Ramón across the desk from me. "You want a scotch?" He looks up at me, completely ignoring Richard.

"Yeah, I'll take a scotch, thanks." Ramón grabbing another

empty glass off the desk and pouring me some. I step toward him with an arm extended and receive it.

"Cheers, welcome to New York City."

"Thank you." We clink glasses and both take a sip.

"You know the owner or somethin'? How come we can be in the office like this with no problem?" "Drinkin' his liquor and sittin' drunk like a fool on his furniture." I dart a look at Richard.

"I know you are not talking about me." His index finger swaying in the air. His leg jolting a bit, and eyes rolling back in his head, then focusing elsewhere than me or Ramón. I'm just not gonna respond. He's completely out of it.

"Well, I do know the owner, and the owner is a *she*, and she is a friend of mine."

"That's cool." "Why come on Tuesdays?" "If you don't mind me askin'." "I guess I've seen a lot of people here like you —this must be the spot, huh?"

"People like what?" "Old?"

"Shit, I didn't mean to say…" "But, uh, yeah." "I guess you're right, that is what I meant."

Ramón nods slightly, looking at me, then takes another sip of his scotch, and so do I.

"Thing is, in New York City, and in gay nightlife, you can be anyone you want to be. Doesn't matter your age, where you're from, what you wear—I mean, those things do matter to some, but for many, it's just about having a good time and connecting with good people." "Good people from all over the world." "Are you good people, John?"

"I…think so." "Why you askin' me that?"

"Just a thought. My good friend Richard over there thinks you're a hit man." He nods toward Richard, nearly passed out on the love seat. Richard springs his hand into the air above his head, but doesn't say anything. "Steve at the bar thinks you're some type of angel investor." Ramón shrugs his shoulders. "Either way, sounds like you're dangerous."

"No, no!" "I'm not either of those." "Sorry for the confusion, I just…uh, I just…" What, what do I *just*? The door opens behind me again, this time slower…It's *Eugene.* He slides into the room, all gallant and swift.

He steps in closer, landing to my left, between Ramón and I. Glances at Richard, rolls his eyes; glances at Ramón, smiles, and then steps closer to me.

"What did you think?"

"What did I think of what?"

"…My performance."

"Oh, yeah." "Yeah, sorry, lots goin' on tonight." "You were good."

"Good?" "That's it?"

Jesus, why am I being so shy? "Yeah…I mean, really great." What else am I supposed to say? "I loved it, actually…" Did I just say that out loud? I take such a big gulp of the scotch, almost leaving the glass empty.

"What are you two talking about?" "Nice for you two to meet, actually." "Ramón, this is…" He chuckles. "Wait, I don't even know your name yet."

"It's John."

"John Pingree," Ramón cracks quick.

"Well, John Pingree, where were we?" "You want another drink after that one?"

"Um, well, I got to call it a night soon, but I really appreciate the drinks. I have to get headed home."

"Where is home?" The light from a lamp in the office hitting his face just perfect. His pupils a black hole with dark-yellow and light-green stardust swirling around—they lift me higher on my toes; collapsing me on the inside at the same time.

"Home is…kinda far."

"Okay, well, are you sure you have to go? Hey! What about that job?" Eugene turns to Ramón. "Ramón, John is looking for work—you got any openings he can fill?"

"You're looking for work?" Ramón's voice curious sounding.

"Uh, yeah. I am, actually." "That is why I have been askin' about you."

Both of them now looking at me like I'm some new carnival game they've never seen at the fair. Don't know how to play it, but might want a go at it. Eugene's face innocent and blank, Ramón's still—intentional.

Shit. What am I saying? What am I doing? Can they see through me?

"I was walking in…Hell's Kitchen"—is that what Steve called it earlier?—"and saw your new space. I need a gig that pays cash. I ran into a fella that told me I could find the owner of that new place here tonight." "So I came to shoot my shot." Phew. Pretty fucking good on my toes! Still got it; both of their faces easing.

"And what makes you think I pay my employees cash?" Ramón replies.

"…Well, I have bar-managing experience and know many bars pay their workers cash—especially illegal immigrants."

"Are you an illegal immigrant?"

"No."

"Why then only cash? Why me out of every bar here in New York City?"

Fuck, I don't know! Because I'm stalking you all the way from Kentucky now, I guess. "I guess I'm a bit of an anarchist—don't like the government or people knowing my information." Their faces back to pinches, staring at me. "And why you? Well, guess it doesn't have to be you…You're just the opportunity now right in front of me." "I guess." Yeah, make him think he's not the target. I hope this doesn't backfire.

"Tell you what, you have any carpentry skills?"

"Yes, sir, I do." I have none.

"Okay, good. I could use help with carpentry work over the next few months before we open."

"Next few months?"

"Yeah, next few months. Is that a problem? Are you looking for work here in the city or not?"

"No, no, it's not a problem at all." "Thank you, sir." I look at Eugene and nod.

"And stop calling me sir." "Just call me Ramón."

"Okay…Ramón, thank you." I nod and actually feel myself smile at him. I look back at Eugene, and smile louder at him. Jesus, Roy. Control yourself.

Ramón takes his last sip of scotch, walks between and past us to the door. We both shuffle politely out of his way. "Gentlemen, I'm done for the evening. Enjoy your night." He opens the door to walk out. "Oh"—he turns back to me—"and John, Eugene will give you all the information. He is one of my best friends and most valued confidants. You can start as early as you want. Nice to meet you." Ramón exits, and the door swings back shut.

Eugene slaps my shoulder and keeps his hand on it. "Hey. Now that I got you a job, how about that drink and I'll walk you home after."

The weight of his hand on my shoulder, his nod, and his eyes pushing for me to say yes. Walk me home? I don't have a home here. And I don't want to say no to you. I smile and nod. "Yeah, let's do it."

27

"Steve. Not another, you mothafucker." I kick the bar wall to spin myself in my swivel barstool. "What time is it, fellas?" The bar now empty, with just Steve pouring us three more shots. I stop the rotation with my elbow on the bar, the room spinning, a laugh popping out of me.

"It's the last one, we promise." Eugene sitting next to me to my left—just how we met, cheers-ing already with Steve, still behind the bar.

I see the single shot left for me.

Fuck it.

It's dark liquor—no more vodka-soda bullshit at this hour. "You fellas are…wild. Fuck me." I grab the last shot and swig it back, pop the shot glass back down, and let out a howl. "What's next after this?"

"After this?" "You gotta go home; it's four forty-seven in the morning, guys. I'm locking up and going home too." "Get the fuck out, cowboy." Steve teasing me like we're somehow old buddies that never lost touch, catching up. Maybe we are? Could I have gay friends? Gay friends in New York City? I think he means it, actually. I should go.

"Who you callin' cowboy?" I grin. "That's right." "I'll be

your cowboy, maybe even your cowgirl, if you're lucky." I spin my stool and position my body back to face the front door and stand up. The room spinning, I lose my balance and fall back down onto the stool. Fuck me, I'm drunk. In New York fucking City, baby. How the fuck did I get here? And where am I now?

"Hey, I'm gonna grab my guitar and shit and come right back, okay? Wait here." Eugene's voice in my ear.

"Sure thing…I ain't going nowhere"—I chuckle—"anytime soon, it would appear." I turn my head and notice Eugene and Steve walking toward the back of the bar. Who would have thought? Me making friends and lovers with some fags in NYC. Mama would be proud. That don't make no sense. I don't know her! Uncle David would be proud. Uncle David…Uncle fucking David. What the fuck am I going to do? You see what your lust has caused? To you and now me?

My eyes set on the back of the front door, a water bottle sliding down the right side of my chest, appearing like magic.

"Here. Drink this, and let's go. I'll walk you home." Eugene's soft, tan, veiny hands next to my nose.

My head tilts back to look up at him. "Sure thing, whatever you say." Why does he make me want to say yes to everything? It's the liquor.

"Whatever I say? That is quite the proposal." He makes a sniffing noise and rubs his nose. Do I make you nervous? He's been rubbing his nose all night. Maybe that's his tell.

"Okay, calm down." I signal with my hand in the air. I stand back up—chugging the bottle of water; crushing the plastic bottle in my hand after it's gone. My balance is fucked, but I think I can still walk. Let's go…

And I'm walking…

"Good night, nice to meet you, John," I hear behind me from Steve.

I throw my hand in the air above my head. "Nice to meet ya too. Thanks for the booze, baby."

Eugene walking on my right. "Night, Steve. Thanks again."

Eugene opening the door for me to walk through onto the city sidewalk. I can't believe people are still out. I mean, it's far fewer than before, but still, it's what? 5 a.m., and cars are still driving, people are still walking on the sidewalk. Where do all these people have to be at 5 a.m., anyhoo? Are they all drunks like me too?

"Which way is home? I'll walk you there." Eugene assertive toward me, with a gleam in his eye.

He's asking me? Which way is home, and can he walk me there? Well, fuck. Wish I fucking knew.

"Uh, left." I start walking left, and he follows next to me.

"So how are you feeling?"

"How am I feeling?" "What do you mean—I'm drunk because of you…you bastard." "What you trying to do with me, anyhow?"

"I'm not trying to do anything. I think I just like you."

"You just…like me?" "You just met me; you don't know anythin' about me."

"Well, yeah, we just met." He bumps his shoulder into mine.

I've liked and noticed every bump or touch he's done to me this whole night.

He continues talking. "But we also just spent the last several hours together and had a good time, no?" "At least I did."

"Yeah…no, it was cool." "You and Steve are cool fellas, 'n' I'm happy I met the two of ya."

Where am I going? All these cars parked alongside the side-walk to my right, cement at my feet and beyond; tall brick town-homes alongside my left—it all just looks the same. I think I'm going the right way?

"You sure you know where you're going?" "Here, let's grab a cab." Eugene steps away from me into the street. I stop to turn to watch him so I don't lose him. His sexy, big hand flexed in the air toward lights shining on him. He looks back at me, still on the sidewalk. "Come on. What are you doing?"

Shit, yeah. "Coming." I stumble over next to him into the

street; the lights on us brighter and bigger. A yellow cab appears, and I follow him into the back seat of it. I've never been in a cab.

"Where to?" The cab driver asking the both of us.

Eugene looking at me…? Oh, fuck, what's the address?… "Uh, 626 Waverly Place." I close my eyes and rest my head back. I think that's the address I went to earlier, where I parked my car? Sounds about right. My head jolts back as the cab driver takes off quick. Damn!

"How do you know my address?" Eugene next to me in the back of the cab.

My eyes staying shut. "Your address?" "What are ya talkin' about?" "Whose address do I know?"

"626 Waverly Place." "The address you just gave the cab driver." "Didn't you just say 626 Waverly Place?"

"Yeah." "My car is there."

"Your car?"

"Yeah, my car."

"You have a car in New York City parked at my address?"

I open my eyes and look at him. "What are ya gettin' at?" "Yeah, I have a car here?" "Look around; everyone has cars here; haven't you seen them?"

"Um, no, not everyone has a car in New York City." "Most people don't." He sets his left hand on the inside of my lap. I look down at it. His hand gentle. I like the weight of it there too. A flashback pops into my mind, of Andrew. Andrew touching me back home, his hand on top of mine in his car in the parking lot of my uncle's nursing home. I jumped from it. I got out of that car so quick. Why am I not jumping from Eugene's? Is it because I'm drunk and we're in a cab that's moving quick? I can't just open the door in the back of a speeding cab and dart into the street now, can I? I look up, keeping my eyes forward, and then close them again and tilt my head back into the head-rest. Keep your hand there. I smile at the thought of Dorian wanting to jump out of my car…twice—who's the pussy now? Me.

"What do you want from me, Eugene?"

"What do I want from you?" He leans closer to my ear. "I want to do wild things to you."

My eyes pop open and dart his direction, my head staying forward. "Wild things?" My head nodding.

"Yeah." A thicker whisper in my ear. "Things wild beyond your dreams…sensations I bet you've never felt." He starts sliding his left hand up my lap. Jesus. My lungs feel like they're closing up.

"Mhmm." "What makes you think I've never felt what you're offerin'?" I turn to look at him, our noses now inches apart.

"Because it hasn't been with me." His eyes seeming to cast a final, inescapable spell into mine, his hand on my lap heating me up underneath. My nose lifts slightly up, his immediately following, and our lips meet. They meet and press into each other. And hold. I keep my eyes shut. Just his lips, that's all I feel, and the weight of his heavy hand near my groin. Nothing else matters. I think I've waited all night for this. And it was worth the wait. I've never felt this type of pulse run through me before.

Exhilarating.

Magnetic.

Right.

I'm dizzy. Is it the booze or the cab driver? Fuck. The cab driver!

I lean back out of the kiss; my right hand pops up onto Eugene's chest and pushes him away. My head and left side tilt away from him. I scan to look at the rearview mirror for the cab driver's eyes. Nothing. The mirror is set at some other angle. Phew. That was a close call.

"What the heck?" Eugene's eyebrows pointing at the center of his forehead. My hand dropping from his chest.

"What?" "The cab driver could have seen us."

"So?"

"So…I don't like that."

"You're not out, are you?"

"What do ya mean…*out*?"

"What do I mean by *out*?" "Oh Jesus, I got a wild one."

A wild one? Why does everyone keep saying shit like this. "A *stray*, you mean?" "Yeah, I heard the reference earlier."

He begins to laugh. "Hey, don't take it personally." "Gay people come in all different shapes, colors, and different phases and times that they accept their real truth." "You're just a little more late to the party than others." "For some you're even early."

"I'm not gay." I turn to look at him.

"…Really?" "Well, what was that kiss, then?"

"You kissed me; I don't know what that was."

"I kissed you?" "That is absolutely not how it happened, sir." "You definitely kissed me, more than I kissed you."

"Oh yeah? Well who is the one that ended the kiss?" "Hm?" "Me." "Now stop talking about it." I look again for the cab driver's eyes in his dashboard mirror; they're on the road.

"Oh yeah? Well who is the one that hasn't moved my hand off their lap?" His speech light and mocking. "Hm?"

I look down at his hand. Fuck. I put my right hand over his and flick it off me. "Get!" I bark at him.

He retracts his hand. "You are something, I'll tell you that." "It takes a lot to grab my attention, and you have it." "And you're not gonna do anything with it?" God, he's cocky.

The cab driver braking. Eugene and I both jolting forward in our seats from the quick stop. Are we here? Eugene paying through some payment machine behind the passenger seat.

"Thank you." Eugene opens his door—"Have a nice night" —and he swings out. Shit, gotta go. I open my door and swing out too. The cab driver takes off, and Eugene walks over to me. He puts his nose back inches from mine. I step back, and my ass falls into somebody's car. My body can't retreat back any further, my right hand back on his chest, flat, my left hand grabbing his shirt in a fist. His pupils digging through mine. I can feel his heartbeat through my palm over his skin.

"What are you doing?" I swallow long.

He glances down, watching my Adam's apple move. "What do you want me to be doing?"

I chuckle and break eye contact to look left, and then lock back quick onto him. "Can't you see? I don't know what I want. I'm a fuckin' mess."

"I don't think you're a mess. I don't think you're a mess at all." "I see a guy that maybe just needs opportunity."

"Oh yeah, and what opportunity is it that I need?"

"To kiss me again, maybe care a little less this time about what people think or where you are." Can I do that? Is this a thought that could be true to try? Kiss a guy and be fine with it? Kiss a fella in a dark street of New York City?

I think something feels alive inside when I'm with you? But I just met you, and we're in public.

Fuck it.

I can try new things. Can't I?

I swallow again. He watches.

My tongue licks my lips. He glances at my tongue, and then up to my eyes. Damn it, I'm in. I'm so in. He has no idea how *in* I am.

I close my eyes slowly, and move my face slightly forward. His lips landing back again on mine. My breath leaving my nose in timid shakes. My hands relaxing against his body. They slide from his front to his back, and I embrace his body into mine while our lips freeze, frozen in a pressed kiss against each other. I don't want this kiss to end. Fuck the cab driver, fuck the people walking around on the sidewalk, fuck everyone. I don't care. I've never felt so alive inside in my life. His kiss sending waves of sensations from his body into mine. And this just through our lips only? I can't resist. I want more. My mouth opens, and my tongue presses into his mouth, opening back for me. We swim together in harmony; our lips rippling back and forth; his hands equally press and shift different directions on my back, as he embraces my body further into his. His hands now sliding together as twins down my spine. They slide over my ass, and he grabs and holds.

I let out a loud "Phew." "Okay, cowboy, let's take a break." My hands coming back forward, slowly pushing his chest away from me. I take a big breath of the New York air, now that I have my mouth back. "I just need a break." His mouth still open at me; his tongue shining, that gleam even shinier in his eyes.

"What's wrong?" "You don't like the way I taste?"

"No, it's not that." "I, uh. It's five in the mornin', and I'm in the middle of some street in New York City. This isn't me." "I don't—"

"You don't what?"

"I don't kiss fellas when I'm drunk."

"When you're drunk?" "So you only kiss dudes when you're sober?" His hands holding my hips, pushing his weight in, keeping my body set into this car. I like the way you say *dude.* Stop grinning at me. I look away and look back. Stop it.

"No, I don't kiss *dudes* when I'm sober either." I grab his hands on my hips, lift them off me, and shove them away forward.

He steps a little back. "You want me to stop, then?"

"Yeah, I want you to stop." "Goodbye." My right foot steps first to start walking away. My car has to be down to the right somewhere? My body and head now parallel with the parked cars, scanning.

He grabs hold of my left arm before I can step too far from him, stopping me. "That's it?" "A cold goodbye, just like that?" "I can't have your number or anything?" My body freezing from his contact. Yes, I want you to have my number. But no. I am returning back home to my wife tomorrow. This was a mistake. *Another mistake.*

My focus on a red traffic light up ahead. No cars left

anymore driving in front or across at the intersection. Just the blaring red traffic light, and dozens of porch lights alongside my view. The traffic light turns green. The clench of his hand on my forearm, not giving any leeway. What is his deal? This guy could have any guy he wants in this city. I'm sure of it. Why me? Why is he not letting me go? And why am I not stepping more out of his grip? Don't turn around, Roy. Keep walking. It's a green light ahead; just step forward more; green means *go*. But what if I'm going the wrong direction? What if all this time, I've always been going the wrong direction? Does this green light mean for me to step further out of his grip, or turn around and plant my lips back onto his and escape into that sensation I never knew existed. I don't know what to do. But, Eugene, don't let go of my arm.

FALL
2012

28

"You really need to call your wife." "She came to visit me yesterday." "She's worried about you, Roy." "It's now been three months you've been gone, and she doesn't even know if you're alive." "Let me tell her you're alive, at least."

"Uncle." "No." "I've already told you that I got a new phone, and that you and Andrew are the only ones to know about this number." "Or that I'm alive, even." "I still need to lay low for a while."

"You're talkin' about the warrant for your arrest, right?" "Lucy told me; she told me everything."

"Oh yeah?" "What did she say?"

"That you hit her, and you were drunk."

"That's it?" No mention of my car found behind the Motel 6? Or my run from the police? Hm.

"And that she just wants to make things right with you." "She knows I'm lyin' to her when I tell her I haven't heard from you." "She loves you; she just wants her husband back, Roy." "Isn't that enough for you?" "Call her from a different phone." "Anything." "Just let her know you're okay." "She is your wife, and you've left her confused and alone." "What is wrong with you, boy?"

Yeah, well, doesn't that sound all too familiar. Guess it runs in the family. You of all people know you can lead a horse to water but you can't make him drink. I'm not calling her.

One day you know who your lover is; the next day they flip on you and become a completely different person—one that abandons and flees. A selfish asshole. I remain silent on the phone. That's who I am now.

"What could be so important that you abandoned your wife." "Your life here?" "Some silly warrant you could probably clear up in a day?" Yeah, I wish it were that simple…

"And why did you get a new number?" "What happened to your old one? You can tell me." "Roy, I will help ya."

Can he help me? How can he possibly help me? I'm here because of him—all his lies and sinful lust from over the years, overflowing, now causing chaos in my life.

"Tell you?" "Even if I did tell you the truth, you wouldn't believe me." "I just have some personal shit I need to figure out." "But I didn't call ya to talk about me or Lucy." "How are ya?" "How's your health?" "I called to check in on ya."

"Well…to be honest." "Not too good." That show *Friends* playing in the background again. I still don't get why that show is always on. Does Andrew even ask him what he wants on, or does he just put that on every time? His speech having more pauses between words than I remember from our last phone call. That was just a few days ago. He does sound different. Weaker.

"Why do you say that? You sound fine to me." "Also, why is that show *Friends* always on in the background? You would've beat my ass growin' up if I had that shit playin' on the TV."

"Is that what it's called?" "*Friends*?"

"Yeah." "I've lost count how many times I've noticed it on." "Why is it always on?" "Andrew put it on or somethin'?"

"No." "I mean, yes, he helps me choose, clicking through channels." "Now that you mention it, I guess I like the way these kids talk to each other." "Free and silly." "Did you know the show was filmed in New York City?"

"No. I did not know that."

"Yep, I guess I like that too." "I never made it out to New York City, and now it's too late for that."

"Yeah." "Well, I'm sorry to hear…" Should I tell him? No.

"Well, I miss ya."

I wish I could tell you everything right now, but I can't. Would the fact that I made it to New York City make him feel better? Or worse? I miss my real phone and my buddies back home. It seems like forever ago that I jailbroke this other one, putting a new number on it and claiming it as my own for my little NYC rendezvous.

What can I share? Nothing.

I shouldn't be unloading any more bullshit on him. Especially now that I'm hearing him different. One thing I actually agree with Andrew on. The sacrifice of withholding information. Or are he and I both making a mistake not coming clean to him? Would the truth be better than tiptoeing around behind lie after lie, hopping from one shadow to the next each day to survive?

I don't know.

But at least in these shadows I can still hop. I have autonomy to move, breathe the same air. It's just in hiding. Pull me out of the shadows and reveal this other side—a fag and destined for jail. Autonomy gone, and I bet the air would be heavier then, suffocating even. Lucy would not come to my defense if she knew the truth. She would not still love me or want to be with me. She would hate me. I hate me.

"I miss you too." I took a long time to respond. He falling asleep on me again?

"Now that you've run out of town and won't tell me where you are—will I ever see you again?" "Sounds to me like you got yourself into some real trouble." "You did promise me you'd come back."

"I hope so." Fucker trying to guilt-trip me? How do you say no to seeing your dying uncle? Would I be able to live with that if I do say no? And he dies with my last words to him in person being "I'll be back, Uncle. I promise," and I didn't? Do I have a choice? Can I actually continue hiding my existence from Kentucky here in NYC? As if keeping myself from being there at the end when he goes would even matter if hiding out here will eventually come to an arrest after an inevitable discovery of me, anyhow? How serious is that warrant? Can it escalate to a national scale? No. The NYC cops have to have more to worry about than a guy from Kentucky that maybe fled the cops once and maybe slapped his wife once. Right?

I don't think he has much time left. At least I hope there is more time than what it feels like now.

"Yeah, well, I hope so too." "I need to talk to you." "And I'd prefer to do it face-to-face." "Not over the phone." "It's too important." "When can you come back?"

Now he wants to talk to me? Now he wants to tell me the truth? To give me answers. Well, it feels a little too late for that. He had the chance already! If I tell him I'm in NYC, it could get back to Sergeant Keaton and Lucy. He'll ask why, and I'm not ready to tell him *why* I'm here. "You mean, what you wouldn't talk to me about before?" "When you had the chance when I was there?" "…The questions I asked about Ramón?" "Yeah?"

"Yes." "I need to tell you the truth about Ramón." "The truth about more things too." Like maybe who the fuck Frank is?

More things? What else could there possibly be with this old man? How many secrets and lies can one pile up behind one's life? And here he is at the end—crippled, with hidden truths that have haunted him, all now coming out. "I can't promise you that I can see you again, Uncle." "I just can't promise that." "I can't promise anything right now."

"…Well, maybe some things are just meant for me to take to

my grave, then." Hm. That's an interesting thought. What if that is true? I'll *never* find out the things I *deserve* to know.

"Yeah, well, maybe you're right." Fuck, I don't mean that. "Jesus, you are so damn dramatic. Maybe you wanna tell me your profession was actually in theatrics too?! Hm? Is that another secret?" "Just tell me over the phone, goddamn it." "I can handle it. Whatever it is."

"It's not about you not being able to handle it, Roy." "It's about…closure for me, I think." "You have more time, Roy. I'm not dead yet. You know where I'm at." "I'm sure Andrew would help sneak you in here, just like how he sneaks his phone to me and calls you so we can chat." "He's a good guy, you know."

"Yeah, yeah, he's decent." "Listen, speaking of him, can you tell him to call me later, please? And I gotta go, I have a thing I gotta get to."

"Okay, Son, I will." "Goodbye."

"Bye." A little curt, but whatever. My hand drops from my ear, phone face up in front of me.

Tap

Andrew Boyd's name disappearing

The background of this phone still the rain droplets that I never changed after receiving it back from being jailbroken months ago. I glance at the time. 9:12 p.m. Where is he?

Could I share this number with Lucy? No. It's too risky. With Sergeant Keaton's threat—and Lucy has to know by now that I lied to Sergeant Keaton about that night being self-defense on my end. I can't believe that's the best lie I could come up with the moment Sergeant Keaton put me in a corner with her questions. Who knows what Lucy actually thinks of me now. I do miss her. But even if I called her and tried to explain, what would be the point? Haven't I hurt her enough? She wouldn't understand. I don't even understand. How could I explain? I think this new truth would actually hurt her more than just thinking I'm dead.

It feels weird and unnatural what I've done, but what has

pulled me into this situation also feels natural too. Actually, the truest, most natural version of myself I've ever felt. If this is the case, why does it feel so bad? I'm torn into two versions of myself, and even in both versions—further confused. My identity, my needs and wants—all confused.

Do I really mean this?

Have three months spent in New York City changed me that much? Is that possible? Is it because I did not know what I know now and because what I did not know actually aligns truer to me? How many others go through this? How many others fall into believing and accepting what is only around them, never to inquire or ask further questions to the different voice that moves inside them—because the voice speaks *too differently*; nothing wrong or deceitful about it, just different. How many are too afraid to face it? To unravel and explore a new truth not yet seen or heard? So they force themselves to ignore it. Convince themselves it doesn't exist? Because it is too different. I wonder. How long can they do it? And at what true cost to themselves and those around? Shit. How long have I done it? Have I done it?

This city is crazy. The possibilities seeming as endless as the height of the skyscrapers in front of me, across the street. Going as high as you can imagine them to go. Even the architecture here is telling you to think past, go further, widen and broaden your views. It's not just the skyscrapers, but all the buildings around them, too, built decade after decade, inspired off each other, coupled with new technology and design—growing, evolving. From the old brick townhomes to the sleek all-glass towers. And between all, the unique community of basement bars, food from everywhere across the world, access to activities from all cultures, all within feet and blocks of each other—the people from all over, all here with dreams, and pursuing the vision for what lives they want, in a landscape that encourages prosperity, uniqueness, and connectivity. Hm.

Who would have known such a place exists? How come I never knew such places existed?

I guess all the thrillers and crime-fiction novels I read didn't serve me any purpose, not inspiring my imagination with anything more than thrillers and crime. No wonder I am the way I am. You are what you eat; I guess you are what you read.

I don't like that David's calling me Son? He never did, raising me, so why now? The man writes in a letter regrets of how he raised me, but today he's calling me Son and still doesn't have the balls to tell me like a man, or a true father, what the fuck is his deal. Little does he know, *I know what's up*. And I'm on a mission to find out more. Am I doing the right thing?

Keeping this all secret?

I take my final puffs from my cigarette and extinguish the butt against the brick wall that I'm leaned on. I flick it in the air and watch it roll across the city sidewalk, under the people's steps, fall off the curb, and disappear into the street. I feel like that cigarette butt right now. Tossed into the air out of my control, landing on tough, hard terrain, to then dive off a cliff I didn't see—into oblivion, alone. With no one to care or notice, and not even me to understand what—or is it who?—put me there. How did I get here? How did I become a cig butt with no light left? Who's responsible for sucking out my flame? Or is it I that sucked it out myself? Maybe life is just a pack of cigarettes. Each cig representing moments of existence and experience. How many cigarettes do we get? Some get more than others. Who lights each one up, lights us within? Some borrow cigs from your pack too. Does everyone refill it back? I doubt it.

I am excited for my date tonight. For so long Lucy was my lighter, and for so many cigarettes—my whole pack. But now there is Eugene. And Eugene feels like a whole cigar, and that flame has just begun. A flame that's larger and thicker, a flame-and-cigar combo that I never knew existed. A combo, now, that I can't get enough of. Is my life upgrading from a thin cardboard pack of cigarettes to a large cedar box of thick cigars? My life should have always been a large cedar box of cigars. Everyone's life should feel like a luxurious, large cedar box of handcrafted cigars, with a thrilling flame that lights them. Thing is, my life *did* feel as grand as a large cedar box of handcrafted cigars with Lucy. But when did it not? I guess I don't know a single gay man back home. It wasn't until we moved to downtown Frankfort that I even saw a gay man for the first time in my life. At least that I know of.

Eugene, a fella exactly my height and with an appearance similar to mine. Well, that's not entirely true. He does wear tighter clothes than me. A fella that is currently late to meet me for dinner and getting on my nerves, our first date. Even though I met him the first day I arrived here in the city and we've been hanging out since. He thought it would be a good idea to have a more formal date tonight. I hate that I'm excited. It's wrong. But I've never felt more giddy.

When he asked me, I had to contain myself. Blushing? Really. Is it truly him? Or is it the adrenaline from being on the run because I'm just fucked up and this is bad. Is that a thing? Am I mixing the two, or are they congruently exciting together, putting me at this new high? The adrenaline of tasting something new that I never knew my body craved. I feel obsessed, and I've never felt obsessed like this for anything. The obsession doesn't just end with him, though. It extends beyond, to others, and now the idea of a new life for me. Here. Is it one I can actually take? Like the rest of these New Yorkers? All coming here, listening to their inner voices. I think. Sharing and growing? Or is this my delusional perception so far of the city and people around me? Or am I just looking for a scapegoat? That New York City is far enough away that my past problems won't find me and that I won't have to face them? Ever? My uncle will die with his secrets, but Andrew will know everything. Where I am, why I came here. He'll eventually probably find out about my warrant and the details of that, if he hasn't already. Would he rat me out? Would he do that? I can't conceal my identity forever here—or could I? Immigrants do it; why can't I? If I do, how will I get his car back to him?

A yellow taxi stops in the street right in front of me, interrupting my thought. Out from the back pops Eugene with a bright smile my direction. From the other side of the car pops another figure into the street. Is that?

Ramón

29

———

Why did he bring him? This was supposed to just be a date for him and me. I didn't prepare to see Ramón tonight. I smile back as they approach, making their way to greet me on the sidewalk in front of the restaurant Eugene and I agreed to meet at—alone.

"Hey." Eugene comes in and gives me a tight hug. I glance at Ramón and give a small smile while Eugene's arms are wrapped around me. He releases his hug but keeps his hands on the sides of my ribs. "I'm sorry I'm late." His touch really does calm me. How can I be mad at you now that you're finally here?

"Good evening, John," Ramón says to me.

"Listen, Ramón didn't have plans tonight, so I invited him and hope that's okay." Of course you did. Eugene's hands drop from my ribs, and he steps a little back.

I smile at both of them. "Of course it's okay." Ramón locking eyes with me. "Ramón, I've been wanting to get to know you more, anyways."

"Well, perfect, I'm happy I came, then." "Y'all have been working so hard opening up my new place, dinner is on me tonight, too, and that's that. Don't fight with me." He smiles at both of us and taps Eugene's shoulder. Really, Eugene? You put me in a corner, with my boss in front of me by the restaurant, and ask if he can join? What the fuck else would I say? "No"? "Get lost"? Maybe this is my opportunity…

Vibrate…

My phone still in my hand, I look down from both of them:

Incoming call from Andrew Boyd

"You boys go on in and grab our table; I gotta take this call." I nod in the direction of the restaurant door to my left. "I'll be right behind ya."

"Okay." Eugene looks down at my phone and back up at me. His expression blank and curious. Same as it always is when we have awkward moments together. Has he seen Andrew's name on my phone before? Probably. But he's never asked, and I haven't said anything either. An arm swings up, and his hand pats the top of my shoulder just as Ramón tapped him. "See you in there." He smiles, and Ramón and him walk into the restaurant. I quickly answer Andrew's call.

"How's it goin'?" "Thanks for letting me get some time with my uncle tonight."

"Of course." "You're welcome." "How are things with you?" "How's the restaurant opening coming along?"

"It's not a restaurant; it's a drag-club thing." "And, yeah, yes." "It's goin' fine; it pays me."

"It serves food, though, right?"

"Yeah." "I mean, there's a kitchen, so I guess it will."

"Well, okay then." "Restaurant, drag club, either-or; it serves food, same thing."

"Okay, sure." "You were right about New York, by the way, when you talked with me about it." "This city is really somethin'." "I was just takin' a second now to appreciate it."

"I see, but when are you coming back?"

"I'm not sure…"

"…Okay, well, I don't mean to cause you more trouble, but your uncle is not doing great." "He's declining." "Soon there

will be nothing more I can do, and he will need more care."
"Hospice, Roy."

"I understand." "How much more time do you think we have?"

"Well, he's in more pain. And he's refusing to eat or drink more and more each day." "So really not a whole lot more time."

"Can't you just force him to eat and drink more? You are his nurse." "Well, one of them, at least." "I need more time."

"It doesn't work like that, Roy." "I am doing everything I can to make him happy. I promise you that." "But if a patient reaches a stage of refusing to eat or drink, there's only so much we can do."

"I don't understand?" "You can force him to eat. You can force him to drink. I don't think this is a hard concept."

"Roy, I will do my best to encourage him to eat and drink, okay?" "I will keep you updated on any changes, as well."

"Okay." "Thank you." "Just try harder." "For me."

"Okay." "Where are you now? What do you have going on tonight?"

"Well…uh, I guess I can tell you."

"Tell me what?"

"Well, I think I met someone."

"You met *someone*?" Shit. Is this a good idea?

I don't know who else I'd tell, and I want to talk about it. It's been three months, and I haven't told a soul. I wanna shout it so loud that the top of this skyscraper in front can hear me.

"Yeah, well, actually I met…him a while ago, and I guess I'm kind of seeing him?" "I can't believe I'm saying that out loud." My face widens in a smile.

"Really?" "Congrats." "I think your uncle would be happy to hear this. Did you tell him?"

"Uh, fuck my uncle." "…Okay, you know I don't mean that." "No. Absolutely not, Andrew. I swear if you fuckin' tell him anything, I will be back in town tomorrow 'n' strangle your ass." "He just guilt-tripped me about going silent on Lucy, and not seein' him too." "I don't think revealing to him that I took off to find his past lover but ended up just fucking fellas in New York City is the ticket to his recovery."

"Okay. Calm down, Roy." "I'm just saying, I think you should tell your uncle. I think it would be good." "I also didn't know that you went silent on her." "Why?"

"I don't even know why I just told you any of this."

"Roy, it's okay." "I'm not gonna tell anyone." "I promise." "In fact, I'm happy for you." "I'm happy that you told me." "You probably need the release. To share things with someone."

"Is that so?"

"Yeah, believe it or not." "I am happy for you and this… journey, I guess you would call it." "When are you coming back? I don't need my car still…but would like it back eventually…" "And I agree with your uncle about Lucy."

"Yeah, well, we will see." "And I will get you your car back."

"We will see?" "Okay." "You're not going to get back here soon and see your uncle?" "I just told you he doesn't have much time."

"Andrew, don't piss me off." "I want to." "I've already told you I need more time." "What's the update on Frank? Have you been able to get any clues or answers out of him?"

"Ugh, I forgot you caved and read that letter." "The one thing I asked you not to do."

"Yeah, well, it wasn't your right to ask—a complete, unrealistic request for me to travel miles away from home to hunt down a stranger and not know the meaning behind it to my uncle, and now to myself. Fuck, you fucking wrote it. You knew how fucked up and twisted it is." "And you still sent me." "Blindly." "You know how fucked up that is, Andrew?"

"Roy, it wasn't that twisted. Your uncle just has regret, and he just wanted to release it by way of an apology. I see it happen all of the time." "It's an honor if you could help him with this release." "It was an honor to be part of, helping to write it." "I don't regret suggesting for you to go to try and deliver the letter."

"Oh, you sure helped him, all right. It's your handwriting, and god only knows how many of those words actually came from you versus him."

"EVERYTHING CAME FROM HIM," he yells. "Don't ever say that again." "I know it's hard to accept, but every single word was your uncle's, not mine." "Get over it, accept it, and move on." "And don't ever question my character again." "Ever."

"Yeah, well, like I said, only God will truly know."

"You're an asshole, Roy."

"Yeah, yeah, I know." "You should know that by now too." "You didn't answer my question." "What's the update on any information on Frank?"

"I don't have one." "I do have conversations with your uncle, as we've had for months." "I've asked different questions to maybe get him to share different things about his life. But never has the name Frank come up." "Ever since you left, his spirit has been dimmed." "I'm as lost on the name as you. Are you sure you don't recall anything?"

"No, I don't."

"Either way, it sounds like Frank was a very evil person, if he is the reason it derailed your guys' lives." "You've read the letter, too, now; you know what your uncle was thinking and what he did when this Frank came back and found you guys. Whoever he was, seems your uncle has buried that memory far down. So far down that he won't talk or even think about it." "Maybe Frank was his past lover before Ramón? Or Frank was a past lover of Ramón's? An employer your uncle stole and ran from? Seems whatever the trauma or heartbreak was, has been buried too far down to ever come up."

"Yeah, well, it's somewhere down there. Keep pushin'; think of more questions." "How's your cousin, by the way?"

"My cousin?"

"Yeah, your cousin. The one you told me was in an accident the day you manipulated me into this situation."

"Oh. Yeah, my cousin…" "He, ah, he's not doing too well, actually." "Actually, in all honesty, he's in a coma still. I'm not sure if he is going to wake." His voice changing high, like he's trying to hold back tears.

"His accident was that bad he got put into a coma? Fuck." "I'm sorry to hear." "How come you never told me this?"

"Ah, I don't think you've really ever asked." Shit, is he right? "I think New York City is good for you." "You've become… softer…nicer, maybe even." "You're still a rough, brute pain in my ass, but I'm sensing a small change in you." "Maybe seeing a guy has opened you up for the better."

"Son of a bitch." Another cab stops in front of me, and two familiar fags I now know pop out.

"What?" "Hate the idea that much that you could actually be a kind and enjoyable human to be around?" "The realization that you might be gay like your uncle was…is?"

"Nothin'." "Listen, I gotta go."

"Hey! Before you go, what's the update on your search for Ramón? You're coming up on three months now there searching for him? Any leads?"

"No." "He never showed that night I told you I thought I'd see him." "Don't worry, though, I'm still searching and will get my answers soon." "I can feel it." Richard and Axel now steps away, in front of me. "I gotta go, Andrew." "Thank you again."

30

"Hey, fellas, what y'all doin' here?" "Let me guess, you're invited for dinner too?" "Eugene and Ramón are already inside." Hopefully my smirk conceals how I actually feel about their surprising arrival. Actually, I'm not that surprised, if I think about it more. Eugene says yes to everything and everyone. Something I like but also hate about him. Especially with these two queens in front of me—his roommates. It seems there isn't one fucking thing Eugene wouldn't say yes to for them. They have him wrapped around their fingers, and I'm sure they know it. They all are obsessed with each other. It's weird. I wouldn't be surprised if they are all fucking, too, behind my back.

"Hey, John, lucky for you we even grace you with our grandiose presence this evening. Why would you and Eugene go out alone, anyways?" Axel smirking back. He knows exactly why. Because we're fucking. And I know Eugene tells these hoes everything. Moron. You're just jealous of me. I'm the one with Eugene, and you're still on standby in the friend zone.

"Hey, slut, what's up?" Richard next to him swiping on his phone. At least this one is always unbothered. Living in his own world on his phone. Bouncing between apps. Instagram, Grindr,

Instagram, Grindr, Grindr, Instagram, Twitter—ignoring much of the real world in front of him. Tuning most, if not all, out. Maybe we can learn a thing from him. To mind your own fucking business and just plant your attention down into your phone.

He never told Eugene about what happened between him and me that day I got here. I never told Eugene either. Does it matter? I still can't believe the coincidence that they all live together. What are the odds?

"Well, I was supposed to have a little one-on-one with Eugene tonight. Now your whole posse is here."

"You got a problem with us, John?" Axel as quick on his toes with me as he's been since I met him, shortly after Eugene and Richard my first night. It's kinda hard not to meet and run into the roommates of the guy you're fucking constantly. Though it's only been a handful of times I've truly been around him where we've had to exchange words.

"No, what makes you think that?"

"Oh, I don't know, your attitude?" "Always," he fires back.

Richard chiming in without a beat missed. "Your secret behavior." "High-key think we are gonna wake up one day and find Eugene murdered or missing." "You know, that shit happens to us; not sure if that is another thing you don't know about gay culture…You are part of this culture? Right? Gay? A faggoty fag?" His eyes pop up from his phone at me and his head leans in. "A godforsaken homosexual?!" Slurring *homosexual*, as if to mock me. What a little cunt. I ought to fuck him. Maybe he would be nicer to me after? Would Eugene care?

Why do they think this of me? "No, I don't have a problem with you guys. I'm just…learning, I guess."

Both of them give a harmonious "Mhmm" and, nodding, stare me up and down. Axel with his hand on his hip and eyes on me. His mustache at my eye height, clean and sharp. Trimmed fresh for tonight's outing. The rest of his face clean shaven. Richard glued back to his phone, swiping—his face like a hairless cat, as always; his eye level at my chin.

"Okay, well, y'all ready for dinner?" "Let's walk in together." "Like I said, Eugene and Ramón are already inside."

"Sure thing, after you, peaches." Axel signaling with his long slender arm for me to walk in front of him. What a *gentleman* he is. *Peaches* because I'm from the South? Can't tell if he's mocking me again or trying to actually be nice to me. I will never understand how these men talk to each other. Maybe he just wants to check out my ass. Do bottoms get off on checking out other asses, or is it only the dick they care about?

"Hey, I'll meet you guys in a few. This daddy wants to fuck me real quick down the block." Richard pointing with his thumb the direction behind him. Ah, so it was Grindr he was on. Actually, that doesn't surprise me. Kid is seriously addicted to that app more than any of them. Every time I've bumped into him, he's been swiping incessantly through it. He can't control his itch before dinner? Lucky for him that he's a trust fund baby and doesn't have to work. I don't think he'd be able to hold a job—he's addicted to sex that much.

"You're gonna miss dinner with your friends for a dick appointment? Seriously?" Axel's voice risen and judgy, per usual. Always talking loud and proud. Telling people his opinion with no fucks. I'd actually respect that if he wasn't such a dick to me all the time.

"I said!" Richard claps his hands twice. "I'll." Claps again. "Be." Claps again. "Back!" Claps one last time with his hands in Axel's face, nearly nipping the edge of his mustache. Richard turns with a spin, and off he goes with a new beat in his step.

"Okay, WHORE!" Axel shouting to the street, prolonging the word *W H O R E* loud and proud. Some people walking by taking notice, Richard throwing his right hand in the air and flipping us both off from behind as we watch his thirsty, juicy ass —that's about to get wrecked—gallop away.

I'm kinda jealous.

Axel looks at me, and we exchange a smile—the exchange actually seeming genuine, natural. Is this how I make friends with gay guys? Is this part of their lingo? Shout out to all that someone is a whore, in the middle of a busy evening New York City street? These people are deranged. I enter the restaurant, Axel following right behind.

"John! Sit next to me." I scan the circular table I'm approaching. Five seats total, three empty, and Eugene and Ramón sitting together. I arrive next to Ramón first, reaching to pull the chair out next to him. "John. Didn't you hear me?" I look across to Eugene, and he's nodding to the open seat to his left. "Sit next to me. What are you doing?" Ramón in his own world looking at the drink menu.

Shit. You'd think after three months of concealing my identity and going by the name of John, I wouldn't make mistakes like this. My name is John. My name is John. When you hear John, fucking drop, roll, cartwheel, do whatever—just respond to it. I'll get caught if I keep ignoring that name when people call me. This isn't the first time. Axel behind me while I push the chair back in that's next to Ramón; I can feel him watching me like a hawk. "Of course, sorry, this chair was just the first one, 'n' I'm just hungry 'n' not thinkin' straight." I shuffle behind Ramón, then Eugene, and sit next to Eugene on his left. That's the best I could come up with? No wonder the posse doesn't trust me. I don't even sit next to the guy I'm supposed to be on a date with. I need to get better on my toes. This is my first sit-down with Ramón. I can't fuck this up. I can't fuck any of this up, for that matter.

Axel sits across, diagonal from me, Ramón to his left. Eugene leans in to my ear. "Hey, I know you noticed already, but I invited Axel and Richard too. They didn't have plans tonight and wanted to come." "Hope that's okay." Here he goes again:

Hope that's okay. I guess it's hard to get rid of your roommates when everyone knows about everything in each other's lives 24-7. And you guys do everything together.

"Of course." I smile. "I like your friends and roommates; I am learning a lot from 'em."

"You are? What exactly is it that you are learning?" Ramón puts his menu down and leans in so I can see him more. Shit, I was speaking a bit louder than I thought. For an old man, his hearing is sharp. Axel with the menu in his face, not paying attention.

"Well, I, uh, as you might know by now, because I know you and Eugene are close friends…I've been, uh, fuckin' guys lately." I let out a chuckle. "It's kind of new for me." Eugene smiling and shaking his head slightly. Wow, that's twice I've said this out loud today. What is happening? It feels good, though, I think. In some way, like pressure that's built up inside of me finally being released and, after a subtle vibe of relaxation, hugging me back.

Nothing about this is relaxing, though. Why or how I am here. The loud restaurant. The 24-7 life buzzing in NYC. But admitting these deep details that I think are true, admitting *me*, feels like pressure is coming out, and I guess the best word to describe how I feel after is…*relaxed?* Who else is listening? Watching me? First admitting to being kind of queer to Andrew back home, and now out loud to an open, public table of queers in NYC.

What am I doing?

"Yes, I know, Eugene has told me. He hasn't told me all of the details, but I know you horndogs are having fun." Yeah…my leg bouncing under the table.

"Yeah, having fun with a guy we know nothing about." Axel's menu drops flat onto the table.

"Axel, give it a rest." Eugene scolding him.

"What are you talking about?" Ramón curious toward Axel.

"Okay, not to be a total bitch and ruin dinner, but the tea is the tea. It's been months since John has been working for you, cash under the table only, and from what I know, we don't know where he is from or where he currently lives." "We don't know a thing about him." Axel puts his elbows on the table, crossing his fingers in his hands, holding slightly to the right side of his face. "Don't you agree these are red flags?" He looks at Eugene, then back at Ramón. The waiter stepping in now to introduce herself and take our drink orders. Thank god. Side conversations then begin between Eugene and I and between Ramón and Axel while we wait for our drinks. Red flags. What does that mean? If it's coming from Axel, it's probably not good.

"I've missed your cock today." Eugene in my ear again. His hot breath and word choice springing my ear hairs up, instantly turning me on when he uses the word *cock*, especially when referring to mine.

"Yeah?" "Good." I grab his hand under the table and slide it from off his leg onto my crotch. "It missed you back." My leg stops shaking.

"How did work at the drag club go today? I popped in a few days ago, and you weren't there. I can't believe how far it's come. It looks like it's almost done." Him caressing my crotch. His hand heavy and feeling sweaty already. I guess it's a little hot in here.

"Good, your friend has me workin' hard." I nod toward Ramón. "But I don't mind. It's been fun." *Friend.* What do Ramón and Eugene have in common where they can actually be friends? Eugene has to be in his late thirties, Ramón in his early sixties?

"Fun?" Eugene wanting to get more out of me, but, happily, the waiter comes with a trayful of our drinks, interrupting us. Three waters, three martinis for the queens, and a double whiskey neat for me, Johnnie Walker Double Black tonight. Fuck yeah. Guess now that I'm partying with the trendy, might as well go big—*bougie*, they would say. Once the last drink is given to me, the waiter jumps into taking our orders. The men all standing by, silent and waiting their turns patiently and respectfully. She finishes with me, and at that same second, Ramón picks up his martini and extends his arm, signaling us to raise our glasses at the table. We all grab our drinks and follow. "Thank you for including me last minute tonight." He glances at Eugene and Axel quickly. "I love you guys." He looks at me. "And John, I appreciate the timing of you coming into our lives, regardless of your background or where you are from." "You've been a huge help to the opening of my new club, and you are a part of this." He looks back at the boys and lifts his martini higher. "Cheers."

"Cheers!" We all follow and clink our glasses, even Axel clinking with mine, though first rolling his eyes at me after what Ramón said. Interesting statement from Ramón; we've said only a few words to each other in passing.

We set our glasses back down, and in comes Eugene's left hand back over my crotch under the table. This time now he unzips me slowly, and my ass slouches further down in my seat to hide my dick further under the table, giving way to his command. He reaches through my zipper, grabs and squeezes my flaccid dick. His soft palms but calloused fingers. A combination that makes me hard. I don't know why I like it so much. Who would have known rough yet soft hands could be such a turn-on. My blood pumping through, dick now not so flaccid anymore, growing in Eugene's squeezing hand. Pumping thicker, combating the force of his squeeze. His hand now giving way to my girth he's worked to grow. His devilish grin at me at the table. Does he get off on public, discreet play? I think so. I guess me too. The evidence is hard and clear. I share a softer grin back at him and focus my attention on my drink and onto Ramón and Axel's conversation.

"Boo!"

Eugene and I both jump in our seats. The loud, random pop shouted between us. The head of my exposed dick slamming into the underside of the wood table. My right elbow firing back simultaneously. Luckily I didn't strike him; I was close though, and that would have been the worst. Mother-fucker! Ouch! My chin down now on my chest and my eyes shut, head leaned over the table. My dick feels like it's been decapitated.

Richard sitting down now to my left, at the last empty seat at the table, between Axel and me. "Gotcha." "You guys ordered drinks without me? You selfish little bitches."

"Us? Selfish little bitches?" Axel firing next to Richard. "Would you like for me to announce to the table why you're late?"

"Go ahead. The dick was good and worth it." "Now my hole is nice and stretched and relaxed for dinner."

Eugene's left hand now on my back and rubbing. "Are you okay?"

"Yes." Fuck, my dick is throbbing. Is it wood on the under-side of this table? Or metal? I'm afraid to look down or touch and find blood. I look left to Richard. "Hi." "Happy it was worth it." "Welcome to dinner."

He smiles at me and flicks his eyebrow up, like he's some hot-shit man doll that everyone wants to fuck. I lean back in my seat and bring my head back up, eyes back to level with everyone else's. My dick throbbing in pain still. I can feel the throb pulsate in my eyes. Phew.

"Why you so startled, John?" "Haven't you ever been scared before?" Axel addressing me and sipping his martini with a floating lemon twist in it. I hope that little zesty yellow twist makes it into your windpipe and you choke and shut the fuck up for once. It's probably not big enough, though, but he's so tall and dainty, so maybe. "Aren't you a little…macho-macho for that?"

"Axel!" "I asked you to give it a rest tonight." Eugene now not fucking around. That's right, baby. Defend me. Fuck your friends.

"It's okay, Eugene." "Yes, I have been scared before, just never with so much *enthusiasm*." I look at all the table, ending on

Richard. The boys all chuckling and smiling at my comment, except for Axel.

"*Enthusiasm* is a good word," Ramón blurts out. He grabs his martini again and extends his arm forward. "Cheers to us, to never stop sharing all of the enthusiasm we want to." He extends his arm higher. "Cheers." All the boys follow, and I make it last, but still cheers and clink glasses with Eugene first, and then with Richard. Why didn't Richard order a drink? He only has water, and, come to think of it, he rarely drinks but is fucked up all the time?

The waiter appearing with other kitchen staff, coming out with our food and setting each plate in front of us. I immediately dive into my New York strip. Each bite tender and juicier than the next, my mouth salivating through each breath I can get in, then breathing out so I can swallow more. Holy fuck, this is good. Steak is good in Kentucky, but steak across New York City is next level.

Fuck.

Another reason to stay staked out here.

Ha ha, *staked out here.* Eugene and Axel's plates are salads. Ramón's eating a real dish like me, too, some type of fish, it looks like. Richard not eating anything at all except a bite or two of table bread.

"Richard, why aren't you eating?" I ask. Many at the table smiling with their heads down, pretending to be focused on their plates. I know these queens enough by now: They are all listening. Shit, I'll ask him what the boys are all thinking. I don't care.

"Really, John?" "Must be nice." "Being a dumb new top with no clue, but all the attention he has thrown at him from these hungry New York City bottoms."

"What?"

"I like to bottom, John." "I like to bottom hard." "Take dick to the max." "Feel it up, through my intestines." "And that takes preparation and sacrifice."

"Uh." "So you don't eat?" Words coming through my

mouth, full of thick red meat and potato. I'm smashing it between my teeth and against my tongue and the insides of my cheeks. It's so good. No way bottoming is worth giving this up?

His chin up, eyes down, face motionless. "No. I don't eat."

"Like, ever?"

Eugene to my right. "John, yes, he does eat. Just looks like not tonight because he wants to be a hole all over town." "Be careful with those two bites of bread, sweetie; it's gonna go straight to your ass." Eugene winking as he puckers his lips and blows a kiss at Richard.

"Yeah, yeah, shut up, Eugene." "It's not just a random night, ladies! I am going to THE circuit party of the year. You won't see my shining, beautiful self until tomorrow morning." "If I make it."

"Oh, boo-hoo, I'll finally have a morning of peace without your cracked-out ass all over the place." Eugene swishing his fork in the air at Richard.

"What's a circuit party?" Did Eugene just say *crack*? "And you fellas do crack?"

Axel across from me. "Okay, that's enough gay education for John tonight." "He doesn't need to know about circuit parties." "And no, they don't do crack; it's just an expression."

"Sure we don't!" Richard blurting to the table and laughing.

"Richard, stop, the man is confused and going through culture shock enough." Is Axel defending me?

"I just gave y'all a compliment that I'm learning from you." "Why is this something to hold back?"

"It's not." Richard peppy and excited. "You guys, I don't know why you hate circuit parties. The men are seriously so fucking hot, and they all wanna fuck, literally anywhere and everywhere."

"So…a circuit party is like a giant sex party? Like an orgy?" The idea and statement putting a smile on my face at the table. Am I ready for that? Yes. Did Eugene notice my reaction?

"Well, yeah, but also no." "People go for the music, the

outfits, the energy, not just the sex. It's a great place to meet new friends." Richard back to swiping on his phone.

"'A great place to meet new friends.'" Axel mocking him. "The last time I went to a circuit party, I stood near the bar like a scarecrow deemed with the plague. No one touched or looked at me. And if they did look at me, they looked at me like I was roadkill two weeks old."

"Axel, you are being dramatic and in your head." "It's a safe space for everyone." "I've seen all types of people there."

"You, my dear, are always douched and delusional." "Yeah, for everyone that is 'hot' to your standards of shaved, white, and muscular." "People like me are not welcome there. Skinny, tall, hipster looking—Ramón, Eugene, back me up on this."

Ramón taking the last sip of his martini. "Well, the last time I went to a circuit party was…decades ago…so I'm out on this one. What say you, Eugene?"

Eugene bounces his eyes between Richard and Axel, then to me, and last back to Richard. Hm? Which side will he take? "Axel does have a point, Richard. The gays that predominantly go to those parties are always shirtless, muscular, and expect the same from everyone else going."

"You guys are the ones wrong, douched, and delusional. Every time I ask for you to come, you say no, so how would you truly know?"

"Did you not just hear me? I just told you what happened when I went?" Axel's head cocking and tone changing, like a parent annoyed with their kid not listening.

"Yeah, yeah, I did, but maybe that day you had an attitude, like you always do, and you weren't approachable. Like how you are now. Think you're approachable now? John, what do you think?" Richard snaps his head toward me.

My silverware drops, and my hands signal at a truce over my steak. "Don't bring me into this. That's unfair." I grab my whiskey and shoot more down. "I see you, Richard." He smirks at me. "You shady bitch." I reply. The table laughing. I think I'm getting this?

"All I needed was one time, and actually, I have been before with you other times; you were just too fucked up to remember, on top of leaving me to go party with your other little muscly circuit friends."

"That's just how the night goes." "Don't take it personally." "You're high on whatever you're doing, or drunk, and you escape into the music and the hot men from all over the world." "It's simple, you just have to dive into it." "Give in, relax, let go. Something your pussy hasn't seen in a decade." Damn, it does sound fun. Also kind of scary. Are they referencing crack again?

"Again, easy for you to say." "The second my tall, skinny ass towers over these muscular, cracked-out queens and they look up at me, I feel like an alien from *Mars Attacks*." The table all laughs, except for Richard. There is the word *crack* again!

"Axel." I can't help but interrupt them. "You just said you guys don't do crack, but now you just also used the word to describe the guys around." "I'm confused."

Richard glancing at me, then to Axel. "I just think you're in your head, like you always are, a Judge Judy cunt, and they see that and don't want to engage. Groundbreaking." "Bye." "This conversation is stupid."

Axel biting his lip, holding back another response he has. That's a first.

"You guys, let's talk about something else. We're supposed to be enjoying a nice dinner that Ramón is treating us to as we near completion of his new club, remember?" Eugene looking at me and then back to Ramón.

"Yes, let's talk about that. What else is left?" Axel immediately jumping on the new topic at the table, turning his attention toward Ramón.

"I actually haven't been there in a few days. John, what do you think is left to be done? You were there just today, weren't you?"

Is this a test? Fuck. I clear my throat, all eyes on me. "It's lookin' pretty good." "I mean, you guys know my context is low, but I like everything you are doin'." My eyes ending on Ramón.

"I'm sure you have more of an opinion than that? You have bar-management experience." Shit, I did tell them that. "From what my partners and I have designed, what do you think?"

I glance at Eugene. What do I think? I haven't thought about what I think. I've been consumed with trying to figure you out and stay incognito.

"Um, well, I guess I haven't thought that far, to be honest." Axel looking at me with his lips pursed, relaxed back in his chair. "Um." Think. Think. "I guess I can say I like that the piano is elevated on a platform from the rest of the room." "Looks like everyone can see it wherever they are in the bar." The table nods, signaling that perhaps that is a given. What else? "I also like all of the whiskey selections I see you've chosen." I raise my glass toward him and take my last sip and set the now-empty glass down. "I am a whiskey-and-bourbon fella, if you guys couldn't tell by now." "And it's cool to see all of the different selections you got." "I don't have the same variety back home."

"And where is back home?" Axel pouncing in. The table silent but for the clinks of the forks and knives of people finishing their last few bites.

"Why is it so important to ya where I am from." "Hm?" "The South," I shout a bit abruptly. My tone changing. This conversation isn't so fun and light anymore. "That good enough for ya?" Axel remaining in his position, Richard giving me a side eye. The waiter swings by, and I tap my glass to signal another double. She asks the others if they want refills, and only Ramón agrees to another.

"Where in the South?" Axel stern and calm; persistent on me. I glance at Eugene. He keeps his attention on his plate. Guess I'm alone on this one. Thanks, fake boyfriend.

"Why do you care?" I respond back. Okay, keep calm. He's

just a prissy, sissy fag with big words. Don't let him expose you. Don't let him get to you.

"We all at this table know where all of us are from." He looks at everyone. "Don't we?" "It's a common piece of information to share." "Richard and I are both from Massachusetts; Eugene is from New Jersey; Ramón is from..." He pauses and looks at Ramón, mouth slightly open and eyes now lost in thought. "Actually, I forgot, I'm sorry." "Ramón, remind us where you are from?"

"Well, my parents were both from Mexico before they immigrated here." "I grew up in Texas, bounced between a few states before I ended up here in New York City in 1992." My eyes widen from hearing it.

1992

I know this really is Ramón, but hearing him for the first time reference something from *our* past makes it really true. What happened with him and my uncle that year? Who can I trust? This has all been so strange—leaving that night and my uncle pushing away every conversation I started about it to understand more, until now near his death. Does Ramón really not recognize me? Would I recognize in my sixties a thirty-somethin'-year-old that I last saw when they were a kid? I don't know?

"Why 1992?" I blurt out loud. *I can't help it.*

The waitress dropping off a fresh new whiskey in front of me and setting a new, crisp martini in front of Ramón. "Actually, can I have what that gentleman is having?" He points at my whiskey neat and pushes his martini away from him. The waitress nods. "Of course, sir." She goes to remove the martini, but Axel beats her to it. "I'll take this drink, thank you." He immediately grabs it and takes a sip.

Ramón looks at me. "That year I had to go through some changes. Not by my willing, and it forced me to pursue a dream I never thought would be possible." He takes a sip of his water. "And it all worked out." "Look at me now, sixty-two years old, healthy, and my dream is coming true of opening up my own club, and with the best people around me to do it."

Eugene between Ramón and me. "We love you, and I am so proud of you; you deserve this." Does he? What makes him so remarkable that he deserves this at sixty-two? Does he sponsor you guys? Give you guys money to live in this expensive city? Can he still fuck? Does he fuck the brains out of you guys too? What is it?

"What changes did you have to go through?" I ask, breaking into a silence in a conversation that had moved on. I can't stop, I need to know more.

"Jesus, John, read the room," Richard snips at me. The waitress coming back and setting a double whiskey neat in front of Ramón.

"What?" "Axel just talked that you guys share and talk about shit. What am I sayin' wrong?"

Axel and Eugene both start to talk over each other; Ramón signals with his hand to cut them off. "Hey. It's not a problem." He looks over at me. "My heart was broken in 1992." "I'm talking the type of heartbreak that changes your life forever." His voice leveling serious and quieter. "I somehow lost a lover I had been with for years, and at the time, he was my whole family."

Axel sets his left hand on Ramón's right hand on the table. "I'm so sorry, Ramón. I don't think any of us ever knew this story about you." Axel looking at Eugene and Richard for a clue. Richard on his phone, Eugene's attention on Ramón. Is Eugene's hand on Ramón's lap under the table like he had his other hand on mine?

"No. You boys don't." Ramón laughs. "That's because no one has had the careless wit to recklessly ask such a personal question at a dinner, unlike here with this new guy." He signals my way with a smile, bringing his whiskey glass to his lips and taking a sip. "I see why you like him." He nods at Eugene.

"See what you did, John." Richard slaps my arm with his

hand as if to hit a mosquito quick. "You just had to kill the vibe."

"Ah well, why don't you just go back to Grindr and ignore us like you do best—haven't found a top yet to fill your thirsty hole? Or have you run through them all and no one wants seconds?"

Richard's eyes pop out of his head, and his jaw drops. "You did not." Loud. His face in shock, scanning the other boys. Eugene covers his mouth as he laughs, Axel's face cracks in a grin, and Ramón sips his whiskey, slightly shaking his head, but a smile is visible through the whiskey glass as it passes in front of his lips.

Ramón starts speaking again my direction, the laughter at the table quieting so all can hear. "You know, in some ways, you actually kind of remind me of him."

31

———————

REMIND ME OF HIM.

Well, no shit. He raised me, so I ought to be somewhat of a mini version of him? I wonder what detail or details about me give it away? And is it truly that? That I remind him of my uncle, or is it I remind him of me, and he just doesn't recall me from when he last saw me long ago as a kid, so all he has is the recollection of David, which I remind him of? Do we move, talk, look similar? We are blood related…No one has told me before, though, that my uncle and I look alike. Maybe it's just the accent that he hasn't heard in a long time? It gives him flashbacks of my uncle talking to him when they were together? Do I want him to remember me? Am I pissed that he doesn't?

No…that's ridiculous.

I mean, why would I be? He didn't mean anything to me back then. But if he didn't mean anything to me, why would my uncle say I would have been better off with him raising me? Did he love me when I was a kid? My uncle actually considered that Ramón being part of my upbringing was a good idea, even better for me than his own company? How can this be? How could he have actually thought two dads would have been a good idea, realistic, a thought to actually consider moral? Was he high on meds back then too? None of this makes any sense still.

Well, I guess it may have been a thought. But I know what he decided, which—is what I would have decided too. I wouldn't raise a child with another man. A further worse abomination than how I am behaving already now—fucking other men as an adult, cheating on my wife. But choosing to expose a child, mold their mind so young that two men can live together —"in love." That's just selfish, wrong. Corrupt. My uncle did the right thing. Making sure I wasn't exposed to Ramón, making sure I wasn't exposed to his sick choices with Ramón. Maybe that is the true reason my uncle left Ramón as he did. Because he was sickened by his choices, disgusted with himself. Wait, that can't be—then why write this ridiculous letter of a long-lost love if he was sick with himself?

Maybe at the end of his life, he just doesn't care how sick he is. He's blinded by the infatuated sickness; it has overcome him. I mean, there is Andrew. Maybe Andrew corrupted him back to how he used to think. Taking care of him, at his sole power, behind closed doors in that nursing home. I could kill him. I could fucking kill him for aiding in this delusion my uncle now has, again. Corrupting him at the end, when he's worked his whole life to stay good. I should be home, saving him from Andrew. My uncle shouldn't die in the hands of a fag after all the efforts he made to escape one before.

My uncle must have wanted to make sure I wouldn't be exposed to Ramón and all these other fags in the world. Did they have other faggot friends around me as a kid? I doubt it; it was such a small town, the risk would be too high.

I can't believe my uncle even allowed this to happen in front of me for all the years it did. What was it, five to fourteen? So that's nearly ten years! That bastard. That fucking bastard! That selfish. Fucking. Bastard!

This IS why I'm fucked up now.

This is why I'm twisted, confused, thinking I'm attracted to men, because my sick uncle exposed me so young. I hate him. I fucking hate him. All my problems would not exist had he not done this to me. Had he not been so selfish. So disgusting. My marriage with Lucy would not be crumbling. I would be back home still, next to her, trying to create our family and pursuing the happiness I always wanted—worked for. God, I miss her. I fucking miss her so much it hurts. Tears slowly filling my eyes. I have to call her. I've made a mistake. I've made a huge mistake. I need to just tell her and ask her for her forgiveness, tell her how much I love her. I grab my phone out of my pocket, dial her number, and stare at it.

12:17 a.m.

Am I sure? Tap the call button, Roy. Tap it.

The balcony door behind me opening, laughter from the crowd inside the stranger's apartment

"Hey, you've been out here on this balcony for a while. Everything okay?" Eugene appearing from the balcony door, closing it behind him and stepping toward me.

I glance behind at him, then face back forward to the city view off this random balcony thirty-something stories up. I wipe my eyes with my forearm quick. "Yeah, everythin' is good." *Lucy's number on the screen of my phone.* I slide my phone back into my pocket.

Eugene now next to me, resting both forearms on the balcony railing, just as I. "We don't have to stay at this house party long. I only wanted to come because I'm not going to that circuit party Richard wants to go to, so just wanted to at least hang here for a few with him and see some friends."

"I get it." My head down, eyes on my shoes. I look up at him. "Don't worry about me; I'm just catchin' some air." I light up a cig and look back at the balcony door, see through the glass all the fags laughing, drinking—their tight, expensive-looking clothes; their shiny faces and teeth glowing through the dark shades of the party. My eyes travel from them to lock with Eugene's eyes next to me, catching him staring at me—

one of the faces, if not the only face, I don't judge. "It's just a lot."

"Is it?"

"Yeah."

"Well, I love it." "So many people, so many things to do." "So many conversations about everything." "Helps that the guys are hot too." He bumps his shoulder into mine.

"What, you wanna have a threesome or somethin' with one of 'em?"

Eugene's face pops a quick, silly-ish frown. "I mean, maybe? What do you think?"

"What do I think?" What *do* I think? It sounds hot; I'm horny—I'm always fucking horny—but I thought you're fine with what we have going on, just us? This doesn't fucking matter! I'm going back to Frankfort, anyways. And I don't want to be like my uncle. I will NOT end up like him, and I am sure as hell not like Ramón.

"Sure."

"Sure?"

"Yeah, sure."

"That doesn't sound too convincing."

"Well, I just really haven't thought about it much, until now you proposin' it." Not true.

"You've never thought of having a threesome with two guys?"

"Uh, well, when you put it that way, I have." Ugh. I have. Why can't I lie to him?

"Okay, so you have?"

"Yeah."

"Okay, well now, combine that fantasy with what you are already enjoying with me, and let's try it out."

"Combine the sexual fantasy of a threesome with men and what I have goin' on with you?"

"Correct." "You don't think it would be hot to see me bent over, getting railed by some hot guy, while I'm sucking that beautiful cock of yours?" He comes close to my face, splats a kiss on my cheek. "Or what about you and I tag team a bottom? Or we both have our dicks together in a hungry bottom moaning how much he wants both of us in him?" He steps back from me. "But hey, not Richard." He chuckles and shakes his head. "Richard is off limits."

"Why is Richard off limits?"

"Because he's my best friend. Why, you wanna fuck him?" His flirtatious tone turning serious on a flat, low note.

"Uh, no?" Shit. Guess Richard really didn't tell Eugene how we met. Looks like the best friend might be holding out on you.

"Listen, I like you, a lot, but if you can't keep your dick or hole away from and out of my friends, it's not gonna work." So he is the jealous type?

"Okay, *sweetie*." "You don't have to worry about my hole, and as far as my dick is concerned, that's my business."

"Are you mocking me? I'm serious."

Yeah, I know you're serious, but, baby, I ain't gonna be here for this bullshit. "No, I'm not mockin' ya, okay. I hear ya and will respect this request." I swing my arms up gallantly and bow my head in his direction.

"Request? Now you make it sound like I'm putting restrictions on you or something."

"I mean, that is a restriction." I take a big puff and stare at him.

His eyes widening and darting to the city lights down below. "Wow, so you really wanna fuck Richard that bad?" "Well, go for it." "Go for it!" He turns and steps back to the balcony door.

I step quick right behind, flicking my cig into the air off the balcony, and hug him from the back. "Eugene, stop." My lips on top of his ear, I hug tighter. "You're the one I'm into, okay?" "I'm not gonna fuck your friend." "No matter how much the thirsty little boy wants it." I hug him tighter and chuckle. "He's not my type—you are."

Eugene lifts my arms off from him, turns around to face me.

His hands slide down to grab each hand of mine. "I'm your type?" "What makes me your type?"

Fuck if I know. "Um, you're my type because…" My dick is getting hard just now here, holding your hands, just you and I, alone in the world on this balcony. I look away into the city view. Why is he my type? Fuck if I seriously know. "Umm." I look back into his eyes, his beautiful, mystic eyes. "Because it feels right when I'm with you, more right than I have felt with anyone in my entire life." Do I mean that?

The balcony door opens, Richard's stupid head popping out. Our moment alone, gone. Lost to time. Just like how everything becomes—lost to time. This may be our last moment.

"What are you bitches doing? Let's party!" "Eugene, come inside."

I shift my hands to break from Eugene's grip. "Go inside with your friends. I'll come in soon."

"You sure?"

"Yes, I'm sure." I glance at Richard, standing halfway through the door, swiping on his phone.

"Okay, see you in there." Eugene turns around toward Richard; I turn around and rest my forearms back on the balcony railing. This view. I'm gonna miss this view. These lights, the energy, the opportunity. But I don't belong here. This life isn't for me. These people are not my people. Do I actually feel "right" with Eugene? Where did that come from? Lucy is my person that makes me feel safe; she always has been. I light up another cig. Lucy…please take my call. I pull my phone back out, tap on the call icon to dial, her number still dialed there.

My thumb over the green call button.

Tap

32

———

RING…RING…RING…

"Hello?" she answers. She actually answered! Oh my god, she answered. I haven't heard her voice in so long.

"Lucy."

"Roy…is that you?"

"Yeah, hun."

"Roy." "Where are you? What happened to you?"

"Lucy, I miss you so much." Emotions overtaking me, I'm going to break open in tears. But I need to speak. "You have no idea what I've been going through." My words barely coming through clearly. This is so embarrassing.

"I have no idea what you've been going through?" Her voice strong, agitated? "You have *no idea* what I've been going through." "Where." "Are you?"

Wow.

I thought she'd be happy to hear from me?

I guess not. "I'm sorry." "You're one hundred percent right. I'm so sorry." "God, I'm so fucking selfish." The idea of Andrew's cousin popping into my mind, in a coma, because I never thought too much of him either. I've been so focused on myself, my uncle. Have I always been this selfish?

"How are you?"

"How am I?" "I haven't heard from you in over three months." "I haven't known to think if you're dead, have left me for another woman, or are locked up somewhere." "How do you think I've been, Roy? Huh? How do you think? You tell me."

"I know; I'm sorry." "I should have called you earlier. I shouldn't have cut you off when I did a few months back." "I'm sorry." "Your last text to me was to leave you alone, and I told myself to do that." "I've been foolish." "I've been wrong." "I've been so wrong."

"Foolish of what, Roy?" "I told you I would have changed my statement to the police." "I told you to come home and we would work this out as a couple. I told you that I loved you." "Why did you leave? And what really happened that night?"

What happened that night?

I fucked two guys that day is what happened. That dumbass Bobby threw your mother's ashes and urn into the garbage, trying to clean my sloppy shit up.

What happened? Fuck.

I don't know what to say. The police were after me since that morning; I think Janice saw me fuck the feller in our living room; me in my car, almost caught hooking up with a random guy in the middle of the night while you were sleeping.

What happened?

What happened was your husband isn't who you thought he was. How do I fix this? Do I be honest? What other option do I have? Lying isn't getting me anywhere. I can't tell her the whole truth; there's no way that's better…How can I save my marriage?

"Roy, are you still there?" "Roy! Just please be honest with me. Please. I can't live like this." "Tell me the truth."

Fuck. Here goes nothing.

"I…I did…cheat on you." My eyes looking across the lit buildings of the New York City skyline visible from here. In an infinite place, give me some infinite energy to redemption.

"I'm sorry." "I'm so, so sorry, Lucy." "Can you ever forgive me?"

"I knew it." "I fucking knew it." "I knew something was off with you more that day." "And when Sergeant Keaton told me your car was found parked behind that Motel 6—why else would you be parked behind a Motel 6 in the middle of the night?!" "…Who is she?"

"Who is she?"

Who is she? Fuck, what do I say? "Why does it matter who she is?"

"WHO IS SHE?" my wife yelling at the top of her lungs. Her rage sending a punch to my eardrum.

"She was just some silly broad that came into the bar that night." "I was drunk and a fool." "It meant nothing."

"What is her name, Roy?"

"I'm not givin' ya her name." "You don't need to know her name."

"Yes I do." "I need to know the whore's name that fucked you in your car! What's the whore's name?"

"Hun…"

"Don't you fucking hun-call me! I am not your fucking honey anymore." She begins to cry, and then there's silence between us. Wow, I have pushed the pastor's daughter into becoming a monster. A crying, angry, rageful monster.

"Lucy…you are my honey, and I made a mistake." "You will never know the heartbreak I feel from the mistake I've made."

"The heartbreak you feel?" "Really, Roy?" "The heartbreak you feel?" "You know what? You are so selfish. So selfish!" "I can't believe I've been in misery, missing and crying over a man as selfish as you." "A man that cheats on me, lies to me, and runs away from me like a coward." "You're a coward, Roy." "You're not the man I married." "The boy I fell in love with in high school." "I don't know who this is."

"Lucy…you don't know how hard its' been—"

"STOP sayin' that!" "You are not the one that gets to be sad and some kind of victim. My daddy was right about you. You cheated on me, have broken my heart, have hit me." "What else have you done?" "Oh yeah, disrespected my dead mother." "Who does that?" " And don't you tell me again how hard it's been for you." "My husband has flipped on me to some stranger of secrets, and I have no answers as to why." "WHY?" "Why, Roy?" "You tell me the truth right now if you care about this marriage."

"Your daddy is right about me?" "What are you talkin' about?" "What does your daddy have anythin' to do with us?"

"What is her name, Roy?"

"Lucy, I can't tell ya that." "Why are you bringin' your daddy up?" "That man has never liked or respected me, and you know that."

"Yeah? Well, now I finally know why—Roy, if you don't tell me her name, I'm divorcing you." "I'm not kiddin'." "I will file the paperwork tomorrow mornin'."

"You're divorcin' me?" "Now that's your fuckin' daddy talkin' in your ear." "Our relationship tossed out the window—just like that?" "Because Daddy says so?" "Huh?" "I never had you to myself, it's always been you 'n' your daddy." "You have any idea how hard it is to be perfect—appeasing a pastor's daughter all my life?" "Impossible." "That's how hard it's been." "Fuck me, Lucy."

"Yes—gone just like that. Because I don't recognize who you are anymore." "And no, Roy, I don't know how hard it must possibly be—because all I've done is try to love you unconditionally, the way the church 'n' my daddy taught me how to love a man and be a doting wife—the way my mama lived; is that so bad?" "I don't think so." "…What is the bitch's name!!"

Who is my wife? What has she become? This is my doing. I have forced this devilish creature to be born and rage inside of her from my corrupted actions. My lies and sneaking around—fucking men like a diseased, sick cockroach. The disease now sickening the most important relationship to me.

"Her name was…uh—"

"WHAT WAS HER NAME!"

"Fuck, her name was Iris."

"Iris? Like ee-rees?"

"Yeah."

"And you met her at the bar near that Motel 6?"

"Yeah."

"I don't know of anyone that name in town, and we know everyone in town. You're lying to me again, Roy."

"I swear to God, Lucy, I am not lying to you. There was a girl named Iris, and she was traveling, and stayed near Frankfort only one night at the Motel 6. I'm not lying." It's true, I'm not.

"So if I called the Motel 6 and asked if they could tell me three months ago if they had a Iris stay, their answer would be yes." Fuck, well I don't know if the reservation was under Iris's name or Dorian's? Actually, based off what I saw on who wears the pants in that relationship—it probably was in her name.

"Yeah, unless she lied to me about her name? Which maybe she did 'cause she was traveling from out of town and could pretend to be anyone she wanted to be."

"Pretend to be anyone they want to be? Is that what you are doin' now? Why you left? Because you want to pretend to be someone else, somewhere else?" "We get hitched too young, and now you're havin' some midlife crisis that I'm not the one?"

"Yeah, that sounds like words your daddy is tellin' ya—ain't it?" "No, that's not why I left. I left because…because…I told you. Because I need to take care of a thing for my uncle before he dies."

"Roy, I can't believe a word you are sayin'. Anything you say and everything you have said is all now a fuzzy cloud in my head of questions and confusions."

"I hear ya, and I am sorry…" "Do you think we can get it back? Get back to where we used to be? Do you think you would ever be able to forgive me?" "I'll be home soon." "I want us back, Lucy."

"Forgive you for what? Cheatin'?" "Maybe?" "I just don't know what else there is to forgive because you aren't bein' honest with me about what is happening to you." "You want me to forgive you? And to save our marriage?" "When are you comin' home?"

"Do you want me to come home?"

"I did." You *did?*

"You did?" "What changed?" "Your daddy in your ear?"

"You just confessed to me that you've been cheating." "And this behavior of yours…I don't know who you are. Going silent on me for months, running from the cops, gettin' a new phone number? Do you think you should be forgiven?" "Is this the qualities of a man that should be raising a child?" "Qualities that make a good husband—*father?*" "I can't go through this again down the line." "I won't." "And I won't put my children through this."

"Lucy, my mistakes will never, ever happen again." Raising a child? Back to this conversation again? "Why are you bringing up children?"

"Because."

"Because why?" "We've tried, and it hasn't happened. It's not in the cards for us."

"Well, actually you're wrong, Roy." "I'm pregnant." "Had you been here and not left, you would have known."

"What?" "You are?" "You're actually pregnant?" "How is that possible?"

"I tried to tell you over the steak dinner I made you." "That's why I made it." "To celebrate and tell you." "Little did I know that my husband would cheat on me hours later."

"Lucy…I don't know what to say." A smile beams across my face. "You're pregnant. I can't believe it. I'm so happy. I'm so happy! I swear."

"You are?"

"Of course I am." "I love you. And I'm gonna love our baby too."

"That's what you want? Me and this baby?" "A family here in Kentucky like we always planned?"

"Yes, I promise you, that is what I want." "Can you believe me? Please?"

"I hear you, Roy." "It's gonna take some time, if ever." "And as of now, I don't know how I'm ever goin' to trust you again."

"So you're tellin' me that you don't think we can get us back?" "Back to how we used to be?" "A better version now that we're gonna have a child together."

"Is me and this child gonna be enough for you, Roy?" "You promise you won't run out on us?" "To never lie to me again on anything?" "Never so much as look too generously at another woman again?"

"Yes, Lucy." "I do." "I promise." "I want my life back, with you and this baby."

"I don't know." "How about you actually come home." "Tell me and apologize in person."

"I will; I can." "I have one last thing I need to wrap up where I am at, and I will come home tomorrow." "Okay?" "This is my new number, by the way. Please just keep it between us." "Again, I'm sorry I left you in the dark for so long; please don't give up on us." "Give me another chance."

"It's late, Roy. I need to go back to bed; I have work in the mornin'."

"I know. I'm sorry for finally callin' and it's this late."

"I'm sorry too."

"Lucy, thank you for telling me." "About the baby." "I'm so sorry I haven't been there."

"I'm sorry too. Good night."

Click

The rain droplets on my home screen in front of my eyes. I can't believe it. She finally got pregnant. And at the worst time. Why, God? I mean, I'm excited, I truly am. But why after all these years—we finally get pregnant at the time I've grown into a mess. I could just drop this phone now. Watch it fall thirty-something stories, see it explode and shatter as it hits the city sidewalk below. Erase the past three months, disconnect myself again, a fresh start back to my old self.

I want my old life back. And I can return to it as a father.

I still got my old phone, turned off and stored away in my car. How many people are down there at this hour? Jailbreaking this phone and running away from my problems here was a stupid mistake. Behaving like a reckless child—running away when they deserve to be spanked and own their shit, to then become better behaved after. Maybe I should let Sergeant Keaton arrest me, face the charges so I can come out of it better? A cleanse.

I want my wife back. My fingers spread out slowly from their grip on the phone in my palm. My hand tilts inward, relaxing open. The phone slides off, and down I watch it free-fall.

SMACK

The phone hits the lit sidewalk, ricocheting into the dark street. A couple people jumping and looking up. I lean my head back, out of their sight.

Phew. Thank god it didn't hit them. Why did I say I cheated on her with Iris? Was that the best move? Telling her Dorian's wife's name? I couldn't think of anything else to say in the moment. I really don't know any other broads. I've always stayed loyal to Lucy in our marriage—never gave too much attention to any woman to not give the wrong impression so I would never be in a position to cheat. I ain't too godly, but that's one thing I've always tried to follow. If she calls that Motel 6, would they share a name from a reservation from over three months ago? Ain't that against the law for privacy matters or something?

It is a smaller town, and Lucy is as sweet as a charm and usually can get her way—also, her father having such a high position as the town's favorite preacher, if she can't get an answer, someone will answer to him. I would have given their last name to her and just told her to ask for that, but I don't know it. Fuck. Dorian's Grindr profile is on my old phone, maybe I can look back and reach out to him. No, that's stupid. Leave it alone in the past, no more looking or thinking back.

Hopefully Iris's name is on the reservation or credit card receipt or something. I can't believe that is something I actually hope for. I need to save my ass. I might need that phone if Andrew calls me with news about my uncle. Fuck. Maybe that was stupid. I flick the bud of my finished cig into the air. I gotta get back to my car and turn my old phone on. Or?

Hm.

What if I just jumped off here too? Free-fall like the phone. Solve all these problems instead. I wouldn't have to face Lucy. Maybe she'd find a better father to raise that baby? One of these idiots would find the letter in my car and give it to Ramón. The mission would be fulfilled, and I would stop causing so much pain. Confusion to myself and to those around me. Stop it, Roy; that's a dumb idea. You just were told you have a baby coming! A new blessing. You're excited! You're gonna be a father, man! You're gonna be the man you're supposed to be.

I gotta get home. What am I going to do about this letter? Do I just give it to Eugene now and tell him to give it to Ramón? Where is Eugene? Do I leave it somewhere in Ramón's new club for him to find?

That would be a fun moment to watch as a fly on the wall. Watching Ramón discover the letter secretly placed in his new club, and then watching his reaction as he reads the contents within. I don't know if he'd laugh, cry, or be scared. If I make it to heaven, think God would allow me to watch that moment from above? Or wait, does God allow people that commit suicide into heaven? Maybe I should rethink this. What am I even saying? God ain't allowing me in. Shit! The adultery, the gay sex, the lies. I wouldn't let myself in either. So fuck it. Better I live the fullest here and now. I got no shot making it up there. It's 2012; we're all supposed to die in a few months anyways.

Enough of that talk.

But wait, what if my redemption is how I raise this child? That makes sense to me. The timing of it all. It has to be. Doing right by Lucy and this child is my lifeline to redemption.

I exit the balcony, enter the house party, into the sea of fags drinking and laughing about who knows what stupid shit. If I give the letter to Eugene to give to Ramón, or leave the letter in the club for Ramón to find, I won't get Ramón's response— which was the main reason I came here to begin with. Is it that important for me to get? To return Ramón's reply to my uncle before he dies? It is the one good thing I set out to do. I'm assuming that is ultimately what my uncle hoped for—a response from Ramón?

But.

Do I enable this behavior further?

I mean, what the fuck, my uncle is about to die, and Ramón is an old, happy, established New York City fag. It's not like they can or would change at all, either way. If my uncle truly thinks he means when he says Ramón was the love of his life, and if Ramón truly thinks he means when he says he was completely heartbroken when we disappeared on him in 1992, then perhaps this last and final thing can be done, and I will go back to Frankfort with some honor. Even though I disagree with the moral of the situation. Let's finish what I came here to do. Give the letter to Ramón and ask him to write back a reply that I can give to my uncle. Simple. It's what I should have done the second I arrived here months ago. But I didn't.

I continue scanning for Eugene as I make my way to the apartment front door. Where is he? I see Richard in the kitchen, holding himself up on the countertop.

What a fucking mess.

His head down, then back up, then down. His eyes opening and closing. He's barely holding himself up. I pause in my step and take another second to assess. Where are his friends? Why is no one around him helping him? He's clearly fucked up, needs water. The idiot is about to fall over and bust his head on the granite countertop. All the men around him, and no one is talking to him, giving him water—they're all just obsessed with each other in their own side conversations around him, laughing among their selfish selves.

I turn back to look at the apartment door. Some fags around me staring and talking. I scan again, looking for Eugene; don't see him. Where did he go?

I step forward toward the apartment door, stop again, and look toward the kitchen at Richard. Fuck. I can't leave him here like that.

———

33

"Hey!" I grab Richard's shoulder and shake. "Richard." "Wake up." "Drink this water." His eyes with faint life in them. Probably can barely tell who I am. My body leaned over him, as he is barely able to hold his balance, sitting on the side of the bed. I'm holding a water bottle in his face, trying to get him to grab it and drink. Jesus. He's a silly, helpless infant. Better get used to this.

"I have never met a fella that couldn't handle liquor the way you can't." I sit down next to him. His body giving way, leaning on me, his head landing softly on my shoulder. My eyes on the back of the bedroom door to my left. At least I got him in here. It's less embarrassing behind closed doors and safer here if he passes out. His head will crash on the bed or carpeted floor.

"Richard." "Drink the water, you stupid faggot." His head lifting off my shoulder, eyes widening, his head shaking at me. That'll wake him up! Just continue insulting him. I know his stupid buttons.

"…Where…where are we?"

"We're at the house party still, numb nut." "Brought you to the bedroom because you were making a fool of yourself in the kitchen." "Remember?" Probably not.

"Kind of." His words slurring. He grabs the water I'm still holding, opens it, and starts to drink it slowly. Our arms touching as we sit on the bed next to each other.

"Yeah, well, drink up." "I gotta get out of here, and I'm not leaving until you can at least walk."

He looks at me, sets his hand on the top of my back. "You aren't that bad, John." He smiles, closes his eyes tight, opens and then brings the bottle back to his mouth to drink. "You aren't that bad." He brings the bottle back down and caps it.

"Go on, drink more." I grab the bottle, open it back up, keep the cap, and give it back to him. "Drink the whole thing; it ain't that much." I stand up and lean on the wall across from him.

His eyes a still gaze, focusing somewhere random on the carpet floor.

"Why you always gotta get so fucked up, anyhow?" "The amount of times I've seen you passed out or like this is a lot." "Why?"

"Who are you to judge me…Mr. John…Bigshot-Pingree."

Hm. Faggot's right. "You know what, you're right." "John Pingree is in no position to judge anyone." "Because…John Pingree doesn't exist." "He ain't real." Half empty, the water bottle back on his lips.

"What are you talking about?"

"Nothin'." What am I doing?

"Who are you?" "Why did you show up that day at my apartment—looking for Ramón?"

"If I told you the truth, you wouldn't believe it."

"Try me."

My ear cocks toward the bedroom door, trying to hear outside. The same loud voices and laughing as the party continues on the other side. People probably think I brought him in here to fuck him or something. Everyone likes to pass Richard around, and he loves it. For fuck's sake. Hope word doesn't get back to Eugene that we came in here together. I'm surprised he actually hasn't come to find me, that fucker. Ugh. None of this still matters! What was that threesome talk? I guess now that it is my last night…maybe it is a good idea. Go crazy one last time before I need to return to my past, dull life. What am I saying? I have a son or a daughter coming! I hope it's a boy. Actually, I don't really care what it is. I'm excited to return back home tomorrow. I am.

"John, who are you?" Richard seeming to come back alive from his messy state. It looks like a little rest and water is all he needed. His balance on the bed much more stable; he's coming across actually sober, as if he was barely drunk at all.

Fuck it—

"My name is actually Roy." "And I was born in a small town in Kentucky." "Near the same town Ramón left in 1992."

"Holy shit. Are you his son or something?"

"Fuck, no." I raise my index finger at him. "Don't ever fuckin' say that again." My hand falls back to my side. "I just know someone he loved in the past, I guess."

"Okay, so why are you here, and why use a fake name?" Richard stands up and steps toward me. Shit, he bounced back real quick.

"Uh, well, I have a letter to deliver to Ramón, that came back to Kentucky as undeliverable here, when it was sent to your place in the mail."

He plants himself a few feet in front of me. "You've been here months; you met Ramón months ago. I don't understand." "Why didn't you give him the letter yet?" "What does it say?"

Across the bedroom, an interior door popping open

Shit, I thought that was a closet? A man emerges, and the light is turned off behind him, the door closing shut. Oh, there is a bathroom off the bedroom. Richard and I both freeze and watch as he zips up and walks toward the door of the bedroom. "Enjoy the party," he says. He opens the bedroom door, slips out, and closes it behind him.

I look back at Richard. "We should go. Actually, I need to go." "You're back to normal, 'n' I gotta get out of here."

"That's it?" "You're gonna confess your darkest secrets and run? Not ask me to not tell anyone—or give me more details?" "What type of cliff-hanger bullshit is that?" "One or the other, man." He cracks a smile and pushes me with both hands lightly; my back taps the wall behind me from his little force.

"I don't know what else to say."

"Why are you still here? In New York? Why did you stay?" "I knew the second I met you, naked, that you weren't from around here." "You stay because you have a little crush on me still?" "Can't stop thinking about finding me masked with my ass up?"

"Ha ha." "No." "I guess I just got distracted." "I've never been to a place so different, so open and alive."

"Yeah, that's New York City for ya." "I get it." "One thing I can actually agree with you on."

"Mhm." "Okay, I'm gonna go." I gotta piss like a Russian racehorse first, though. I walk around the bed toward the bathroom door that guy came from. "I'm gonna piss and then go," I holler out as I stretch my hand to open the door.

"Wait, you've been here watching Ramón for months, undercover?" "That's crazy; you're fucking crazy." "I knew it but didn't know you were that type of crazy." "I have to tell him."

I remove my hand from the bathroom door handle, my body turning back toward him. "You're not gonna say shit to him." "You got that?"

"And why is that?" "You gonna finally beat my ass up like you should have the first time we met?" He turns around, pulls down his pants to show me his bare ass.

My body jumps in his direction; he pivots back in front of me. I stand right on top of him, kick my foot up to claw the top of his pants and bring them down to his ankles. My right hand grabs his balls and pulls down. His torso shifting from the force of the pull, closer into mine. "Listen you numb-nut-faggot piece of shit." "You say one fuckin' word about this to anyone, I'll fuckin' rip your nuts off."

His face inches from my chest, his body still. What you gotta say now, pretty NYC boy?

His breathing stopped. "Yes, sir." Is he smirking?

A creak from the bathroom door behind me

My head turns. Eugene emerging from the bathroom. Eugene? He steps into the bedroom and stops, his face with an expression as if meeting winter's first cold burst of air. I let go of Richard's balls, push him away from me into the wall, and turn to fully face Eugene.

"What were you doin' in there Eugene?"

"Uh-huh." "You're joking, right?"

"Does it look like I'm joking?"

I can hear Richard behind me, scrambling to pull his pants up.

Eugene's eyes bouncing from Richard behind me, back to my eyes. "What's going on here?"

I look back at Richard, now fully dressed. There is a smirk on his face! Did he know Eugene was in the bathroom with a guy this whole time?

"It's not at all what you think." I turn back to Eugene.

"Yes it is." Richard in a stern and sassy voice behind me. I could rip his vocal cords from his throat right now. I'll go to prison for murder; I don't care.

I turn to him. "You're a fuckin' liar."

"I'm a fucking liar?" His index finger pointed inward at his chest. "Did you just hear the last five minutes of what you just told me?" Shit, did Eugene hear anything I just said? Why did I tell Richard any of this??

I look back at Eugene. "Who was the guy you were in the bathroom with?"

Eugene nodding. "Who was I in the bathroom with?" "Why

the fuck are you in a bedroom alone with my best friend, naked, at a party?"

"We are not naked." "See—my clothes on." I pat all over my chest and thighs. "These are clothes—all fully on."

Richard still behind me. "He was making a move on me." "I told you not to trust him, Eugene."

In a flash my body turns toward Richard, my right hand clenches, and my arm throws a punch through Richard's face, knocking his head into the wall. The back of his head ricocheting off the wall, sending his body forward and onto the ground. I step out of the way. Eugene hops over the bed, landing next to Richard. "Jesus fucking Christ, John!" "What is wrong with you?"

Richard turns around on the ground, some blood coming from his nose. He tilts his head back at me. "His name is Roy, Eugene." "And he has some weird obsession with Ramón, not you." "You're just a pawn in his plan to reach Ramón."

"What are you talking about?" Eugene holding Richard, Richard tilting his head back further to stop the blood and plugging his nose with his fingers.

"He's right." "You've been nothing but a pawn to me." "I came to the city for Ramón, and I'm leaving the city now." Some rolled-up towels in my reach on a dresser against the wall to my right. I grab them and toss them to Eugene and Richard on the floor. "This was never meant to happen."

I turn, open the bedroom door, and exit.

"Wait."

Is that voice coming from behind me? My pace on the city sidewalk putting me already a couple blocks away from the party. Eugene? I turn around. Eugene approaching me fast.

"What the fuck, John? Or is that not really your name?" He arrives, stopping a few feet in front of me.

"What?" "You couldn't hear what I said from the bathroom with that guy's cock in your mouth?" "Get out of my face." I turn around and walk.

"John!" "Stop!" I hear him right behind me. "I'm not gonna chase you all through the city tonight." "Come on." You should, you cheating bastard.

"Good," I holler out, cocking my head into the air to the right. "Be gone!" "We can pretend it never happened," I shout, tilting my head up to the sky, "all of it." "None of it matters."

"That's what you want?" "That's what you truly want? To pretend?" "Aren't you done pretending? Haven't you pretended enough in your life?"

My feet stop, and my body turns to face him. "I am not pretending. I have never pretended my whole fuckin' life." "You don't know me."

He puts his face close to mine. "Really?" "Not once?" "Not once you have ever pretended to be anyone you're not?" "I highly doubt that." "And, yes, I do know you." "You're like every other closeted man to ever exist—afraid to fully accept that he's gay."

"I'm not gay!" I shout at him, my head shaking. "I haven't pretended to be anything I'm not." Have I?

"Who is Roy, then?" "Why did Richard say you're lying about your name?" "What did you do that you came to the city and changed your name? Jailbroke a new phone? Only work for cash?" "Just tell me." He grabs my hands. "I love you."

What? Words I never thought a man would say to me. No. No, he can't love me, and I don't love him.

NO.

My arms fling out to the sides, tossing his touch off me. "Eugene, it doesn't matter." "Okay?" "None of this matters." "I have to get back home." "I have responsibilities back home." "Coming here was a mistake." "Meeting you was a mistake." "I'm sorry." I turn back again and start walking. Tears building up inside of me. This is stupid; control them. Seriously? *Tears?*

"Didn't you just hear me?" "I love you! Does that not matter to you? I don't matter?"

I keep walking. "It doesn't matter; I have to go," I holler again to the side. I don't look back.

"Yeah, well, I think you're just being a pussy." Eugene shouting behind me. "You felt something truly real for once in your life, and it terrifies you. Look at you now. Physically running away from it." "From me."

Keep walking, Roy; you have to let go. It's not real. You don't love him. You don't.

I don't.

But if I don't, why does it hurt so much?

34

———————

2:17 A.M.

My old phone back on.

Searching…at the top left corner.

Come on Lucy, I hope you didn't disconnect me. I hope you kept paying the phone bill. I'm coming home, hun. Come on, come on…Yes!

Verizon at the left corner; I'm back. Old Roy is coming back.

I set the phone down, plugged into my car, charging.

Hm. What is Ramón's schedule tomorrow? Damn. After all this time, I still don't know his number. I'm gonna just have to search for him. I'll try the club first; from there, if he isn't there…I'm sure someone at the club will know where he is or can give me his number. I don't think I've ever seen him there before 10 a.m. My eyes jump to my car clock, 2:18 a.m. I got time to kill. What should I do? My hand grabs my phone, my fingers swipe over to Grindr, and my eyes watch as all the profiles upload. Then I scan through them. A few notifications and messages coming through, voicemails, texts…bullshit I don't care about now. Who's online? Who's looking? It's my last night, fellas, and I'm a free man.

Wait…What about that circuit party tonight Richard was talking about?

What was the name…? I don't remember. I remember Richard saying Eleventh and Fifty-First, though, at dinner. I could just drive there and look for a bunch of fags on the street and follow them? Would that work?

I shouldn't…

But fuck—I want to.

Excitement and nervousness in my gut. I remember this feeling. I'm in New York City, and it's my last night. Just one more night, and I'll never look back again. I'll never make these twisted, sick choices again. I'll return back to Kentucky, become the doting husband I'm meant to be, to Lucy, and a great father to our soon-to-be newborn. Become the best father to him or her—better than my uncle was to me, better than my own that died too early on me.

I will spend the rest of my life making up for my sins by becoming the best doting and faithful husband and raising a child to be the same way. To treat and respect a woman, to find passion in work that serves others, and know God. I can do that. I'll do it all right, I promise.

But…tonight, I gotta let my desires roar, just one last time, one final time to end this fucked-up diseased beast, to kill it inside of me with a final blow. Serve it its final meal—a last and final delicious meal that fills it for a lifetime. A meal so satisfying that it's never craved again because it was completely and wholeheartedly fulfilling; deliciously oversatisfying, turning to a point of me hating it. Is that a thing? Can you become sick of something from overindulging? I'll make it a thing. I'm gonna go so crazy tonight that I'll never want to touch a fucking man again. Crazy to the point that it makes me sick of them. Like overeating and then vomiting and then never being able to eat that type of food again—indulge to the max so that I'm maxed out, no other option left but to turn a new direction, a direction back to where I belong, back to what I know, back to who I am.

What if Richard's there?

The excitement fleeting, darkness and an evil warm rush filling its space. I hate him. I already gave his pretty little face a bloody nose—that faggot won't be out nowhere tonight. He cares too much about his fake appearance.

What about Eugene?

Would Eugene be at that circuit party tonight? I don't know. We did just break up. What if he is? So what if he is! Fuck it. It's your last night. You owe him nothing. He owes you nothing. Don't make it complicated, Roy. I don't love him. I don't.

I open the glove box of my car, grab the letter. A small piece of paper flies out with it and lands on the seat. I fold the letter and put it in my pocket. I guess if for some reason Ramón is there tonight, I can just handle this tonight and not chase him tomorrow across the city. Kill two birds with one stone.

I pick up the piece of paper on the seat, bring it in front of me, and scan—

Kentucky Motor Vehicle Registration

Oh, it's Andrew's registration. I extend my arm toward the glove box to put it back, my eyes still down on it.

Isaac Jones

Wait, what?

I bring the paper back close to my face. *Isaac Jones*, followed by the address, date of birth, etc. I scan for Andrew's name everywhere on it. Nowhere. I look back at *Isaac Jones*—Who the fuck is Isaac Jones?

35

————

WHY WOULD Andrew tell me he has two cars when one of them is registered to a different person? I scan to see if the registration is up to date. It is. What the fuck? I'm calling his ass—I don't care how late it is. I swipe to his name and tap to call. I hit the speaker button.

Ring…ring…ring…Grindr messages popping up at the top of my screen…Ring—

"Roy?"

"Hey, *babe*." "Long time no chat."

"Uh, hi." "Why you calling me this late, and on your old phone?" "You okay?" "I'm at work."

"How's my uncle?"

"He's okay…" "Still not eating or drinking much, to be honest." "Our head nurse noticed his decline, and the doctor will be coming to assess him later this morning." "Roy, if the doctor says he's declined too far, he'll be transferred to hospice tomorrow."

"What?" "Andrew, you have to stop them." "Listen to me: I'm coming home tomorrow." "I found Ramón, I did." "I actually found him a while ago, and I'm giving him the letter tomorrow and coming home."

"A while ago?" "What do you mean 'a while ago'?"

"It doesn't matter." "Just keep him there, okay?" "I trust you; you know how to care for him." "You know as I if he goes to hospice, he won't be taken care of as good as with you." "I fucking trust you." "You have any idea what that means that I actually trust you?" Is that possible?

"Roy, it's gonna grow out of my hands." "I'm just a nurse." "I'm not a head nurse here, and I'm not a doctor." "I don't call the shots on decisions like that."

"Andrew. Get creative, man." "Are you a fearless fag or not?" "Always having to overcome bullshit from everyone around you?" "You can do it; don't bullshit me that you can't." "I've seen you in action." "I've seen others in action." "Keep him there."

"Roy, I'll talk with the head nurse, let her know that family —you, are coming home tomorrow and that you would appreciate for them to wait until you are back before they transfer him." "Okay?" "I can do that, and maybe that will buy you some time." "I'll do my best, I promise."

"Okay." "Thank you." "Now we're talkin.'" "I knew you had it in you—you just need a little push sometimes."

"I don't need any type of push; you're the one that needs a push."

"Oh really?" My face lightening up, the corners of my mouth reaching to my ears. His voice soothing to me. In all this chaos, his voice surprisingly relaxes me.

"Yeah, you need lots of pushing, let me tell ya."

"Mhm." "Well, I don't know or agree with much of what you're sayin'." "So whatever."

"How are you?"

"How am I?" *Grindr notifications popping up more at the top.* "Horny and frustrated." "How are you?"

"Horny and frustrated?" "That's your reply? Horny??" "Okay…"

"What? I'm just bein' honest." "I'm a man with needs." "What can I say?"

"Honesty is good; I appreciate that." "Honesty is hard to come by these days with anyone."

"Yep, horny and hot as a dog in heat on a summer day."

"Ha!" "You know you just referred to yourself as a horny bitch, right?"

"What are you talkin' about?"

"Well, (a), you just referred to yourself as a dog, and, (b), only female dogs go through heat, not male—so you referred to yourself as a horny bitch." "You finally let someone put it in your butthole?" "It's about time." "Good for you, big guy."

"No." "There ain't nothin' ever gettin' put in my butt." "I'm sure you'd love to try, wouldn't you." "I know how much you'd love it."

"Yeah, well, I'm sure you want to know if I would want to try."

"Hm." "Okay, that's enough, creep. Speaking of honesty—" "What?"

"Well, the real reason I'm callin' ya…Who is Isaac Jones?"

Andrew silent for a few seconds. "How do you know that name?"

"Don't avoid the question." "Who is he?"

"You know, Roy, I've done a lot for you." "More than for any other patient's family, by far." "Why are you messing with me?"

"Why am I messin' with ya?" "Are ya kiddin'?" "Why are you messin' with me?"

"What are you talking about?" "How am I messing with you?" "How?"

"How?" "You told me the car I'm borrowin' is yours. Come to find out, it's registered to some Isaac Jones, hm?" "So who is he? And why do you have his car?" "Why am I drivin' Isaac Jones's car?" "And why don't the fella need it for months?"

"How did you find out the car belongs to Isaac?"

"What difference does it make?"

"Roy, how did you find out?"

"Andrew, whose car am I drivin', and why did you lie to me about it?" "Everyone in my fuckin' life I feel is lyin' to me." "The one person I'm beginning to trust turns out to be lyin' to me too." "Why?"

"Isaac is my cousin, Roy." "The one still in a coma." "That's why you've had it for months and I haven't said anything about it, though I didn't know you'd be gone for this long."

"Oh." "Shit." "He's still in it, huh?"

"Yeah…I just told you hours ago that he was. His parents actually came into town today." His voice changing tone. "Tomorrow they are going to decide if they pull the plug or not"—he begins to cry—"and I have no say at all." "No one cares what my opinion is." "No one," he croaks. Soft weeping coming through. His pain on my speaker phone filling the silence of my car—well, I guess, Isaac's car—so…real and true. I don't know what to say. The incessant Grindr messages still coming through—now annoying me. I turn the phone upside down. His cries still coming through uncontrollably. Damn. He and his cousin must have been very close.

"Andrew…" "Andrew." He can't catch a breath. "Andrew."

"What!" His crying even louder. A wailing cry I've never heard come out of a man before. Fuck. Control yourself.

"Andrew." "Control yourself; it's okay." "You're not close with your aunt and uncle?" "Hm?" "They don't listen to ya?"

"No, it's not, Roy; none of this is okay—you have no idea. No idea in the world how none of this is okay." "Don't ever tell me 'It's okay,' ever." His crying leveling, his words coming clearer.

"Are you done?"

"Fuck you, you asshole." "God, you're such an asshole." He takes in a gasp. "Such a fucking asshole." Is he chuckling? "How did you make it this far in life being such a fucking asshole?"

"Honestly, I don't know." "That's a good question." "I'm surprised I'm still here, to be honest."

"What does that mean?"

"Nothin'."

The phone silent…

"Your aunt and uncle don't care what you think?"

"What are you talking about?" "My aunt and uncle?" "I don't have any aunts or uncles." "Why do you keep saying that?"

"You just said your cousin's parents are in town and will decide tomorrow on pullin' the plug." "Aren't they your aunt and uncle?"

"Oh." "Yeah, I guess technically you're right—they are." "We just aren't that close, so I don't consider them my aunt and uncle."

"Ah, okay." "Well, I'm sorry, Andrew." "Is there anything I can do?"

He chuckles on the other end of the line. "I don't know." "My world has crumbled into pieces, right before me, faster than I had hoped, and I'm just sitting in the front seat of a train on tracks headed off a cliff, with no brakes." "…Isaac was my tracks." "He grounded me." He begins to cry again.

This poor guy. "I'm comin' back tomorrow, Andrew." "I will be there." "I'll be your friend." "I will help you find your brakes, okay?" "You're gonna make it through this." "Hm?" "You hear me?"

Nothing on the other end of the line, no breathing or words…nothing

"You still there?"

"Yeah, I'll believe it when I see it, Mr. Runs Away for Months and Gets a New Number." "A new life." "Have you talked to Lucy?" "She's visited your uncle a few times." "You should call her." "She even asked me if I knew anything. I told her no."

"Did you know my wife was pregnant?" "And not tell me?"

"…I did."

"What the fuck, Andrew?" "I thought we had…we have a relationship? Mutual respect?" "How could you not tell me that my wife is pregnant?"

"I'm sorry." "I didn't know what to do." "You're in New York City on your secret mission." "I figured if you knew, it would add pressure."

"I deserved to know." "You fucked up with me again." "You keep fuckin' with my life, and it boils my fuckin' blood." "First my uncle, me, and now my wife." "What is your problem?" "Why can't you just leave me and my family alone?"

"I made a mistake, okay?" "I should have told you about Lucy. I'm sorry." "Okay?"

"I hear ya." "I don't trust ya, but I hear ya." "I'm comin' back tomorrow; ain't nothin' stopping me." "And yeah, I did talk with her earlier; she needs me." "My uncle needs me. I guess now you need me—even though I'm not entirely sure how much help I'll be, but I'll try." "Even though now I'm pissed at you again." "You've done so much for me and my uncle." "I am grateful to you for it."

"Well, it's been my pleasure, Roy." "What time are you coming home tomorrow?"

"I don't know yet; it's over an eleven-hour drive, I guess twelve with stops 'n' shit." "I'll get there as soon as I can." "I'll come see ya first." I turn my phone back over to check the time. 2:43 a.m.

"Really?"

I swipe to unlock. My Grindr app with a red badge in the corner: *37*

Holy shit, thirty-seven messages. Thirty-seven dudes want to meet with me. Thirty-seven horny, hot NYC dudes…

"Yeah, really." "I gotta go, Andrew. Good night." "See ya tomorrow."

36

Taking loads on 53rd and 9th

Couple here

Benny

Ash

NYC Daddy

Looking

bttm for top

Fist me??

E

Visiting

9 inches

Looking 2 suck

My thumb flicking up and down as I scan through the Grindr profiles. My ass sore from sitting in this car too long. My eyes blink and bounce to the car clock. 3:17 a.m. I look through the windshield to across the street from where I'm parked.

Eleventh and Fifty-First

All right, where are these homos at? I should be in the right place. I look out all the car windows at the sidewalks, storefronts, restaurant fronts—people out still, but no one, no group of gays specifically telling enough to follow. What am I doing? I can just pick one off Grindr, unload in him, and move the fuck on.

Fuck—I wanna experience that party, though, just one time. Just one final time before I leave back home in a few hours. Never to look back. My eyes back on my phone, a red badge over the green phone icon: *2*

I tap the phone icon: two voicemails. Who left me voicemails? How did I miss this when I first turned the phone on? In three months I only have two voicemails? Damn. Maybe no one really does care about me back home. I don't recognize one number. Wait? That's the number that called me before and I hung up on them; the other voicemail from Lucy. I tap the voicemail from the strange number, *314-555-1516*. It has to be one of Sergeant Keaton's people?

"Eh, Roy, listen, I'm callin' because I'm an old friend of your uncle's. I know he ain't doing too well; I'm sorry to hear that. I promised him I'd reach out to you. Give me a call."

That's weird. My uncle never told me about a friend that would maybe visit him, or a close-enough friend that my uncle would give my number to—let alone my old number. Well, I for sure as hell ain't calling him back now. Okay, Lucy, what did you call me about?

Tap

"Roy, I don't know where you are and what's still goin' on. I don't even know if you're alive. I've left you so many messages and calls. I've gone from sad to now angry…Anyway, just wanted to let you know a man came to town here lookin' for ya. My daddy says he's an old friend of his. Small world, I guess. His name is Frank. Nice fella—I met him. He came here to the apartment. Asked me questions about you. When are you comin' back? Please come home to me. I'm so angry at you, but I still love you. Bye."

Frank. That son of a bitch has turned up all of a sudden. My wife calling him nice? And her father, Pastor Paul, knows him too? Looks like I'm the last person to meet or know this feller?

When was this? I scan to see when Lucy called. *Tuesday, September 11*. What's today? Friday, September 28. Hm. A couple weeks ago. Why didn't she say nothing earlier tonight about this?

She forget or something? Maybe I blindsided her, calling her in the middle of night after months of silence—from a random number too. When did Frank call? I scan to see. *Wednesday, September 12.* A day after. Is that what my uncle meant by "more things"? More bullshit I gotta clean up before he passes.

Wait.

Frank already had my number three months ago.

My uncle gave Frank my number a long time ago, then? But didn't tell me? How much more bullshit am I returning back to tomorrow? I'm done with these secrets and lies! Fuck, maybe I should just stay in NYC. Eugene and I have a good thing going. Well, we did. My thumb flicking back through the profiles on Grindr. Who's on?

Hyatt Hotel

Drinks?

Visiting from FL

Horny

E

Sam

Dad4Son

twink looking

Dating ONLY

Hm. A lot of hot guys over here in Hell's Kitchen. I wonder what Eugene is doing?

Fuck. What if he tried reaching out to me after our fight?

He doesn't know I dropped my phone off the balcony on purpose. What if he's calling me right now? Texting me? I don't want him to think that I'm blowing him off. I don't want him to think that at all. I'm sure Richard is all in his ear, talking all the shit to change his mind on me. That fucking prick. Telling him I just used him as a pawn to get to Ramón. It ain't true. Is it?...I should have smashed his face into that wall harder. Thinking of his smirk and the yapping bullshit out of his mouth, my fist clenches, nails putting an imprint into my palm. I could kill him. If I see him ever again, I could fucking kill him.

E

Wait a minute? It can't be. I tap on E's profile.

87 feet away

I scroll through the description: **6'1, 185 lbs, vers, Just looking**. Eugene doesn't live over here. No way. My eyes dart up to my rearview mirror: a group of men approaching behind on the sidewalk. Barely any clothes, shorts riding up their cracks, and itty-bitty tanks over their muscled chests, they look gay. And all the same, like a group of steroided white minions. Ha. They all talk like minions too: yippinjabbingibberish! I look down at the profile. What if he is at this circuit party? That little shit. He was on the prowl tonight, after all. Asking me about a threesome and hooking up in the bathroom behind my back. What a sleazy little shit. I guess who knows how many guys he's been hooking up with all this time. We never really made rules. I'm not one to do well with rules, anyways, it appears…You want a threesome, babe? I'll come find you in that crowd and fuck the both of you —whoever you're with. That's what you want? Hm?

I turn my head to get a better view, the faggots now passing my car on my left. Got them. That's a big group. Maybe ten plus. I can blend right in, walk in behind them. My hand grabbing the inside car door handle, the car door opening, and my body whipping out onto the sidewalk. I close the door, hitting the lock button on the key fob as I walk away quick behind the group. All right, where ya boys headed to? Show me.

Show me everything.

My phone in my hand, I tap E's message icon on his profile, type, and send:

You fucker.

37

I LIKE IT HERE. No one can see me; I can't really see them. Should I take my shirt off? It's so hot it's steamy, and everyone else has their shirt off.

The moans of different men all around me, the music from the party hovering over all of us. How do I find one? How does anyone find anyone in here? Maybe that's the point? Just feel the bodies around until one clicks with you. Feels you up, and it's a match—a secret, silent, dark match.

Fuck, what if someone has something? Can't see diseases in a dark room. I don't care.

Fuck it.

I'm taking my shirt off

Ah…better. Moist, hot bodies rubbing against my bare, colder skin as they pass by. Why are these men so hot? And I so cold? Maybe because I just got here. Maybe these fellas have been in here awhile.

No words from anyone—at least none that I can make out over the different variations of moans and the loud bass of the music. My hands glued in my pockets. My body retracting them out; setting them by my sides.

Relax.

My body inhales, filling my mouth and lungs with the scents and density in the air trapped behind the black curtains. My dick growing in my pants immediately. Figures all shades of dark, right next to me and far away. Heads below, at, and above mine.

This is fun. This is fucking wild.

A hand landing on my chest, the touch of his forearm gliding across, and then his hand again, the pressure of his fingers pressing different directions on my chest muscles, not that they are at all huge or anything compared to those of other men around. This hand feels familiar. My hands relaxed at my sides. Free, with no constraints. But this time, I *really* like it.

Am I just too drunk to care?

No, can't be. I haven't had that many in recent hours. Is it because it's dark?

Don't stop touching me; keep touching me; grab whatever you want. I love it.

"Hey." Did he just say "hey" to me?

"Hi."

The breath from his mouth nearly in mine. "You're hot." His lips and tongue smashing into mine. My mouth already open to receive. One hand of his groping my hard dick, the other cupping my ass. The scruff sensation from his facial hair on my lips, felt for the first time. My tongue responding to his instinctually. I grab his face with both of my hands. Lean my face back out of his mouth and spit.

He moans at me. "Ugh, yes." "Fuck, you're hot." "Can I suck your dick?"

"Yeah."

He starts kissing my chest as he unbuckles my pants with both hands. His knuckles nudging into my lower abdomen as he fights to get my buckle undone. I love it; unbuckle me slower. But also hurry up. His lips on my torso, traveling down. The head of my dick pressing into his forearms as he works. Fuck, baby, open your mouth for me and drop further. Stop the tease, I can't take it.

My dick pops out and lands right in his mouth. I start moaning like everyone else. The inside of his mouth feeling like a mini whirlpool, working in swirls to drain the cum out of me. "Holy fuck." The dark figures moving around us. Maybe some heads looking at me, looking down at him. I can't tell. And I don't care where they are looking. This feels so good. His hand jerking my shaft, and my tip down his throat. He sucks so good. I'm gonna bust; fuck, I'm gonna bust. Wait, can I cum in here? Of course I can; who cares? He probably wants it. I think I would want it too if our roles were reversed. Should I try after him with someone else?

"You want some poppers?" His voice down below, too dark to see, so it's like my own dick is talking to me.

"What?" What the fuck are poppers?

"Poppers." A whiff of something I've never smelt. Woah, I don't like that. What the fuck is that?

I step back, flip up my dick, and pull up my pants. "I'm good." Jesus.

I start walking through the fellas—like glow-in-the-dark bumper cars. Some of them with glow-in-the-dark colors. Defeats the purpose of a dark room, but who am I to say anything?

The scent still stuck in my nose of some weird…*chemical?* Poppers. Why didn't I ever learn about poppers? Kind of sounds familiar.

Where is the exit?

I stop to turn and look. Another hand landing on my stomach. The shape of his dark torso below my sight. Okay, you're sexy too; maybe I should stay. I'd like to grab your body and feel it against mine. It's glistening, almost, visible from a soft light ricocheting from something. Someone's glow thing or maybe light from the club bouncing down on us from the ceiling. I set my hands on his traps and squeeze.

He moans at me that it feels good. He leans in and starts kissing my neck. Fuck, I forgot how much I like that.

My knees weakening, and ripples of pleasure spreading from my neck to my toes. His hands now on my ass. His relentless thirst, sipping and biting all over my neck. His hands holding my ass underneath my jeans. Easy now…even Eugene hasn't touched my ass like that.

Fuck, it feels good, though.

His grip strong on each cheek; massaging in a circular motion and then also just holding and squeezing.

"Your ass, man, uh. I love it." He comes up from my neck for a breath. A finger of his slipping into my crack. I grab both his arms immediately, extending mine to hold his out, away from touching me. "Don't touch my ass."

"Why not?" "You seemed to be liking it?" Was I? "Want me to fuck you?" he says.

"No, I'm a top." "Never done that."

"How do you know you're only a top then?"

"I just know." I let go of his arms and start to walk away, pushing and stepping through the open crevices of figures around.

He grabs my ass. "Come on." Another whiff of that weird chemical shit entering my nose from somewhere. I said don't touch my ass.

My body turns and throws a punch into the dark shade of where I think his face is. The men around notice. A loud thud of my knuckles knocking through his cheek. "I said I'm good, faggot!"

A bunch of dark figures all around me, facing me:

"Get this guy out of here."

Who said that? Did I just hit someone's friend? Do friends all come in here and fuck together? Why the fuck do these guys care?

"Get on, go! Get the fuck out of here."

A guy's face right on mine, his bubble chest like rocks against my arm—

"This place isn't for you."

I thought the gays were inclusive. Guess the fuck not. My steps stalling. I don't see any crevices to walk into. I don't want to go. My hard dick gone. My curiosity and lust still strong. I'm sorry. I won't punch anyone else or call any of y'all a fag.

"Can you not hear? Get the fuck out!"

A different guy on top of me, too, his hand grabbing my arm, pushing me some direction. I start walking, pushing fellas with my body as I am pushed through myself from behind. Hey, you know what, I was trying to find the exit earlier, so thank you for leading me. My body walking the direction the guy is pushing me. He keeps his hand on my arm with a tight grip. Feller, I'm leaving, whatever.

"I see the exit." I jerk my arm forward to release from his grip. I'm almost there. A colorful slip from the club lights, between the tall black curtains. I'm here. A push from several hands simultaneously on my back, throwing me through the slip, back into the open, lit dance floor. I catch myself on my feet from their push, almost knocking some people over. I stumble getting my balance, using people's shoulders. "Sorry." I nod and look at the floor. I look up.

No fucking way

That little slut. I can't believe he made it out here. The guy railing him a hairy beast. Someone order a gorilla? His thick hands cupping Richard's face, fingers slipped inside his mouth, pulling Richard's face back, holding his cheeks like handles— rapidly fucking him in front of everyone on the dance floor. I can't…not look. Richard's head bouncing, tongue flicking out like a dog—agreeing in the pleasure coming from that dick smashing behind him in his ass. He must like the public fucking. Look at him, not a care in the world—getting off on the atten- tion of guys in line to plow him next and of the other guys standing around and watching, stroking their hard dicks, all out on the dance floor to see too. I see him looking at them looking at him. Fucking slut…should I get in line too?

My body moving forward in the crowd in their direction. More men dancing around, glancing at the show, but also not giving too much attention. Hm. Guess Richard isn't as hot as he thinks he is. Anyone else here that I know?

Eugene…where are you? Why aren't you here?

My head scanning the crowd around. Everyone is shirtless and hot, just like Richard said at the dinner table. He wasn't lying; I'll give him that.

Where are you, Eugene? *I miss you.*

38

"Whiskey coke."

"You got a preference on whiskey?" The bartender looking barely out of high school. I get it, fella; I literally was you, just in Kentucky.

"Sure, Jim Beam. You have it?"

"We sure do." He winks at me. "You want a shot, too, I'll buy it."

Ha. May look like a boy, but he ain't acting like one. Sure. Shoot your shot, kid. "Okay, sure, thanks."

He pours my whiskey coke fast, says, "I'll be right back," and dives somewhere else in the zoo of bartenders. This place is packed!

My eyes forward into the mirror along the wall behind the bar. I don't think I've ever seen so many shirtless men in one place. I guess, why would I? How come I never came to one of these things sooner? I guess Eugene took a lot of my time while I was here. He didn't want to come to these parties. Was that a mistake? I could have been at these parties all this time. Having cute boys buy me shots; random hot men touching me and me getting into fights with them. How fun, all the excitement I missed…I grab my drink and take several gulps, then turn around to check out the crowd better.

What. The. Fuck.

My first real second taking it all in. I slipped right into the dark room as soon as I got here. Saw some hot men sliding through the slit of them black curtains, and my body followed. Couldn't help my curiosity, couldn't help my hard dick pointing where it wanted to go. A grin on my face. Guess I was nervous. Not nervous anymore, with a drink and my knuckles warm. Men all various shapes, sizes, colors—all wearing skimpy clothes, barely anything. I look down at my jeans and cowboy boots, my belly button exposed. Not in a dark room anymore but in a very, very lit club. I do look really different from all these men. Is that a good thing or a bad thing? At least I have my shirt off. I blend in enough within this madhouse of faggots.

Wonder what God truly thinks about these…people? Are they *his* people? Or are they just here to test the rest of us? Test me with this lust I have that is a sin? A challenge set by him. I can overcome it. I just need to go back to ignoring all of it. Pretend it all doesn't exist, and then eventually, it won't exist. But does that mean part of me won't exist?

Damn it, Roy, that's too far. Jesus.

I don't know. But one more thing—if God put them here just as a temptation for the rest of us, what happens to their souls after they die? Seems a little cruel for God to design a flawed human, only for the benefit of testing to see if his other humans would fall into sin with them. Could this really be their only purpose?

What if they don't want to be gay? And they find a way to choose to be straight? Would it be fair to deceive all of those around that they are straight? Though God created them to really be gay? I'm so confused.

"Here you go!" I hear behind me and turn back.

A pink shot placed in front of me. "What is it?"

He smiles and cheers with his in the air. "It's a cosmopolitan shot." "That sexy guy over there actually bought it for you." He nods to his right, and I look. A stranger to me, staring at me. Did we chat on Grindr? I don't recognize him.

I look back at the bartender. "A what?" I look down and pick it up. "It's tequila or something?"

"No, it's vodka." He clinks with my shot and shoots his back. I follow his lead and shoot mine back.

"Thanks." I raise the empty shot glass in the air in front of him and set it down. Not bad.

"You want another, stud?" "This time I'll buy it." He winks at me again. What is with NYC bartenders always winking? Maybe that's how they make their tip money—flirting with the gay patrons, or do all the bartenders want us to fuck them at the end of their shift, in the stock room? Sounds like a good gig to me. Free booze, meet hot men from all over the world, and fuck them after your shift. Guess I have time to find out. I take out my phone to check.

4:12 a.m.

Okay, maybe I'm pushing it. I should get some sleep before my long-ass day tomorrow. I should try to look half decent for Lucy. Andrew and my uncle, too, I guess.

"Sure." "I can't stay for long, though." Not sure why I'm telling you that, but whatever. I turn back around to face the crowd. I look right and lean to find that guy—is he still there staring at me? I don't see him. There are so many people here. Of course I don't see him. I've already forgotten what he looks like.

My head turns left. Two feet in front of me he stands. "How's your night?" Yeah, this is him.

"It's…good." "How's yours?"

"It was going well. Nice to catch a break out here, out of the dark room." "Have you been in it?"

"Uh, yeah, I checked it out."

"What did you think?"

"It was cool. I wasn't in there long." The music loud, I'm practically in his ear shouting.

He smiles at me. "Nice, I was in there too." "Guess we didn't bump into each other." "Otherwise I would have said hi."

I lean back to check him out more.

I don't think so?

I guess he's the same height as both the guys I fucked around with. Should I touch his body to see if it feels familiar? No, that's weird. Maybe grab his face? Jesus. I shake my head. "I guess not."

He nods at me slow, eyes squinting a little. What is he thinking? "How was your shot?"

"It was good, thanks." "I don't think I've had that type of shot before."

"Really? You haven't?" He steps to my left and sets his drink and hands down at the bar. "Let's do another."

He's cute.

Sure. "Yeah, okay." I nod. "Why not?" Maybe I'll get off with him and move on with my life. He's good enough.

He smiles and nods. "Yeah, why not?" He sips his cocktail, staring at me. Flags the bartender and orders more shots; looks back at me—checking me out. "Where you from?"

I hate this question. I hate sharing details of my identity with people.

"Ah, I'm from…" Guess it doesn't matter anymore. I don't need to hide anything from anyone here, I guess. "I'm from Kentucky." "I actually drive back in a few hours."

"Oh, you are?" "Lucky me, I'm catching you before." His smile kind of making me feel suspicious. But why? "Nice." "I've never been." The shots appearing in front of him, he hands the bartender his card to pay.

He points for me to look across the club. "See the DJ booth over there?" I take one step and look that direction.

"Down yonder?" "Where?"

Him behind me. "Keep lookin' in that corner, you'll see it." My head feels kinda funny. I don't see it.

I turn back to him and step back. "Sorry, I don't see it, too much goin' on in here." "Why you want me to see it?"

"Oh, I just am friends with the DJ. Was pointing him out to you."

"Okay…cool." Why does that matter? My attention still on the dance floor and away from him. Did Eugene ever come? Do people like meeting the DJ?

"Here's your shot." He nudges my arm with my shot glass in his hand, his other hand holding his. "Cheers to new friends."

Friends? I thought he was flirting with me? I turn to cheers him and take the shot.

He continues to ask me more questions; I keep trying to avoid direct answers. I don't think I'm into him? But the free booze was nice. How do I get out of this? Twenty minutes stuck in this conversation is enough. I keep scanning the crowd, practically ignoring him. Why are the figures now blurry and the lights beginning to spin? Wow…*I feel drunk*. I put the bottom of my forearms on the bar to rest. Why do I feel more drunk than I should? Hm. I've only had a few gulps and a couple shots… recently. *Right?* Wait, what have I had? It's hard to count. How many at dinner? Maybe three. And the house party, a beer and…? I can't think. I look at the guy, my vision pulsating a bit and my ability to keep focus fading fast.

"What is your naame?" My speech changing.

"You don't need to know it."

Ouch. My lips pressing against each other. I mean, I get it. I lied about my name here for months to everyone. I guess that's what I get. *"Karma is a bitch"* comes out under my breath.

"Did you just say 'karma is a bitch'?" His hand appearing on my forearm.

"Yeah." I want to say more, but I can't. My balance giving. My hands and fingers spread with pressure down; I'm forcing them to hold me up at the bar.

The bartender's boyish face in front of me. "You okay? Hey! You okay?" He snaps his fingers in front of my face. What does he want? I don't want anything else to drink. And I can't tell him, the words spiraling away from me in my head.

I close my eyes and shake my head, my head falling forward, down, chin against my chest, forehead continuing down, planting on the bar. I can't come up. I'm drained. How did I get so drained? My fight or flight kicking in and fighting to keep me balanced and not let me fall over. My mind on a loop of thoughts, but I can't keep a single one. My knees losing their lock, giving way to my weight; I can't let them. The pulsating sensation from my eyes, now in my kneecaps.

My right ear:

"You really don't remember, uh, do you?"

Is that the same guy talking to me?

My head popping up from the bar counter, looking left. Where am I? The bright, colorful lights spinning faster and flashing brighter. I'm stuck, falling in a rainbow to death. My legs unable to hold my weight up. Eugene, where are you? What do you even look like? I can't remember your face. Your beautiful, majestic face. I wish we had more time.

My torso all of a sudden embraced. Someone is holding me? A person? Can I let them take my weight? I don't have a choice. My eyes closed. The darkness and music sending me to a different universe. Am I dying?

This is it, isn't it. I'm finally paying for my sins.

God is done with me. Finished with me.

Disappointed to the point of not coming back. Killing me in the place that I should have never come. What I deserve. Lucy, I'm sorry; at least you won't see it. And now you can really move to someone better for you.

"John." "John!" Something shouting in my left ear. "Roy!" "I got you!" "Hey!" "Wake up!" A sting across my face. "Wake up!" Another sting and pressure on my cheek. My eyes fight to open. A thing I recognize. *Richard*

39

THIS LEATHER SMELLS GOOD. My eyes open. My body lying sideways somewhere. Fuck, my head is pounding. A camel-colored leather chair sideways a few feet from me, with chrome armrests. My right cheek against a stiff pillow. I lift my head up to look at the clean chair up to my right, the chrome so shiny and bright that I follow the light bouncing off to look across further to my right—windows larger than I've ever seen. Wow, the glass from the floor all the way to the ceiling. Black blinds halfway down from the ceiling. Where am I? The living room lit as if I'm outside while a dark storm blows in—a still, ominous gray. Hm.

My eyes scan through the windows to see across. Glass buildings, further reflecting the hue. Fuck, what time is it? And I need a Tylenol.

"You're awake." "Good," I hear coming from the direction of my feet.

My head whips left as fast as it can under the throbbing pain. A man sitting with his legs crossed in an identical camel-colored leather chair, just opposite the one next to me.

Ramón

I try to sit up to get eye level, but struggle.

He puts his hand up at me. "Take it easy, Roy." "You're okay."

I stare directly at him, my elbows propping me up. Wait. "You know my real name?"

"Yeah." "I do know your real name." His voice calm. Calmer than I would have ever expected when imagining him learning who I am.

A smile comes across my face; I can't help it. Subtle and small but, still, a smile. I finally feel lighter.

Wait, why is he so calm?

I force my torso up more, bring my knees to my chest and turn my body to sit upright on the couch, then put my feet down on the floor. My head pounding louder. Shit…maybe that was too quick. A fluffy black blanket that was on me falling down to the floor off the couch. I lean down to pick it up. My eyes level with and inches from the coffee table.

Oh my god

Is that…? My body freezing with my chest on my knees.

Can it be? Or am I imagining?

I squeeze my eyes shut and open them again.

The letter

My uncle's letter. It's opened, Andrew's handwritten words finally exposed. The envelope right next to it: *David Stevens* from Kentucky and *Ramón Ramirez* from New York. My fingers spread through the plush cloth; I close them to grab the blanket; my torso leans back until it hits the back of the couch in a resting position—my hand releasing the blanket next to me, on my right.

I look left to him. "So…you found my letter."

"Yes, I did."

Silence between us. Okay? What now? Why isn't he saying anything?

"Um." I clear my throat. "How did I get here?" "Why am I here?"

"How did you get here?" "You don't remember?" Is he

giving me shit? Why not just answer my question? Clearly I don't.

"Uh." I look right to see past the half-exposed windows, the light too much for me. My hand pops up to shade my eyes, and my head lands back forward toward the coffee table, eyes back on the letter. I did it; son of a bitch finally got it. "By chance you got a Tylenol or somethin'?" "My head feels like oversized balloons keep poppin' off." I glance his direction. No movement at all. "Did you hear me?" I shut my eyes and keep my head down and my hand shading my face. I can hear my breathing; it's so quiet.

"Yeah, I heard you." "But I have a question first."

Oh? Fuck. "Yeah, whatever." "Ask." "What is it?" "Anything to get some water and some fuckin' meds." "You're holdin' me hostage here." Is there a bathroom nearby? I glance at different corners of the living room. I'm not sure. I don't think I can stand up yet, anyways. I shut my eyes back.

"Something I guess we might have in common?" His reply confusing to me.

"In common?" I shake my head. "What are you talkin' about?"

"Nothing." "Here's my question." "How old is that letter?"

How old is the letter? Why the fuck does that matter? "What?" "That's your big question?" "Out of everything that letter says and finding out who I am—your only question is how old is it?"

"It's not my only question, but it's the most important." "How long have you kept that letter from me, Roy?" "David always dated everything he wrote—that letter doesn't have a date on it." He nods at it in front of me. "Who wrote it, and when was it written?"

My right hand comes off from covering my face, and my eyes open, my left arm sliding on top of the back of the couch and my body shifting to face him more. "…Summer, this year." "A few months ago." I look at him and then look down. "I came here to give it to you—to New York City, that is. For him." "Didn't you see the envelope?" I nod at it on the coffee table. "For some reason he mailed it to where Eugene and Richard live." "And someone wrote 'return to sender.'"

"Is he still alive?" "Why didn't he just call me?" "Why send his nephew to spy on me?"

"He didn't." "He doesn't know I'm here, actually." "I chose to come." "Well, kind of was forced to, actually…" More silence between us. "And 'why didn't he just call'? I don't know; you'll have to ask him." Ramón scanning me like an opponent scans the other in a high-stakes game of poker. What is he searching for out of me?

"Is he alive?" he asks again.

"I think so." "My…friend, Andrew, is, well…was one of his nurses at a nursing home he's in—he's the one that wrote it for him." "That's his handwriting." "My uncle has stage-four lung cancer and recently had a stroke that paralyzed most of him from the neck down."

Ramón still with his legs crossed, remaining silent, observing me. What else should I say? "Last night I talked with Andrew. He said this morning some head nurse or whatever was gonna make the call to transfer him to hospice." "I guess he ain't eatin' or drinkin' no more." "I guess he's been that way for a bit." "I begged him to stop them, at least until I get back." "I'm driving back today…now, actually—what time is it?" I have to get home. I need to talk to Andrew. My hands skip to my lap and feel nothing. I push my pelvis up, sliding my hands under my butt—where is my phone? "Ramón, where is my phone?"

"Your phone?" He's as confused as I am.

"Yes. My phone." My voice louder.

"You didn't have one on you when Richard and Eugene brought you here."

"Richard *and* Eugene brought me here?" "Why?" "I don't remember that." "And who emptied all my pockets? Huh?" "Why did they do that?"

"The boys brought you up a few hours ago." "You passed out at the bar, Roy." "Richard and Eugene carried you out, brought you here." "Richard thinks someone drugged you." "Do you remember any of it?"

"For fuck's sake." "Can I have a bottle of Tylenol, please?" "Somethin'? My head hurts." No, I don't recall if someone drugged me. That's the point of getting drugged, ain't it? So the stupid son of a bitch drugged doesn't remember shit.

What is my last memory?

Ramón uncrosses his legs and stands up quickly for his age. Finally.

"I'm sorry, I forgot you asked. Yes, I'll grab you some water and something to take now." He walks away, in the direction of the kitchen, across the room, forward from me. His place is so… clean. Tall and nice. Random art everywhere. Paintings on the walls, art pieces of various sizes on end tables, and stand-alone pieces by the windows and the staircase. His largest wall art being Michelangelo's *Creation of Man* I think it's called? But an artist added rainbow colors to God's hand. Hm. That's an interesting take.

Does he live here? Eat here? I've never been in a model home, but this could be one. All this time…I never made it to his place, until now. Had to take getting me drugged by some fags at a circuit party to get my ass here. I look up. *Thanks for that.*

What's your last memory, Roy? Think. The group of fags on the street; I followed them into the club—the dark room. Yes, I went into the dark room. Did I make it out? I can't remember past the dark room. Poppers. Fuck, that shit smelled nasty. Bleh. My body squirms at the thought—a memory I wish I could've forgotten.

"Hey, what are poppers," I blurt out toward him across his apartment. Maybe that's what drugged me.

Noise coming from the kitchen as he searches in cabinets. "Poppers?" I hear him question far away. I pat my pockets again and then push my hands inside all of them; they really are all empty. Nothing. Not so much as even an empty gum wrapper. My phone, my car keys. Fuck. Who took all my shit? How am I gonna get home?

He appears in front of me, setting down three reddish-brown pills and a bottle of water. "Why are you asking me about poppers?"

"Is that what drugged me?" "A fag—guy I met in the dark room." Okay, here we go…am I doing this? Talking about the dark room with Ramón? Fuck it. "Offered me poppers, and then I got a whiff of somethin' nasty." "Is that what did it?" "And what are those?" I nod at the three pills.

"Ibuprofen."

My body doesn't move to grab.

"Take it." "Three is good for you; it will clear your headache up." Can I trust him? "It's 9:02, by the way." Phew, just a bit past 9 a.m. I'm on schedule, then, to make it home at a decent time. Good. I grab the pills and chug them down.

"No, it wasn't poppers that fucked you up. Probably something else." "Some form of G."

"G?" "What is that?"

"Why didn't you tell me who you were?" He sits back down in his seat and crosses his legs again, arms lax on the shiny armrests. Why are you ignoring my question?

My throat clearing. "Listen, I'd love to play this weird father-son catch-up thing." My hands zigzagging in the air between us. "But I gotta get back to Kentucky. I gotta somehow find that club first, see if they have my phone and car keys."

"Your car keys are here." "They are by the door on the hallway table." "Eugene drove your car here." Thank god. Finally some good news, at least. Shit, I wonder if I said anything stupid to him fucked up?

"You know where he parked my car?"

"Yes, it is in my building garage; I have an extra spot."

"Maybe your phone is in the car." "As soon as you're ready, I'll walk you to it."

"Okay." "Thank you." The cold bottle of water in my hand, halfway empty. My headache slightly less awful. I chuckle to myself—I actually found Eugene, but my dumbass doesn't even remember it. For sure I made a fool of myself with my last interaction with him forever. Probably for the better. Make a fool of myself so we can move on from each other easier.

"What's so funny?"

"Nothin'." I shake my head. "Just nothin'."

Silence between us. A few car honks in the faint distance from the city street below, outside his windows. "How far up are we?"

"Why haven't you told me who you were all this time?" "Why didn't you give me that letter when we first met?"

My head down, eyes forward, looking at the beautiful flowers in the center of his coffee table, freshly bought—he have a maid or something? Or does he do all of this on his own? Clean and decorate his place like a woman. "I don't know, Ramón." "I don't know anything."

"That's not true." "You do know some things."

"Oh yeah?" "What do I know?" "Please, enlighten me." I look at him and bounce my eyebrows up, eager to learn what this geezer has had to offer all this time. What'd I miss? Please. Do tell.

His face reacting as if I just slapped away his inner thoughts as insignificant. "You now know the truth about your uncle, truth about me." His voice agitating me. "Truth about Frank." Frank. "Question is—do you know the truth about yourself?"

"Truth about myself?" What the fuck is he talking about? "And what about Frank?" My attention serious. An answer finally about Frank—he has to know something. "What do you know about Frank?"

"What did your uncle tell you about Frank?"

"Tell me?" "He hasn't told me a goddamn thing." Thinking

about his secrets and escapades of deceit soft boiling my blood. "That's why I have to get back to Kentucky today." "Last we spoke, he told me he would tell me in person—I figure it's more bullshit I gotta clean up for him before he dies." "Why?" "What can you tell me now about Frank?" "My uncle owe him some money?" "Sleep with his wife, and he wants vengeance? I have a brother out there somewhere I don't know about?" "Or how 'bout another ex-lover-boyfriend thing?" "Frank a fag you two had a threesome with that went wrong?" "Fuck, ain't nothin' can surprise me now."

"Stop using that word." Ramón's voice commanding, strong.

"Or what?"

His posture still, expression like a lion watching prey limping in front of it. Don't you feel sorry for me. There ain't nothing to feel sorry for. Why are you looking at me like that?

He hesitates from a breath in and presses his lips closed, and then finally spits it out. "Frank is your father, Roy."

40

———

"My what?" What in the godforsaken hell is he talking about? "No, my father's name was John." "And he died when I was five."

"No." "Your father's name is Frank." "You were lied to." "And stop using that word, because if you're gonna talk with me, you're gonna respect me."

"Or what?"

"I won't share with you anything else—how about that?" Ramón puts his hand in front of his face, tracing his goatee with his thumb and fingers. I can stop saying that word, *fag*, *faggot*, whatever. I've tried to stop before. I can do it. I don't know why I keep saying it, anyways.

Is he telling the truth?

If Frank was my real father, why did my uncle run from him? Lie to me that his name was John, keep me from him? I need to know. Play nice, Roy. You sure as hell ain't getting answers from your uncle, so squeeze it out of Ramón.

"Okay, I'll stop sayin' it." "And I'm sorry I didn't give you the letter sooner." "That part about my uncle sayin' I would have been better off had you raised me—had me curious, I think, to maybe get to know you." "I see now it was kinda weird; fucked up—a mistake." "I'm sorry."

His hand comes from his face, back to resting on the armchair. "Why do you think your uncle wrote this to me? His last, dying words?" Ramón's energy shifting. I think hearing himself say that out loud, *last, dying words*, is doing something to him. Is Ramón still single? It's a little late for that, anyhow…

"I don't know." "I guess that's why I stayed here, to find out; I just told you that." "None of this makes sense." "And now you're tellin' me I was lied to about my father." "By my own blood?" "His own brother?" "Why?"

Silence between us. He doesn't want to speak.

"Three months ago I heard this crazy story that a man was the love of my uncle's life; then I find out he believes this man should have raised me instead of him; to now he's sitting in front of me, and I've seen his gay life in New York City." "It's been a lot." "Wouldn't you be curious if you were in my shoes?" "It's been a roller coaster of confusions, to be fuckin' honest." "And I thought this ride was near over, and now you're tellin' me this." "I should have just given you the letter the day I met you and been done with." "Done with it all."

"And what have you thought?"

"What do you mean, what have I thought?"

"What have you thought about New York City? And me? And Eugene?" "What do you think about all of it?"

"Why does it matter what I think?" "I have a wife back home; a baby on the way." "My life is happy in Frankfort."

"A baby on the way?" He uncrosses his legs and leans forward.

"Yes, I just found out last night that my wife is several months pregnant." "I need to get back to her; I've been away too long."

He nods. "I see." His eyes roll and land somewhere off looking into the kitchen. "Congratulations." "Your father would have been proud." He almost sounds sarcastic? Who is he talking about? Did he know Frank, or is he talking about Uncle David? He crosses his hands and sets them in his lap. "You think returning back to Frankfort and your old life is best for your wife, and that baby?"

"What type of question is that?" "Of course I do." "I've always worked for and have wanted to have a family."

"That is what truly makes you happy?" "You're thirty-four; why did it take you so long?" "Being loyal to Lucy…and raising a child with her?" "Are you sure?"

Wait a minute.

"How do you know my wife's name is Lucy?"

His eyes bounce off me and head turns slightly down.

I ask again, "How do you know her name is Lucy?"

"Your uncle told me."

"What?"

"He wrote to me last maybe ten years ago." "We used to exchange letters here and there throughout the years." Hm. That would've been around the time Lucy and I got married.

"You did?" "Why?"

"I don't know." "Maybe it was nice to catch up with an old friend."

Ramón is staring at the envelope on the coffee table. A tear falls down his cheek.

"If he wrote to you ten years ago, why did he have your address wrong?"

"I moved; where Eugene and Richard live is my old apartment." "Your uncle had no way in knowing that." "I actually own the building." You own the building? How rich is this guy?

"So Eugene or Richard wrote 'return to sender' on that letter?" "Is that what you're sayin'?"

"I don't know." He wipes the tear off his cheek and rubs his eyes. For a second I was thinking you were the one that wrote the *return to sender*. Why would Eugene or Richard do that if they are, like, your best friends?

Silence between us.

"Tell me about my father." "This Frank."

He shakes his head.

"Did my father, Frank, come back for me in 1992? And my uncle was too selfish to give me back?" Heat of anger spiking through my veins. That lying bastard. Or is Ramón lying to me now? But why would Ramón lie to me? My father came back for me, and my uncle kept me from him. Rage. My veins filling with rage. To be lied to for this long; taken for a fool my whole life.

Noise from a door opening behind the wall of the kitchen, echoing through to us in the living room

Who is that? Who does Ramón live with? I thought we were alone. My ears and eyes search for clarity; a voice I know, it sends a new quake inside. My veins hot as lava, and this voice a mist over them, sending calm—relief. It's his voice. I hear his voice! He's here. *Eugene.* Come out from the hallway; I'm here. Let me see you. I ache for you now. I need to see you to believe it. I didn't go anywhere. I'm right here. You found me.

41

"THAT WAS QUICK." Ramón speaking louder toward the kitchen. Eugene entering, holding two plastic bags.

Richard behind him.

A flash of Richard getting plowed on the dance floor by that gorilla shooting back to memory. Good! Yes! That was after the dark room, and then I went to the bar—looking for Eugene.

I was looking for him.

My eyes now on his real presence. He's here. He looks good. A yellow tank, his olive skin looking tan in the overcast daylight filling Ramón's apartment, arm muscles popping from the strain of the bags he brought in. His thick veins that stretch from his shoulders to his wrists. I smile; I can't help it. I'm so happy to see him, and I'm sober now. I'm gonna remember this. We can talk; we can leave things on good terms—I hope.

"Yeah, line wasn't too bad." Eugene sets the bags on the kitchen counter. Richard walks past behind him and rummages through the cabinets, finds plates, and sets them out.

"How are you feeling?" Eugene's eyes into mine from the kitchen. "Richard and I got breakfast for everyone. Are you hungry?"

I look left at Ramón, catching him observing me, and then

look forward at Eugene. "Yes, ahem…please." "I would love to eat some breakfast with you guys." My headache gone.

"Good. We waited twenty minutes for this food, so you better like it and be grateful." Richard yapping out with sass. I'm actually gonna miss this little slut.

Eugene and Richard come from the kitchen, each of them holding a plate of food in each hand. Richard hands Ramón a plate and sits next to me on my left. He's wearing a hat, *MC* in big letters in the center of it.

Why does that look familiar?

MC…Where did I last see that? And what does it stand for? There is a McCormick's Construction company back home. But that can't be it?

Eugene hands me a plate and goes to sit next to me on my right. Just before he sits, I pick up the blanket. Sit next to me under it, please—for us to share it. He accepts my offer and gets comfortable next to me, pulling the blanket over himself. Our thighs touch underneath. The warmth of his body sending a flurry to my chest.

His eyes level with mine, our shoulders touching, too, the heat of his bare skin against me. "How are you feeling?" he asks.

"Good." "What happened last night?" "Do you know where my phone is?"

"I tried calling and texting you." "You never replied, and then I found Richard near the entrance of the club, carrying you out with someone else."

"I actually was looking for you." I can't hold it back.

"You were?"

"Yeah, the phone I had—I lost." "So I had my old phone and phone number, a phone number none of you have." "I figured you might be at the party, from Richard talking about it at dinner." "I didn't want you to think I would ignore you."

He smiles at me, chewing through his breakfast sandwich. Even with his mouth full of pieces of bacon and egg, I'd still kiss it. I'd kiss it anywhere with anything in it. Well, maybe not anything?

Would I do that with Lucy?

Have I ever felt this way about Lucy? Or a woman in general?

Of course you have, Roy; you just have lost sight of it. Don't compare the two. There is nothing to compare. These emotions are not real. Get it together, eat your sandwich, and go. You've spent enough time already chitchatting and wasting time. I bite big into my breakfast bagel. God, I'm gonna miss New York City food. Why is it always so good?

"So, we read your uncle's letter." Richard to my left, chewing, with sauce dripping from the corner of his mouth, unwilling to wipe it clean. You probably like that feeling there, don't ya? I shake my head. The *MC* on his head still puzzling me. I never forget things. Why am I forgetting this?

My eyes look back down at the letter, then glance at Eugene, then to Ramón, then land on Richard, and then back to Eugene. "You *all* read it?" "Why?" "Isn't that like an invasion of privacy?" "Why would you guys do that?" "What's wrong with y'all?"

Richard coughs and chuckles as he swallows. "What's wrong with us?" "Honey, you do realize you invaded all of our lives, hiding who you are, were—and now you want to point at us like we are the bad ones invading privacy for reading some letter that should have been read months ago?" "But hey, I finally understand at least your urgency that day on Grindr." "And why you didn't fuck me after all." He lunges his shoulder into mine —trying to be silly. None of this is funny. God, this kid is relentless at every hour of the day. Is there an off button somewhere? Can someone drug him, please? Maybe I won't miss him. I chuckle to myself.

It feels kind of good to finally be seen, I guess. No more hiding. In this very moment, they are seeing me for me. A mess, but at least a truthful mess. At least, I'm being truthful to them.

Not gonna be truthful much longer here today as I figure out my next hurdles to get my old life back.

Ramón raises his hand up. "Give it a rest, Richard. It's okay." "It's better that all of us now know the truth." The truth? My uncle likes that line—*truth will always set you free*. Is that biblical? I can't remember.

"My uncle liked the line, 'Truth will always set you free.'" "I do feel as if a weight has been lifted." "I'll be returning to Frankfort today and tell him his truth was set free today with you, Ramón." "If that's what you wish." Ramón silent, eating his food—with grace and small bites, wiping his mouth after each. "Is there anything you want me to say to him—from you?" "You wanna write something down, or tell me something to say in person to him?"

He continues chewing and swallows. The boys next to me completely silent, all of us waiting.

"Yeah." "Tell him that I forgive him and I am here now, healthy and alive, and I will be here for you too."

Here for me too? What? I don't need you here for me. Why are you saying that? "Uh, okay." "That's nice of you…I guess. I will tell him that." "And I don't need anythin' from you." "But thanks."

"Roy, I'm serious." "I wasn't able to be there for you before, for unfortunate reasons that I now know why were kept from me, but I can be here for you now, in anything you need."

I don't need anything. Well, if one thing—can you teach me how to get rid of this…disease?

No, you can't.

Teach me how to be anything BUT you and my uncle? Can you do that for me? I don't think so. So there really is nothing you can offer me.

Why are they all being so nice to me? This one here on my left I punched in the face hours ago; Ramón, you I've stalked and have lied to; Eugene, I've led on, selfishly. "Why are you all bein' so nice to me?" My attention on Ramón. Hands in my lap, holding my bagel half eaten, my rumbling appetite feeling gone.

"I'm treating you no different than I would treat my friends sitting right next to you."

"I mean all of this." I nod at the food, blanket, and letter in a circular formation. "Allowin' them to bring me on your couch." "To not havin' a bad reaction to finding out who I am." "Y'all feedin' me breakfast this mornin'." "Sittin' here eatin' together like everything and all of this is normal and okay?"

"We are friends, Roy." "This is what friends do."

"Do what?"

"Show up for each other." "Even when it's hard or you don't understand every detail, but you trust and know your friend might need some grace." "Some empathy."

He thinks I need empathy? Why?…A light bulb turns on in the deepest depth of my brain. "You've known all this time who I've been, haven't you?"

Ramón looks down, and then back up to lock eyes with me.

"Haven't you?!" "Say it!"

Eugene setting his hand on my arm. "Roy…it's okay."

"Say it!" I shout louder. Richard pressing his face back into his neck against the couch. His tell gives me more evidence.

"I did," Ramón admits with confidence.

I don't even know what to think. "Why?"

"Why what?" Ramón says.

"Why let me make a fool of myself?" "…I understand your statement now." "You kept me hostage, withholding information that would set me free." "You think I did the same to you."

"Yeah…well, something like that." "Looks like we both may have been curious about one another."

"Well, all good things come to an end, whatever the fuck this was."

My left hand lifts the plate off my lap, tossing it toward the flowers in the center of the coffee table. My right arm shoving forward to release Eugene's hand. I stand up, and the blanket falls off to the ground, pulling his breakfast plate down with it, the hardy food and orange hot sauce rolling across Ramón's white carpet. I step over the blanket and food. "I have to go, I'm already behind schedule." I start walking toward the kitchen to slip into the hallway I think the boys entered the apartment from. I holler back, "Ramón, you're walkin' me out, remember?" I slip past the wall and find the hallway to exit.

"Roy, come on, don't end things like this."

"Come back here."

I don't know who is hollering that to me from the living room. I don't care. I need to get back to Frankfort. The mission is over.

A bench and table down to the right, next to the apartment door in the hallway. I walk to the bench. My emotions unhuman —no human could interpret or understand—I sit on the bench and scan the table. Is he coming or what?

My keys

They are here, thank god. "Ramón!" I shout. "Come on!" "Let's go." "I gotta go." My ears stretching for a clue—*movement of some sort, their voices among each other.* "I have to go now!"

My attention on the inside of Ramón's apartment door, I hear soft steps approaching behind me and no more voices. I turn my head to see the geezer finally coming.

Eugene

Why? Can't you just leave me alone?

42

"Roy." "Stop!" I hear behind me.

My keys crunched in my hand, I don't know where I'm going. An exit door up ahead, down the hallway outside Ramón's apartment. That has to lead to the building stairs. I'll find the parking garage myself.

"I can't believe you're doing this to me again." "Running." "Why am I wasting time on you still?" His voice cracking. "If you want to leave, go!" His shout and cries fill the hallway behind me. My body reacts and stops walking.

I don't want to leave you, Eugene. But I have to.

I turn around. He's sitting on the floor with his back up against the wall, knees popped up; his hands over his face, face between his legs. I walk over to him. How can he think he feels this strongly about me? I mean. What are we? What were we?

I squat down in front of him, my hand set on his knee. He glides a hand over it and keeps his other hand trying to cover his crying face. His chest and throat shaking. Jesus, Eugene.

As calmly as I can: "Eugene." "I have to go." Another quake inside of me, erupting larger than I thought could happen. Shit…this is what I was trying to avoid. Tears filling my eyes, the lava inside nowhere to go but out—and it's true, lava *is* inside; real, hot, emotional lava.

"Eugene." "I'm not the one…or the guy for you."

His hand falls from his face. He wipes it clean on his thigh, his face red and cheeks wet and dewy. "That's not what you said to me last night." "It's not." "You don't know yourself, Roy." "You don't know yourself like I do."

My throat swallows. *Said to him last night?* What did I say to him last night? "It doesn't matter what I said last night—Eugene." I lean my head in. "I have a wife back home; her name is Lucy." "I have a child on the way." "She is pregnant." "My uncle is dying." "I need to return back home." "I need to let my uncle know I found Ramón and gave him the letter so he can rest in peace. I need to be a better man to my wife, a better father to my soon-to-be son or daughter." "You have to understand this?"

"That's truly what you think?" His cries gone. Now trying to breathe through his congested nose. His mystic, wet eyes on me, challenging me; pushing me—questioning me? God, I never want to forget these eyes. But I have to. I need to forget you.

"Yes, it is truly what I think."

"I don't agree."

"You don't agree?"

"No, I don't agree. I don't think that's best for you—for your wife, and for that child coming."

"Well, it's not up to you to agree or disagree." I stand up from my squatted position away from him.

He stands right up with me too. "Don't you get it, Roy?" "Don't you see how your uncle has all of these regrets? You don't have to be like him. You don't have to live life the way he did." "You can make better choices for yourself, and those around you."

"I don't know what you're talkin' about." "I am not my uncle. I am NOTHING like him." I get in his face.

"Yes, I think you are." "You know you are."

"You have no idea what you're talkin' about." "You read that letter." I point past him at Ramón's apartment door down the hallway. "My uncle fell into sin, thinkin' he was in love with a man." "His lust takin' over and poisoning his mind into delusions." "I am not my uncle; I will never be in love with a man." "I will never touch a man for the rest of my life." "This was all a mistake." "What don't you get?" "I am not like him, or Ramón." "I don't want this life—or you."

A pit in my stomach.

Am I telling him the truth? Am I telling myself the truth? It doesn't matter.

He steps back, the open hallway behind him. "That's not what you said to me last night."

"Enough with what I said last night, Eugene." "I don't even remember!" "I already told you: What I said last night doesn't matter." "I was drugged, and drunk." "People say 'n' do shit all of the time when they are drunk, and—especially drugged." "Have you ever been drugged before?" "Hm?" "How did you behave and what did you say?" "Did you mean it all?"

"You're not even gonna ask me what you said to me, are you?"

"No." "And don't te—"

"You told me you have never felt for anyone ever before, the way you feel for me." "You said we are a cosmic connection." "One in a billion." "Your words, not mine."

I actually said that? No way I said all that shit to him. No fucking way. "Well, like I said, I was drunk and drugged." "I didn't mean it." My voice stern, my fist clenched, resting on the hallway wall at eye level between us. He glances at it; so do I. He has seen how this fist swings.

"I think you did." "And you wanna know what I said back to you?" His stance still and calm.

"No, Eugene, I don't." "Just stop." "Please." "I don't!" I can't break his eye contact, my body can't break facing him.

Turn around and walk, Roy. I can't! What did you say? My heart a rumbling volcano.

"I told you that I feel the same way." He responds softly. "I also told you—"

"What?" One word snapping from my mouth, my teeth now shut tight inside. Don't say it…Don't say it.

"Roy, I told you that I love you."

The volcano erupting, flooding my insides. The lava, sensations of euphoric heat. My brain stormy clouds sending rain down. It's not how it feels. It's a lie.

"Eugene…" "Where did you park my car?" "I have to go."

43

I love you.

The words and his face saying them on constant replay in my mind. *I love you…I love you.*

What does he know about love?

What we had. What we were doing. That wasn't love. Love is between a man and a woman. Love creates life between a man and a woman. Love between a man and a man is just… wrong. Sick. God is challenging me with this sin to live with, and I am failing. I am failing, and all those around me are suffering from my failure.

What good has come from *all* of this? Nothing. Ever since the first guy I met. His face wrecked by me; another man I watched get hit by his wife in front of their kids. And me? I hit my own goddamn wife.

And what about my uncle? What did he benefit? Nothing either.

He's dying alone. Shitty wife in the end who isn't by his side —maybe she knows. Maybe Sheila knows about my uncle and his gay affairs. Maybe she saw one of the letters between him and Ramón over the years? But why would she stay with him? And for all those years? Either way, he chose to give light to this sin and now deserves to die alone. No kids. No wife. His body giving up on him, unable to live with or hold the sin anymore. I don't want that. I won't have that. I'm gonna do things right. I can control this. I am in control.

I glance at the car clock. 1:17 p.m.

Traffic ain't that bad, given it's lunch hour. My phone face up, plugged into the car, charging. Thank god I found it on the floor in the back seat. Andrew must be sleeping—after several calls and no response. I'm sure he'll call me back as soon as he wakes. I need an update on my uncle. I hope they didn't transfer him to hospice this morning.

I guess I could call the nursing home? Would they tell me? Maybe that's not a good idea…More people would know I'm returning back to town. And I don't know the status on my warrants. What am I doing? Is making it to my uncle in time before he dies worth going to jail for? I need to return back, regardless. I can't run and hide forever.

Jesus, Lucy. Call me back. I need to know what I'm getting into. How much of a cover do I need to keep?

Incoming call from Lucy Stevens

Perfect!

"Hey!" "How's your lunch hour? I'm on the road and making good time." "As you can also see by now, I got my old phone back."

"Hey." "It's okay. I'm not feeling too well, actually." "Took the day off and stayed home."

"Are you and the baby okay?"

"Yes, I think we both are." "What time are you gettin' in? You're comin' straight here, right?"

"Yes, of course." Guess I have to now. It's fine, I can see her first, and then chase Andrew and my uncle down after. My priority is Lucy. "Um." I scroll to the GPS on my phone. "I'll be home a little bit after ten. Will you wait up for me?" "I can't wait to kiss you 'n' hold you."

"Yeah, I'll wait up for you."

"Great." "I'm lookin' forward to seein' ya, hun, and the baby bump." "I bet you look so beautiful."

"Roy."

"What?"

"Nothing." Her voice sounds like it has more to say? "I'm lookin' forward to seeing ya, too, but I'm still angry at you."

"I know, I know." "I hope and pray in time you'll forgive me." "We can move past all of this, like it never happened." "I promise."

"Well, it did happen." "Might be a little harder for me to forgive and forget than you hope." "I can work on forgiveness; I'm not so sure about *forget*."

"Lucy, I promise you I am returnin' back a better man." "This quest I got put on to make my uncle rest well before he goes has opened my eyes." "They are open for you, for this baby, for us." "It was one mistake; it won't happen ever again—I swear to god." "I'll stop drinking." "I'll never lie to you again."

"Really?"

"Really."

"You swear to God it won't happen ever again?" "That's a big oath." "You know I take a promise to God seriously."

"Of course I do; we've been goin' to the same church together since we were kids; I know this, Lucy." "…Yes, you go more than I, and your faith is probably a bit stronger, but I will work on mine." "I swear to God I won't ever hurt you again the way I have."

"Okay." "I hear you."

"When was the last time you saw my uncle, by the way?" "Also, the warrant for my arrest? What did you do about that?"

"Um." "I saw him a few weeks ago." "I went to visit him, checked on his health, also asked if he's heard from you." "He told me he hadn't." "His health has really declined." "You should see him as soon as you can."

"I will; thank you for tellin' me." "What about Sergeant Keaton?" "Her and I spoke a few months ago. She told me about the warrant." "Do you know if it's still active or somethin'?"

"I don't know, Roy." "I told you I would go to the police and retract my statement. I'll do that today while you are drivin' here."

"Really?"

"Yes." "Really." "We can start fresh." "I want to try." "I do believe that you love me."

"I do."

"Okay." "I'll see you later then when you get in."

Another man's voice in the background

"Lucy, who is that with you?" I ask.

"My daddy."

"Why is your daddy in our apartment?"

"I called him and told him I wasn't feelin' well today; he brought me some soup."

"I'm sorry." A feeling of shame, deep shame wraps over my skin tight. "It should be me bringin' ya soup."

44

10:36 P.M. I look past the car clock up at the back of our apartment building. I made it. I'm finally back home. My journey on the run over.

Why didn't Andrew call me back all day? Let me try him again before I go in. I swipe to my call list and tap his name. Did something happen to him? Shit, maybe that meeting didn't go well about his cousin?

Ring…ring…ring…ring…ring…ring… "Your call has been forwarded to an—"

I remove the phone from my ear.

Tap

He knew I was coming back today. Why would he go MIA on me? He sounded fine yesterday. Hm.

Okay, go inside, say hello to and kiss my wife, and then I'll drive up to the nursing home and see if my uncle is still there. I've already snuck in before; shouldn't be a huge deal to do it again. Or maybe this time I should just ask a nurse working there if my uncle is there or not—maybe avoid having the cops called again on me.

I hop out of my car and start walking to my apartment. I wonder if she looks different and all with a pregnancy glow. I can't wait to see her. This Kentucky air, I missed it. Smells… clean, fresh. Good ol' country air. New York City offered many things; fresh air was not one of them.

"Mr. Stevens."

A voice behind me my body recognizes. *Why is she here?* The hairs on my back zinging.

My body stops in its tracks and turns around to see if it's true. Lo and behold, dressed in her uniform, it is her. "Sergeant Keaton." "Good evenin' to ya." I nod at her.

She appears from darkness between a line of parked cars, stops a few feet in front of me, and sets her hands in front of her with her thumbs tucked into her belt. "You're gettin' in pretty late. Where ya comin' from?"

Why are you here? "Is it late?" "I couldn't tell from the darkness and all." "The sun did set, didn't you realize too? Or do you need your vision checked?"

"Cut the shit, Roy." "You're in serious trouble, you know that?"

"Am I?" "How so?" "If you haven't noticed, I've been out of town for a bit, so I'm not too sure what you're referrin' too?"

"You think we let people run around here—hittin' their wives and gettin' away with it?" "Murder suspects run wild without bein' questioned?" "Or flee a scene from us in their cars like teenage kids caught smokin' pot?"

"I don't know what you're talkin' about." "I told you someone stole my car." "Did they flee from you?" "I'm sorry to hear that." "Anybody get hurt?"

"Don't act like you care about me or my officers." "Don't try to play me, Roy." "I am not the one." "I am your enemy." "I suggest you start bein' nice." "And start by tellin' the truth."

Be nice? Hm. "Why are you here now?" "How did you know I would be here?" Did things not go well at the station when Lucy went to remove her statement earlier? Fix that police report from that night? "It's almost eleven o'clock. Don't you have a life?" "I do." "And I'm tryin' to get to mine right now, if you'll excuse me."

"This is my life." "Work is my life."

I want to turn around and walk into my apartment building. But from the way she is standing and looking at me. I can't.

"So you're workin'?" "Right now?" My body transfers weight to one foot. Try to relax, Roy. *She's working.* The fear is creeping in.

"Yes, I am." "And you're under arrest for the suspicion of murder, domestic assault, and fleeing and eluding the cops."

Did she just say suspicion of murder? "Murder?" "What are you talkin' about, of murder?" "And domestic violence?" "Still?!" "No!" "Lucy told me she was goin' to the station today to fix this." "To retract what she said on that police report." "She didn't see you today?" She said she was sick; maybe she didn't make it? Or maybe her daddy talked her out of it. *Son of a bitch.* I thought this was handled!

She continues speaking gibberish "…*You have the right to remain silen*—"

"What?" "No." "You don't understand. I'm not goin' to jail. I can't!" "AND I'm not your guy." "I haven't even been here?!"

"…*Anything you say can and will be used against you in a court of law*—"

"Sergeant Keaton! STOP. Please." I turn and point to my apartment. "My wife is up there now. She's been expectin' me. She's been waiting for me all day—months actually. I haven't seen her in months. Go now!" I nod up at the apartment. "Knock on our door and see her waiting for me, go!" "We'll go together."

She's not letting me get a word in—"*You have the right to talk to a lawyer…have a lawyer with you during questioning*—"

"Why are you doin' this to me?" I screech. Should I run? No, I've run enough. Should I run to my wife? Sergeant Keaton will follow and be forced to speak with her—see her face-to-face. Will that work?

I need to see my uncle. Fuck, I should have gone to him first! I didn't come this far to get arrested in my fucking parking lot.

"*…If you cannot afford a lawyer, one will be appointed for you—*"

"Are you listenin' to me!" I holler. I can't help it. She's pushing me. Why isn't she listening to me? It's probably not a good move to yell at a cop when they're telling me to be nice. "MY WIFE IS UPSTAIRS AND WANTS ME TO COME HOME." "Stop this goddamn bullshit!"

She finally stops her gibberish and stares at me blank. "Roy, your wife is safe, away from you and with her daddy," she says calmly, then nods behind me. I turn around, and a wave of shock stifles me.

Lucy?

Standing on the sidewalk, her daddy next to her with his arm around her, holding her tight some thirty yards or so away in front of the back apartment building door…

It can't be.

"You MOTHERFUCKER!" My middle finger in the air at her daddy. "This is your doin', Paul, I know it!" "This is what you want—your daughter's husband put away?" Lucy beginning to cry. I can tell from the sound I hear and the jerks of her head. It's dark; I can only really see the dark masses of the two, but I know it's him and her. I turn back to Sergeant Keaton. "You don't understand: This is all her daddy; this isn't what my wife or I want." "She forgave me." "She understands I made a mistake—haven't you ever made a mistake you wish you could take back? I know you have!" "I've seen it!"

She holds her posture strong at me. Are you considering my comment? Hm? "Roy, I have to book you tonight." "Don't make this harder than it has to be." "I told you this would happen." "I warned you." "Now turn around and put your hands behind your back."

"No." My head shaking.

"No?" She surprised by my answer.

"NO." "This isn't what my wife wants." "This isn't what I

want." "Over half the things you're barkin' at me that I did—I didn't do." "What would *you* do if you were in my shoes?" "Hm?" "An innocent man."

"Roy, how about this…I have to arrest you tonight. There is no changin' that." "But I promise I will reach out directly to your wife, hear her side more, and help you." "Okay?"

I stand staring at her. Can I trust her? Can I trust Sergeant Keaton? Why should I? She's a woman that probably hates men like me. Men that are drunks and take shit out on their wives. It was one fucking accident. If only she knew. If only she knew how much I've grown and have changed. She would know I don't need to be arrested—booked, any of it! My body shakes, standing in front of her, lost in thought. How do I get out of this?

"Roy, turn around and put your hands behind your back." "Your wife is watching. Do it for her."

What type of bullshit manipulative cop work is that language? "My uncle."

"Your what?"

"Sergeant Keaton, my uncle is dyin'." "I was told he was maybe goin' to hospice today." "I haven't seen him in months, and I need to see him." "You can't arrest me right now—you can't." "Please! He's the only blood family I have left. I promised him I'd make it back in time." "Please, please don't do this." I fall to my knees, my hands flat on the concrete parking lot, her black boots in my peripheral vision. I've seen these boots before like this, just last time on the floor of my uncle's room. "I beg you." I can't believe I'm here again.

"Arrest me tomorrow, fine!" Yeah, that's a good idea. My head pops up from the ground. "I'll come in tomorrow. I will drive myself straight to the station after I see my uncle." "I swear it." "Put a tracker on me if you need right now, tie a location device on my ankle—whatever you want." "I ain't goin' anywhere." "I promise."

"Roy, get up from the ground and put your hands behind

your back like a man." "You're under arrest for the suspicion of murder, domestic violence, and fleeing and eluding."

My head dropping back down to the ground, *like a man*. Maybe Lucy's right: Maybe I ain't a man. Maybe I'm not the man I thought I was. I did think about turning myself in before —getting through this legal hurdle and then working to get my life back.

All right, Roy, stand up. What other options do I have?

Own your shit.

She said she would help you. Have a little faith in humanity. Her. Have a little faith it will all work out. Stand up, put your hands behind your back, and face Lucy with confidence. Show her your obedience to Sergeant Keaton as a way of committing to her. But letting Sergeant Keaton cuff me at my will shows Lucy I agree that I am guilty. I'm not. Well, aren't I a little? Come on, Roy.

I make my way back to standing. Look at Sergeant Keaton. "Okay"—I turn around, put my hands behind my back—"but I ain't commit no murder or flee from y'all, you have to believe me." I look to where Lucy and her daddy were standing.

Nothing. They're gone.

Maybe she didn't wanna see me get arrested? Maybe her daddy forced her back into the apartment against her will? More thoughts come to me to shake Sergeant Keaton's mind— the cold, hard cuffs circling my wrists—and she pulls my arm for me to turn around. My head laser focused on the back entrance of our apartment building.

I almost made it. Lucy?

I thought you were gonna give me a second chance? What happened? What changed? Why did you just stand there and do nothing?

45

Murder?

How did I end up becoming a suspect of murder?

Feels like I'm in a TV show, waiting in this jail cell, waiting to be questioned like some murderer? Did something happen to Dorian or Iris that night I called 911 on them?

Was my DNA found on Dorian, and he finally snapped and killed the bitch—but somehow pinned her murder on me? That's insane—kinda smart, though…and I guess possible. He was off to New York; it would be easy to murder her in some town on the way, find a local to pin it on, and leave. Was he capable of that? Was his intention to meet a guy on Grindr to then pin his wife's murder on after sucking his nuts out? He seemed kinda like a pussy to plan such a scheme.

But who knows?

Who knows what people are capable of when pushed into certain corners. Fuck, I've done it myself. I've snapped and done things I shouldn't have.

"Roy Stevens."

An officer I've never met, standing on the other side of the bars from me.

"Yeah?" I pop up from the hard bench and walk over to

him. I've only been here an hour or so. It's a slow night, but who am I to think that? I've never been arrested, processed, in jail before, just seen it on TV. It went quicker than I thought. But when can I get out?

"You get a phone call tonight. You want it?" he says, talking casually like tonight is just another walk in the park for him.

"Yeah." Duh. Where is the phone?

He unlocks the jail-cell door, opens it, and signals for me to walk in front of him. I do, and keep walking as he advises me to turn down different hallways.

Who do I call?

Lucy? She just stood by and watched?

Am I alone in this now? Did she change her mind about me? What about Andrew? He never returned any of my calls today.

Eugene?

The idea of Eugene dismissed real quick into the air, my head cocking right and up. No. The thought even coming into my mind angers me. No.

I cannot call Eugene. Ramón? He did say he would be here for me—whatever the fuck that meant. Why am I even thinking about those New Yorkers? I don't even know their numbers. And they're in New York, you dumbass. That chapter is ended. That life is gone. I see it: the old phone mounted on the wall.

Fuck, who am I calling? *Dad?*

"All right, you get one phone call tonight; it's a collect call, and I'll give ya five minutes," the officer says behind me.

I step right in front of the phone, turn to look at him: He's planted a few yards away, leaned on the wall, scrolling on his cell phone. You on Grindr there, too, buddy? Give me back my phone and I'll chat ya. I chuckle to myself. *Really?*

"What's so funny?"

Shit. "Nothin', I just was thinkin' how silly it is I don't remember a few phone numbers as I should."

"Yeah, well, you'd be surprised how many folks nowadays

don't know anyone's number." He nods at the phone. "Go on, you're wastin' your five minutes."

Okay, who do I call? *Who* do I call?

I pick up the phone. An idea comes to mind. My thumb over the metal numbers, I don't know why I'm remembering this number so vividly. Here goes nothing: I dial *314-555-1516* —I think that's it…The phone now ringing in my ear. Come on, pick up. Pick up!

"Hello?"

"Ah." "Hi." "Who is this?"

"You called me. Who is this?"

"Is this Frank?"

"Whose callin' me? How did you get this number?" "Tell me right now, or I'm hangin' up."

"Don't hang up!" "Ah, it's Roy." *Your son. I think.*

"Roy?"

"Yes." "Sir."

"Oh." "I've been trying to get hold of you for months?" "Where are you?"

"Well, actually, that's why I'm callin'." "I've been arrested." "And I need your help." "I don't have much time." "I'm assumin' they will post bail or somethin' soon? Can you pick me up?" "Please." "I'm at the Franklin Regional County Jail." "Are you nearby, by chance?"

"Are you kiddin' me?" "Pick you up from jail?" "Why would I do that?"

Don't say it. Don't say it. "Because you're my father?" It just blurts aggressively out from me into the phone. "Is it too much to ask for one thing from you after all of these years?" "Hm?" "You are the one that called me first." "I didn't even know you were alive until recently." "And I don't know what happened between you and my uncle, but can you just help me out now?"

"Who told you I'm your father?" "And all these years, you thought I was…dead?"

"Bastards" is said under his breath.

Ramón told me…but can't say that. Um…"Your brother, man. My uncle, Uncle David." "He thought it was finally time." "Figured because he's now leavin', I should know you exist." "I know it's fucked up."

"He really said that?"

Shit. I don't know what he would say. "Yeah, he said that." "Can you come get me or not?" "You are my one call."

"Sure."

"Yeah?"

"I'll be there first thing in the mornin'."

"In the mornin?" "No." "Can you come now?"

"No, I'm tied up now." "I'll come out for ya in the mornin'." "Okay?" Fuck! I wasted my call on him. After years of nothin', thought maybe he would show up for me now. Should've called Lucy. Fuck! I don't know what I was thinking?

"Okay." "See ya in the mornin', I guess."

"What are you in there for?"

"I don't know, some bullshit charge for some murder. My father-in-law is probably tryin' to stick it on me."

"What else?"

"Uh." "They're tryin' to pursue a domestic violence case or somethin' against me, but my wife and I already have that sorted out." "They also think I fled a scene a few months ago in my car, but it wasn't me; my car was stolen that night."

"Stolen?"

"Yeah, stolen." "And what else do you think there would be?"

"I'm just askin'." "I'll see ya in the mornin'." "And I know who your wife is." "I met her." Shit. That's right. Lucy left me a voicemail saying you went to our apartment asking questions about me and that you're an old friend of her daddy's. "Sweet and pretty girl—you did well."

"Okay." "Bye." I hang up the phone. I don't know if I trust him. But he was my one call, and at least he's coming tomorrow to get me.

"Hey"—I turn to the officer—"that was less than five minutes. Can I make another call, please?" "I should have called my wife the first time." "Please."

He glances up from me off his phone. "Sure, make it quick." "You're lucky it's Friday and it's slow tonight."

Fuck. It is Friday night.

How long will it take for me to get out of here?

Are jail cops working on weekends? They have to be. The lives of people locked up can't just stop because of a weekend?

"Thank you." I quickly pick up the phone and dial her number. Lucy…please pick up…please—

"Roy?" How did she know it was me?

"Hi, hun, yes, it's me." "Are you okay?" "What happened tonight? I thought we had a plan?"

"Yeah." "I'm okay."

"How did you know it was me callin'?"

"Well, you're the only one now that calls me from numbers I don't know, and I thought you might try to call tonight from jail." Okay…

"So…you knew I was going to be arrested?"

"Yeah."

"What the fuck, Lucy?"

"I did try, Roy." "I went to the police station earlier today." "Turns out, it doesn't matter right now if I tried to retract my statement from months ago; the police are already aware, and I guess they now pursue charging you themselves." "I'm sorry." "It is what it is."

"'It is what it is'?" "That's it?" "That's all I get from you?"

"Yeah." "That's all you get, because there's more." "They questioned me today about that whole day before you ran off."

"Okay?" "And I didn't run off; I had to take care of something, and I was always coming home." "I was always coming back home to you."

"Well, you ran off to me." "I was the one left without a husband." "Pregnant and alone." "Scared and alone." "And physically harmed by someone I thought would never touch me like that."

"Okay, we can argue about this later; I don't have a lot of time." "So, the police questioned you?" "You were at work all day, I came home late from the bar after seeing that my car was stolen, and you found me drunk in the shower, and then we had a fight." "What more is there to question?"

"Someone was attacked in front of our apartment earlier that day."

Attacked?

"Okay?" "Attacked?" "What does that have to do with me?" It might have everything to do with me.

"Well, that guy that was attacked…died today at the hospital."

"He died today?…From an attack that happened months ago? I don't get it?" "What happened to him? Who's this guy?" I glance at the officer; he's not paying any attention to me, I don't think? Reminds me of Richard, glued to his phone. That bitch.

"His name is Isaac Jones." "Did you know him?"

Isaac Jones

Hearing my wife say his name…a nail hammered into the center of my skull. My nerves turning numb.

Waves of fight or flight ripple from the impact inside my brain, a confused insanity within. What do I say? This might be a recorded call? "No, I've never heard that name before in my life."

46

"How do you know *Isaac Jones*?" The detective across the table from me.

Please stop saying his name and looking at me. I glance above his head at the clock on the wall. 11:16 a.m.

11:16 a.m. on my first Saturday morning back in Kentucky, and I'm stuck in this room with these fuckin' I D I O T S. Sergeant Keaton next to him, with her little notepad, as if she really adds any value to anything. Fucking bitch, locking me up in here. Maybe she *will* help me out; maybe that is why she is here. Working on a Saturday morning. Or her life is so boring outside of work that she was actually looking forward to this. Fucking bitch! Maybe I should have ratted her ass out years ago for who I saw her hooking up with behind my bar. Maybe she wouldn't be in this town anymore if all knew the real truth about her. That she's a dyke. Why have I kept that secret for her all this time?

"How do you know Isaac Jones?" the detective asks me again. Shit. Did I not speak?

A pause in their faces, looking toward me. I remain silent and keep a relaxed expression. Keep it cool, Roy; you are innocent, you know nothing. *Which is technically true.* Well, mostly nothing.

The detective again. "Son, can you hear me?" "How do you know Isaac Jones?"

Do I know him? Was he the fella I had in my apartment that morning? I don't know. And how the fuck did I end up having his car—that Andrew gave to me, telling me it was his?

My eyes on Sergeant Keaton. "I don't." "Sorry, I was thinking if I do, and I don't." "I didn't sleep much last night; I've never been arrested." "I'm not your guy."

"You don't?"

"Correct. Can you hear me? I don't know Isaac Jones." "I'm not your guy." "I've never met the guy in my life."

"Why are you driving his car, then?" That's a great fucking question. Ask Andrew; maybe he killed him and gave me his car to frame me?

"Whose car?" Nice, keep it up. Stay ahead of them.

"Why are you driving Isaac Jones's car, if you don't know him?"

"I don't know what you're talking about. My friend, Andrew Boyd—look him up, I've been also trying to get ahold of him— a nurse taking care of my DYING uncle, who I should be seeing right now, lent me his car."

"Why did this Andrew Boyd lend you Isaac's car?"

"I don't know." They sit still. "I." "Don't." "Know." "Why don't you ask him?" "Hm?" "Call him up right now, put the phone on speaker between us." "Andrew told me he had an extra car; I needed to do an errand for my uncle; I thought it was Andrew's car." "…Is it not?" Smooth…

"What errand did you need to do for your uncle that put you MIA for three months?" Um, I don't have an answer for that. I don't even know myself why it took that long.

"That question isn't important; that's between my uncle and I." "Now may I please go." I look at Sergeant Keaton, my eyes trying to convey desperation, but I'm so tense inside, it probably looks like I'm trying to cast an evil spell on her. I would if I knew one.

Sergeant Keaton finally saying something. "Roy, we can't release you until a judge sets your bail."

"Okay, when is that gonna be?" My hands in front of me in cuffs hiccup in the air. I'm losing my patience. I spent all night in a cold jail cell. My eyes are heavy; barely slept. I'm freaking out when I shouldn't be freaking out.

"Not until at least Monday morning." Is she serious? The words coming out of her mouth like pliers ripping off my nails.

"Monday mornin'?!" "Are you serious?" A holler I can't help.

"Serious as a heart attack," the detective chimes in, backing her up. Both of them with no grins or smiles. Just zombies with an agenda to fuck me.

I bounce glances at both of them; my approach isn't working here. What else can I try, say? I'm drowning over here in bullshit. Having stayed in New York City seems like the better option right about now. It's cold in here; I'm tired; no one seems to care about me. The *real* me.

"Detective." I glance at him, chin down. "Sergeant Keaton." Chin remaining down, and I look at her. "I'm a family man." "My wife misses me; she is pregnant." "She needs me." "Can't we work out some temporary arrangement here?" "Frankfort appears to be a small town, where everyone knows everyone."

"How does Andrew know Isaac?" The detective back on me. "Answer a few more questions and maybe we can make a deal." Really? Make a deal? I like the sound of that. Sergeant Keaton's eyebrow pops in the direction of the detective.

"I already told you, I don't know anything." "I swear." "Jesus Christ!" "How many more times do I have to say it?"

"You shouldn't use the Lord's name in vain." Sergeant Keaton scolding me. Really? Coming from you, ya sinning dyke? Just go with it; you need both of them on your side.

I nod at her. "Fine…I apologize." "As you can imagine, this situation is extremely frustrating for me. I came home from a long trip to see 'n' kiss my wife, see my uncle who is very ill, and I was blindsided with an arrest just outside my home—ambushed, and am bein' accused of murderin' a person I've never met, seen, or have heard their name before." "Can you level with me at all on what that frustration might feel like?" "Hm?"

"So you've never seen Isaac Jones?" "You've never talked to him or hung out with him?" The detective not missing a beat, replying with more questions after everything I say.

"Hung out with him?" "What are you guys smokin'!?" "Is everything I'm sayin' goin' in one ear 'n' out the next?" "Am I just talkin' to the wind here?" "Hello00oOOooo?" "Anyone there?"

"No, I'm listening to you." "I just don't believe you."

Are all detectives this stupid? I'm not your guy. Domestic violence? Sure, I slapped my wife; it happened one time. I'm gonna work on that. Fleeing the cops—good luck proving that was me. Poker face. Seconds of silence between us three.

The detective glances at Sergeant Keaton, then back at me. "Roy, we have a witness that says Isaac Jones was in your apartment the day he was attacked."

Fuck. *That guy was Isaac Jones* AND *he just died yesterday?* No way. I can't believe it. I won't accept it.

A witness? And who could that be? Shit. Keep your poker face. Fuck, I'm nervous as hell and confused. My leg bouncing under the table.

Janice from across the street?

Keep your poker face, keep it! Roy, you're innocent. You. Are. Innocent. You know nothing, you've seen nothing. Don't show them your fear. "Who? Janice from across the street?" "She's just a drunk gossip, always on her phone, watchin' St. Clair Street all alone from her sad, empty apartment." "You should talk with her more; you'll see what I'm talkin' about."

Shit. Is that the best play? "Of course…she will feed you more gossip, and that's all that it is…gossip."

"No, not Janice, but thank you for the tip; we will reach out to her." Sergeant Keaton jotting down that tip—F U C K… Who, then?

"What witness, then?" "Lucy's father? Pastor Paul?" "That man has always had it out for me. I've never been good enough for his daughter. You guys have any idea how hard it is to live up to a preacher's daughter's standards? Hard. I'm sure now that she's pregnant and he's gonna be a grandfather, he don't want nothin' to do with me in raisin' that child—but that is MY child, not his. I am the father, and I will be the best father to that child." My finger darts to point at the detective.

"No, Pastor Paul is not involved in any way in these cases." The detective crossing his arms.

Okay?

What. The. Fuck. *Who*, then?

Maybe they're fucking with me to get me to confess more shit…shit that's not true just so they can pin crimes on me. They do that on TV. Wait…there *was* potentially a witness that day. I completely forgot about him. *Bobby.*

I look at the detective and Sergeant Keaton. Can they see it in my eyes that I know who the witness is? Maybe I ain't getting out of here today.

Okay, say it with confidence.

Anything and everything can be used against you. Remember. I've already said so much…"I think I need a lawyer."

47

$150,000 BAIL SET.

I can't believe that's the judge's ruling. Based on what evidence? Would have been less without the murder and fleeing-the-cops charges—which they WILL NOT be able to prove. What did happen to Isaac after he left my apartment? I remember blood on his face, and the shattered urn…but I didn't kill him? *Murder him?* Was somebody staked out on St. Clair Street, following him?

Why didn't Lucy or Frank come to my arraignment? Maybe they didn't know. I do have a *no-contact order* against me. If I contact her, I risk making the domestic violence charge worse. And she knows not to contact me…Fucking domestic violence cases—I had no idea they were this dramatic. I wish I could have seen her today. I wish she would have shown up for me. Probably doesn't help the domestic violence charge that the court didn't see her today…They don't know she misses me… and wants me home.

Maybe she doesn't?

She could have called the jail; she could have learned about my arraignment and showed up.

But she didn't.

Pretrial is set for four weeks from now; *$15,000* needs to be paid now in some sort of bond to get me out of here. I don't have that kind of money; Lucy doesn't have that kind of money. Even if we did, I'm not allowed to see her or talk to her about how to find or get it.

Maybe she does want me locked up in here. I did hit her… and put her on a roller coaster of emotions, going silent on her these past several months. Confusing her too; leaving her in the dark, alone. Maybe she resents me.

Hm. Chasing Ramón and men all over New York City.

Maybe this is what I deserve. My eyes begin to water.

I'm stuck. There's no way out. I'm gonna rot in here for four weeks, awaiting my further doom. This is my punishment. I've failed. I have just…failed. I'm a fucking failure. Ain't no other way to put it. I've been pinned into some corner, right where they want me. Useless and powerless. I do deserve it. Maybe I'm right where I need to be. Can't hurt anyone or sin while locked up—can I? I could hurt myself…Would Lucy then work harder to get me back? To be with me? Maybe…What else am I gonna do, locked up in here?

Wednesday morning, my fifth day behind bars…It is Wednesday, right? No communication from my wife, no update from my new, arisen-from-the-dead, deadbeat father. Nothing from Andrew or my uncle—I guess how would he find out I'm here? Maybe I should have called Eugene, or Ramón. Maybe those guys would have showed up for me. Not let me rot in here. It doesn't matter. *Should* I memorize one of their numbers if I get the chance? In case this happens again? Just for emergencies? Yeah, emergencies only…Eugene's number.

The hexagon metal pattern above me, holding the mattress above it. My body lateral on the first bunk in this bunk bed. They ought to give me a book or something? Sitting—well, lying—here like this all alone, subject to only your thoughts, is…torturous. How many thoughts need this much time to be dissected?

Or how much time should you be allowed to spiral into a certain thought itself? I guess I could talk to the other inmates. Nah, I got nothing in common with these criminals. Why would I talk to them? There ain't nothing in common that we have. Except maybe that we like butt stuff. I chuckle to myself. Is that a myth or true? I'm not looking to find out. Speaking of butt stuff…

I miss him. I hate it, but I do.

Why do I think about him when all is silent around me. When no distractions are around—from my duties to my wife, baby, and uncle to how I'm gonna get my old bartending job back. Every night here when I've tried to fall asleep, it's him I think about. Wait, have I really thought about him every night? *I have.* Eugene. The way he looked at me, the way he looked at everyone around him. The way he talked with me, the way he talked with everyone around him. The way my body felt when he'd touch me. The idea of his body touching some other body in front of me, with me, too—a threesome with him would have been one of the hottest things I've done in my life…Blood rushing to my dick, making it hard under these orange pants. Fuck! I missed out when I had the chance!

Okay, calm down. Can't hide a hard dick under these prison pants. Last thing I need is some wacko-ass men seeing my dick hard and getting the wrong impression. Either raping me or kicking my faggot ass. I turn my body in the bunk so it faces the cinder block wall the bunk is cornered against.

It's not even just the sex…His body next to mine, touching mine—just, close to mine.

I felt…more. Maybe our legs touching Friday morning before I left—my body knew it would be the last time; maybe that's why it felt *so* much inside. Or was I just sad? Sad to leave it all. Sad to say goodbye to the what-if had I stayed. Or was I just fucking horny like I always am?

Or do I *love* him?

Impossible. How can that thought even come to mind? I

can't. It's not who I am. And it's not natural. These feelings…
these feelings are just disturbed, delusional sexual impulses.

…If it's not natural, then why does it feel *so* natural, *so good*.
Why is my dick still hard from the thought of his gaze at me,
him speaking to me, touching me? It's making me wanna jerk
off right now into this wall. Shoot my load all over it. I can use
this crummy blanket to wipe it off.

Fuck it.

I lean my head up to look behind me through the jail-cell
bars. Anyone around? Any cops or inmates walking by? No.
Would they see my body wiggling if I jerk myself off in this
position? Fuck, I want to. I don't care if they do. Yes I do. I rub
my shaft with my palm, grab it with my fingers and stroke it
through these thick cotton pants. Fuck, it feels good.

I haven't cum in a while. When did I cum last? My dick
needs to feel my warm touch. I slide my hand under my pants
and grab it. I can feel the ridges of my dick veins through the
grooves on the inside of my hand. My eyes shut, then open and
peeping back behind me. I can at least hear footsteps if
someone comes? Right? I don't hear any.

I'm more horny than nervous, so I know I'll cum.

I stroke my dick fast, squeezing tighter. It feels so good; I'm
gonna bust so quick. I'm gonna bust all over this fucking wall.
Fuck this jail. Thank god I don't have a bunkmate or maybe
he'd wanna suck me off and I'd save this wall from shame. That
would be kinda hot. A little risky, though. My eyes back shut,
facing the wall, my ears alert for noise around, the imagery in
my head…*Eugene.* His eyes, his mouth, thinking about all the
times I was inside him, thinking about hi—S P L A T.

My cum ejecting from my dick, landing on the flat surface
and channels of the white painted cinder block wall. Some cum
getting on the bed between me and the wall. The cum releasing
a sweaty-ball-like stench, or maybe that's just my balls? I like it.
I'm so fuckin' horny. So alone. Still? I peek over my shoulder.
Still no one. The stench and visual of my cum right near my

face. Should I? I've never…I look down at my hand still on my hard dick. Cum circling the insides of my thumb and index finger. I bring it up to my nose, take a whiff, and my tongue pops out to lick it clean. Bleh! Also…not bad. I take the same hand and collect the drips of cum running down the wall on my index finger. Gooey like heated sugarless frosting but also loose like water, my tongue circling my index finger like getting the last bit of a popsicle off a stick on a hot summer day. I wonder what Eugene's cum tastes like. I wonder if it tastes like this? I should've had it when I had the chance.

The cinderblock wall with a sticky sheen. I got every drop. The aftertaste in my mouth still. I take the crummy blanket and wipe the sheen away—that ought to do it.

Okay…Roy. What should I do next?

Maybe be honest with yourself…Dig…What do you have to lose thinking about this more? You're already at your bottom. How much lower could I possibly get?

Okay, well, if I'm being honest…I always thought the feelings inside that I had when I'd been with Lucy to be…*it*. The highest level of what humans can feel for another. But now…I think…maybe I might have been wrong. Eugene is proving something's different in me. But just because I think it feels like more, or different, doesn't mean it's right or natural. It doesn't mean it's what God expects of me. I am a godly man. Godly men marry and respect women—their chosen wives. And those women respect their husband and are faithful to them back. They have kids together and raise those kids to do the same thing as men and women should be doing. And how those kids turn out is a test of our discipline and faith.

Lucy is pregnant. I will not fail her. Fail us. Fail God. I cannot. I am a man with responsibility to a wife, and now my soon-to-be child. I'm disgusted with myself. Disgusted that I jerked off thinking about Eugene, disgusted that I ate my own cum like a kid trying ice cream for the first time. You're fucking disgusting.

I hate myself.

Why me? I guess…why any gay person for that matter. Why does God challenge them with this burden inside? Making this emotion feel so real, when it is a sin and unnatural. WHY DO THIS? I don't get it. Why make something natural, that feels so right, one of the most immoral and disgusting sins known to humanity? I guess that's the point…Keep the temptation so high that if you are disciplined here on earth, your reward is higher in the afterlife? Damn. Fags have it rough. I have it rough. I've already gone through so many theories in my head, I'm tired of thinking about them. Trying to figure out what's right.

Maybe I should end my life now. Keep me from fucking up more here. A tiny bit of aftertaste still left. A dribble, a gooey bit of cum on my tip, leaking out under my pants. I just referred to myself as a faggot…Faggots probably eat their own cum, and you are what you eat. I'm so fucked. Maybe prison *is* where I belong. Or maybe I don't belong here at all. What value does a father add to raising a kid when he's in jail? Or a cum-eating faggot outside of jail? Nothing. He has no value at all.

48

———

"GET UP." "You made bail."

Someone banging on the jail-cell bars

What? My eyes open and look; a police officer standing there, one I haven't seen before.

"Get up. I don't have all day; I got other things to do. Let's go; on your feet."

Really? I made bail?

But how? Who paid it? What knight in shining armor has come to my rescue? What if it's Eugene? When did I shower last? Brush my teeth? Shave? Does my breath still smell like cum? Bleh. I don't want him seeing me like this.

Wait. For real, how is this happening?

Ugh. Why is he coming to mind again? God, snap out of it, Roy. Eugene IS GONE, nothing left but a fragment in my memory, and I need to get rid of that fragment too.

I swing my legs off from the bed and place my feet on the floor, then look left at the officer. "I don't understand?" "Who paid it?" I thought I'd be locked in here forever. Forgotten and not cared for. Not loved.

He bangs on the bars. "On your feet; let's go."

Okay, okay! Fuck, I just woke up. I stand up, turn around

and look at the bed and floor to grab my things. Jesus, you dumbass, you're in jail. You don't have shit here. I turn to face the officer, walk toward him and nod.

He opens the jail-cell door, allows me to walk through in front of him. I think I know my way out of here? I know where to go to get processed out. I can't believe this is happening. Maybe there is a God. And he doesn't think I'm that bad.

Thank you, God, for whoever you sent to bail my ass out. I promise—I promise to do right by you. I swear on my life. I promise.

I get my clothes back, my pack of cigs, my phone, my wallet. That's all I had on me when I was ambushed on Friday night.

Good to go? I nod at the final police officer as they signal for me to walk through the last door into the public, free lobby. I push through it.

The cooler air in the lobby feeling lighter on my face. Is the temperature lower here? Or am I just relieved? I start walking toward the main exit—I'm so excited to see it! Unbelievably, it's there in front of me.

An old man sitting on the bench against the windows near it. A few other people sitting on other benches around. A couple police officers chatting, down the room, in the corner near some vending machines—should I go ask them who posted my bail? No. I don't wanna see or talk to another police officer again in my life. I continue walking in the direction to run out the exit. The old man staring at me as I approach closer.

Why is he looking at me? Do I know him?

Should I know him? He continues looking me up and down. His expression intense. His posture in a slump, and his hands rested on top of each other over a black cane in the center of his body. Should I stop looking back? Just walk past him and nod—

He's seconds away from me; my eyes bounce from him to everywhere else. I can't help but bounce them back to check if he's still eyeing me.

I'm right in front of him.

His attention still locked on me.

Okay, feller. What do you want? I break eye contact and keep walking past. Does he recognize me from Grindr or something? That's ridiculous, Roy. You haven't been here in months.

"You're just gonna walk past me?" "Not even say 'thank you'?" A blurt from him.

I stop and turn. Could it be? "...*Frank?*"

He nods. His nod continues as he checks me out more. Haven't you checked me out enough?

Holy shit. This man is my...*dad*. My biological father.

Is it really him? He stands up. He's maybe in his fifties. I didn't realize he was so much younger than my uncle. How did that happen? Do they have the same mom and dad? I don't even know.

He steps toward me. "You ready to go?"

"Go where?" I'm not legally allowed home, where my wife is. I can maybe see if a buddy of mine will let me crash for a few. I guess I have Andrew as a last resort. Andrew! I grab my phone out of my pocket and turn it on. The apple coming on the screen as it fires up.

"To go to your uncle's funeral."

My eyes jump up at him. "My uncle's funeral?" What?

He nods. "Died in his sleep Friday night." "He's with the Lord now." "They arranged his funeral to happen today." "It's happening right now."

49

———————

My phone turning on completely.

12:55 p.m.

I look back up at him. "My uncle is dead?" "My Uncle David?" "Your brother?"

He nods again. And he's not sad; his emotions…There are none, just a stern face.

I don't believe him. I don't believe this. I just talked with my uncle a few days ago; Andrew said he was going to hospice—which meant to me that he still had some juice left. I NEED to tell him I found Ramón and share how Ramón replied to his letter. Is he sure? "When did it happen?" I want to cry, but I can't. I'm pissed and confused. How could this happen? And why are you here for me? Here for me now all of a sudden?

"When did what happen?"

I have to control myself to speak calm and direct. "When did he die?"

"I just told you, Friday night."

"Friday night?" Friday night? The same night I got arrested? The same night I just drove in? No way. No way the world would be this cruel to me. Cruel to him? Or would it?

"Yes, Friday night."

Wait a minute…"You knew he had died when I called you late Friday night to come pick me up here?" "And you didn't tell me?"

He pauses. "No, I did not." He shakes his head. Why is his thought lost? "I found out over the weekend, Saturday."

"How did *you* find out?"

"Pastor Paul." "Your wife's father called me." Of course he did. Lucy must have been called, and then she told her father.

"Why are you bailing me out?"

He stands up slowly, pushing his hands over the cane to keep his balance center and forward. "An investment."

"An investment?" Now I'm totally lost.

"Yeah, I'll get my money back." "Don't you worry about that." Hm?

"I mean, yeah, I'll work to pay you back." "One hundred percent." "…I didn't think I was getting out scot free."

"You won't need to work." "You already have the money."

An awkward chuckle comes out of me. "I wish I did, but really, I don't."

"You do." He nods.

"No." "I don't."

"Your uncle just died." "That house he owned, it now goes to you." "You're gonna sell it, pay me back the fifteen thousand dollars I just spent to bail your ass out, on top of paying off a debt he owes me."

"My uncle owes you money?" I knew it! I knew he ran from you because of money. It's always about money with people. I don't know why he couldn't have just told me that.

"Yes, he sure does."

Got your message loud and clear, Dad.

50

———

WHY DID my uncle run from you? Keep me from you?

Didn't you want me back when I was fourteen?

He's not really acting like he's happy to have finally met me. *See me again.* Maybe because I just cost him $15,000 just now… though he just told me his plan to get the money back, and more.

Why didn't my uncle give me back to him? Why did he lie to me my whole life about his real name and make me believe he was dead? It doesn't make sense. He was barely a part of my life. Maybe he kept me as a hostage to use against Frank for something between them?

His car is a mess. I thought I was a messy person. There is shit everywhere, from everywhere. Fast-food wrappers, old napkins, cigarette buds, the windows with a haze of white from god knows what.

Who cares, though.

I'm in a moving vehicle and not that jail cell anymore. Anything is better than that jail cell. Even being next to my estranged father. He did just bail me out—I have to mean something to him?

"What happened to you?" "When I was five." "Why did my

uncle lie to me?" "Tell me that you've been dead my whole life?"

He almost looks at me, but doesn't; he keeps his attention forward on the road, and he isn't saying anything. Is he going to speak?

My mouth feels disgusting. "You got any gum in here?" I open his center console. Two handguns in plain sight inside.

"Don't open my shit." "Just sit there and don't touch nothin'." He slams the lid down shut with his elbow fast.

"Shit." "Okay." I put my hands up in a defensive way. "My bad." "Don't know when's the last time I brushed my teeth is all."

"I ain't got no gum." He reaches into his pocket and pulls out a pack of cigs. "Here"—he extends his hand in front for me to grab—"just have a smoke."

Sure…yeah, I guess that will help. "Thanks." I grab a cig and light it up with a lighter I find in his cup holder. He grabs a cig, too, and grabs the lighter from the cup holder after I put it back. We both crack our windows at the same time.

"So, are you happy with Lucy?" "Happy you married her?" "I know she's pregnant now and all." "That's a big responsibility." And you would know that how?

"Yeah…I love her." "We've been together forever." "She's all I know."

My uncle's death starting to hit me more; it's got me thinking that Lucy is all I have left and she don't even want me no more. A crack in my heart widening, deepening. Wait, where do I sit if Lucy is there? I'm not supposed to be in the same room as her. Maybe she won't say anything. The court-appointed attorney warned me of the consequences if I talk to her—an exception has to be made for us to be in the same room today—it just has to?

He continues scoping me out still. His body leaned the opposite direction as mine, his lips in a frown. I don't think he trusts me?

Maybe start with easier questions, and then he will tell me the truth? "How do you know Pastor Paul? My father-in-law?" That one has been itching at me too.

He coughs, catches his breath, and shakes his head. "We met long time ago, in college." "Studyin' to become pastors."

"Oh?" "Really?" That's interesting. My real dad is a pastor too? "You're a pastor?" You sure don't look like one.

"No." "I never finished." Okay, that makes more sense…

"Why didn't you finish?"

"I got busy with other things."

"Like what?"

He sits silently, adjusts the radio to a different channel. I didn't even realize it was on. "That's enough questions." "When are you listing that house of his to sell?" "He owes me money." His cough continuing—just like Uncle David's. You might not tell they were brothers standing next to each other, but listen to them both cough, and they sound exactly the same.

"My uncle's house you're talkin' about?"

"Is there another house I should know about?"

"I don't think so?" I chuckle a bit, actually. "Turns out my uncle was full of secrets, so who knows if he owns other property or has money stored 'n' hidden somewhere. I bet his wife Sheila ought to know."

"My brother always had secrets." "Sheila?" "His wife?" He sounds shocked to hear it.

"Yeah…he was married." "You didn't know that?" "I'm assuming she will be at the funeral." "They have been together since…like, when we moved here twenty or somethin' years ago."

"You moved here twenty years ago, and he's been with this Sheila ever since?"

"Yeah…" "Why?"

"In 1992?"

"Yes, why?" He remains silent…

Hm. There it is, the same year Ramón and Uncle David talk

about too. The year you found them—*me*, apparently according to my uncle's letter to Ramón. "Did you hear me?" "Why?" "You never knew where we were?"

He won't say anything.

What the fuck.

He continues smoking his last few puffs, then extinguishes the bud in the cup holder. "No, I never knew where my brother went after he kidnapped you."

"Kidnapped me?" So my hostage theory might be true? What did you have on Uncle David? "You're sayin' your brother kidnapped me from you, and you never knew where we ended up? You never knew we moved to Owenton, Kentucky?"

He's searching for words. Come on, spit it out! "No, I never knew until Paul called me a few months ago."

"Why did Pastor Paul call you?"

"To tell me my son beat his own pregnant wife." He glares at me.

I look away.

My father-in-law has always had your number? Pastor Paul has known who my real father is and has also kept this secret from me? Why?

"I didn't know she was pregnant at the time." "Not that that matters," I correct myself real quick. "It was an accident."

"I called you a few months ago." "I got your number from Paul." "But you were short with me on the phone." "And then I could never get a hold of you after." Yeah, I was in New York and thought you were a cop trying to find me…So it wasn't Uncle David that gave you my number, then. "Paul told me David was very ill, too, so I came to see him too." "Can't believe that the biological son of mine married the daughter of my old buddy from college." "A random coincidence." "As I live and breathe, here you are in front of me." " I went to your apartment too." "To meet Lucy, see it for my own eyes." "See who you've become." "Then she told me you had run out on her." "Didn't know where you had gone." "Where did you go?"

We turn into the funeral home. Damn. It's a busy day at the funeral home. Lots of cars parked out. I scan for Lucy's; I don't see it. I don't recognize any of these cars. Actually, wait, there is Sheila's. Wonder what show she'll put on for everyone to see today.

Where did I go? I went on a trip for Uncle David. This fucking bastard couldn't hang on for me just a bit longer. I almost made it. "It's a long story." "I'll tell you later."

"Okay." "Bet."

51

———————

I missed the funeral.

And I missed him before he died.

My last memory of him will be me promising him that I was coming back. But who cares about that promise? He was a pathological liar, a thief, a perpetual sinner. Should I really care for him at all?

My fist rises and bangs on the table. I can't help it.

The reception hall filled with old people I don't know, people that didn't know him the way I did. Or thought I did. Frank next to me, sitting at the same table. Just us. My plate of food barely touched. I know my body is starving, but my appetite is gone.

Frank leans his head in over his food, looking my direction. "What's wrong with you?" "Control yourself." "You'll draw attention to us, and you don't need no more attention your way." He's right. I should control my anger, my emotions; all eyes are on me now. The whole town has to know about the charges against me. People talk here, and everyone knows everyone. They're probably speculating right now how I got out on bail; wondering who's sitting next to me.

I thought my uncle was the only one I truly had in my

corner, but now, is it Frank? And what about all the years we missed out on?

Maybe it was a good thing that I missed his service, missed seeing Lucy. Maybe I need to stay out of sight—for her, and myself.

My focus forward, Sheila and Dr. Pingree three tables away. I can't believe she brought him or he voluntarily came with her. Neither of them acknowledging me. Scattering their eyes else-where every time I look over. I don't have a no-contact order for Sheila; I can go up to her and say anything I want. In fact, I think I will. I look at Frank. "I'll be right back." I get up and make my way to their table.

"Well, well, well, ain't this all too familiar of a picture?" "Hm?" "Dr. Pingree." I nod at him. "Looks like your prediction was pretty spot on." "Guess that's why they pay you the big bucks." I slap his shoulder with my hand and grin, keeping my hand pressed on top of him.

I look at Sheila. "How are ya?" "Miss me?" "I know it's been a minute." "I've sure missed you."

"Is that so?" Her voice squeaks.

"Yep." "Hey, I gotta question for ya about my uncle's house?"

"What of it?" Her chin going down along with her pitch.

"You think it belongs to you?" "Or me?" "See that man over there I'm with?" I nod for her to look behind me.

She leans to look, then leans back, centered in her chair. "What of him?"

"His name is Frank." "He's come to collect a debt my uncle owes him." Her pupils flit with life, her hands squeezing the plastic utensils to death.

She leans back to look at him, then pops back to the center of her chair again, hiding behind my cover so I'm blocking her from Frank's sight. "Roy, listen to me." "That man is not safe." "Trust me." "You need to get away from him."

Not safe? What would Sheila know about Frank? She's never

cared about my safety since I've known her; never cared about my life.

"Not safe?" "That man just bailed me out of jail." "That man is what is keeping me from rotting in prison like a dog." "That man has just saved my ass." "That man, he is my true father."

"I know." "And that is why he is dangerous." "*Because* he is your father."

"What are you talking about?" "What do you know that I don't?"

"*Roy.*"

The voice sending a lightning bolt down my spine. Is it possible? Is it? My body turning quick, the bolt hitting my feet and spinning me to face—

Eugene

AND *Ramón*

I swallow and take a breath in. I look past them and around to see who's watching us. The room filled with maybe thirty or so people—it's not a lot. Two men standing near one of the front tables has to draw a lot of attention, especially men that look like they're not from here; from New York.

We all take a second to take each other in. I can feel my eyes want to water, I'm so happy to see him. I'm so happy he's here. I can't show it, though. Do I think he can tell? Can he tell how weak inside he makes me?

My lungs finally inhale a breath to speak that won't spew out into tears or anger. I'm somehow calm. "What are y'all doin' here?"

"*Ramón!*" I hear Sheila behind me.

The sound of her chair scooting back as she stands quick

She walks behind Dr. Pingree, around and over to Ramón. "Hi, Sheila." He smiles and nods at her, and she hugs him tight.

What is happening? They *know* each other? Eugene standing next to Ramón, calm as can be. Not a reaction at all to this random country woman embracing Ramón like a long-lost brother.

Sheila and Ramón stop embracing. Eugene to Sheila: "Hi, Sheila, I'm Eugene." He extends his hand to greet her, and she gives him a hug. His face surprised and his eyes on me. She lets him go and turns to me.

She steps in closer. "Your uncle and I had an arrangement."

"An arrangement?"

"Yes." She nods cautiously. "It wasn't at first, and then it grew into one." "How do you think Andrew got the letter your uncle wrote to Ramón that got returned back to our home?" "Me." "Last time they wrote to each other was over a decade ago, but I recognized the name and address."

"*Roy, are you gonna introduce me to your friends here?*" Frank appearing behind Sheila, popping between her and Ramón. Sheila and Ramón both subtly jump. Their bodies both cut to face him directly, and then back at me.

"Uh." "Yeah." "This is Sheila, my uncle's wife—well, widowed now."

"I'm sorry for your loss." He nods at her.

"And these two are…" Their outfits really placing them definitely not from around here; what do I say? I nod their direction. "These two are…"

"I know who this one is." He nods at Ramón. "Where ya been all these years?" He extends his hand toward Ramón.

Ramón looks down at it and then back at Sheila. "What are you doin' here, Frank?" "What do you want?"

Ramón knows Frank. *Have they met?*

"What do I want?" "My brother just died." "I'm here mournin' his death, just like the rest of ya." "Ain't that what family does?" He has a subtle grin. "Not to mention bailing my dumbass kid out of jail." He nods at me. "What do you mean what do I want?" "What type of stupid question is that?" He leans in and steps closer to Ramón.

"David may have been afraid of you." "But I'm not."

Ramón takes his hand to pull back his coat, revealing on his left side a holstered gun.

Frank glances at it. "You ain't gonna shoot me; faggots don't have the balls."

Eugene grabs it in a flash out of Ramón's holster and points it at Frank, between us all five. "He might not, but I do." His stance firm, arm locked. Oh my god, Eugene.

Frank puts his hands up. "Well hold on now, calm down there, boy." "You better not."

"Eugene!" "Put the gun down." I step closer, in front of and facing him. My shoulder touching his flexed arm, the gun pointed at my dad behind me. "What are you doin'?" "Stop." "He's my father."

Eugene darting eyes to Ramón, back to me, and then to Frank. "He's not, Roy; trust me." His eyes oozing desperation for me to listen to him.

"Roy's coming with us." Ramón says.

I'm what? "No, I'm not."

Eugene glares at me. "You're coming with us." "Please, listen to me."

I glance at Ramón for a clue. Is this him showing up for me? Is this what I need? People in the room have stopped eating and are staring at us.

Frank standing there calm. I glance over my shoulder at him. "Who is this, Roy?" "Who is this man to you?" he asks.

My head aimed back forward at Eugene, I set my hand and arm on his arm that's holding the gun at my dad, my touch soft, not forcing his arm down but allowing the weight of my arm to be on his, our eyes locked. "He's…nothing." His arm loses its strength, and it falls, the gun now at his side, pointed at the floor. My arm back at my side. "He's nothing to me." "I don't know these men."

"Sure looks like to me that you know 'em." Frank scowling behind me.

Sheila with a whispering haste in her voice: "You boys need

to get." She nods at Ramón and Eugene. "Look at all these folks around—one of 'em probably, if not more, called the cops already. Go!" she barks.

Ramón and Eugene take her note, then turn to scan who's watching, who's staring? I take note too. How many people are staring? Who's on their phone? Who or how many called the cops already? I look across to the exit. And in the doorway, standing, is that…?

Andrew

52

I WALK FAST TO HIM. His face is red, his eyes a thick haze like he's stoned. Is he? Just the sight of him lifting weight off me. I might be happier to see him than I was seeing Eugene? I don't know. The emotions are different. But both good.

I get to him and embrace him; I hug so tight. He begins to sob in my chest. I'm uncomfortable, but I also don't care who can see us. I'm probably going back to jail; I ain't gonna see these people again. Let this little—man cry in my arms. Why am I emotional too? My eyes releasing emotions that've been held back, my chest hiccuping as the tears come out. We cry together for a moment.

"Why didn't you answer my calls Friday?" I pull back from our hug. My hands still on him.

"I'm sorry. A lot happened that day." Our eyes on each other's. His filled with sorrow. I didn't know my uncle meant so much to him too? Or maybe I did and just ignored it? Or was I too much of an asshole about it?

"Are you okay?" I let my hands drop off from him. I'm afraid to look behind me now to actually see how many people are staring. I step around him for him to follow me into the hall outside the reception room. He walks in front faster, turning down the hall and asks me to follow him—okay? Again? Where are you going? I can't run anymore.

53

____

WE REACH a chapel inside the funeral home. No one is in it. Okay, this looks private enough. We dart right into the chapel once we get past the doors; I follow quick and he continues walking down the center aisle. My attention on his back, trying to keep up with his fast pace.

"Where are we goin', Andrew?" "We are already alone in here?" I chase behind him still, until he stops at the last bench in front of the altar. I stop next to him and look forward at what he's looking at:

An open casket with a man our age in it

54

———————

My heart stops. And then beats heavy like it's three times its size.

The man lifeless, and his face familiar.

I've tried to imagine this whole situation is a lie, unreal. Not a crazy coincidence. How could it be? There really is a dead person in front of me. Our age. Someone *did* really die. The actual body is in front of me. And Andrew is next to me, standing in disbelief, still. My eyes stuck on the body, studying it. "Who is this, Andrew?" I turn to look at him.

Don't say it. Please, don't say it.

His hand over his face, covering his mouth. "He's…my…" He can't control himself to answer. "My…my…" His head drops, and he begins to sob more.

"Your cousin?" "Is this your cousin, Andrew?" "The one that was in an accident?" "The one that fell into a coma months ago that you told me about?"

He steps closer to the casket, his knees landing on the kneeler, his sobs becoming louder and chaotic, with no rhythm. I guess his aunt and uncle did decide to pull the plug…

What do I do? My instincts want to hold him, let him cry in

my arms more, share the pain with him. But if someone sees us? Sees me holding and consoling him?

I step closer to him. He's on the right side of the kneeler, his face down in front near the dead body's stomach. Should I kneel next to him on his left? That puts me closer to the body's face. I don't wanna be that close to it. I don't want to see it.

Ah…the hell with it.

I kneel next to Andrew. I set my right hand on his shoulder and just leave it there while he cries with his head down, forehead against the edge of the casket. I didn't realize he and his cousin were that close. Or maybe, all this time, after all—

"It's okay, Andrew." "He's in a better place." Andrew's arms crossed in a pretzel against the casket, his nose stuffed in the middle between them, fighting to get air. I slide my left hand across the edge of the casket toward him to grab one of his hands. He grabs it back and squeezes while he continues to cry. Both of my hands now making contact with his body. I scan behind us to see if anyone followed—no one. What happened to everyone?

We are alone.

I turn my head forward to view the face in front of me: pale and lifeless as a white piece of old paper. I've never been this close to a dead body. I look from his Adam's apple to then his lips, up his nose, and at his eyebrows. The heavier beat of my heart unchanged. I do know him.

A scar above his right eyebrow near his temple

And his scalp with a five-o'clock shadow, but I remember it shiny and bald after he took off his black Nike ball cap. Am I sure?

My hands retracting from touching Andrew. "What happened to his face?"

Andrew pops his head up from crying. "What do you mean?" "They not do his makeup good?"

"Huh?" "Oh, I don't know about that?" "Is he wearin' makeup?"

"Yeah, they put makeup on all dead bodies, Roy."

"Oh." "Weird…okay." I gotta ask him again. I need to know. I swallow and point with my index finger at the scar. "I'm talkin' about that scar on his face." "The one above his eyebrow, near his temple." "How did your cousin get that?"

"That's where he was attacked." "The cops found him on the sidewalk on St. Clair Street, unconscious." "His attacker… just left him there, bleeding out to die." "Like he didn't mean anything." Andrew begins to cry more, dropping his head. "Who would do such a cruel thing?"

"I don't know."

My body stuck, stuck and locked into observing the body of *Isaac Jones* more. The fella I accidentally killed.

Andrew slides his left arm under my right arm, his shoulder and face now leaning against the right side of my body.

I have to ask him to verify. It's my last and final question, my body forcing it out. "Andrew, is this Isaac? Isaac Jones?"

He cocks his head out from me. "Yes." "Who else would this be?"

"Ahem." "I don't know." "I'm just makin' sure." "…I'm sorry for your loss." My head turns to face his, still cocked out from me, our arms still entangled. Our eyes inches from one another's. His crying seeming to be all let out now. My organs shaking inside as if a bomb went off, leaving everything lifeless inside. He looks down at my lips; I look down at his. Our heads pull toward each other as if we're a modern-day fucked-up Lady and the Tramp. I can't stop it, the invisible spaghetti between us getting smaller.

Our lips meet.

Our heads stay still, our lips softly pressed forward into each other's. Tears leak from the corners of my eyes and slide down my face.

He pulls back first, and I stay stuck. I open my drenched eyes at him.

"Run away with me, Roy."

Did he just say—

"There ain't nothing left for me in this town anymore except sad memories." "And a past that is no longer my future."

I untangle our arms from each other and lean my body away from his. I look back at Isaac.

"*…We can go to Atlanta, Chicago, Miami, New York City! Anywhere you want. Just you and I…*"

My right ear perking up: Did he just say New York City?

I stand up from kneeling next to him. Imagery of Isaac leaving my apartment months ago, when he was alive. Angry and confused at me—to now his dead body in front of me. *I did this.*

"I can't." I look down at Andrew, still kneeling. He stands up next to me and grabs my hand. I retract it.

"Roy, there has always been something more between us." My chin jolting back into my neck.

I shake my head. "Andrew, I gotta go." "You need to forget about me." "I'm sorry again for your loss." I start walking. Walking away from the body, the altar; walking down the center aisle of the chapel—

"He wasn't my cousin!"

I stop halfway down the aisle. I can hear him walking, trying to catch up to me. I turn to face him. "Stop!" I say. He gets to me. I put my hands on his shoulders and lock my arms out. "I know he wasn't your cousin." My insides getting feeling back after the explosion. "I know." My head starting to nod fast, I shake his torso violently. "I know, and I am sorry!" "You'll never know how sorry I am." Because I fucked your boyfriend, and accidentally killed him after. I start bawling. "I have to go." I grip his shoulders harder and push. "I can't explain it to you, but I have to go."

He sets his hands on my face. "Stop."

You don't know who you're touching. "Andrew, don't touch me anymore, please."

"Your uncle left something for me to give to you." "Don't run away from me." "Don't disappear again."

I can't ignore the statements. But I need to run, I need to leave. My eyes behind Andrew again, on Isaac's body. "What?" "What did he leave for me?"

"A final letter to you, just in case this happened." "Just in case you weren't able to make it back in time." "You really need to read it." "There are also journals he kept hidden throughout the years." "He told me where they were; I collected them for you."

"Did you read the journals too?"

He removes his hands off my face.

"I know you wrote the letter, I'm assumin', based on past history." A bit of attitude darted at him. I can't help it. I'm the one that is the enemy—the true, crooked person—but still, I hold anger at you.

"Roy, I'm not your enemy." He steps forward and hugs me. His voice lower and closer to my ear. "No, I did not read any of his journals." "And, yes, I wrote the letter for him." "You really need to read it."

I push him off me slowly and turn us, my hands back on his shoulders, holding his body away again from touching mine. I get lost in his sad, hopeful brown eyes. Trust me, you wouldn't look at me this way if you knew the truth.

"Roy!" My name like a loud crack of thunder fills the chapel.

My head whips toward the direction of the sound. Frank is standing in the center of the aisle, just inside the chapel, under the doorframe. His feet planted hips' length apart. A gun in his right hand pointed down. Is that Ramón's? Or one of the two from his car? No one else around behind him. We didn't hear any shots? Did we?

"You," Andrew blurts out, a bit under his breath, and squints at him as we both step away from each other and face him. Wait a minute…

"You two have met?"

"I saw him leave your uncle's room before he died Friday night." "Your uncle never made it to hospice." "He died at the nursing home."

"That's Frank." "My dad," I say loudly enough for Andrew and Frank to hear.

Andrew looks at me. In a heavy whisper: "I know." "Run."

55

———————

THE PAIN. The guilt.

The confusion.

How did this happen? It's too much. I can't breathe. My hands are shaking. I'm a disease that has gotten out of control. *I really am.*

I glance at the clock in Andrew's truck, his real one: *7:17 p.m.*

How poetic, taking my life near sunset. Going down like the sun on the earth—just, this time, for good.

Why me? Why me, Lord? I can't handle it. I can't do it. Look who I have become. And look who I've hurt around me. *Killed.*

I glance at the envelope closed with my name written on it: **Roy**

A stack of my uncle's journals below it. What's the point in reading what he left me? It's too late. I'll join you up in heaven, and you can just tell me there—if I make it. God forgives all his sinners? Doesn't he? At least that's what's been taught. And it's at least what I hope. It's my only hope.

But me? A killer and a fag? Why would God want me in heaven? He wouldn't.

But maybe Satan would take me? And that's terrifying.

Nothing you wrote in this letter can change the way I feel, change the way other people feel, change the fact that I killed someone accidentally—

Someone loved him. Andrew loved him. And I took that away from Andrew. And Isaac.

I don't deserve to be here. I don't deserve to share and breathe the same air these people do. I should have done this a long time ago, when I noticed the signs, but I was a pussy. They were always there. I just ignored them.

Signs that I was different, signs that I liked men, when I started watching porn of men in my twenties. It was probably my teens, if I'm truly fucking honest. I just didn't have the balls to take my life then.

I have the balls now.

I have no way out here on earth. No way out from the cops, no way out of my own sins I keep doing. I've tried. It's too late for me. I'm too *possessed.*

Vibrate…vibrate…

My phone upside down in the passenger seat next to the journals. I told Andrew I needed some space after dropping him off at his place. Just give me some fucking space! I grab my phone, turn it over to read on the screen who's calling: *314-555-1516.*

Frank

That son of a bitch. He just stood there with a gun held out, watched us as we ran off through the chapel to exit the back of it. What did he say? "*I'll find you, boy*"?

What the fuck was that about? The anger in his eyes before Andrew and I darted to the back. Luckily, we found an emergency exit.

Why was he so angry?

I landed at the driver's side of Andrew's truck. As soon as Andrew made it to the passenger side, we bolted. I didn't see him come out chasing behind us.

Why the gun? Why the threat?

He looking to kill me, and then he's next in line for all the money in my uncle's house? I guess that makes sense? But worth killing me over? His son?

I press the side button to stop the vibrating, then slide the phone into my pocket. Leave me alone, too, you bastard. You'll get your money soon. Just gotta wait until the morning, when the cops or some loser fishing finds my floating body in the river. This drop is high enough to do it, right? Let's see. I glance at my name again on the closed envelope. My body grabs it, and I open the car door at the same time to swing out. I walk across the two-lane road on the bridge, get to the thick railing, and look over.

Phew. I'd say it's gotta be more than seventy yards down.

White caps and bubbles from the rolling river flowing under the bridge

Must be good-size rocks down there under the water; if I hit one right, that'll do it. I should fall headfirst; quick and easy. I throw my right leg over the railing and saddle myself in the center of it. I look forward and behind me on the road; no one around. That's good. One fewer person I traumatize. The sun setting to my left, the warmth on my left cheek still; it's peaceful, but my right cheek feels a brisk wind blowing in the direction of the sunset. Blowing me toward the road; toward Andrew's truck. Is the wind a sign?

No. This is what I need to do.

Why now all of a sudden would there be a sign to keep me here. Keep me living in this trap. My weight on my hands in front of me, bottoms of my fists pressed on the railing, and my ass bones too. I'm equally balanced at all four pressure points. I just have to shift the center of my weight off to the right, relieve the inside of my left leg from holding me centered on the railing, and down I'll fall. Just like the old cell phone of mine. Down I will go and explode into pieces, just like it. Easy peasy. I glance at the white caps, the boulders on the sides of the river. I can do this. Go!

I shut my eyes and shift slowly.

I stop. I look right into the air, following the river up, and scream. I take a breath and scream again. My head shoots down at the letter in my right hand. Clenched tight between my thumb and index finger. *Read the letter, Roy.*

Fuck it.

I quickly open the envelope and toss it in the air off the bridge. The pages now inside unfolded and flat in front of me. What? What were your last words to me, you bastard too?

Roy,

Just in case you don't make it back in time, I asked Andrew to help me write this one last note. I changed my mind that some things should go to my grave, never to be said. Some things need to be said, even if it comes this late, and I'm sorry for that.

You need to know the truth, for your safety, and well-being. I'm sorry it took this long. All this time I thought I was protecting you. Doing right by raising you the way I did. I don't think I got it right. But I really did try my best.

Your real father is alive. He did not die when you were 5. His name is actually Frank, not John. I lied to you that he was dead, and that his name was John, in hopes you would never, ever find him, and that he would never, ever find you.

Frank has come to Owenton. Pastor Paul came to pray over me, and after told me that all this time, he's known who we really are. And that he called Frank recently. You see, when your grandfather died, every penny from him went to me, and nothing to Frank, and I used it all to buy that house. Frank wants that money now, and also wants to meet you. And now, I can't control him or protect you because I'll be gone.

Before the age of 5, your behavior from other boys was

different. You did behave like a boy, but also showed interest in things girls showed interest in. Behaviors like wanting to play with your mother's makeup, walk around in her heels left out from her night out before; to even preferring her perfume on you. Most boys played with toy monster trucks, you preferred Barbie's pink convertible. And Barbies too.

Frank noticed you were more comfortable being around and behaving more like the girls than the boys. He shared this with me and your grandfather. Turns out, he also shared this with his best friend from college, Pastor Paul.

At first it terrified him, not knowing how to fix it, and then as your behavior didn't change over the years, it grew to disgust him. He started to hate you. He stopped viewing you as his real son.

Right after you turned 5, your mother was all of a sudden out of the picture (I still don't know what happened to her, but I know he blamed her for the way you were) and he didn't want to have you anymore as a son. The idea of his son acting more like a girl than a boy, he couldn't handle. Back then, we all knew what men those types of boys grew into, sissies, faggots. So he chose to get rid of you. To leave you behind and forget you ever existed. He dropped you off at a Baptist orphanage near the town you lived in, and left. I think he wanted a fresh start entirely somewhere else.

I got a call from your grandfather. Frank had told him he got rid of you and took off, that he was leaving town, and he also told our father the reason.

My father and I had actually never met you. We only knew that Frank had a son, and what Frank would say about you.

My father called me and told me to pick you up, told me to raise you. Told me that he would pitch in financially to help. Truth be told, and you might already know this, but I never wanted kids. Our father forced me to take you in, raise you up—told me no grandchild of his would be left to rot in an orphanage or end up elsewhere outside the family, even if he was a fag. Our father was at least progressive for his time in that way, more at the end of his life.

So, I went and picked you up. My father and I had a good relationship. I respected him, unlike your father. They didn't have a relationship.

My father and I agreed that we would never tell Frank what we did. That I came and got you. At least not until we knew more information, observing you more as you would grow up.

Your father had made several statements throughout the years of his hatred towards gay people after and before he left you—we all did. That is how we have always behaved towards them. But your father's hatred was at another level. So strong he'd say things along the lines that he thought God expected us to convert gay people around us to be straight, and if they didn't convert, that it's our right and will to cleanse the earth from them. To kill them. He convinced himself this destiny was true. He would say comments like this often, but I never believed he would actually let his hatred turn into action, into murder. Until the day he saw us.

You might recall when you were 14, Grandfather Walter died. Frank came to the funeral. I didn't think he would come because he and our dad weren't talking before he died. Frank saw you, and me, and Ramón. As soon as I recognized Frank was there, I kept my distance from Ramón, and you. I didn't want him to see me and Ramón together, or recognize you…but he did.

I was outside the funeral home having a smoke alone. He came up quick behind me. "Is that my boy in there sitting next to that fag you're fuckin'?" I didn't know what to say, but I think he saw the fear in my eyes, and I will never forget the rage in his, and his next words:

"You better run, brother. Because after Dad's funeral, I will find you, and all three of you are gonna be buried next to him. There ain't no one left to protect you." He pointed and looked up at the clouds in the blue sky with crazy in his eyes. "Think heaven has a place for you?" It was such a pretty day that day to hear such a twisted and dark thing. He then said, "Actually, wait…fags like you and my boy don't go to heaven. They will burn in hell, you're a man of faith, you should know better." He then punched me in the gut, nearly making me collapse right then, and took off walking into the parking lot.

I tried looking to see which car he got into, but lost him. Right then I knew, I knew I had to take you and run. I never told Ramón the truth. I picked a fight with him later that day, and then took you and left that night. Ran. If Ramón knew the truth, it would have made things more difficult. Ramón was a fighter, I was a runner. One of the few things we didn't have in common.

Though I never wanted kids, and I was forced to raise you against my wishes, you were the one thing that gave real meaning to my life, besides Ramón before. I didn't have him anymore, and the company of women didn't fully satisfy me, as you might get by now. I vowed to myself, and our pops up above, to raise you as best I could. Raise you in a way that would protect you, from the world seeing who you might really be—because the world isn't kind to anyone that is too different than the majority. It isn't kind to things they don't understand. Things that the Bible says that are wrong. Many people use religion to justify their cruel actions derived from their fear and hate—when really I think religion should have been used to justify more actions of love and compassion. But that's just me in my final hours trying to make sense of it all. Why we're all so fucked up.

Thing is, Roy, I think I was wrong. Ramón tried to tell me, many times. Tried to get me to relax and allow you to play with the toys you wanted, or dress the way you wanted—dance the way you wanted. I didn't listen to him. You didn't really like baseball when I signed you up, if you remember, but…I didn't give you a choice. I was rough on you every time your behaviors didn't align with how other boys behaved. Rough on you when there were other boys that were sissies around so you'd learn to hate them. I forced you to play baseball. In my eyes at the time, you needed to be a regular boy that loved baseball, just like the others. No sissy boys played baseball.

I think that's why you worked to become the best pitcher, how you grew to love it. Because you chased my approval through baseball. I forced you to want to love that sport, to make you think that in return, you'd receive my love. My approval. That's why I never went to a game. I never wanted you to stop chasing it. For my plan for you to stop working.

It was my new purpose in life, to raise you not to end up like me, protect you if Frank ever found you, make my dad proud. Condition you out of the version your natural self was behaving. I thought that was best for you, that I was doing right by you. Right by God, even.

And, maybe some of my choices did work out to protect you. Pastor Paul knew who you were the second he learned your last name after he met you, when you and Lucy got together in high school. He knew whose son you actually were. But he never told Frank. And he's been watching you silently ever since.

But maybe I was wrong, Roy. Maybe it should have been dance class I signed you up for, instead of baseball. You loved to dance so freely. Had Ramón been in the picture, maybe you eventually would have made it to a dance class, and maybe that dance class would have led to more peace and happiness, because it was what you actually wanted to do.

Sometimes I think, had I not conditioned you into a version of a generic boy I thought you should be, maybe your life would have been easier as an adult, or different now—maybe better off than how it has unfolded. I don't know what's happened to you now, and why you've been running from the cops, but I can't help but feel that it's all my fault. Because I didn't know how to love you as a kid should be loved.

My voice is tired. Andrew's been such a good sport, helping me. I hope I see you in person, that you never need to read this letter, and I hope I have the courage to tell you. To apologize. To say to you, don't make the same mistakes I made. Who you truly are on the inside is nothing to be ashamed of, to live in fear from, to hide. I did this my whole life, and I feel it in my bones now that I was wrong.

I think as long as something feels natural, gives you joy, and you are not harming others around you, I think God has a design for. I was wrong to allow my fear of my brother to control how my life ended up—control how strict I was with you. Control my love life, limit the passions in my heart that felt natural.

If I could go back in time, I would have told Ramón what Frank said that day. I would have listened to Ramón more. Parenting from a place of true love, regardless if gay or straight, has to be the purest form in raising kids right. I took that away from him, me, and you. I broke our little, secret family apart, breaking all of our hearts in the process. And perhaps a family that didn't need to be kept a secret. I didn't know how to grow out of the shell I had shielded my whole life behind. It's all that I knew that was safe.

I see Lucy is pregnant. Congratulations. If I can leave you with anything: Learn how to be your authentic self for that child. And learn how to encourage him or her to do exactly the same for themselves. I'm sorry I didn't teach you this. I'm sorry I didn't know how to be my authentic self.

I am in no position to tell you what to do or on how to handle your life with your wife and now baby on the way. But please don't make the same mistakes I made. Nobody wins. Learn to know and love yourself, and then you will be able to know and love your child as they should be known and loved. I am proud of you, and I think you have the potential to be a great father.

Love, your true father, David

I can feel the cold tears streaming down and collecting into drops on the bottom of my chin. There is no hope. I don't know who I am. And I hate who I've been, who I am now. I don't wanna be this way. I glance right to look down at the river, my tear drops falling off my chin and all the way down.

*Vibrate…vibrate…*Who the fuck is calling me now!? Ignore it. It doesn't matter. You read his letter. There is nothing else left to do. I have all the truths now. Maybe it does matter? My hand retracts and slides down my front pocket to grab my phone. I bring the screen to my eyes.

314-555-1516

The phone vibrating in my hand. My hopelessness turning into rage seeing his number. Son of a fucking bitch. Don't answer it. It doesn't matter. *Frank.* my thumb slides across the screen to answer. "What."

"Where are you?"

"What's it matter to you?" "Huh?" "Think you're fulfilling God's work?" "Cleansin' the earth still at your age?" "What's your count now?" "How many fags you kill?"

"I should have aimed and pulled the trigger in that chapel."
"Where are you?"

He just admitted it.

"Well…hate to burst your bright bubble, but you will fail this time." I stare at the boulders on the edge of the river. I'm ready to go.

"I will go to earth's length to find you, boy. You wanna test that? You'll be runnin' for the rest of your life. I won't stop until I find you." "Ask your uncle." "Oh." "Wait, I already took care of that one."

He what? A new weight forms in my stomach. "You killed him?" "Didn't you?" "Why?"

"I didn't do anything that the Lord wasn't already in the process of doin'." Wow. My uncle really did do what he thought he needed to do to protect me from you.

"Why is my life so important to you?" "His life?" Why does my life feel more important to him than it does to me?

"Leviticus 20:13—'If a man also lie with mankind, as he lieth with a woman, both of them have committed an abomination: They shall surely be put to death; their blood shall be upon them.'" "That is the Lord's word." "Plain and simple, and there's more of it." "No seed of mine will be living in sin like that." "Or brother of mine."

"Living in sin?" "Aren't we all living in sin?" "Isn't that the point of the Church?" "To teach us that we all live in sin by default, and teach us how to embrace it and do better?" "Why does me with a fella have to be the sin that deems my life to be worthy of nothin' but death?" "Why is this such a big fuckin' deal to you?"

"Your sin is immoral; your type of people are repulsive, fundamentally wrong. I am doing God's work." "He tried in the eighties with AIDS, but it wasn't enough, and now the rest of us have to take matters into our own hands."

"That is really what you think?" "WoOw." "You are so

fucked up." "Holy shit." "My uncle was right to hide me from you." Now this is a *true* monster. I see where I get it from.

"Your uncle was a walking plague of sin. He should have repented years ago; I know he never fully did. I know the sick mind of my brother, and now the sick mind that has been passed down to you." "Your mind is too far gone." "There's only one way to handle you now." "Where are you?"

"You're right." "I do feel I don't belong here anymore." "That my mind is too lost with no hope of return." I lean my torso right, the drop down clearer as my body stretches more over. But I keep the resistance of the inside of my left leg on the wall of the railing. "You know what's so stupid, you fuckin' idiot?"

"What?"

"You don't even have to kill me." "I'm already killing myself."

"Good." "You should!" "Do it right now; I'll stay on the phone." "You have a gun on you?" "I wanna hear it."

56

I don't.

I wish I did. It would be easier. Less scary, and faster than this fall and crash. I look back at Andrew's car. A white pickup truck. Hm.

A white pickup truck

My uncle comes to mind, bashing me for ever thinking I could have a white truck, and here I am borrowing one to my death.

What if the fall doesn't kill me? And I become paralyzed like some vegetable, just like what I did to Isaac—payback, *what I deserve*. Fuck! Why do both options of living or suicide suck for me?

"I don't have a gun on me, but trust me. My plan will work."

"Goodbye…*Dad.*"

"I was never your dad; you keep that name towards me out of your faggot mouth."

"Dad!" "DAD." "Hey D A D!" "Your son is a FAGGOT!!" I shout as loud as I can into the phone, into the sky, and down below into the air between the river and my boot. "*Your* son! Your biological son—that *you* created—is. A. FAGGOT!"

Silence on the phone, all except for his breathing and mine, the sun now gone, hiding behind an overcast that's blowing in. "Go on, boy, do it." "Maybe God will then forgive you." "I pray that he does." "Why the hell not." "Maybe he will give you grace for relieving yourself from this sin you've chosen."

Chosen. That word stinging my spine. "Sin I've chosen?" "You think I chose this??" "You actually think *I* chose this…this thing inside me?" "I didn't choose this." "I didn't *ask* for this." "I sure as hell bet Uncle David—my true father—didn't ask for this." "Nobody asks for this." "Or wants to choose this."

"I saw you point blank—with not one, but two men today in front of me, no will or power to stop." "You're out of control."

I can't believe a person has so much hate for something that feels so natural and innocent to me. My own father.

"Bein' this way." "People bein' gay is not a choice, Frank."

"Yes, it is." "Everything you do is a choice." "Different types of sin tempt us all every single day." "That's how the devil works." "You have chosen to live in this sin." "You choose it every time." "You think I don't have temptation daily?" "Repent now, or sacrifice your life." "This is the only way God will accept and forgive you."

"To live and bury how my soul naturally feels?" "Or accept I cannot do that, and take my own life?" "Those are my options designed for me from God?" "For all gay people?"

"The way I see it, yes." "If you don't bury it and learn how to control this lust, take your life now." "Do it for Lucy." "Do it for your baby."

"For Lucy?" "My baby?"

"Yes, if you can't control yourself and live a pure life." "To set the right example to your wife and child, then give up now." "Save them from this misery." "…Or I'll do it for you." "And I'll make sure your child is raised right."

Can I bury this *lust* again? Am I certain it will never come back out? Is this really best for Lucy and my baby? But what if my son or daughter grows up to be like me? What will Frank do to them? This cycle will repeat all over again.

No.

"You're wrong, Frank." "It is not just lust." "There is so much more." "These gay people all around—your brother, my uncle—it is not just a sin from lust." "It can't be."

"You just like the way men taste more than women." "It's a sin; a disease in your head, boy."

"You're wrong." "It's more than just the sex." "The fucking." "It's more." "It's *love*." "I think, the truest of love possible."

"No it is not." "You have chosen this sin far too long, continued to live in this sin, and now you are lost." "Too far to come back." "Now a liability to all of us around, to children around—"

"That man you saw me with, that I kept from blowing your brains out." "Eugene." "And maybe with Andrew, the other man I was in the chapel with." "With them, what I feel inside, it is not just…lust." "It is a natural, good attraction." "That could only be designed intentionally." Is my brain believing in what I'm actually saying? I feel a little less darkness for once.

"Don't try to tell me differently, boy, what I know to be true; you are deceived by your own repetitive sins." "There ain't nothin' natural about two men together. Not one goddamn thing."

The memory of Ramón's Michelangelo painting in his apartment, revised to add shades of rainbow to God's hand, popping up in my brain. Huh. I think I get it now.

"Frank, I'm tellin' ya." "I don't even know why I'm wastin' my breath on ya." "It's more." "God has to have some good and intentional reason for all of this." "For all gay people." Why am I even fighting with him? Come on, he's not your father, Roy; there is nothing left there. Nothing left to save or grow.

Just slide away. Shift the center of your weight more off your ass, and fall down into the river. It'll be over soon.

No.

I don't want to fall. Maybe there *is* more for me.

"You're disgusting," Frank says. "Diseased." "God has no

desire or purpose for you here." "Go on, do it! I'm tired of hearin' ya speak." "Just kill yourself now!" "I don't see you changing." The wind still against my face, blowing my body the direction back toward Andrew's white truck. *Run away with me.* Andrew's voice and face in my head. How am I now really just noticing the color?

His gay white truck. Hm. Funny the timing on this. I did always want one.

I glance back down at my uncle's last letter to me, then to the white caps below—now appearing more terrifying all of a sudden…Frank is wrong, though. I didn't choose this. I didn't ask for this. I don't believe now that this life is a sin. I don't believe my options morally are to hide it or to die. Yeah, I don't have all the answers, but I know I experienced love. A love that I never knew the heart could be designed to experience. This intensity can't be by mistake. It can't be a sin punishable by death.

"Being gay isn't a choice out of lust, Frank—well, maybe some of it is." "But I know with Eugene, there is something more I feel." "Something…sacred." "More worth living for, that God designed for me and him to experience and enjoy together." "It feels too pure to be wrong." "It was love." "It is love." Am I finally seeing it? Admitting it? I think I am. It's *more* than his taste.

To all in the LGBTQ+ community that were ever made to feel unworthy of love, dignity, or purpose.

They are wrong.

AUTHOR'S NOTE

Thank you so much for reading my novel!

The story of Roy Stevens is just one example of the millions of stories LGBTQ+ people experience.

If my writing entertained or resonated with you in any way, please share with your friends, or leave a review online to help more people discover it.

THANK YOU.

RESOURCES

If you or someone you know needs resources regarding suicidal thoughts, domestic violence, or overall LGBTQ+ support, please reach out. You are not alone.

These are resources in the US that I have verified myself, and I hope they add value to whoever needs them.

Suicidal Thoughts

- **US emergency number:** If you're in immediate danger, call **911**.
- **988 Suicide & Crisis Lifeline:** If you need to talk now, call or text **988** or chat online at **https://988lifeline.org**. This is free and confidential.
- **Crisis Text Line:** Text **HOME** to **741741**.

Safety from Violence and Abuse

- **National Domestic Violence Hotline:** Call or text **1-800-799-SAFE (7233)**.

- **StrongHearts Native Helpline:** Call **844-7NATIVE (762-8483)**.
- **love is respect** (regarding teen/young-adult dating abuse): Call **866-331-9474**, text **LOVEIS** to **22522**, or chat online at **www.loveisrespect.org**.

LGBTQ+ Support

- **The Trevor Project** (for LGBTQ youth and young adults): Call **1-866-488-7386**, text **START** to **678-678**, or chat online at **www.thetrevorproject.org**.
- **Trans Lifeline** (peer support run by trans people): Call **877-565-8860**.
- **LGBT National Help Center**
  - **LGBT National Hotline:** Call **888-843-4564**.
  - **LGBT National Youth Talkline (≤25):** Call **800-246-7743**.
  - **LGBT National Senior Hotline (50+):** Call **888-234-7243**.
- **SAGE National LGBTQ+ Elder Hotline:** Call **877-360-LGBT (5428)**.

ACKNOWLEDGMENTS

To my beta readers—Anne Sagan, Cameron Delphinium, Tyler Bennett, Anonymous, and Anonymous—thank you for your enthusiasm and support. Your honest perspectives helped me fine-tune areas and also believe in myself more as a writer. I am so grateful to have had all five of you be beta readers for my first novel.

To my editor, Anna Barnes, thank you for editing this piece to help make my vision for it become clearer and polished. You are truly amazing at what you do!

To my cover designer, Diego Sanguino, thank you for your enthusiasm and cooperation to help my vision of the colorful details added to Michelangelo's concept look amazing.

To Benjamin Sharkey, thank you for your friendship and support with creating renderings of the artwork to help my vision become a reality.

To my mother: Your standard of love, class, perseverance, and kindness is unmatched. We don't get to choose which mothers we get, and I won the lottery with you. People always say you and I are alike, and that is the highest compliment anyone could ever give me.

To my best friends, Shawn and Alvaro: Your unwavering support as my cheerleaders is one of my secret sauces to happiness in life. I hope everyone in life gets to experience the greatness of having a best friend, as you both have been to me. What a gift!

To Henrique: You were the first person I shared with that I wanted to write a novel, the first to believe in me. "I think you should too" is what you said, and I've run with that moment. Thank you for your love and support always. Thank you for being my spark that ignited this journey!

To my BSD family—Joe, Will, Valdet, David, Andy, Cory, Nick, Jake, Shaun, Lucas, Jason, and Hernan: We've been through a lot together. I'm grateful for all of the sharing, memories, disagreements, love, and depth in connections we have. The stories we have together…oh my! What a journey our lives have already been, and I can't wait for what more yet we get to experience together.

To my Century 21 Curran & Oberski and Title One work families: Working alongside you all is a joy, and I appreciate your personal and professional support throughout the years. My work setting actually first inspired this writing path. It is my pleasure to work alongside such fun and passionate people!

To Terry Knickerbocker, thank you for the second chance. It did change my life. I hope your studio is everything, and more than you dreamed of. I'm so proud to be from the first graduating class of 2016.

To CC: If you ever read this novel, I hope you learn something from it. You did teach me a very real, unfortunate life lesson—people don't always get closure on everything that wrongfully happens to them. But what control we do have is how we reshape our attitude and move forward.

To Jessica: I forgive you. I never thought for a second I would be in this position where I would have to learn forgiveness in this way. But life is larger than what we are limited to here on earth. Maybe you trusted that, and maybe I will see you again someday. I hope so. Love you, sister.

To Tyler Petree, thank you for reviewing and providing feedback on scenes that I know you have proficient knowledge in. I want my stories to reflect the honest truth in every way of the human experience, and I thank you for being a part of this.

To my friends in Kentucky—Aidan, Donovan, Alyce, Tracy, Sharon, Corie, Carlos, John, Allen, Jayde, Charlene, and David—thank you so much for believing in me and sharing knowledge to help me create this story with the most truth. I hope you enjoyed it!